A WILD JUSTICE

CRAIG THOMAS

A WILD
JUSTICE

HarperCollins*Publishers*

HarperCollins*Publishers*
77–85 Fulham Palace Road
Hammersmith, London W6 8JB

Published by HarperCollins*Publishers* 1995
1 3 5 7 9 10 8 6 4 2

A catalogue record for this book is
available from the British Library

ISBN 0 00 223927 2

Set in Linotron Meridien by
Rowland Phototypesetting Ltd, Bury St Edmunds, Suffolk

Printed in Great Britain by
HarperCollinsManufacturing Glasgow

for
Terry and Angela
with love and thanks for
25 years of friendship

'The first of the leading
peculiarities of the present
age is, that it is an age
of transition . . . when almost
every nation on the continent
of Europe has achieved, or is
in the course of rapidly
achieving, a change in its form
of government . . . Mankind will
not be led by their old maxims,
nor by their old guides.'

J. S. Mill: *The Spirit of the Age*

PRELUDE

'It must occur to every person,
on reflection, that those lands
are too distant to be within the
government of any of the present
states.'

Thomas Paine: *Public Good*

'Nice overcoat – I wonder why his killer left it behind?' Alexei Vorontsyev muttered, his cheek turned into the hood of his parka against the chilling slap of the wind.

Behind Vorontsyev, Bakunin, the GRU colonel who had also received an anonymous telephone call summoning him to the scene of a murder, stamped clumsily back and forth on the rutted snow. Smoke from his cigarette whipped past Vorontsyev.

'I like the suit he's still wearing,' he continued, calling out to Bakunin over his shoulder. The GRU officer appeared profoundly indifferent, as if all he desired was to return to whichever warm room he had come from. 'By rights, this corpse ought to be stripped naked.'

He tugged the body away from its bed of stiff grass, his hand behind it as if he were about to commence some ventriloquial act with the corpse. The body had been reported as having been accidentally discovered. There was nothing in the pockets, he'd already checked. Cleaned out by whoever had found it, or the killer.

He turned on his haunches and glowered at Bakunin – who paused in his patrol to attend to him, lighting another cigarette as he did so.

'American tailor – Washington.' He let the head of the corpse loll. 'One wound –' His words were repeated into a small Japanese recorder by his inspector, Dmitri Gorov. '– straight into the base of the skull and thrust upwards, from behind.' The pathologist would, in all probability, be able to tell them little more, just the approximate time of death. There were two explosions of a camera's flashgun. 'Do you have to do that at this time of the morning?' he growled, letting the corpse fall back much as

3

the murderer must have done, hours before. 'What's this – ?'

It looked very much like a professional killing. They'd had a few of them recently, one gang of drug-dealers or black-marketeers sorting out another gang; a territorial or profit-based dispute – newly imported capitalist crimes. Here, one stranger had approached another, unsuspecting, stranger for no more than a moment, ending a life. The wind numbed him through the parka. Nothing in the pockets, except . . . He held it up.

'Recognise that, Colonel?' he asked, then added with sour humour: 'Yours the same colour?'

Bakunin snatched away the slip of stiff plastic. The labels had been left in the suit, and perhaps the card had, too, as a statement. If it belonged to the dead man.

'Is this him?' the military intelligence officer snapped, his voice husky with a lifetime's cigarettes.

'If it is, then he must be from one of the American companies – oil or gas, or one of their suppliers.' Vorontsyev looked at the rimed soles and uppers of the dead man's shoes. Small, fringed leather tags, once-soft leather. Expensive, and hardly broken in. No thief had found this body, or he or she would have been away with everything here, including the underwear. So, the killer must have been the one who called the station – and who had called Bakunin, too. The murder was some kind of statement that required publicity.

Bakunin handed back the single, unwalleted credit card with gloved fingers. It had appeared to be trapped in a back trouser pocket, as if overlooked. *Allan Rawls*, it claimed. An Amex Gold Card. A lot of Russians carried them these days – waved them like badges. Especially in front of *babushkas* and the other endlessly queuing poor. Gold Cards had all the power and credence the red KGB cards had once had.

The body had a youngish face, early thirties – maybe as much as ten years younger than himself. Snuffed out.

Vorontsyev climbed to his feet and stamped them to rid them of the icy cold, grunting at the numb ache in his legs. Bakunin, arms folded, confronted him like an implacable machine, or an assertion that nothing had changed. Military intelligence was as it had always been, dim and certain and eternal; all's right with the world, Lenin's still in his heaven. Behind Bakunin, Dmitri Gorov hovered, his round features pale with cold. Uniformed men waited as awkwardly as if it was the funeral, not merely the discovery of the body. Their cars and the morgue wagon were parked like abandoned toys.

There were rutted wheel tracks everywhere, leading from the road that ran past this shrivelled little copse of stunted firs. He rubbed pine-mould from his gloves. The red dawn was coming up behind the group of men and vehicles like a wound. Frost sparkled in the headlights of the parked cars, the frozen snow blued and reddened alternately by their slowly flashing lights. Late autumn, Novyy Urengoy, Siberia.

The first of the MiL helicopters droned along the flat horizon of the snowbound marshes, making itself a black spot on the sun's curled lip as it ferried the first of the day shift out to one of the gas rigs that were skeletally all around them in the day's earliest light. Rigs topped with needles of flame and thin, desperate smoke signals lay across the landscape like preliminary sketches for sites of human habitation. Vorontsyev shivered.

'Well, Major?' Bakunin asked peremptorily. Vorontsyev wondered why whoever had murdered Rawls had wanted the GRU here. Security wasn't involved, this was no more than a *crime*; *his* jurisdiction as chief of detectives.

'Ask a doctor if you want a diagnosis.'

'I'm asking you. Why are we both here to inspect a corpse? He's been murdered by one of your economic criminals . . . hasn't he?'

'It's likely, Colonel.' But possibly not the case.

Bakunin was just another military intelligence officer whose superiority over him resided entirely in their distance from Moscow. His own authority as chief of detectives for the gasfield town of Novyy Urengoy was civilian and insignificant. Not that the military ran things – that was done by the entrepreneurs and the gangsters and the foreign investors – there were merely more of them. In reality, people like Bakunin no longer even irritated him. He was just one of many of the hundreds he vaguely disliked and without whom he attempted to get by; creatures called other people.

5

There were lights from the town and, scattered and pitiful, from its surrounding villages and dachas, lodges and peasant smallholdings. Novyy Urengoy was on the southern edge of the tundra, where the forest petered out into marsh before the northern barrenness and the Kara Sea. His responsibility – except that the police were the district's three fabled monkeys who had no ears, eyes or voice for any serious wrongdoing. More like traffic wardens. The local bigwigs and his own chief saw to the effective castration of the force. No one should interfere with the holy mission of getting gas and oil out from beneath the permafrost.

'It's saying to us that it's professional,' he murmured, as if to Dmitri rather than Bakunin. Gorov was nodding in agreement. 'It's screaming the fact out loud.'

'Yes?' Bakunin snapped, as if the temperature was still the only matter to which he could give his attention.

'But then there's a credit card so clean it must have been kept in a wallet or billfold – which tells us exactly who he is. It's there *as if* it's been overlooked.'

'But why was *I* telephoned?' Bakunin asked angrily.

It might have been drink, more than lack of sleep, that rendered Bakunin's chilly, broad features as coarse and brutal as they appeared; it was neither. The man *was* brutal, the reddened eyes like those of some malevolent boar glaring at a hostile world.

'I don't know, Colonel,' Vorontsyev replied. 'Someone evidently requested your presence. You'd be involved eventually though, wouldn't you, with the murder of an American? Perhaps our mysterious caller was just saving time.'

Another big helicopter transporting workers out to the well-heads and rigs passed low over them. He waited until the rotor noise began to fade, watching the ugly, tenement-like blocks of apartments and offices that were Novyy Urengoy, as if puzzled by his location. The streetlighting was fading as the day lightened. The near-tundra of the frozen marshland stretched shadowy and empty to the horizon in every direction. The town was sitting in the landscape like a spilt box of building-blocks, isolated and bleak, ringed by the watchtowers of the gas rigs.

6

'Someone wanted both of us to know about this death. I don't know why. Does the name mean anything to you, Colonel? You move in more exalted circles than myself, after all.' Dmitri's mouth cracked like a cold sore for an instant, behind Bakunin's shoulder.

'Not immediately. I'll have it checked.'

'Are you assuming control of the investigation?'

Bakunin shook his brutal head. 'You're the detective. It's just a murder – for the moment. The motive was probably robbery –'

'He didn't walk all the way from town in those shoes. If he was brought, then he knew his murderer . . . at least, knew who he was coming to meet or who drove him here.' Bakunin nodded like a pedagogue, lighting another cigarette, cupping his hands around a gold lighter.

'How long has he been dead?'

'Who knows? I doubt the pathologist could be accurate. I'd say three hours, roughly.'

'My call came two hours ago – yours, too?'

Vorontsyev nodded. 'Whoever wanted us to find him was keen we should get on with it. He wouldn't wait, just in case someone found the body and . . .' He paused, then added softly: 'In case someone walked off with the clothes and the Amex card.'

He glanced again at the makeshift town hunched in aggressive defence on the frozen land. Lights on in the tower blocks, unlit streetlights straggling out towards larger homes and to scattered copses sheltering new hotels. Rawls would have been booked into one of them, probably the best, the Gogol. Hyatt part-owned it, had part-paid for its construction. It had the biggest lobby and the best whores. The Japanese, the Germans, the Americans, all had bought into Novyy Urengoy . . . flats, hotels, company offices. The town had trebled in size in four years. There were dozens of companies involved in leasing, owning, exploring and exploiting the gasfield, some with Russian partners, some not. Rawls had belonged to one of them.

'I don't understand,' he announced.

'What?' Bakunin returned.

'People like him are normally sacrosanct. Remember – no,

7

you wouldn't, it was a small matter. An oil company executive got mugged in the summer, outside his hotel. The culprit was knee-capped by one of the local mafiosi, just to enforce the holiness of golden geese like Rawls. So why has he been murdered? It's usually the gangsters and racketeers and the drug-dealers who *execute* each other.'

'You're suggesting he was a gangster? All the best ones *were* American, weren't they?' Even the smile was sadistic, leering with command.

'I don't know.' Addressing the corpse, he added: 'Who are you, Mr Rawls? Why are we supposed to take special notice of you, dead as you are?'

Bakunin stamped his feet, as if bringing a royal audience to an end. He turned away, waving one gloved hand and calling: 'I leave it up to you, Vorontsyev. *You're* the policeman.'

Dmitri Gorov grinned as Bakunin all but lost his footing on the rutted snow as he walked towards his limousine. The driver flung away a cigarette and snapped open the rear passenger door.

Vorontsyev turned back to the body as Bakunin's ZiL lurched out of the slight depression where it had been parked and onto the main highway. A car tooted its intrusion into the fast lane, but the horn was muted, as if the military insignia had suddenly been recognised.

Rawls' hands, even with the nails blued, were soft and manicured. The man, when alive, would have reeked of power and money. The wind rattled the leafless birches and swayed the firs of the copse. Novyy Urengoy seemed more alien than a minute before, and the landscape that tolerated it more vast than ever.

Someone had *ordered* this corpse, and demanded it be made to look like a professional hit. Was it intelligence work? He glanced towards the highway but Bakunin's car was already out of sight. Gangsterism, or something else . . . ?

We were meant to notice –

– but *who* is being *warned*?

PART ONE

The Wealth of Nations

'Their market is not confined
to the countries in the neighbourhood of the mine, but
extends to the whole world.'
                    Adam Smith:
              The Wealth of Nations

ONE

Family Portrait

He had walked through the last sunshine of the brief afternoon, the leaves brown and crackling beneath his shoes. John Lock's cheeks were chilly, then almost at once stingingly warm as he entered the lobby of the Mayflower Hotel, shrugging himself out of his overcoat. It had been an invigorating walk from the State Department, pleasant even as the early autumn dark closed on Washington and the streetlights glared out. Aircraft, navigation lights winking, had thundered overhead, but he had been able to hear and see them impassively. He wouldn't be travelling again for a good while. The city had begun to fit itself comfortably around him, just as his office had already done; as the whole of the State Department had agreeably done.

The barman recognised Lock with the slightest lifting of heavy eyebrows and his favourite drink was silently remembered and served. The olive fell into the martini like a small bird's egg into clear oil. He toasted himself, then glanced at his watch, smiling. Just time for two drinks, then back to the apartment to change. He felt a reluctance that he wouldn't have time to play even one of the batch of new CDs he had bought during the lunch-break. The latest *Marriage of Figaro*, a new Handel recording, something special in the way of a Beethoven cycle – all very promising. He grinned. It was, after all, Beth's birthday. Anyway, he no longer had to snatch at hours with the hi-fi or novels or the book he was trying to write. And wouldn't a while yet. State had given him a tour of duty at his desk in the East Europe Office. Definitely a *minimum* of travel involved.

Even his answerphone messages, each evening, possessed an unexpected, comforting charm. Fred with tickets for a basketball game; the prim, severe lady who was secretary for the early music group in which he occasionally sang baritone – he was supposed to be editing a performing version of an obscure seventeenth-century opera for them; his dry cleaning ready for collection, which was a statement of intent rather than just a message. He was staying home, staying put. He grinned, shrugging his shoulders as if into an old and comfortable jacket.

The mobile phone bleated in the pocket of his topcoat as it lay across his knees, ruffling his mood like a brief wind. The barman passed him, ice like Latin percussion in his cocktail shaker. He unfolded the phone's mouthpiece.

'John Lock.'

'John-Boy!' It was Billy, his brother-in-law.

'Hi, Billy. I haven't forgotten the party, if that's what –'

'Your sister wouldn't let you, John-Boy.'

'I remember her birthday, anyway.'

'Sure. Say, is that the second or third martini?'

Lock smiled. 'So you guessed. But it's the first.'

'OK. Look, Beth – me, too – we want you to come out to the house as soon as you can – there's nothing wrong, by the way. We just want to see something of you before the guests arrive. So, drink up fast and get over here. Beth's orders.'

'Right. Thanks, Billy.'

He slipped the cellular phone into his topcoat. At once, a hand fell on his shoulder, its grip almost immediately doubtful, as if the hand's owner wondered whether he would be recognised.

'John Lock! This still your favourite watering-hole?' The man was taller than Lock, even when he hitched himself onto the adjacent barstool. Thicker-set and somehow more loosely arranged. Or designed for activity no longer undertaken. 'I haven't seen you around here lately.'

'Bob. Good to see you, man!' The lobby bar was beginning to crowd with office workers and government people. Bob Kauffman was Company – the *other* government. 'How're things on the farm?'

'I'm still working.' A shrug. Bob Kauffman had been a senior case officer in the field. Reagan, Gorbachev and Thatcher – lately, Yeltsin and Clinton and Major – had foreclosed on him like realtors, just as on most of his breed. 'Jeez, I wish State would take me on like they did you. Lucky sonofabitch.' It was said entirely without resentment. 'Maybe then I could get away from the sour smell of guys waiting and wondering, kicking their heels . . . This administration's gonna dump the Company, man, like it was politically non-correct!' He clicked his fingers and a bourbon on the rocks appeared magically. 'Unless you're a desk-jock, an image analyser or a computer whizz – or you recommend we do nothing about the world – forget it!' He swallowed at his drink.

Lock, smiling, murmured: 'I guess things are tight all round. I've just been confined to my desk myself, though I'm not complaining. What have they gotten you doing, Bob?'

'When I'm not being bored out of my skull in meetings and committees, I ride shotgun on a bunch of college kids and their computers. Middle East stuff mainly – the ayatollahs and the rest of the bandits. You know the kind of thing –' He shrugged dismissively. 'I'm like their grandfathers. A dinosaur. You?'

Lock studied their images in the mirror. Kauffman seemed, at that moment, like an unwelcome drunk narrating his history. And, as he had described himself, out of time and place. Lock's own slimmer, dark-haired, more youthful form stared back at him, looking like the future, just as Kauffman represented the past gone to seed. Loose-jowled, disgruntled, grey-eyed, while he appeared sleeker, more tanned, like a business executive watching the world from behind sharp blue eyes.

'It's mainly trade, investment, that kind of thing.'

'But you're still hanging around the old places, the old crowd.' Kauffman made the Cold War seem like a college fraternity, viewed all the more romantically with twenty-twenty hindsight. 'The nearest I get to the old action is when my college boys discover our old friends have sold a bunch of tanks or missiles to the ayatollahs. Or a scientist –' He grinned sourly. A second bourbon had appeared in front of him, another martini near Lock's hand.

'Sell a scientist?' he murmured to humour Kauffman. He'd heard other, more substantiated rumours echoing around State, and during his own travels in Russia. Scientists were going south and east, a few west. The poorly paid bastards were dribbling out of the former Soviet Union. But it wasn't wholesale, they weren't shipping them out like books or machine parts.

'Some crazy theory. College boys! They think our old friends are selling brains now, to whoever will buy. People. All those redundant atom guys, germ warfare experts, you know. Jeez, you wonder why I get nostalgic for Afghanistan or Europe – even 'Nam?' His glass was empty again. 'Let me buy you another, John – very dry martini, right?'

Lock paused, his eyes halfway to his watch, listening to the warmth of two dozen conversations on the eternally fascinating subject – power. Hillary's latest dressing-down of a senior insider, the snub of a meagre Clinton working lunch, the President's ratings slump, the situation in obliterated Bosnia, those asshole Europeans . . . The politics of power and the power of politics. It would be churlish to reject Bob Kauffman's offer. He was the kid with his nose pressed up against this most wonderful of candy-stores. It would be arrogant to demonstrate to him how far outside he was.

'Thanks, Bob. Though I must watch the time.'

Kauffman ordered the drinks. The occasional tourist conversation was hemmed in securely by the political gossip. Lock felt comfortable within those verbal walls, just as Kauffman felt shut out.

'Your college boys are exaggerating. There have been some disappearances – a trickle, no more. The Russians have a very real interest in keeping their top guys at home, and happy.' He grinned. 'Look, Bob, a job at State these days is just as much out of the old line. I get to study Russian economics.'

'Is there Russian economics?'

They both laughed at the joke.

'What have they turned you into – a salesman or an insurance assessor?'

'A little of both.'

'Some brave new world order, uh? Like letting the Bosnian Moslems go down the tubes. The old guy with the Grecian 2000 wouldn't have done that. Cheers.'

Their conversation rapidly became desultory, as if they were both misplaced among the political chatterers. Lock occasionally waved to people he knew from State and other departments of government. Kauffman evidently wanted to enlist his aid, solicit information and maybe introductions; yet knowing all the time that the State Department would have no interest in a semi-redundant CIA case officer. Meanwhile, the names of the great and the good, their deeds and misdeeds, flew about them like paper missiles.

Kauffman became progressively maudlin. Instead of *Yanks Go Home*, the walls of the world told the spies of the world they were surplus to requirements. *Not wanted on voyage.* And the Clinton administration told them, with equal certainty, that the world was no longer their playground or their policeman's beat. The rest of the planet was not America's 111th Precinct, and Langley its Precinct House. Instead, the CIA headquarters was a slaveship full of bitter, displaced and betrayed men; a factory making the wrong goods in the wrong age.

Suddenly, he tired of Kauffman and the scents of their professional past, eager to be at Beth's birthday party. The memories of other birthdays, mostly spent apart, were easier to shrug off now. His own uncelebrated days – always bleak and snowbound, it seemed, with himself occupying an icy corridor, staring through tall windows at the white fields of the expensive private school. Their years of separation had now thankfully come to an end. Unheated dormitories and the glad escape of sportsfields and music from the brusque, suspicious indifference of boys who were not orphaned. He had found basketball and a singing voice and a fascination with musical scores rather than the printed pages into which Beth, in her isolation, had retreated. She'd discovered books – any books, all books.

He smiled to himself. He had always suspected that her own horror stories of lonely birthdays were fictitious, invented to give him sympathy. She had always generated a strong magnetic field that attracted other people, bound them in orbits of friendship. She'd never have been alone on any of her birthdays. Just like this one.

He quickly finished his drink, ordered another for Kauffman, and announced:

15

'It's my sister's birthday, Bob. I'm running late. I still haven't wrapped her present. Great to see you – '

He was shrugging himself into his topcoat as he spoke, already a few yards from the bar. Kauffman watched him with a gored bull's distrustful, enraged eyes. Lock waved his hand and Kauffman returned the gesture, his glance softening.

Lock shook off the man's infectious world-weariness. He'd never known Kauffman well, he had never been a friend. They'd come into contact in Afghanistan in the '80s and hardly ever since. Kauffman was a 'Nam veteran of the Company, an intelligence field officer who still moved through an imaginary world of inferior races and ideologies.

He was blithely recovered by the time the doors slid back and the street's cold air struck him. He moved into the lamplit cold, turning up the collar of his topcoat. Leaves rattled like tin along the sidewalk. Gas was sharp on the air. He began to hurry, grinning with childlike anticipation.

Alexei Vorontsyev put down the telephone and announced: 'They're sending someone over to the hospital to identify the body. The shock-horror sounded genuine enough. From the description, it sounds like it is Rawls.'

Dmitri, licking his fingers and putting down a second receiver, nodded then said: 'You're going to love this.' He shook his head in the direction of the telephone.

'What?'

'By the time Forensic – your pal Lensky – got to the morgue, someone had had the shoes off the corpse. The body must have unfrozen just enough to – '

'Deliberately?' Vorontsyev snapped.

'What?' Dmitri was chewing on another huge bit of something that approximated to pizza. As a breakfast, its prospect made Vorontsyev queasy. 'Oh, I see what you mean. No, it looks like opportunism. Probably one of our uniformed buggers taking advantage.'

The office smelt powerfully of pungent, burned herbs, anchovies, tomato. And of their wet boots standing forlornly near the single radiator. The snow flew past the large window. The

16

morning was all but obscured. The frontier town had, for a thankful moment, vanished behind the onset of winter. As had its drugs and gangster epidemic. He heard a truck skid, then collide with something four floors below.

'OK, let's assume it *was* Rawls. Why did someone have him turned off?'

Dmitri hunched his shoulders, wiping his mouth with a large, grey handkerchief. He did his own washing now — not very successfully. Vorontsyev's laundry was much neater; fastidiously so. Arctic white and aseptic as the flat he occupied. Dmitri's home was untidy and grimy with grief and neglect. He couldn't take his washing along to the Foundation Hospital and ask his mad wife to do it for him. He went there just to sit beside her. Not *with* her; she wasn't with *anyone* any more.

'Do you think he might have been involved with the local crap — the *biznizmen* and the mafia?' There was a tone of fervent, reawakened hope in Dmitri Gorov's voice. It was a sign of obsession rather than anticipation; everything, for him, had to be to do with drugs and the local mafia.

Vorontsyev shook his head and rubbed his unshaven cheeks with both hands, as if they still retained the chill of the copse beside the highway.

'There's never been any hint of an American connection. Rawls was a senior executive of Grainger Technologies, not even part of the Grainger-Turgenev set-up. I can't see him dabbling in cocaine or heroin as a bit of private enterprise. Seriously, Dmitri — can you?'

Reluctantly, Dmitri shook his head, an intense disappointment on his features. He rubbed one big hand through his thinning, lank dark hair, then around his big-jowled face.

'I suppose you're right. Look, Alexei, this murder isn't going to get in the way of our drugs bust, is it?' He was all but pleading.

Vorontsyev shook his head.

'I don't know why Bakunin didn't grab it straight away. He will do, though. There's kudos in dealing with the Yankees, with Turgenev. Security is bound to take it over. After Bakunin's had his breakfast — and maybe masturbated himself into a better mood.' Dmitri laughed explosively. 'No, we'll concentrate on the drugs — as always.'

Dmitri seemed pleased. He picked up a report sheet from his side of the desk and passed it to Vorontsyev.

'The Aeroflot flight up from Islamabad arrives at eight tonight. Nothing's changed. Hussain is booked onto it.' Dmitri fidgeted with excitement.

'The apartment block stakeout's all set?'

'All in place. There's nothing much happening at the moment — but that's not unusual.'

'OK. Tonight, then. The stuff *will* be on the flight?'

'That's what I've been told. It's the usual method of transport, and Hussain's the carrier — for the Pakistani connection, that is.'

'The Pakistanis are all we have. We know it comes in from Tehran and from Kashmir, but we don't have any leads. Hussain from Rawalpindi is *all* we've got.' Vorontsyev realised he had begun to sound hectoring, a distributor of blame. He added: 'Yours is the best lead we've had so far. We have a flight number and a name — at last. We know it's coming from down there, the Moslem Triangle, and we guessed it was coming in by air, brought by casual workers on the gas rigs. But we never had a name and a precise flight. Now we have both.' Suddenly, he banged his fist down on the desk. 'Christ, the number of shipments that have been brought in under our noses! We're not going to lose this one, Dmitri.' He saw Dmitri's features darken with what might have been some obscene hunger. 'I promise. *This* time we'll gut the bastards, sweat it out of this Hussain, follow the trail we persuade him to give us, pick up the distributors . . .' He knew, to his own embarrassment, that he was feeding a sickness in Dmitri. Revenge. But, Christ, the man deserved his revenge if anyone ever did! 'Planeloads of workers coming back off holiday, and every time a new consignment of heroin. Simple — when you know how.'

He studied Dmitri's face. He had successfully lightened the atmosphere. Two years ago, Dmitri's only beloved daughter had overdosed on heroin that hadn't been sufficiently cut. Revenge might never compensate him for her death, nor make up for the post-breakdown, vegetable state of his wife in the hospital.

18

But it might help. Two years ago, some of the local pushers hadn't had the expertise to cut the heroin for maximum profit while leaving their customers alive for more. Now, they did.

The drugs had followed hard on the heels of the Germans, the Yankees, the Japs and the market economy. The local gangsters had discovered distinctly Western ways of making money. The bad old days might have been bad, but *now* . . . ? Vorontsyev rubbed his face. The bad old days *had* been bad. Always remember that, *and* what you're supposed to be doing about the new days . . . despite a corrupt police force, seniors on the take or in the pockets of the *biznizmen* or the remnants of the KGB and the GRU and the local powerbrokers and the gas companies. Just remember, *you're* holding the line.

They *had* to strike lucky tonight. They'd waited so long for a break. They needed a success – the arrest of Hussain and whoever would be at the flat they had under surveillance, where some of Hussain's relatives lived. A whole shipment of Pakistani heroin suddenly taken off the streets would dry up supplies – temporarily. By which time, they might have begun to make inroads on the smuggling and distribution organisation. Begun climbing the greasy pole towards whoever *ran* things.

'You stay here and monitor the surveillance,' he announced. 'I'll take Marfa over to the Gogol and search Rawls' suite. We ought to appear to be doing our best when Bakunin takes over.' He smiled. 'The answer might be sitting on the bedside table – you never know.'

He tugged on his boots, then thrust his arms into the sleeves of his topcoat. Wound his scarf around his neck, donned his fur hat, and opened the door of his office. At once, it seemed, the barnlike space of the Criminal Investigation Department became a scene of noisy indolence; as if a schoolmaster with a Party card had arrived. The duty detectives glanced furtively at him – as if he were likely to ask some of them for his cut of their black incomes. Or simply ask for results; a greater coronary threat than their drinking and their fatty diets. The air was heavy with cigarette smoke, but the place didn't even *smell* Russian any more, the dark, pungent tobacco having been abandoned in favour of American cigarettes. The only real Russians remaining in the room were a kid who needed a fix and couldn't pay for one, a whining old peasant woman in black, her face like an eroded rock formation, and the drab, youngish woman being interviewed by Marfa. The younger woman had a black eye and split lip.

The other suspects and complainants in the echoing, smoky, littered room were mostly well-dressed and either relaxed or demanding. One padded neck wore a vivid silk tie, and Voronts-yev noticed an astrakhan collar on a dark coat. He smelt cigar smoke.

He looked momentarily at the beaten, drawn woman, her hands twisting like strangers suspiciously circling each other, then studied the intensity of comfort in Detective Second-Class Marfa Tostyeva's face. She was leaning her narrow body forward across her desk; her hands seemed engaged in some constant series of military forays of sympathy towards the other woman's hands. Her cheeks were pale, her eyes glittered. Vorontsyev tapped her on the shoulder. Her reaction was that of someone woken from a deep sleep.

'Hand this over to someone else —' She was already shaking her head in protest, but then acquiesced. '— I want you with me.' None of the others in the room would give this victim of domestic violence the time of day, but it couldn't be helped. It seemed almost his duty to wean Marfa forcibly away from her addiction to lost causes; at least for short, recuperative periods of time.

Marfa patted the woman's unceasing hands, whispering intently to her. Then she browbeat a junior detective into taking over the interview, before she followed Vorontsyev out into the chill of the corridor. It smelt strongly of disinfectant where the linoleum had been washed down.

Marfa sniffed loudly, repeatedly, as they went down in the lift.

'Cold?' he asked, grinning despite himself. Marfa Tostyeva wasn't a hypochondriac — merely someone always surprised and disappointed in herself at the onset of minor illness. Perhaps, at twenty-six, she still felt immortal.

'Flu, probably. I expect you'll get it from me.'

20

'Thanks, Marfa.' He felt obliged to ask: 'That woman. Her old man beat her up?'

'Naturally! Rig worker – when he's sober. Obviously thought he's start his two-week vacation with a little exercise. Bastard.' It was said without malice and without cynicism. Marfa still believed that life possessed *oughts* and *ought nots*. Imperatives. Rules of behaviour. She was the angriest and most passionate member of the CID. Which was why he trusted her.

She sniffed again, her pale blue eyes looking more watery than usual. She would battle the cold or flu or whatever it was as violently and unremittingly as she did domestic violence, theft, drugs, cruelty to animals. Joan of Arc. He masked his smile. He'd have trouble sending her home if it was flu.

'Where are we going?' she asked, glancing back at the interior of the lift as they left it, as if she had somehow betrayed the young, drab, beaten woman.

The foyer was a casual litter of humanity that lounged, slumped or moaned on benches and in tiled corners, observed by cynical militiamen or brushed and mopped around by cleaners.

'The dead body this morning. It was staying, when alive, at the Gogol. I thought we'd go and see in what style it was entertaining itself before going into the dark. OK?'

Marfa glowered at him. Rich men's crimes hardly interested her. The Gogol Hotel was another planet, and one whose atmosphere was malign.

'OK,' she replied.

His car emerged from the last trees of the avenue that shrouded the climbing drive and his headlights splashed on the Georgian façade of the house. Though splendid, it was too far out along the George Washington Parkway, in Virginia. It overlooked the Potomac and the rushing waterscape of Great Falls. Its twenty-acre grounds nudged the Park. The immaculate mansion whispered of money; owned variously by eighteenth-century landgrabbers, a retired Civil War general, a steel baron – and now temporarily in the custody of Billy Grainger. Of which John Lock approved, since the house had been his sister's sanity.

21

Billy's black Porsche, his company limousine and the cruiser stood marshalled to one side of the house. Floodlights let the manicured lawns creep to the edge of eyesight and greened them. A few last brown leaves – overlooked by the gardeners – lay like liver spots on an old hand. There were two other black limousines from the Grainger fleet, parked regimentally alongside Billy's cars. Billy must have flown in some business associates. He shut the door of the small Nissan and walked towards the portico, which was supported by four white columns – like the White House. He smiled. Billy's mansion was slightly smaller. The flagpole thrust up into the starry evening, the flag itself furled. The huge lamp above the doors was gleaming. Windows glowed with light, welcoming and secure.

And he no longer had to worry what he would find inside, as he had during the months when that façade had been a lie.

He felt no instinctive hunching of his shoulders, so often in the past the reaction he had been unable to avoid on coming to the house, wondering and even dreading what he would see. Beth's drugs, her drinking, her breakdown – caused by Billy's infidelities. He understood it now; they had come through it, his sister had been put back together again, good as new. He smiled to himself in anticipation of her appearance. Now, he could even understand Billy's behaviour, because it had caused no lasting damage to Beth. Billy had simply cracked under the pressure of marriage to someone cleverer, purer, brighter than himself. The women he chose as mistresses had always been glamorous, they were never intelligent.

Then she was on the steps, as if it were her twelfth or thirteenth birthday, not her forty-first, hovering excitedly beside Billy's English butler in a silver sheath of a dress that bared one of her narrow, pale shoulders to the light.

'Hi, Sis –' She was hugging him, childlike rather than in the desperation he had seen her through. He held the gift-wrapped present behind his back and felt her hands search for it. Her lips giggled warm little breaths against his cheek.

'Johnny –!' she exclaimed in mock disappointment and temper, pouting. He handed her the present and she held it against her girlish breasts for a moment, before taking his hand and

22

half-dragging him into the mansion's broad, high-ceilinged reception hall.

'Excited?' he asked.

'I got through forty – I'm going to *enjoy* forty-one!' A maid offered him a champagne flute. Stillman, the butler, regarded his mistress and her younger brother indulgently, judging them to be adolescents, but acceptably well-mannered. Beth drew him into her parlour.

There was a log fire in the hearth. Subdued lighting glowed on the marble fireplace and the gilded clock on the mantel, and reflected in the pieces of furniture she had gathered to the room. American and English. Beth thought French too fussy, even vulgar, to the horror of a number of Washington matrons and climbers of her acquaintance. The drapes, and carpets, like the furniture, were her choice, not the diktat of a high-priced designer. Which was probably why he liked the room. Two Sisleys and a small Cézanne were the only paintings; there were books everywhere else.

Books by their father, still regarded almost thirty years after his death as one of the best historians of the Civil War – books by Beth, from her doctoral thesis to her last and best-selling volume, the one she called her potboiler. Books on history, music, art, many of them Dad's library recreated here . . . and one half-shelf left mockingly empty, or put there as a challenge. The one reserved for his own books, whenever she finally goaded him into writing them.

Beth let him take the room in, as she always did, just as if she were a tour guide, or perhaps a mother who had kept his old room exactly the way he left it, year after year, waiting for him. She squeezed his arm in shared, silent memory. Then, breaking the reverie, she all but pushed him into a chair, her eyes bright. Not with drink or cocaine any longer, or even with a determined pretence of happiness. Just because – now – she *was* happy.

'How was Russia, Johnny? Are things *any* better, for God's sake?' She asked as if she had near and endangered relatives there; the impression she always gave about any place or state or war zone she cared about – and she cared about most of them. Organised, donated, *went* sometimes . . . she wanted to accompany him to Russia next time he went. Strangely, she had never travelled with Billy. He would have seen nothing with her eyes, and she required someone to share her perceptions. 'How were things? Come *on*!' she added, as if his silence teased her.

'It's not good – though I met an honest cop.' He grinned,

'You were arrested?'

'No. He interviewed me, over a fight in the hotel bar. Sort of a fight,' he added quickly as her face clouded with concern. 'Just an argument, really. Since I was State, I rated the chief of detectives himself. He seemed more amused by me than concerned. He was about as cynical as you could get, but I quite liked the guy. Other than that, Billy's investment's safe, though what the Russian government and people are getting out of it –'

'Pete Turgenev's here, with Billy. They flew up from Phoenix just today.'

'Has Vaughn come up with them?'

'No – he's a little tired –'

'Nothing wrong?'

'No, he's fine. I think he overreached, presenting Pete Turgenev and his executives to major stockholders. He's not Billy's father in name only.' She smiled.

'How was your trip to New York? I get back from Russia, and you're not even in town!' he mocked gently.

'You know. Rich students listening to a debate on the Third World's hunger – how much can it mean to them?' She spread her long-fingered hands. Diamonds glittered in the firelight, sparkled at her ears and throat. He did not remark the irony. 'Well, maybe one or two were impressed by the UN. The others either wanted us to send the Marines or get the hell out.'

Images of her radicalism, her protesting and marching, flickered in his memory. He realised he was still staring at her in a doctor's searching manner, and that it amused her. Recognising old contempts and angers in her expression was like seeing signs of returned health.

'So, you're entrenched as official caring professor at Georgetown, sister of mine?'

'I'm not politically correct –'

'– so you're not popular.' He grinned. Beth held onto her academic tenure because she was dazzlingly bright, Billy had established a professorship in geopolitical studies, and she had written an academic treatise on Eastern Europe's economies that had fluked its way into the non-fiction best-seller lists. Criticism was silenced by the power of the successful word.

He wondered whether she would nag him, even tonight, about his own book – the project that had accompanied him for years like a faithful but ignored hound. At State, they said every good boy needed a hobby, so the brightest and the best turned out monographs, papers, journalism when allowed – arts reviewing was favourite and he'd done a lot of it himself – but books, as he always protested to Beth, were *real hard work*, at which plea she would wrinkle her small nose with the mild, dismissive superiority of someone to whom the mind was a familiar room.

'No, I'm not popular, but that doesn't matter – not any more.' She sighed, stretching like a small animal in the warmth and firelight. Once, it had mattered. His had been the only approbation she had been able to recognise. Billy's fooling around had been a rejection. 'Who did you meet?' she asked.

'Just a deputy prime minister – who's in favour now but might not be by the weekend. Yeltsin's shuffling them like cards, trying to keep the hardliners fed but not bloated.'

'Is it all going to hell in a handbasket?'

'Maybe – maybe not.'

'Billy says their economy is coming around.'

'Billy would – he's a great guy, but he still believes trickle-down economics is enough to keep the peasants happy.' He raised his palms in a gesture of peace. She would defend Billy like a bear its cub, now that she felt loved again, felt that her stability and happiness were not under threat or siege.

She smiled. 'Grainger-Turgenev must be doing some good.'

'Some. There are Russians driving Porsches in Novyy Urengoy now. That's got to mean something – I guess. But you and Billy – ?'

'Fine.' There was no hesitation, no uncertainty. 'I lost sight of what Billy and I had together – so did he. Everything's fine now.'

'Good.'

He sipped his forgotten, tepid champagne. Relaxed in the firelight that threw their shadows together on the wall.

'Open your present.'

She snatched it up from the arm of her chair and tore at the wrapping. Her eyes widened. The small, gold-framed ikon, a flat, cartoon-like image of the Virgin haloed with stars and heavily painted – like a whore, he thought irreverently – gleamed like the furniture.

'It's beautiful.' She kissed him, and edged herself onto the arm of his chair. They admired the ikon together.

'Black market, in Moscow. An old woman. She must have kept it under her mattress for decades.' She seemed to disapprove. 'I gave her a decent price, Sis, I really did. She's suddenly rich, and in dollars.'

There was a knock at the door and the imperturbable figure of Stillman, the butler, appeared; an adult come to summon children.

'Your guests have begun arriving, Madam,' he announced sepulchrally. Lock, sipping at his champagne, controlled a giggle.

'Thank you, Stillman – I'll be right out.' The door closed behind the butler. Beth sighed, but it was a noise of pleasure, then stood up, smoothing the sheath of her dress. 'Come to lunch tomorrow. I want time to talk to you . . .' Then she smiled, touching his hand with her fingertips. 'No, just talk. I am going to *enjoy* my party!'

She glided to the door and he followed her. There were gowned women, black-tied men in the reception hall, where the lights seemed suddenly stage-bright. The grand staircase climbed to the gallery, the chandelier glittered, hired-in maids took topcoats and wraps. A few politically incorrect furs, swathes of silk scarves and bright shawls. Jewellery gleamed as if the bare-shouldered women posed deliberately beneath the flattery of the chandelier. Beth squeezed his hand, then floated forward confidently to greet her guests.

Lock took a cold glass of champagne from a passing tray,

relieved and glad. Almost at once, a powerful lobbyist bore down on him and he, too, was drawn into the eddies and whirlpools of power and money and pleasure, the elements of the occasion.

The suitcase lay open on the bed; forlorn in appearance only because Vorontsyev knew what had happened to its owner, lying in his underclothes in the mortuary of the Grainger Foundation Hospital. He had sat on one of the large room's upright chairs for ten minutes, staring at the suitcase, aware of Marfa's sniffles and the flatulence of the central heating pipes. Then he knew that the suitcase, packed before Rawls was summoned or taken to his appointment with a professional hit man, had been searched. Expertly, delicately – but searched nonetheless.

There was no briefcase, no Filofax. There was a suit still in the wardrobe, together with a pair of shoes and some underwear, and little else except the toilet bag and its contents in the bathroom. Anonymous. It was too anonymous. There should have been a briefcase, papers, a passport, other things.

He picked up the telephone. Unlit, the room was shadowy with the snowblown day outside the window. He pressed for the cashier.

'I want to know whether Mr Allan Rawls left anything in your safe – yes, the dead man. Yes, the police.' His identity had little effect. It was a measure of the passing of an aristocracy. A revolution had occurred and people were no longer cowed by *KGB* or *police*. They genuflected before other, imported, gods – Amex Gold Cards, money, well-cut suits, fast cars. He was *only* the police and no longer counted here, in the best hotel in Novyy Urengoy where, uncorrupt, he could not afford a room.

'Mr Rawls put nothing in the hotel safe,' came the reply.

He put down the telephone. Marfa came out of the bathroom.

'Found any pills your family can use?'

She frowned, then nodded.

'He must have had trouble sleeping over here. He got some tablets from the hospital, apparently.' She rattled them, then put them in her pocket. Marfa's sister-in-law had trouble sleeping. The gas company injury insurance and the disability pension paid to Marfa's brother were inadequate to meet the demands of the town's new Westernised economy. He'd lost an arm in a rig accident. Soon, they'd have to move somewhere where it was cheaper to live.

'*I* have trouble sleeping *over here,*' he murmured.

'Nothing else, sir?' She slumped into a chair, and then at once was aware that her posture made her appear exhausted and sat bolt upright, leaning eagerly forward. Her black woollen scarf reached almost to the pale carpet, and swathed her throat like the folds of a python. Her small, narrow, pretty face was already clouding with the onset of her cold.

'No, nothing. Listen, take the next couple of days off –' She made as if to protest but he held up his hand warningly. 'You've got a cold coming. I don't care *how* much you want to put our drug-smuggling friends out of circulation. One sneeze at the wrong moment and you'd blow the whole thing! So, don't plead with me.' She was angry, her frustration that of a child – or someone deeply just. Innocent, anyway. 'OK? You'll just have to leave us incompetent males to tie the parcel.' He smiled.

Eventually, after her face seemed to have wrestled itself into acquiescence, she said: 'Agreed. Just don't cock it up, sir.' It appeared she was about to add a homily of some kind; probably concerning the dead or damaged victims of the heroin operation, their bereaved families. He really needed her on the drugs raid. How many of his people could he *really* trust not to fire off a warning shot that would look like an accident or the result of over-stretched nerves – or sound a car horn to warn the pushers and the suppliers? 'What about this business, sir?' she added, gesturing at the room. To her, it was a matter of indifference; a crime among the rich with only well-heeled victims.

Vorontsyev rubbed his hand through his greying hair. 'Who knows? He was searched and stripped of everything by his killer. The same man must have searched this room and removed his briefcase and any papers. Agreed?'

'Just a minute, sir –' She sneezed, to her own anger. She pulled the telephone off the bedside table and returned to her chair. Consulting her notebook, she dialled a number. Her impatient breathing was loud in the room.

'Antipov?' she asked. 'Police – yes, it's me. You're the night

28

commissionaire at the Gogol. I don't care if I woke you up, I've got some questions for you.' She paused, listening. 'Good. An American guest at the hotel, Mr Rawls – medium height, dark hair, small build, dark topcoat . . . he left the hotel around two or two-thirty this morning. Did he ask you to get him a cab?' She sniffed with exasperation. 'How many guests are in and out at that time? Look, we know you're on the take from the whores, do you want me to come around and ask you about that? Right. You remember . . . ? Good. Taxi. You know the driver – what? Noskov. Address? Cab number?' She scribbled in the notebook perched on her knee. 'What? Yes, I see. Don't leave town, someone will be around this evening to take a statement.'

She put the receiver down loudly. Expelled an angry, mucus-thick breath at the ceiling.

'Well?'

'I'll check on the driver, sir – after I've had a couple of aspirin and a lie-down!'

'Was there anything else?'

'Antipov said he thought Rawls was going to get into a limousine. A black Merc. It had been waiting outside the hotel for half an hour or more. But it wasn't for Rawls. It just drove off in the same direction, following the taxi.'

TWO

An American Tragedy

'You know what's wrong? You guys from State – and there's no offence in what I'm saying, nothing personal – but you should all butt out and let guys like me and Billy Grainger go in there with a free hand!' The CEO of an oil exploration company had Lock backed into a panelled corner of the vast dining room, so that his head was almost resting against the large splash of a Jackson Pollock. 'I mean – you guys with your *handouts* and your Harvard outlook, where's that going to benefit us or the damned Russians either?'

The man's tall, blonde, decorously glamorous wife, a lump of polished diamond on her finger glittering at him like the eye of a snake, appeared bored, hanging on the man's arm like a cloak to be wafted enticingly in the face of all the bulls in the world. Lock tried to smile disarmingly, but the woman was proof against everything unordained by her husband.

'I know what you mean,' he offered, 'but it's just not as simple as that –'

'Simple, hell! It's not any real problem,' the man replied, and Lock witnessed his tame lobbyist sidling unobtrusively towards them, calculating the worth in nanoseconds of a conversation with a roving junior executive from the State Department. 'Just let us in there, with a free hand!'

At once, before he could adjust his governmental mask, Lock snapped: 'I remember a whole bunch of Indian agents used the same argument, Sam.'

The wife's eyes flickered, momentarily, with amusement. Before the man could respond, Lock smiled affably and said: 'Sorry, Sam, we'll have to debate capitalist ethics some other time. I think my brother-in-law needs me.'

30

The lobbyist was assuring Sam that Lock was unimportant even before he was out of earshot. Sam seemed to think that Lock had been infected *by some of the crazy ideas over there*, and then they were gone, and his enjoyment was undisturbed. Any Washington party was a swim in the open ocean where one encountered the expected sharks and suckerfish and octopoid residents of the political deep. He assured himself he had gotten used to it, without any more longing for pot parties where Frank Zappa or The Grateful Dead blared from the hi-fi system, and the world seemed simple, its problems easily solved.

That past life was something still fondly remembered. He recalled parties in other parts of the world, from his time with the Company as well as his time with State. They marked his gradual maturity with their increasing glamour and formality. Until the only parties he ever seemed to attend were grand black-tie occasions like this, beneath high ceilings and surrounded by jewellery and painting-cluttered walls. The parties and the world's problems continued, unchanging.

The noise in the dining room, voices above cutlery and crystal, dinned around him; a coterie. Every Washington party was the same, people came just to *find* themselves in a coterie, among the familiar, inhaling the incense of power and money. He sidled through lobbyists, businessmen, the occasional hemmed senator or congressman. He queued behind plump, bare shoulders at the buffet, and smelt expensive perfume and cigar smoke as he was helped to caviar, prawns, salad, quiche, salmon and a glass of good claret, before the caterers turned away to the next customer. Then he moved towards his brother-in-law and Turgenev, after checking Beth's whereabouts automatically. Her slim arms waved above her head and the heads of those who surrounded her. The pleasure was genuine, not fuelled by drink or coke, the extroversion her own and not implanted by an analyst.

'John-boy!' Billy was his effusive self.

He turned to his brother-in-law, whose gaze flinched away momentarily, as if he always remembered Lock's angry, violent words when they had finally quarrelled about Billy's infidelities and the havoc they were wreaking in Beth. While she was

31

having her stomach pumped at Walter Reed, Billy had confessed that Beth was too hard to live with and too hard to live without. Billy had never really held that night against him, but there was always this fleeting shadow of it whenever they met.

The chandeliers dripped diamond glass. Real diamonds on pale, dark and black throats were offered up towards those peculiar, vast, imported ikons suspended from the ceiling. The dining room had a cupola of stained glass.

'Billy – Pyotr.'

'It's Pete here, surely,' Turgenev retorted with a smile.

'For a lot of these guys, *Pyotr* would require a brain transplant,' Billy offered as Lock shook hands with the Russian.

'You've been in Phoenix?'

'Let me tell you, John-boy. We had a presentation to major stockholders – what Grainger-Turgenev is doing, how we see the next five years, the whole bit.' Billy had been drinking, though not heavily, and his broad hand patted regularly on Lock's shoulder.

'How's Vaughn?'

'Dad's just a little tired. I guess Beth told you, uh? No need to worry, John-boy – he'll outlive both of us!'

Sharks and smaller fish nibbled at the edges of their group. Turgenev, who was CEO of Grainger-Turgenev in the Novyy Urengoy field, had three or four other Russians with him, vaguely known to Lock. There were two of Billy's executives, one a youngish woman wearing a stunningly peeled-away black dress sparkling with diamanté, as well as himself and Billy. Billy's party had moved with the eddies of favour and debt, money and influence, back and forth along the dining room's length during the last hour and more. Beth performed circles and pirouettes with her friends or amid audiences more academic or more impressed by academe. The activity around her was less intense than that which followed and surrounded Billy like the debris of a comet. For Billy was *into* Russia, had congressmen and even the occasional senator *in hand*; Billy had government funding *coming out of his ears*. Billy was a buzz-word.

Turgenev was taller than Billy, less powerfully built. They might have been a double-act for a buddy movie – which, in a way, was what they were; Billy short, dark, broad, Turgenev slim, pale-skinned and pale-eyed.

'How are you, John? Sorry I wasn't in Novyy Urengoy when you were last there. But Phoenix is warmer at this time of year – *any* time of year!'

The tide of the room was already beginning to eddy Billy and Turgenev away from him, and Lock was prepared to let them go. As they moved away, Turgenev's face became suddenly intent, as if a mask of affability had been removed, and he bent to say something to Billy; something peremptory and demanding. There was shock on Billy's face, as if he had been informed of Vaughn's death or the collapse of Grainger Technologies' stock on the Dow. It was the kind of disquiet he had seen on Billy's slowly comprehending features when he had finally confronted him on Beth's behalf; as if he had been shown something unacceptable, even despicable, about himself.

'Something wrong, Billy – Pete?' he called.

'No – *no*,' Billy replied, waving the matter aside but unable to remove it from his eyes.

It couldn't be Rawls' murder. Billy had told him of it earlier, and had been surprised, even shocked. But not *moved* in the way he was now. He'd just said, *The guy spent all those years in Washington only to get himself murdered in God-forsaken Siberia . . . eaten by a wolf, maybe, but mugged to death?* Rawls was replaceable, he wasn't family.

Billy had still not recovered from whatever he had been told, but Pete Turgenev was smiling and there couldn't be anything really wrong. Their party, shepherded by pilot fish towards other sharks, drifted amenably, knowing its power.

'Catch up with you, John,' Turgenev called.

The noise of the party gusted against Lock as he was left, for a moment, on his own tiny area of carpet. Food had been trodden into it, near his shoe. Beth wouldn't worry; this was the party carpet, after all, the one put down for such functions. Normally, the long dining room gleamed with polished wood blocks, flared with huge old Persian rugs.

Hurriedly, he picked at the caviar and the salmon and sipped his claret. Red wine with fish, dear me, he observed. But it was

33

room temperature and best French. Billy-boy, you're throwing one hell of a party for my sister's birthday! Even if it was maybe a kind of belated apology for fooling around and ignoring her for years . . .

A colleague from State drifted past with a small wave. A lobbyist and his client had the man from State between them like prisoner and escort. Lock grinned back, acknowledging the wave with a waggle of his fork. This was Indian country for civil servants and politicians.

Billy and Turgenev, on the other side of the room, were in close counsel with a Democratic senator who had ambitions to head the Senate Committee that overlooked the administration's assistance to Eastern Europe and the Russian Federation. Turgenev was affable, as always, while Billy's face was still clouded with some new and worrying knowledge. Lock realised that he might require a bolthole – preferably in the shape and glamour of a young woman with brains – before he was summoned into the dialogue as the State Department's resident expert on Russia. But he could not turn away from the image of the taller Turgenev and the somehow reduced and *shrunken* Billy. The unflurried, relaxed Russian looked as if he'd been moving in Washington circles for most of his life.

But then he had, in a way. He'd been a young but already senior KGB officer in Afghanistan during the '80s. He and Billy had met Turgenev during the last days, when the Russians were about to get out. They'd helped supervise the withdrawal, the prisoner exchanges, obtained guarantees of safe passage from the *mujahideen* commanders. They'd found themselves comrades-in-experience, the two men from the CIA and the KGB colonel. They'd all *liked* each other, under the strangest circumstances and in the most unlikely place. He had a snapshot somewhere of the three of them, posed against snow-capped mountains like good ol' boys on a hunting trip.

It had been the beginning of Billy's association with Turgenev, and when the Russian had appeared in Siberia, reincarnated as an entrepreneur, he and Billy had set up what had become the behemoth of Grainger-Turgenev, the largest exploiter of the vast Urengoy gasfield.

34

They drifted purposefully out of the dining room, leaving the senator in their wake – just Billy and the Russians; as if fleeing the party. Business? Beth would *not* be pleased; her liberal credentials did not extend to excusing a lack of etiquette in herself, Billy or anyone else.

His claret was refreshed by a murmuring waiter, moving smoothly as a machine about the room. There was a desultory exchange of greetings with a journalist, but no real conversation. The man was after bigger game. Russia was unfashionable this month in the *Washington Post*. Bosnia had the inside track on international news. A department junior introduced his girlfriend, a small-faced young woman hiding behind huge spectacles who gushed her awe of Beth. She'd been one of the students his sister had taken to the UN.

Then he was alone again for a moment, surveying the guests, before a hand touched his arm. His delight that it was Beth was at once tempered by her clouded expression.

'What's the matter with Billy?' she demanded, as if Lock were responsible.

'What's up, Sis? Great party –'

'Billy's locked in the study with Pete Turgenev and some other Russians. I want him out here, not ignoring his guests.'

'Sis, it must be important –'

'John, go and drag him back in here, please!'

She smiled at a passing compliment on the buffet and her hair from a blue-rinsed matron who was a congressman's wife and a member of the same country club, then the affability was gone in a moment.

'There's nothing to worry about, Sis,' he soothed. It was as if her new confidence was the merest façade. She would not interrupt Billy herself, just in case a chasm yawned in an angry or impatient refusal. He nodded. 'OK, I'll go roust him out.'

'Thanks, thanks –' And at once she plunged into a conversation regarding the current production of *La Forza del Destino* at the Washington Opera, the young woman from her class hanging on her every pronouncement. He was relieved to miss that discussion, because Beth would inevitably want to show

35

him off as her musicologist brother – which he wasn't, not unless he eventually *did* finish that damn' book on Monteverdi . . . Beth was severe when he excused it as a *good reason to spend time in Mantua and Venice, Sis, nothing more* . . . all of which reminded him he had to return the call on his answerphone from the lady at Washington Musica Antiqua tomorrow. Tomorrow, definitely – just as soon as he thought up a good enough story for the delay with the performing version of the opera.

There wasn't too much wrong. He wandered to the broad, dark doors of the dining room and across the hall. At the foot of the staircase, seated on the bottom step of the sweeping flight, an aspiring painter Beth was patronising was insinuating himself with two senior executives of a bank. Like the bank's profits, the price of his paintings was set to rise. Maybe the bank should invest . . . hustle, hustle. He smiled, then knocked at the study door.

He could hear raised voices on the other side of the door – which was locked, he realised. He knocked again, sipping at his claret. He could distinguish nothing of the conversation – quarrel, was it? Then Billy eased the door open like someone afraid of the cops or the landlord.

'Oh – John.' He was sweating and he had been drinking bourbon by the scent of his breath. He was in shirtsleeves, his black tie loosened and dangling on his chest, which heaved as if he had been running. 'Beth sent you, uh?' Lock could see Turgenev seated in a leather armchair, long legs stretched confidently out. The Russian turned his face towards the door. He was smiling, untroubled. 'Well, did she?'

'Yes. You know what a stickler – '

'I'm busy, John. Just get lost, uh?' He manufactured a disarming, reassuring smile. His eyes were drunk, tired and – unnerved.

'OK, OK, I'm just the messenger.' Lock raised his hands in mock surrender, and Billy nodded, closing the door and relocking it at once.

Even before he had moved away from the door, he could hear Billy's raised voice again; protest, anger, defiance. He shook his head. A disagreement over profits, what else? He'd have to soothe Beth.

He looked at his watch. Eleven-thirty. He had an early meeting with the Secretary of State, who wanted his face-to-face impressions of the Russian situation. He'd leave soon.

He looked back at the study door, as if drawn to the disturbing eddies and waves of emotion he had sensed as vividly as static electricity during the moments that the door was ajar.

He yawned. Not your business, he advised himself. Just soothe Beth, nod in the direction of the faces that were important, talk to the people he liked, then make tracks. Pete Turgenev was a hard-nosed bastard, but then so was Billy. It would be an interesting contest –

It was like the most undeserved and repressive surveillance, glancing through the small square of window in the door to the ward. He could make out only the shape of the wife beneath the bedclothes, her features hidden by a mound of pillow. Dmitri Gorov sat motionless on a chair beside the bed, staring at the hand that lay unresponsively in his own. It was a scene, Vorontsyev guessed, identical to every other visit Dmitri made. A tableau depicting the aftermath of a tragedy. His wife was evidently sedated on this occasion. There were more awful visits, he gathered, when she wept uncontrollably, when she was conscious but did not know him, when she was a girl again.

He could not understand why Dmitri came so regularly. Was it self-flagellation for the dead daughter? Was it memory, love?

Vorontsyev turned away, ashamed, his boots echoing in the hospital corridor. He had come to collect Dmitri, but the man was evidently not yet ready to abandon the silent, unconscious madwoman.

The pharmacist had confirmed that he had prescribed sleeping pills for Rawls – four days ago. The executive from Grainger-Turgenev had identified the body in the mortuary. Vorontsyev had the autopsy report in his pocket. It told him nothing he did not already know. Rawls had been dragged into the copse, but had not walked any distance. The taxi must have dropped him and headed back to town. He must have been meeting someone he knew − at least, someone he had no cause to fear would do him harm. There had been no sign of a struggle, no physical damage to Rawls other than the single wound to the back of the head. The Russian who'd identified him had no explanation. He had expected Rawls to leave on the morning flight to Petersburg.

Why would he have been killed, except to rob him? the Russian had asked.

Agreed − except . . . why was he out there, in the icy dark-before-dawn without even overshoes and not a suspicion in his head?

Vorontsyev looked at his watch. Turned back towards the ward and Dmitri. It was time to leave. Rawls was a larger matter, like a drama seen in the shapes of clouds; it was perhaps significant, but also illusory, a trick of the mind. The drugs shipment they were expecting that night was real, part of the world of facts which was all that should interest the chief of detectives in a raw town in Siberia. He tapped on the door, then pushed it slightly ajar. Dmitri, roused from his empty contemplations, nodded, then released the expressionless hand, folding it back under the bedclothes. He stood up, picked up his fur hat, paused for a moment, then hurried to join Vorontsyev.

'Sorry −'

'No problem. But it's three already.'

'Anything useful?'

'On Rawls?' Vorontsyev shook his head. 'Nothing.'

'Where do we go from here?'

Their footsteps hurried along the corridor, echoing ahead of them and behind, as if a platoon of soldiers were quick-marching through the Foundation Hospital.

'Nowhere, I should think. What can we do? The guy was robbed. Everyone says so.'

'Except you.'

Vorontsyev shrugged. He had, involuntarily and perhaps while he was unguarded, recalled an early visit to Dmitri's house for a weekend barbecue in summer. Remembered the vivacity of both wife and daughter, their unexpected ease in front of him, the certitude of their family life. Midges had plagued the patch of garden behind Dmitri's home on the outskirts all afternoon, but it had not seemed to matter. It had not diminished the laughter.

'Maybe. Maybe not. Who knows what Americans think they're doing?'

They reached the bottom of the final flight of stairs, and the foyer where the Outpatients Department had created its encampment of people with limbs in plaster or patched eyes, loiterers, children who sniffled and roared and ran around shrieking – and, as if the Soviet ethic could never be entirely expunged, lounging porters in brown overalls. But he had been informed that hospital porters throughout the world were similarly ossified.

The day, declined into late afternoon, was bruised with cloud on the horizon. Vorontsyev pushed open the fingerprinted, smudged glass doors and the cold struck against them with a promise of winter violence. Their boots crunched on the freezing snow as they crossed the car park. Dmitri's bulk slithered on glassy ice, and Vorontsyev grabbed his arm, righting him.

The cellular telephone nagged in Vorontsyev's pocket. He opened the mouthpiece and said: 'Yes?'

'The flight's on time, sir. The weather's OK, they should get in more or less on time.'

'Good.' He folded the instrument away like the empty wrapping of a toy, and thrust it into his pocket.

'Well?' Dmitri had forgotten his wife.

'It's in the air – and coming our way.' Dmitri's face was as excited as that of a child. He sensed the same pleasure in himself.

He was warm in the car park's freezing air. The lock of the car door opened easily, without his having to heat the key. They bundled themselves into the car, as if setting out for a party, and Rawls and Dmitri's wife, Anna, had never existed.

The aircraft bringing gas workers up from Pakistan would land in a little less than six hours. They'd be at the airport to meet it, would watch the unloading and the passengers filing, ghostly, in night-glasses across the tarmac. They'd follow the bus or taxi back into town, then wait for the Pakistani called Hussain to walk into the glare of their surveillance at the block of flats. How much heroin didn't matter, it would be something; a satisfactory consignment. It would be *real*, unlike the cloudy speculations that surrounded the murder of Allan Rawls.

He started the car. Dmitri, beside him, was now tense with excitement, and guilt at the opportunity to forget his wife for a few hours. The engine coughed, then became an assertive roar. He had wandered out of some abstract drama which refused to make its meaning clear into the last act of a play that offered a genuine climax. They were going to *do* something, have something to *show* –

The telephone drew him slowly up from a deep, dreamless sleep. The room pounced familiarly as he switched on the bedside lamp. Four in the morning. He could hear rain against the window.

'Yes?'

There was a moment's hesitation, then: 'Do I have Mr John Lock?'

'Yes? Is this important?'

'I'm Lieutenant Faulkner, Mr Lock. I'm calling from Mr William Grainger's house –'

'Wait a minute, there. Are you police?'

'Yes . . . Mr Lock. Washington PD.'

The man's reluctance worried him. He felt stunned by a detonation he had hardly begun to suspect.

'What kind of policeman are you?'

'A homicide detective, Mr Lock.'

He was silent, hearing the rain against the window, the tick of the alarm clock, the breathing of the man on the other end of the line. A solitary car in the street below.

'Mr Lock –?'

'Yes,' he said in a stony, gruff whisper.

'I'd like you to come out here, sir – to help us identify the –'

'No!' It was not his answer to Faulkner's request. 'What's happened?'

'There have been some homicides. If you could make it now, it would help us.'

'Bodies?'

'Yes. There were servants, I understand?'

The ridiculous spring of hope, broken-winged, was down in an instant.

'A butler. A housekeeper. *How many bodies are there*?'

'You've accounted for the other two, Mr Lock.'

Immediately, he felt the nausea choking his throat as his stomach churned.

'Hold on –' he blurted, then staggered across the bedroom to the bathroom.

After he had vomited, retching until his throat ached, he stared into the bathroom mirror at a stranger's face – white, drawn, dislocated. His mind reeled as if he had been awoken from a drunken stupor. His thoughts raced with images of Beth and Billy and of the house, the gardens falling to the Great Falls, the long drive up which his headlights had climbed, Beth and Billy, Stillman the butler, and Beth and Beth . . .

There was no escape. He was locked in a padded room where the scream, the only activity left to the stranger's face in the mirror, wouldn't be heard by anyone.

Beth had been murdered –

Twenty minutes late, the Tupolev dropped out of the clouds and rushed towards them, Aeroflot emblazoned on its flanks like the desperate cry of a lost cause. Vorontsyev watched it inspect the runway, wobble, hurry and then settle as quickly as a migrating duck onto the strip of darkness between the lights.

He swept the glasses after it as it rushed away again, not appearing to slow until it turned like a wounded animal, slowly and clumsily. A hundred passengers crammed into it, standing-room only as was *still* the habit of Aeroflot, especially with Iranians and Pakistanis and whoever else had been gathered up in Islamabad to fly into winter. The plane nosed back towards them, once more looking like a shark, sleek and purposeful, nosing the darkness for its appointed parking slot. Dmitri twitched and shuffled beside him. On that plane would be handheld heroin, furtively concealed, nestling in clothing or in toothpaste tubes or talc containers. Just enough to keep the

41

streets of Novyy Urengoy supplied until the next flight, a fort-night later.

The plane came to a halt. He continued to watch it through his night-glasses, staring at him like a ghost-shark.

Iran, Pakistan, Kashmir, the Moslem Triangle, as the press and agencies of a dozen countries called it, had come to Siberia. Just a small sideline. The Foundation Hospital addiction unit, courtesy of the American conglomerate whose name it bore, was stuffed to the ceiling with the victims of that sideline. The passenger door had opened in the flank of the Tupolev. A collective sigh was audible from the surveillance team. And – *and*, it was being delivered into his hands, here and now. He sensed – shared – the excitement like the freshness of a cold wind.

The passengers began to descend. Whispers identified or rejected them. They were waiting for Hussain, even though they understood that there could be two, three, even six carriers. The plight on the streets had been evident to them for days. A new supply was *urgently* required. The drugs community was rippling like dead flesh responding to the expansion and contraction of the gases of decay. It *hurt* – they *needed*.

The Iranians and Pakistanis and others trooped towards the terminal, while the luggage tractor nosed like a piglet against the sow and the bags began appearing. He glanced at Dmitri beside him, leaning against the other side of the car, his breath smoking in excited little signals of anticipation and desire. The stars were hard in the sky, there were a few grey blobs of cloud, and the airport lights showed a straggle of passengers.

He fitted the night-glasses once more against his eye sockets. Those bags, they could contain more drugs. There were no searches of returning workers. Everything was done like some parody of Western commercials for holidays – *Siberia welcomes you*. The operation could, of course, be far bigger than Dmitri's sole contact – an Uzbek he had charged with sodomising the son of a local government official related to a deputy prime minister – had ever revealed or known.

He admitted to himself that he had almost *indulged* Dmitri in his pursuit of the drug-pushers who had fed his daughter the heroin on which she had overdosed. It had seemed more congenial than having to watch his best subordinate disintegrate at his desk.

The troop of passengers had entered the terminal.

The town's addiction problem was increasing like algae under sunlight, covering the surface of the place. The politicians made noises, then forgot, returning to their habitual fawning on the foreign companies who possessed the real power. Nobody wanted to know – not really *know* – about heroin.

The R/T, as if to emphasise the insistence of his thoughts, clamoured with reports. Hussain was in the terminal, they were making for the luggage carousel, then customs. Usually, they passed through customs with not even a perfunctory search. Tonight would be the same.

'Where's Hussain?' Dmitri's excitement was palpable on the air, like the scent of petrol; something inflammable.

'Baggage carousel. He doesn't seem worried.'

'He wouldn't. He must have done this trip dozens of times.'

The Uzbek had been a small-time pusher, but he'd pointed them towards an apartment block, rundown and colonised by the families and relatives and hangers-on of gasfield workers. He picked up his cut heroin there. There was a courier named Hussain, a Pakistani. The heroin originated in the Moslem Triangle. That was it. In exchange for the information, the sodomy charge had been kept from the father of the boy. The boy, an addict himself, fervently desired anonymity.

Vorontsyev glanced at his subordinate, all but envying him the sense of purpose that strained his features like those of a hunting dog close to its quarry.

He shook himself; the nervous tension was infectious, the voices from the R/T a discordant chorus of anticipation. Hussain had collected his luggage – two bags – and was on his way through the customs green channel. No one stopped him, but his exit from customs was reported.

'Anyone else?' Vorontsyev asked quickly. Dmitri was puzzled. 'Get hold of the cabin crew, the hostess or the purser. Find out who he sat with – one of you, get on with it. You're not needed in customs any more.'

'Yes, sir.'

43

There had – now that he really thought about it with stretched nerves – to be more than one courier. Diminish the risk, increase the supply. The addicts had begun queuing at the Grainger Foundation Hospital's unit for the heroin substitutes, giving their names, addresses . . . the supply was so overdue.

'Get me the passenger list – and I want every one of them checked out with Grainger-Turgenev and RossiyaGas and SibGas and all the other companies. Wherever they work, I want links between them, if they're there, uncovered. Got that, all of you? Tomorrow's schedule.'

Dmitri, for an instant, laid his gloved hand on Vorontsyev's arm, a gesture of gratitude. Vorontsyev felt a small, sneaking shame but Dmitri didn't even resent his elbowing his way in, taking control. Nor did Dmitri's look remind him that he had shown no more than an occasional – even if fervent – interest in Dmitri's lead via the Uzbek sodomite. Both of them loathed drugs, badly wanted results. But, Vorontsyev admitted, he had always believed Dmitri more of a crusader than a policeman.

'He's getting into a taxi.'

'Tail-car?' Dmitri snapped.

'We've got him – don't worry, Inspector.'

'Let's go,' Vorontsyev said to the driver, and they heaped themselves into the rear of the ZiL.

The car skirted the terminal building and hurried towards the airport gates and the highway, the suspension thudding on rutted, frozen snow. In the distance of the night, the narrow flares from the rigs pricked out like campfires. Ahead of them, the town glowed, the outlying apartment blocks seemed skeletal, pocked with lighted windows. Block after block, retreating towards the centre of the town. Some larger houses, cottages, fenced gardens now under snow, churches, a cemetery, old-fronted shops and narrow streets; Urengoy had been the administrative centre of the province, and Novyy Urengoy its suburb. Now, it housed a hundred thousand people, and maybe fifteen or twenty thousand more lived in trailers, shacks, lean-tos and sheds. Workers from the Urals, the Ukraine, Iran, Pakistan, Soviet Central Asia, imprisoned for two weeks at a stretch for twelve-hour shifts on one of the fourteen hundred gas wells.

They passed a huge hoarding that informed him that Novyy Urengoy produced two-thirds of all Russian gas, fourteen trillion cubic feet every year. The word *Soviet* had been painted out, and *Russian* substituted. The place was – as it enlarged before and around them – phantasmagorical, almost nightmarish. Beside the highway was trailer park after parking lot after windswept collection of shacks. Lights glowed fitfully and feebly in the vast darkness, remote as stars from each other and from him. The place was a company town, his enforcement of law tolerated and often ignored. It was like a huge, Tsarist factory complex, except that no one was actually *poor* here any longer; desperate, futile, greedy, envious, crooked, but not destitute. They chose to live like derelicts and peasants because of the money. Six or seven hundred roubles for a week's work. A thousand, two thousand a week for anyone with the slightest degree of skill or responsibility.

Stunted larch and birch, and sheds littering the ground beneath their inadequate shelter. Then the sodium lamps flared beside the road, masking the detritus of greed.

'Hussain's taxi still in sight?' Dmitri asked over the car radio.

The canyons of apartment blocks enclosed the car, and Vorontsyev could hear the wind noise above the sound of the engine and the crunch of the snow tyres on the rutted street. Hunched figures hurried through the icy weather.

'We're right behind him –'

'Don't alarm him!'

'It's *OK*, Inspector, everything's under control.'

'Where are you?'

'Junction of K Street and 14th. We're both at the lights.'

'Keep me informed.' He turned to Vorontsyev, his eyes gleaming. 'Just on the edge of the red-light district. He's heading straight there.'

He kept the radio microphone cradled in his hand, like a weapon or a lifeline. The car halted at a set of lights strung above the junction of 9th Street and K. They were five blocks behind the tail-car and Hussain's taxi. The old town slunk away into semi-darkness to their left, wrapping itself in the night and the twisting, narrow streets and patches of blankness. Ahead, the main street was swallowed in the glare of lights from bars, hotels, clubs, strip-joints, whorehouses, cinemas. K Street was a tunnel of neon.

The car skidded. No one bothered to clear the snow this early in winter. The heaviest traffic was workers' buses taking men out to the well-heads and rigs, and large trucks moving pipes and heavy equipment. When they wanted to move, the streets were snowploughed. Otherwise –

'What's that?' he asked, tapping the driver on the shoulder. A blue light was struggling to announce itself amid the neon glare and the small, gathered crowd.

He felt Dmitri about to protest.

'We have time,' he said. 'Just make sure the tail-car doesn't lose him.' Then to the driver: 'Pull over. If they've picked the wrong situation, they could start a riot.'

It didn't happen often, but it did happen – drunks who kicked back, or whose friends didn't want them taken in. A brawl like that had lost them two officers through serious injury and one they'd had to bury.

Ambulance and police car, the former drawn up at the black entrance to a side alley. The patrolmen were watching from beside their car, not quite indifferent but hardly concerned. Vorontsyev got out of the car and they stood to attention and pretended attentiveness. He nodded.

'What is it?'

One of the patrolmen pointed to the alleyway.

'Dead druggie in there – OD'ed, by the look of it, sir. *This* one –' He jabbed his gloved index finger against the rear window of the patrol car. '– was trying to get the clothes off the body before it was cold. Says he's a *friend* of the deceased and he wouldn't have minded!'

'Is the one you've arrested an addict?'

'Looks like it, sir. He's in a bad way. Really needs a shot in the arm.' He grinned indifferently.

Vorontsyev nodded and crunched his way over to the two ambulancemen, who had placed the body on a stretcher. The small crowd was already beginning to drift away towards the warmth and expense of clubs and bars. He heard laughter; it

46

wasn't cruel, merely indifferent and at something else entirely. The addict had already been forgotten. The wind howled out of the blackness of the alley. He sensed others in there, derelicts. Huddled in cardboard boxes and drinking anything that offered oblivion. The cold stars were visible above the alley, undrowned by neon.

He turned to look at the body as the ambulancemen hoisted the stretcher. A thin, stubbled face, red-eyed and staring. Probably eighteen or nineteen; he looked Russian. His clothes smelt vilely even in the icy temperature. He watched the stretcher put carelessly into the rear of the ambulance, then saw the other addict, the grave-robber in need of a fix, so badly in need, staring at him with a dead, white, expressionless face.

He shrugged.

'Go easy,' he murmured, to the surprise of the militiamen. 'Just lock him up – get him some of that heroin substitute from the hospital. OK?' he added as they stared at him, astonished.

'Yes, sir.'

He nodded, surprised himself. Then, as he got into the car, he saw Dmitri's face as that of a driven, fanatical monk from Dostoyevsky, battling for the soul of Novyy Urengoy. He'd often employed the image of Dmitri as a religious fanatic; now, it seemed not as risible as before. There were worse delusions in which to believe . . . though one needed a daughter's death, probably, to thrust one into a state of mind like that.

'There's a call for you,' Dmitri said, and mouthed, *Bakunin*.

Vorontsyev took the mobile telephone from Dmitri. 'Yes, Colonel. What can I do for you?'

'I've decided to take over the Rawls investigation,' Bakunin announced. 'Send me everything you've got. I take it that doesn't amount to very much?'

'Not a great deal, Colonel. Is there a security angle?'

'I'm upgrading the investigation to keep the Americans happy. You don't object?'

'Suits me, Colonel. I wish you good luck.'

He switched off the phone and put it between them on the bench seat. Shrugged.

'Bakunin wants Rawls to himself?'

Vorontsyev nodded. 'Seems so. He's welcome.' He rubbed his hands. 'Let's get *our* job right.'

'He's paid off the taxi. Going in, carrying both suitcases,' the radio announced.

'Fine with me,' Dmitri sighed, his anticipation vivid.

The Maryland countryside blazed with late fall colours. Across the rush and boom of Great Falls, there was a fine day. Virginia and Maryland, peaceful; he in a trance-like state of shock and dammed grief. He stood on the terrace at the back of the mansion, looking over the gardens that sloped down to the Potomac. His breath smoked no more than the cooling coffee in the mug he cradled in his hands. He felt cold and numb inside his topcoat.

Yes, that's my sister . . . yes, my brother-in-law . . . the house-keeper, yes, the butler, Mr Stillman . . . and, beneath a tree near the main gates, *yes, the security guard . . .*

And that was all there was to do and say. Lieutenant Faulkner was polite, grave, attentive, businesslike. And sensitive enough to let him wander away soon after the identifications, into the kitchen where the crocks and crystal from the party were stacked and ordered, ready for collection by the catering company. There was a scent of abandoned food. He made himself coffee, nudging away the insistent, hundred reminders of her that every surface, utensil, cup and tile seemed intent upon thrusting at him. Beth had looked – just dead; not agonised, not even surprised. Just – still.

Jewellery, yes . . . empty boxes and caskets in her bedroom . . . *Yes, a Pissarro, I think yes, quite valuable . . .* Other empty frames and lighter squares on the walls of the library and the main drawing room . . . *I don't know how much my brother-in-law kept here, in cash or securities . . .* The safe in Billy's study had been opened with explosives. Silver missing, he thought, some valuable jade pieces, other paintings, ornaments and statuettes . . . There were shreds of packing, polystyrene bubbles, wrapping –

– professionals. A gang. Maybe even stealing to order. So surmised Faulkner. *Did they – usually kill?* he had asked. *Sometimes. Not always. In this case, they weren't prepared to wait until the house was empty . . .*

48

End of story. End of Beth's existence. Snuffed out. *For things, for damned things!* he had protested in his only moment of wildness.

Maybe two million dollars' worth of things, Mr Lock, Faulkner had murmured in response, gripping his arm. *Maybe more . . . I'm sorry. It happens.*

The police had found Beth's guest list, Faulkner had told him. There'd be no need to trouble him on that . . . *you left when, Mr Lock?*

Then Faulkner had moved away, finally, at the door to the kitchen. The downlighters had hurt his eyes. He had fled them – the house, really, and the memories of the previous evening and of Beth at some pinnacle of ease and beauty and happiness, ready only to fall.

Now, all he could see was the child four years older than himself, forcing herself not to cry when telling him that Mom and Dad had been killed in a road accident. Both dead. It had pressed and pressed on him while Faulkner had talked, however much he had tried to force it back. It was, now, the only *real* memory of her, and it was awful.

He sipped at his coffee, but it was already cold. Angering him. He flung the mug away from him, over the stone balustrade down towards the lawn. A squirrel hopped into bushes, alarmed. The grey coffee streamed through the air like a comet's dull tail.

His hands were shaking now they had nothing to hold. He stared at them as they ached for something on which to do violence, have revenge . . .

Oh, Jesus . . . The vivid, red-gold-green countryside mocked, the bright morning indifferently serene. He heard crows calling, other birds. Oh, Jesus . . .

THREE

Raised Incorruptible

Dmitri was staring through the grimy windscreen, which the car's heater managed to prevent fogging up, at the blowing snow and the trodden distance of white between them and the dilapidated block of flats.

The car's interior was hot with their tension. Vorontsyev could make out the humped, whitened shapes of the other unmarked cars. The two vans that had contained the TacTeam were parked well out of sight, the members of the unit crouched in doorways, leaning against pillars, masked, waiting.

He lifted the R/T to his cheek, then bellowed into it and the car radio. 'Go – *go*!' Icy air as Dmitri opened the door. '*Go!*'

The wind, the taste of snow, the uncertainty of the surface under his feet, all caused him to stagger as he followed Dmitri. He watched the first members of the TacTeam approach the entrance to the flats. Snowbound steps, a grimy glass door shattered like the image of a star. He could visualise the grubby, graffitied foyer with its thermoplastic tiles in grim grey. The lifts might not be working, but then that was what the TacTeam trained for. The flat they were interested in was on – running now, thudding and lumbering across the snowy street – the fourth floor. There were a handful of windows lit, fewer curtained. A block of flats so rundown only the families and hangers-on of the least-rewarded gas workers inhabited it.

Dark shadows flitting up the steps, through the doors. There were lights in the windows of the flat they wanted, burning steadily. No one up there was alarmed.

Dmitri steadied him as he slipped on a patch of ice. Other men in overcoats and parkas. Handguns bristled in fists. There

50

was a heady, collective excitement, something dangerous, communal. Wanting to do damage.

They clumped breathlessly up the steps and burst through the doors. One black-overalled figure was waiting at the lift, others he could hear thudding up the stairs. The porter was not in evidence – unless the ancient, bemused woman huddled against one scratched and filthy wall was the superintendent of the block. He didn't think so. She was just a terrified old woman –

'Lift?' he bellowed. The TacTeam officer shook his head. 'Stairs!' to Dmitri.

They crowded after the overalled specialists and two younger detectives in wet-stained overcoats. The omnipresence of pistols. He would not be able to prevent shots, fatalities –

– they needed, at least, Hussain alive. He'd stressed that, time and again, but all the sober nods and grimaces of agreement in the squad room had been replaced by a mad delight in antici-pated, violent success.

First floor. Dmitri was panting like a huge dog, gripping the loose handrail as he lumbered after Vorontsyev. The R/T's cacophony was uninterrupted, irresistible. Two team members were already on the fourth floor, *turn of the stairs, nothing moving up here*, their breathing like that of large, fierce hounds. He heard the clicking-off of safety catches. Second floor. A startled child, wearing only a vest that did not cover his tiny penis, was peeing in the corridor, presumably not against his own front door. His eyes were black holes in his dark features.

Third floor. The detective ahead of him had trodden in some-thing that had spilt from an abandoned rubbish bag, and was swearing.

'Shut that noise!' he snapped at him. Their boots, still wet with melted snow, slithered like reptiles in panic on the stairs. *Still nothing moving, sir*. The noise of a radio, a child crying, a deep male voice quarrelling. The noise of a slap. A door slammed.

'What – ?'

'Sir, someone in the corridor. Old man –'

'Get him out of there – quietly!'

Fourth floor. He lunged against the two detectives he had pursued up the stairs. There was staining, rubbish, dogshit on

51

the cracked linoleum flooring. The two overalled Tac-men were bustling a shrivelled, nightgowned old man – Iranian or something like – along the corridor towards them. Terrified eyes stared at Vorontsyev above the gloved hand that was clamped over the old man's mouth.

He nodded reassuringly, to no effect, and told one of the younger detectives: 'Take him out of the way. Make sure he doesn't wander back up here!'

Others crowded behind them now. Three in overalls, another plainclothes detective. He ignored the old man's continuing terror as he was roughly bundled away.

'He didn't come out of the flat we want, sir. Further down the corridor.'

Vorontsyev nodded, listening. Arab music from behind one peeling, flimsy door. The sound of an argument, or perhaps merely an exchange of information. The wet smell of cabbage mingling with more spicy scents, the smell of ordure and decay and mould. The walls were icy with frozen leaks and condensation. Their breaths whitened the air.

'OK – positions. Wait till I give the word,' he instructed in a hoarse whisper, breathing heavily; excitedly. Dmitri stared into the coming moments as into a huge gift-parcel. 'Try to keep alive, try to keep *them* alive!'

The TacTeam members moved along the corridor in short, jerky little shuntings, constantly overtaking each other as in the steps of a strange dance, then positioning themselves on either side of the door behind which Hussain, others, and the heroin, waited. Four overalled figures below bright, angelic faces turned to him. This was *it*. For a moment, none of them was corrupt, on the take, indifferent. This was –

He nodded and the largest of the overalled men raised his foot and jabbed stiff-legged and violently at the flimsy door. It cracked and folded inwards with little more noise than he would have made stepping on a twig. A small sound –

– swallowed, at once, by a roar, a bellow of noise. A sheet of flame engulfed the TacTeam man at the moment he regained his balance. Two other figures fell back, screaming. Then the flame was gone. The man on the floor burned, then simply

52

smouldered. He could still hear screaming – he thought. It was hard to tell in the deafened condition to which he returned from numb shock. Slowly, the screams became louder. Not from the member of the TacTeam. The concussion as much as the flames had killed him. The noises came from inside the flat.

He moved clumsily. The shockwave had robbed his legs of strength. Someone beside him, as he moved, was muttering. *No, no, no, no* . . . it sounded like. It was Dmitri, robbed of his gift.

He imagined that there had been screams; Beth's protestations against whoever had invaded her life and was about to rob her of her self. He did not wish to do so. His hand closed around a thick-cut crystal glass where whisky swilled with all his barely-suppressed grief. He kept looking at the glass and the swilling, gold liquid rather than drinking from it.

He glanced at the answerphone as if it posed some threat. It was almost filled with messages of sympathy. He'd listened to every one, and answered none of them . . . and the woman from the music group was sorry to bother him again, but . . . she obviously hadn't read the newspapers or connected Beth with himself – and Fred who, with a lot of deep breathing and genuine, awkward compassion, still had the tickets for the basketball and wondered what to do with them . . . the Library of Congress enquired through an austere female voice when he intended making use of the books he had listed before his last trip to Russia . . . and more expressions of sympathy, the disconnected, ugly, unreal gulping of people who saw him on the edge of an abyss and didn't know how to save him. He'd unplugged the machine. That way, the voices couldn't enter the apartment.

Billy had not had time to reach for one of the various firearms he kept around the house. He had been shot in the bathroom, and was found slumped over the basin. His head was arranged as if on the block of a guillotine, twisted sideways, blood from the wound on his cheek streaking over his chin like thin vomit into the white china basin. Beth had hardly moved in the bed – he was grateful for that, at least – the bedclothes barely disturbed. Only marked with two black holes that then passed through her and into the mattress. The sheets had looked slightly arranged, too stiff and smooth. That had been the blood sticking them in place like licked postage stamps.

He stared at the window of his apartment's lounge, into the midday sun, the light splintering through his tears. The nausea becoming onmipresent.

He was preoccupied with anger, hatred; searching for a means and opportunity for revenge. Wanted to *know who*. He could not have anticipated this sense of being *cheated*, as if Beth had been some porcelain creation of his own smashed by a stranger's intrusion. He swallowed the hypnotic drink at a gulp, and choked on it, and fled to the bathroom to vomit.

When he came back into the lounge, the phone was ringing, seeming to have achieved a pitch of impatience at being ignored. He picked up the telephone before realising it was what he least wanted to do.

'Yes?' His voice sounded strange, as if it didn't belong to him.

'John?' An accent. Not American.

'Yes – this is John Lock. Is this important? I mean, I'm sorry, but –'

'John, it's Pete. Pyotr Turgenev . . . I understand why you didn't recognise it was me. I rang to say how sorry – how *angry* I am . . .'

Lock's throat was stretched and dry. His mouth was vile with the taste of bile and the hours of drinking. He began to realise he had not eaten, but had not simply stared at the glass, either.

'I don't want to *talk* –!' he wailed, shocking himself.

'John, I *understand*,' Turgenev soothed. 'I can't help *feeling* it – without intruding on your special grief, John, I feel it, too.'

'Thanks, Pete.' He grabbed at the intuitive empathy as if to drag it down into the deep place where he felt himself to be. There was someone else down there after all, who knew what it meant.

Unlike the *Washington Post*, lying open on the small table beside the telephone. In its habitually reined-in style, it announced in a subordinate headline the *Grainger Slaying*, and trickled towards its report with subsidiary heads that acknowledged *Arts Patron Among Victims* and *Dow Slump Expected for Stock in Grainger Technologies*. It was all so neat, so encapsulated, measuring the worth of Billy and Beth on the markets of industry and the arts. What other headlines could any good American wish, having been violently done to death?

'You still there?' Turgenev asked, his sympathy insistent now, almost proprietary.

'Yes, sorry –' Beth's brilliance of mind and her qualities as a Washington hostess achieved parity in the *Post*'s report. Billy's dash in intelligence and the market followed as almost equally admirable – now that he was dead. 'Look, Pete, I really can't talk right now –'

'I understand. I just wanted to *tell you* I understand.'

'Thanks.'

'Was it robbery?'

'Oh, yes,' he answered. 'Maybe as many as a dozen paintings, all her jewellery, things like that.' He realised he was repeating Faulkner's words exactly, as if he had been programmed like some PR guy to give out only so much and no more.

He felt his stomach churn again and squinted against the light burning through the net curtains. Beth had bought them, put them up –

'How terrible.'

'Yes.'

'I know . . . no, I don't need to say it, John. I just want you to get in touch if there's anything, simply anything, you might need or want. Even someone to talk to . . . Should I talk to Vaughn just now?'

'No, I'll do that. He's on his way up from Phoenix.'

'He must be broken up.'

'He is – is there something else?'

'No. Just sympathy, John. Understanding. You take care now.'

'Yes, Pete.'

'We all loved her, John –'

'Yes.'

Lock put down the receiver with the care he might have expressed in stroking a small, hurt animal. Pete Turgenev, Jesus . . . who'd have thought the KGB had such depth of feeling . . . ? At once, the small, self-rescuing joke foundered. The phone call had stranded him farther than before on the reef of his sorrow. Vaughn Grainger's arrival that afternoon loomed, a species of interrogation and pressure he felt he would not be able to undergo without himself coming apart.

He wandered to the window and stared through the glaze of the net curtains. The apartment was half of the first floor of an old Georgetown house, student lodgings become the necessary domicile of a civil servant. Except for those currently in power who bartered the mansions of the suburb at every election or Presidential whim. It possessed the atmosphere that much of Georgetown exuded, with the bright young men and women who did not have to stray too far from Harvard and Yale and the other colleges when they came home from power-broking and nudging and lobbying each evening. The couple downstairs were lobbyists for the soft drinks cartels, the guy who shared the first floor a poet who had not written a line since his last National Book Award.

Only rarely had women stayed – slept over, as kids called it, and it was almost as small an occasion as that – and only once had one moved in, taken up wardrobe as well as bed space. Even changed the drapes and the cologne in the bathroom. For a while, Johanna had been very real. He had surrendered to her, opened all the closets of his privacy and his secret life. When she had left, because it was still not enough, he had been devastated. No woman had slept in the apartment since. It had slowly reassembled itself as it had been, growing and healing around him like a broken carapace. *You have a cold place in you no one can reach – and God knows I've tried*, Johanna had said, a week before she moved out. Only one person could reach him – and she was dead. Johanna had been right, in a way. He had never wanted to share, be part of someone else. He had never wanted to give all his secret self to someone who wasn't *entitled*, like Beth was.

Had he ever gone into analysis, the shrink would have identified that snow-covered-ice stretch in a Vermont forest where his parents' car had gone off the road and struck a fir. In its facile way, it would have told him what he already knew, all too well.

The trees were red-gold along the quiet street. There was no ice in the whisky he had thoughtlessly poured. Two kids kicked up heaped, fallen leaves –

– turned away at once from that image. Too like, too like . . . He and Beth, kicking up New England leaves as children. As his older sister she would shower him with them, then brush him down so that Mom would not berate him. He turned quickly from the window, sensing that other, even stronger images, a whole army of them, were on the point of attack.

On his retinae was the image of a car, just beyond the shrilling children and their kicking legs and the flying red leaves. He did not want to turn back, but did so. The image was still retinal, that of a topcoated, hatted, squat man getting into a black sedan, and another man, taller and well wrapped up, getting out; an exchange of guards. He looked down into the street. The car was moving away from the kerb, its exhaust wintrily smoking. The man who had gotten out of it flicked behind a tree-trunk. The children played obliviously.

Lock realised he was under surveillance – who, why? The questions came immediately; that instinct that long training had placed there and State had not allowed to fall into disrepair.

Then another realisation. That the void he had been speaking into and imagining while he was on the line to Turgenev – *and* to Vaughn Grainger, earlier – was not entirely the void of his own grief. The hair on his neck tickled with curiosity, and fear. It had been that special kind of void, that added distance, that only occurs when a phone is bugged.

Even zipped up in their black bags, the bodies were not less damaged, less shocking. They lay like the victims of a road accident or a war zone, side by side, in the corridor. If Vorontsyev turned his head even slightly, the bags appeared to him like a black snowdrift. He turned his head frequently, such was his frustation and anger; as if blaming the bodies.

Because there was no drug shipment in the ruins of the flat . . . no trace of drugs. Maybe a month-old powdering of spilt heroin vacuumed up from a corner of the room by Forensic. There were two TV sets that might have been stolen, stored in the bedroom where condensation had frozen on the livid

57

wallpaper; there was little food. There were four bodies. The occupants, Hussain, and another man whose face wasn't quite intact, someone Vorontsyev thought he vaguely recognised – though not criminally, not from a mugshot or an arrest.

Hussain had brought *nothing* with him. That was Dmitri's all but anguished conclusion. They'd been *had*, and how. Someone – maybe even one of the officers in the ruins with them – had provided a tip-off. Hussain would never have thrown the heroin from the taxi. He'd stopped nowhere, except for traffic lights. He'd been watched closely at the airport. There'd been no switch –

– someone else's luggage? He didn't actually *carry* the heroin? Vorontsyev stamped his feet on the thin, purple carpet, waking his toes back to life in the wet boots. There were bootmarks all over the carpet, superfluous to the exploding cooking fat that had splashed it and the walls and the bodies. That was what Forensic suggested. Cooking on a faulty paraffin heater, spilt fat, explosion – *poor sods*. They were all burned, scarred by flying fat and paraffin. The heater or stove had gone off like a bomb. They'd been gathered round it to keep warm.

But there was no heroin, his thoughts insisted like an addiction. The information was certain, Dmitri persisted, Hussain had been scheduled to bring in heroin. He *must* have had it with him, mustn't he?

Which left a switch or a blind. Either way, he and Dmitri had been tricked. It had been a set-up for them, a charade, two raised fingers – probably originating from somewhere at head-quarters, someone on the payroll of whoever controlled Hussain. The drugs had come off the flight in another bag or in the cargo.

He glared towards the open door of the flat and the icy corridor and its black body bags. That containing the TacTeam officer lay alongside the others. He'd get a better burial, with a flag over the cheap coffin. The flat reeked of paraffin and other, un-nameable, scorched odours. Cheap carpet, furnishings, fat and muscle –

He cut off the thought there.

'We were set up – all the way from the plane!' Dmitri whined

58

beside him. Vorontsyev glowered at him. Undeterred, Dmitri continued. 'They sacrificed these poor sods just to cover their tracks!'

And, without doubt, they had done just that. Hussain, who must have been a good courier, the two others who were packagers, cutters, distributors.

'It could have been an accident,' Vorontsyev corrected his own thoughts, Dmitri's words.

'Like it was an *accident* there are no drugs here?'

They were standing in the middle of the room, on the most scorched area of the thin carpet, like a couple engaged in some depressing marital quarrel. Forensic fussed at the tag-end of their examination, searching as much for merit badges as for clues.

'Their stove blew up,' Vorontsyev tried to insist.

A bright, chilled, young face stood beside Dmitri, smiling as breath clouded around it. Dmitri held up a clear polythene envelope.

'Lubin here found some of these scattered around the room. Embedded in the furniture and walls,' Dmitri announced.

Inside the envelope were metallic slivers, tiny steel diamonds glittering through the clear plastic.

'What are they – Lubin?'

'I think they're from a fragmentation grenade,' the young man replied, as if suddenly thinking better of a wild, improbable piece of guesswork.

Vorontsyev turned the envelope in his fingers and the steel splinters caught the light. Dmitri appeared to be silently urging the young forensic officer to continue, as if his own conviction was dribbling away like water into sand.

'There are fragments of what might be a child's balloon!' Dmitri eventually and incongruously burst out. 'Some of them embedded in the victims' skin – tell the Major, Lubin!'

'I've – er, I've seen this kind of thing before, sir. It's normally a terrorist device.' The wind gusted through the shredded curtains of the room, making the remnants float like seaweed.

'Yes?'

Most of the others had left the room, drifting out of the gap where the front door had been.

'I think the balloon and the grenade were inside the heater, sir. I wouldn't have guessed, except I've –'

'– seen it before. You said,' Vorontsyev interrupted impatiently.

'Yes, sir,' Lubin replied shamefacedly. 'The balloon would have heated up inside the stove,' he hurried on, as if successfully overcoming a violent stammer, 'probably had water in it, enough expansion to pull the pin out of the frag grenade, which would then explode. The heater was old, the metal thin, the fragments would have come flying out – ripping the poor sods to shreds.'

'Couldn't these be fragments from the heater?'

Dmitri shook his head. Lubin's similar gesture was slower in coming, but as certain.

'They're too regular – see, sir?' he offered. Steel needles. 'A gas or liquid in the balloon, sir, heated up . . . it's possible, sir. I mean, it's not clever or anything, just messy. It can be done.'

Again, Lubin wound down like a clockwork toy, confronted by Vorontsyev's scepticism. Or perhaps he didn't want to believe it, he told himself. Too much like another warning, like Rawls' single, professional wound? He cleared his throat. Glanced around him, then nodded towards the door of the bedroom. Dmitri and Lubin followed him.

It was colder than the living room and smelt of paraffin, dirty clothing, soiled bedlinen, stale food. All three of them were engaged in some laughable conspiracy, or a dream. He turned to confront Dmitri. The envelope between his fingers caught the light once more and the steel splinters gleamed mockingly.

'Your boy's well coached,' he murmured.

Dmitri appeared wounded. Lubin said abruptly:

'I came to Inspector Gorov with the idea, sir. The balloon, the shards of steel, the force of the explosion.'

'Enough to kill the TacTeam man who kicked the door down? Why wasn't it he who triggered the explosion? Or was he just unlucky?'

'There may have been something wired to the door. I'm not sure about that –'

'Or about *this*?'

Their breathing smoked like a burning fuse in the icy bedroom.

'I can't be *certain*, sir – at least, not yet. But I've seen it done *before*.' His hands sculpted the room's stale air. His parka rustled with the small, intense movements. 'To find out *how* exactly, in this case, I'd have to run tests at the lab. If you doctor the pin mechanism, it doesn't need much force to explode a grenade.'

'Alexei –!' Dmitri demanded at once, as if he had been waiting for his cue. He turned Vorontsyev aside from Lubin and pressed close to him. 'Why don't you want to believe it? Eh, why not?' He was tugging at the sleeve of Vorontsyev's coat like an importunate, wheedling child.

'It's too fancy and too pat,' he snapped back.

'Lubin saw what he saw. He's not a fool – and he's not working to any script of mine! This was a set-up, a false lead!'

He sighed aloud, irritated at surrendering to the nonsense woven by Dmitri and the young, enthusiastic Lubin – who, he remembered, had diagnosed more than one murder as mafia-inspired and not the consequences of a brawl. He didn't need more conspiracy theorists – he already had Dmitri and he was sufficient unto the day.

The thought would not be ridiculed into submission. Rawls' murder had been an assassination and meant to appear as such. It was a declaration, a warning . . . were they connected, then? That *was* crazy . . .

The wind rattled the loose metal windowframe of the bedroom. He could hear, quite distinctly, the rustle and creak from the corridor as the bodybags were lifted and moved. The Tac-Team man, Hussain, the other bodies . . . one ragged face he had vaguely recognised. He'd have to look at that face –

'You're *certain* these slivers are from a frag grenade?' he snapped with unreasonable anger.

'I'm – pretty sure, sir.'

'Then bloody *make* sure!' He snatched them away from Lubin's gaze and carried them into the wrecked living room, still dimly lit by its single bulb. An image of the paraffin stove exploding made him nauseous for a moment. The steel slivers glinted in their clear plastic envelope. Regular, small, needlelike. 'Bloody

61

make sure!' he repeated over his shoulder, hearing them follow him from the bedroom.

'Yes, sir.'

If Lubin's nonsense was true . . . as true as his own conviction concerning Rawls' murder . . . then *someone* had gone to all this trouble to eliminate their only lead to the drug-trade in Novyy Urengoy, and to *tell* them what they'd done.

Lubin was at the door of the flat, examining the charred frame. He was nodding to himself with intent, silent satisfaction.

Vorontsyev sensed the malevolence and the organisation that could make a deadly practical joke out of an exploding paraffin stove and a bomb-wired front door. You have been warned. We know what you know. We're untouchable.

He placed his hand on Dmitri's shoulder, who looked up at him like some faithful and rather singleminded hound. He realised his own features were bleak, as if he had been standing face-on to a storm. The smell of the flat nauseated him and the wind through the broken window carried snow into the room that stained the cheap purple carpet as violently as blood had already done. He shrugged Dmitri's shoulder with his hand, gripping it fiercely. The warning off made him edgy – and angry. Very angry.

Lock turned from the door closing behind the bellhop, and saw unmistakable fear in the collapsed posture of Vaughn Grainger. The old man was slumped into the chair, and his heavy, lined features were quivering. Lock shook his head as if to clear his vision, but the stigmata of fear rather than grief remained on Grainger's face and body. Then he appeared to become aware he was being studied and roused himself in the chair.

The sitting room of the suite in the Jefferson Hotel was pale-walled and draped, the furniture heavily antique. Grainger had been drinking on the flight – too much – but he wasn't drunk. It wasn't the alcohol that blurred his features and made his hands shake. Afternoon light gleamed through the net curtains.

'You OK?' Lock asked quietly. 'You want something to drink?'

Grainger shook his head. 'I'm all right, John-boy. OK.' His

right hand waved in front of him as if to ward something off. Was he afraid of his own mortality? Billy's murder had hit him like a stroke.

Lock poured himself a large bourbon and swallowed eagerly. He didn't want to be in the room with Billy's father. He wanted to be outside, where his own grief could be distracted by other people, things, lose itself in the indifference of the streets. The car journey from the airport had been claustrophobic and now the suite pressed in on him like a migraine. He swallowed more bourbon, his back to Grainger, aware of small, shuffling movements, the creaks of the chair, the aimless, lost slapping of old hands on old thighs, the rub of fingers against stubbled cheeks.

'You – don't mind Beth being – being buried with Billy? In Phoenix? There's no family plot or anything, is there?'

Lock ground his teeth together at the sense of appropriation he felt. He couldn't say he wanted her to be buried near his parents in New Hampshire, in the country churchyard; not in the burned dryness of Arizona . . . because it was stupid. She was gone, and that was it and all of it, and it didn't matter where her – *remains* lay to desiccate.

'No, Vaughn. They – should be together, right?'

He vigorously crushed *all* memories of the many visits he and Beth had made to that country churchyard, deep in leaves or grass or snow. From the first visit, when there had been coffins and dizziness and dislocation and eventual nausea and fainting, to the last, they all reminded him of Beth and his parents and there wasn't the least thing *good* about any of them any longer.

'Thanks, John-boy,' Grainger murmured. 'I – maybe I'll have that drink now.'

'Bourbon?'

'Sure.'

He poured two more drinks. Grainger took his with a deliberately firm hand. His eyes were self-aware, concerned with presenting himself in a certain way; masking things Lock might have noticed. Why?

Why do I think he's afraid – really afraid? Because *I'm* afraid, unsettled by the car that tailed me to Dulles and then followed me back into the city? Disturbed by the man on the street outside the apartment, the man outside the hotel now? He smiled concealingly at Grainger and sipped his bourbon. Grainger's face was half-hidden by his hands as he lit one of his long Cuban cigars. Part of the suite's claustrophobia could be put down to his sense of being under surveillance. And not knowing why.

'What do the police think, John? Really think?'

Lock perched himself on the edge of the chair on the other side of a deeply polished table. The net curtains were a sheened blankness beside the table, as if both men sat on a bare, modernist stage set, waiting to begin a play.

'Robbery was the motive. There's maybe three, four million dollars' worth of paintings, jewellery, other stuff missing. The lieutenant in charge of the investigation called me, gave me the insurance assessor's estimate. It couldn't be anything else – '

It was not quite a question, but it alerted Grainger's body like the sting of a small insect.

'What else could it be?' he protested.

'Billy had enemies – in business. Who doesn't?'

'Do they go around killing –?' Grainger's reply was throttled by a growling sob. He shook his head, staring at his cigar. A cocoon of ash had fallen onto the carpet. 'He wasn't into things that could cause . . .' He looked up, his eyes flintily grey, harsh. 'He ran Grainger Technologies, not some gambling palace, whores, stuff like that. Jesus, it's so senseless, John – so damned *senseless*!'

'I know.' He swallowed grief, more bitter than the drink.

'They will find these animals?'

'The police department – maybe, they say. If some of the stuff, the paintings for instance, comes onto the market. They may have had a shopping list,' he added. 'It might never see the light of day.'

'You mean people *order* stuff they want, to fill up their houses, from animals like that?'

'You – we both know it happens, Vaughn.' His own unsatisfied need for justice – revenge – was reflected in the old man's face. 'They must have had the place under surveillance –' He swallowed, aware of the window near which they sat, of 16th Street below, of the man on the other side of the street in the sunlight. '— for days, maybe weeks.'

'Then why didn't they go in when Billy wasn't at home?' Grainger all but wailed.

'The alarm system, perhaps. They must have bluffed their way in — maybe pretended they were caterers, something like that. It was *easier* to kill Beth — and Billy and the others. Maybe.'

The ringing of the telephone on the Colonial writing table startled both of them. Lock stared at the spilt drops of bourbon staining his dark trousers, then he got up jerkily and lurched towards the phone.

'Yes?'

'Sir, a Mr Turgenev is at the front desk. He says he's a friend of the family. He'd like to come up.'

Lock placed his hand over the receiver and relayed the information to Grainger. 'He wants to come up. Are you — ?'

The fear was back. Grainger was rigid in the chair, the disregarded cigar held loosely between his fingers. The eyes moved rapidly, like wideawake dreaming or as if in search of a hiding place. Lock didn't understand.

'Pete wants to pay his respects, express his sympathy,' he told Grainger as Turgenev came on the line. 'Can you go through with it — say for five minutes?'

Grainger nodded as if in spasm. The hand holding the cigar was once more fending away something unseen. 'Sure,' he said throatily. 'Pete's a good guy — '

'Yes.' Then, into the receiver: 'Come on up, Pete. Just don't stay long, OK? Vaughn's tired out from the flight.' He put down the telephone and stared into the white-gold blankness of the net curtains. Grainger gradually relaxed. 'Another drink?'

'Hell, why not? It isn't drowning anything but it takes the edge off it.' He held out his empty glass, his features controlled; reinvested with grief and loss.

Lock refilled the glass and hesitated over his own before deciding he didn't need another drink. Not just yet. As he handed Grainger his glass, there was a discreet knock at the door. As Lock moved to open it, it was as if the old man was preparing himself for a bruising encounter or a game of bluff.

Turgenev's good looks were arranged in appropriate, sympathetic lines and planes, his eyes saddened. He took Lock's hand in his own, murmuring:

'I'm so sorry, John.'

Then at once he moved into the room, his topcoat over his arm, his Russian fur hat in his hand, and gestured to Grainger to remain seated as he placed his hand firmly, empathetically on the old man's arm. Bending over him, he made Grainger seem shrunken. Against the window's blankness, it was an affecting tableau, a frieze that belonged on some classical temple.

Then Turgenev lowered himself into the chair opposite Grainger, hat still in his hand, coat over his arm, his voice low and soothing.

'There's nothing I can say, Vaughn, I know that . . . but believe me, I understand your loss. I feel it myself . . . just like I feel for John –' A glance towards Lock, hovering by the drinks tray. Turgenev shook his head at the proffered bottle and turned back to Grainger. 'You're not to worry about anything, there'll be time for everything later. Nothing is urgent,' he impressed. Grainger was nodding emptily.

Lock turned away, but the two men at the table remained in the gilded mirror that confronted him. Turgenev leaning forward across the small space between them, his features heavy with sympathy, Grainger hunched into himself in the chair, staring at the smouldering cigar between his fingers. The frieze had altered, suggesting an ambiguous image; grieving old man being comforted – or old man being instructed on his determined future, as if being given news of his placement in a retirement home after the death of his family. The peculiarity and vivacity of the image struck him, but it was more than momentary.

In the car – of course. He remembered now. Vaughn had made some scattered references to Grainger Technologies and its future, after Billy. Turgenev was a stockholder in a major way, there was the suggestion of a buyout. Vaughn ran the Grainger Foundation, the charitable corporation based in Phoenix. Would he surrender that to others now, too? In the mirror, he appeared resigned to a blank future. The impression was too powerful, too personal.

Lock remembered Billy, appearing at the door of his study, sweating, angry and somehow powerless beneath the intoxication. Just like his father now. Turgenev's long legs stretched out in comfort. In power. Power *over* . . .

He glanced back into the mirror, then away from it again. He wanted to think it was paranoia, but the self-mockery would not quite come. It was in a log-jam, trapped between the man who had gotten out of the car opposite his apartment and skulked behind a tree, the tail-car to and from the airport, the man outside now on 16th Street – and Turgenev. Billy's cowed, abrupt dismissal of him at the study door, Vaughn's abasement now even though all Turgenev offered was sympathy. Vaughn making it look like threat.

He disliked the insistent, feral intuitions. They took him back into the field, back to the Company. To the time when he and Billy had met Turgenev, he reminded himself. It had been years since Pete Turgenev and his past had evoked old instincts, habitual suspicion. But now in the mirror, Turgenev seemed to loom over Vaughn Grainger like a great, dark bird.

What the hell is happening here –?

FOUR

Extremely Old Professions

The desert sunlight struck back from the bright shovels, from the chrome on the funeral limousines, from the cars of dignitaries and businessmen and politicians. The glints of hard light caught at his fugitive glances as he tried to avoid the omnipresence of the coffins and the dark hole into which they would, in another moment, be lowered. The vast, cloudless sky was as high as only desert air could be, but it nevertheless pressed down upon the large group of mourners in black clothing. They were seated in rows as for some college class photograph, facing with fortitude the pastor's closing remarks. It was the easy bravery of remaining alive in the face of the death of others. Cars could be heard from the noisy highway beyond the cemetery.

A Phoenix morning, already hot. Cactuses like a via dolorosa stretched away towards the mountains. Vaughn Grainger's weight and the old man's scents pressed against his side and his senses as Billy's stricken father rocked slowly, inexorably as a pendulum, on the adjacent chair.

Vaughn Grainger leaned on him now as he himself had leaned on Beth at that other funeral, when they had been made to sit beside their few relations in falling snow in front of the grave into which their parents were lowered. That was when his head had wanted to burst and he had felt dizzy and sick. All through it, Beth had gripped his hand to still his shaking and tears. When she released it, it was numb and bruised inside his glove from the pressure of her own undemonstrated grief. With a pain always easy to recapture, he remembered a neighbour's comment that Beth *didn't seem upset. A strange child. You'd have thought she had more feeling . . .*

He felt the tears threaten, and heard the echo of the sounds

68

he had wanted to make then, but could not. *You don't know anything! You don't know my sister at all!*

He blinked the tears aside. The desert light had begun to prism through them. He pressed away the memories with strong, practised, mental hands.

Most of the mourners were unknown to himself and Beth. The state governor and his dumpy wife, Phoenix celebrities, receivers of Grainger Foundation charity, businessmen, some people from government, the state senator and his retinue, a few faces from Grainger Technologies he had seen at the Virginia house – rows of strangers' faces, as if they had been hired to make it some funeral of the year, something worth putting in the local society magazine.

Sunlight flashed semaphore from windscreens climbing Camelback Mountain, and the city's high-rises watched the cemetery from an assured and lofty distance. He felt displaced here, separated from his own grief, from any sense of connection with the bodies in the two trestled coffins. Three days ago, the contents of one of them had been his dearest knowledge, his best companion. She had been a great distance away when he had seen her in the police mortuary, grateful amid the formaldehyde and clinical steel that she had been shot in the torso and the sheet had continued to conceal the wounds. Even so, memories of bodies had come back, from Afghanistan and other places, his mind eager to substitute a brutal reality for the quiet detachment of the place. The images of the coffins being loaded aboard Vaughn's Learjet brought back more formal, uninvolving times, coffins draped with the flag arriving from distant wars with which he had no connection.

Vaughn had crumbled like an old adobe wall, staring at Billy's dead face. Just as he now leaned against Lock's shoulder and arm, a scarecrow no longer defying a wind.

Beth's coffin was raised by professionally gentle hands the ropes arranged, then it was lowered into the dry red earth. The old man tried to straighten himself for long enough and Lock scooped earth feverishly and cast it onto the disappearing lid. The silver nameplate mocked in reply. Then Billy's coffin. The old man's body pumped like a feeble heart, nothing but rushing,

69

thin blood under ricepaper skin. Lock pressed some fragments of earth into Vaughn Grainger's hand and the crumbs feebly followed Billy into the grave. The pastor murmured like an insect. Then it was done and other murmurs converged on them, the whole place a whispering, breeze-like enclosure of sympathy from which he wanted to flee. Earth began to rattle drily as he turned away, holding Grainger's elbow; holding him upright, steering him towards the cab-rank of black limousines.

Lieutenant Faulkner had called, just before the funeral cortège had set out. Some of Beth's jewellery, he thought. They were sweating the guy who'd bought it – a record going way back to the Flood, he'd talk for sure . . . Yet there was a lack of expectation in the police officer's voice. The paintings and the really valuable stuff – and thus the killers – remained as remote as . . . Beth, now they were filling in her grave. As isolated as his own fantasies of being watched and followed. Were these some grief-crazed projection, maybe, or an attempt to escape his present into the weird certainties of his intelligence past? Fantasies that couldn't survive under a desert sky in a temperature in the thirties.

He guided Grainger's boneless, motiveless body through the shower of murmured sympathy and proffered hands, into the rear of the leading limousine, then climbed in beside him. Leather squeaked, the air-conditioning purred. He felt his forehead prickle with sweat. His eyes were dry.

He wanted to be alone and a long way from Phoenix. Way beyond the Superstition Mountains, beyond the desert, out from under that immense sky that even the tinted windows could not keep at a safe distance.

The limousine pulled out, made a slow, respectful turn on the gravel, and headed for the cemetery gates. Beside him, Billy's father was sunken in a dumb rage and fear. Maybe it was as if death had bullied its way into his study or bedroom, or appeared beside his pool – threatening and immediate in a moment of relaxation. Was he thinking of his own death? Billy's? Beth, of course, fulfilled some kind of consort role in Grainger's universe. Billy had been married, his wife should properly be buried beside him; very little more than that. No . . . perhaps it was the possibility of his own violent death that Grainger seemed to fear.

He rubbed his eyes as the car drew out into the traffic of mid-morning. It was as if death was infectious. Vaughn Grainger seemed terrified that death would come for him soon.

'You OK?' he murmured.

Grainger shook his head. His skin was ancient and grey, loose about his jowls like a poor disguise.

'Scum killed him.' Lock winced at Beth's unimportance. 'In his own *house* . . .' He saw the brutal side of the old man's nature, the one that had suited him to Special Forces in 'Nam. The nature that Billy, too, had possessed and revealed in Afghanistan. His gnarled hands strangled something invisible on his dark lap. Yet the hands were defeated now, with no known enemy; without authority. He couldn't burn their homes, raze their village – whoever had killed his son.

He heard a stranger's voice ask: 'What do I do? What's left for me, now?'

Vorontsyev stared down at the dead features caught in the glare of a flashbulb, shunting the enlarged photograph between his fingers. Then he looked up.

'So, he leads nowhere?' Dmitri shook his head glumly, once more the cheated child. It was becoming his habitual, frozen expression. 'A male nurse at the Foundation Hospital. We know everything about him, you've checked his room at the hostel, you can account for his movements, habits, friends, sexual inclinations – everything except why *he* should have had an interest in meeting Hussain?' Dmitri nodded with a shamefaced expression. 'He wasn't even an addict?'

'No.'

'And there's nothing in his room to suggest he was a pusher?'

'Nothing.'

Vorontsyev sighed, shaking his head. His eyes were still gritty with sleep. Beyond the window, the day seemed reluctant. Frost starred the windows.

'OK – so, finding no heroin in Hussain's possession or in that flat, we've checked every suspect, every lead . . . to come up with precisely nothing.' At once, he sympathised with Dmitri, who wriggled like a boy on his chair. Vorontsyev could not excoriate failure more than Dmitri himself was doing. *Mea culpa.* 'Look, I'm not *blaming* anyone,' he insisted. 'Except whichever bastard on the take tipped someone off in time for them to set the explosives! But not you, and not Lubin, who spotted it was deliberate.' Lubin grinned, rubbing his hand through his thick hair, then at once assuming a lugubrious expression which he evidently felt suited the discussion. 'So — what do we do? It can't actually *be* terrorists, can it, Lubin? I mean, some group from outside? Raising funds for weapons and bombs by smuggling heroin?'

'It's one of the usual sources of income, sir — do *you* think so?'

'No. The only terrorists around here are the Yankees and the Russian entrepreneurs.' He smiled with a scowling, cynical relief. 'It's too neat. Terrorists wouldn't have warned us off quite so obviously — would they?' Lubin shook his head. 'Which means this is a properly run *business.*'

'Part of something bigger?'

Vorontsyev shrugged. The sun was climbing tiredly above the car park's close horizon.

'I hope not. But terrorists — no. They're out of the picture. They'd not have resisted blowing up a gas well or a length of pipeline, just to keep their hand in. Who would they be, anyway — Arctic Reindeer Freedom Fighters? This country's full of shit, but they're crooks, mafiosi, gangsters, not *political.* Who cares about politics?'

'We — we have to go back to the hospital, then,' Dmitri said. 'Grill some of the poor bastards in the Addiction Unit —'

'— or the knocking shop. Everyone's favourite brothel?' Vorontsyev offered in response. 'We had it under surveillance, before Hussain's little trip got us all excited. Worth putting a team back on it?' He tried, too late, to suppress a yawn. 'Not a comment,' he added. Sleeping was often impossible in the neat flat to which hardly anyone ever came. When the music palled and the books failed to interest and his thoughts were as sombre as the face that reflected back from the uncurtained windows — there was nothing to like, nothing to expect.

'We weren't acting on any hard information.'

'I know that.' He got up and crossed his office to the coffee percolator. Black-market coffee. He filled their cups, then his own. Coffee might aid the sense of conspiracy that he needed almost as much as Dmitri did.

He was angry. Very angry.

'We thought we had something four months ago, when those two addicts overdosed on heroin smuggled into them − *that* dribbled away down the drain. We thought the knocking shop could be a distribution centre, since it caters for the R & R requirements of the gasfields, and the outworkers were the means of getting the stuff into Novyy Urengoy − *that*, too, drained away into the permafrost.' He leaned towards them over his littered desk, his knuckled hands resting on two untidy heaps of files and reports. Abruptly, he sat down. Lit a cigarette.

Relieved, Dmitri and Lubin scrabbled for cigarettes. The fug of collusion, of planning their way through frustration, filled the office.

'So? Which is it? The cleaners, orderlies, nurses at the Addiction Unit − or the girls and their clients at the best whorehouse in town?' He blew smoke expansively at the ceiling.

Lubin beamed. Welcomed aboard, unofficially promoted into confidentiality − trust.

'We could try a raid on the brothel − before word of what we are up to gets −' Dmitri hesitated, rubbing his round face with both hands.

'It's all right. We need to remind ourselves −' He looked darkly at Lubin. '− they have a source inside this building, maybe a dozen people on their hook. Fact of life.' He drew on the cigarette. Marlboro. Cowboys smoked them. He coughed. He smoked too many of them, through the sleepless nights, the impotent days. 'OK. We'll raid the place tonight. After all, we've looked everywhere else for the bloody heroin − it can't *all* have been cut, sold, injected already, in two days. So maybe it's there . . .' He opened the first file that came to hand, then a second, a third. Names, dates, suspicions . . . hospital orderlies, cleaners, working girls, gasfield workers coming in for R & R; to get drunk, pay for sex, fight in the streets . . . smuggle heroin

73

back to the gasfield, or into town when they came back from the God-forsaken places where they'd originated.

He dismissed the files with a gesture.

'What about the TacTeam, sir?' Lubin asked. 'Aren't they on our side?'

'No. They just blame us for getting one of their boys killed. And demand we find whoever did it. But as to helping –? Forget it.'

'So we're on our own?' Dmitri seemed pleased at his realisation. The sun was losing its blood colour now, still low over the car park.

'Looks like it. What *was* that male nurse doing there? He had to know what was expected. He wasn't related to the flat's tenant, didn't know him as far as we can discover. Drugs and a hospital – better cover than a brothel.'

'But it's more or less run, as well as funded, by the Yankees. More dangerous to use that than the knocking shop,' Dmitri offered.

'Teplov owns the brothel, but he's not into drugs. We've established that.'

'There's nothing from the passengers on Hussain's flight, not so far. Or from the crew. Most of the workers are out on the rigs now, anyway. Company buses collected them.'

'And your contact – our *only* contact?'

Dmitri shook his head mournfully. 'He's keeping away. Or trying to. Or they're keeping away from him.'

'OK, then we'll raid. Brief a team, but don't tell them where.'

There was a quick knock at the door and it opened before he could speak. Marfa Tostyeva entered, dragging her woollen hat from her head, unwinding the long scarf from her neck. Her eyes appeared blurred and her nose reddened.

'You better?' Vorontsyev asked.

She slumped on a hard chair, breathing stertorously.

'Fine. I've just caught up with the taxi driver, Noskov. Want to hear what I found out?'

She drew her notebook from her coat pocket and opened it, oblivious of Vorontsyev's puzzlement until she once more looked up.

'What is it?' she asked, shrugging.

'Taxi driver?'

'The man who picked up Rawls, the American, just before he was murdered. Remember – sir?' The sarcasm was obvious.

Vorontsyev squinted against the sunlight streaming across his desk. The frost glittered on the windows.

'It's not our case,' he offered. 'It's been taken over by GRU –'

'Do you realise how much *effort* it was, with a stinking cold, tracing that driver? He was never at home, I couldn't get Traffic to help –!'

He held up his hands.

'All right. Make your report. I'll pass it on, with *your* compliments. By the way, we're raiding Teplov's place tonight.'

'I heard about the other raid.' She looked gloomy. 'I'm sorry it fell so flat,' she offered to Dmitri, who shrugged in response. Then she looked at once at her notebook and announced: 'Apparently, this Noskov ferried Rawls around for most of the week . . . unusual. Rawls didn't use a Grainger-Turgenev limousine, or drive himself. Noskov has one of the newer taxis, I'll admit, but it isn't a big ZiL or a Merc.' She cleared her throat, not looking up. 'Rawls made most of the calls you'd expect, around the Grainger-Turgenev headquarters, other companies – twice up to the rigs, five times to the hospital, in all . . . must have had the trots.' She smirked.

'Anything important?' Vorontsyev asked impatiently.

'Sorry – not sleeping again, sir?' Marfa replied.

'Don't push it.'

'Sorry,' she replied stiffly.

'I'll pass that on to Bakunin.' Marfa closed her notebook audibly, to the accompaniment of a strained sigh. 'Right. Tonight. We know Teplov's made money on the side renting rooms, cupboards and outside privies to illegal workers on the field. He's hidden them, fleeced them, covered for them, even supplied papers . . . perhaps he thought he *would* dabble in heroin, after all!'

The empty glasses littered the tables around the pool. The evening breeze off the desert was warm. Napkins blown from the tables lay like jellyfish at the clear bottom of the pool. The last guests had long gone, flitting blackly in the afternoon sunlight, away from the intensity of grief Vaughn Grainger had been unable to conceal. Or perhaps from his own reticent, intense quiet, repelling as surely as an electrical field. A guard fence.

John Lock sat down at one of the tables, the umbrella above his head crackling like a flag in the breeze. Phoenix was emerging from the darkening desert in strips and gobbets of neon; as if the contents of a foundry ladle, some incandescent metal, had been spilt on the desert floor. The mountains were distant, like barely cowed great animals waiting for the night. He shivered unaccountably. Poured a glass of champagne, the bottle slithering in the melted ice of the bucket. The house behind him threatened insistently. He had no idea, nor possessed any wish to know, where in the house Grainger was. The housekeeper or the butler could see to him, for the moment.

He had, out of habit rather than the remotest interest, paged his answerphone at the apartment. More messages of sympathy – so that he wished he had not reconnected the machine – the early music group, the woman's prim voice grating on him like that of a disliked teacher, the Kennedy Center regarding reserved tickets he had ordered for himself and Beth as a late birthday surprise . . . and Johanna, diffident and awkwardly offering a pinched, embarrassed sympathy – *I'm really sorry, John* – but all the messages seemed like indecipherable signals from distant galaxies, meaning less and less.

He wished – Christ in Heaven, how he wished – not to feel as he did. But there was nothing to fill up his emptiness. The place he inhabited was devoid of everything, and he didn't have the ability, the will, to refurnish it. It would remain empty.

He swallowed the barely cool champagne and poured himself another glass. The city brightened in the dusk, spread out below Camelback Mountain. Grainger's estate was perched amid new trees and a security fence on the mountainside, proprietorially overlooking Phoenix. An aircraft drifted towards Sky Harbor airport, its lights against the first stars. A napkin hurried across the tiles towards the pool like a bird to the water. The hummingbirds had disappeared with the sun.

He had to get away. Vaughn had the servants – and there was nothing he could do to alleviate the man's mental distress. He could only be another servant in the house – the house which oppressed him with illusions of peace, with the suggestion of a place outside time. He needed to get back to Washington, back into some kind of numbing routine. But the old man clung to him, as tightly as a blind man stranded on a crowded freeway.

The maid appeared at the open windows, and he waved her enquiring look away. She disappeared. The patio's Italian tiles gleamed palely in the gloom, the great hacienda-style house glowed with curtained lights. The doctor had promised to sedate the old man before he left.

The telephone rang, startling him, his hand automatically reaching out for it. Someone must have asked to make a call earlier, and the phone had been brought out to this table. He picked up the receiver before remembering that one of the servants could have answered it.

'Yes? Sorry – this is the Grainger residence.' His servant-like tone caused him to smile.

'I wish to speak person-to-person with Mr Vaughn Grainger. Please put me through.'

'I'm sorry, he can't take your call right now –'

As if another and entirely different conversation had begun, he heard: 'I wish to convey my sympathies, condolences . . . I have read about the death of his son.'

'I'll convey your message, Mr –?'

'I wish to convey my sentiments personally to Mr Grainger.'

'I'm afraid he's under sedation at the moment. I'll get your message to him as soon as he wakes. It's Mr –?' Someone Asian, he knew from the sibilants, the slight slitherings around consonants.

Then, as if it were a third conversation, one from another context altogether: 'Tell Grain – Mr Grainger that it is urgent I speak with him. Soon. My name is Nguyen Tran.' Vietnamese then. 'You will tell him.' It was not a question.

'I'll tell him. He has your number?'

'I am here in Phoenix at the moment, on business. I am staying

77

at the Biltmore.' A deliberate softening, then. 'I am an old friend of Mr Grainger.' But an old friend who didn't come to the funeral, Lock thought. Then the abrupt demand of: 'Nguyen Tran. I know he would wish you to wake him. I suggest you do so. I'll be waiting for his call.'

'Goodbye,' Lock offered to the hum of the receiver.

He put down the phone, outraged on Grainger's behalf at the insensitivity of the Vietnamese man. Some business deal, some document or loan or investment – Jesus! The guy evidently wasn't a Buddhist . . . He grinned. Then either the breeze or the chill of the words made him shiver. Nguyen Tran was . . . threatening Vaughn Grainger. He had power over him, his impatience would unnerve the old man. The substance of the message was that Grainger couldn't afford to keep the Vietnamese waiting for an answer.

Someone else, he reflected, just like Turgenev – someone Vaughn Grainger is afraid of, or is expected to be afraid of . . .

The house seemed insubstantial now, and perched in an act of madness or hubris on the mountainside. And the breeze was colder. He could explain neither disconcerting impression.

'Look, Noskov – my chief wasn't impressed with your story. I'm back to make sure you make it sound better.' Marfa Tostyeva grinned at the taxi driver as she slammed the door of his cab. It was third in the rank outside the Gogol Hotel. Other drivers stamped in the morning air, slapped their hands against their arms, breaths fuming.

'I gave you the whole story. There's nothing else – *officer.*' He swept his hand along the dashboard behind the steering wheel, as if removing dust. The three-year-old French saloon was without smells, its heater worked, its upholstery was unstained.

But why did Rawls use it? He had access to a gas company limousine, a Merc or a stretched ZiL, which Grainger-Turgenev used to impress their Russian credentials on officials from Moscow. He'd taken the Renault on an exclusive-hire basis. For less money, he could have hired a better car from Hertz.

'What's the American done?' Noskov asked slily.

'Got himself killed. Don't you read the papers?' She relaxed into the passenger seat, luxuriating in the warmth of the heater. Noskov looked as if he was contemplating broaching the subject of a bribe, the universal currency.

'I saw that – you told me, anyway. But you sound as if you're after him, not the killer?'

No, she thought. And I'm not supposed to be here at all. Off limits. But she was – because the major had rubbed against her enthusiasm with his indifference, and the use of the taxi for the whole week of Rawls' stay in Novyy Urengoy intrigued her.

'Just be more expansive, Noskov.'

'Or what?'

'I can make trouble for you – small trouble, maybe, but irritating. OK?'

'OK,' he replied sourly. His clothes smelt of stale sweat in the warm interior. Why would Rawls, with his manicured hands, want to sit behind this man in his old, stale donkey-jacket for a whole week?

'You took him to the hospital, you drove out to one of the nearer rigs, you took him to the helicopter for his other trip out. Tell me everything about the last evening, when you picked him up from here and took him out there to be killed.'

'I didn't have anything –!'

'Well, tell me, then. Maybe I'll even believe you.'

'You bloody cops!'

'That's right. Shame you aren't being questioned by one of your pals from headquarters ... All right, all right, I'm not making enquiries about whoever you pay or do favours for or who's got some hold over you. Just Rawls. That evening.'

He shunted the cab forward to second in the rank. One of the expensive whores had disappeared into a battered American saloon, a chiffon scarf trailing from the shoulder of her mink. High heels, slim legs. Made you envious just to look –

Noskov, watching her, was grinning with insight.

'That evening,' she announced like a threat.

'Like I told you, I drove him out there and he said it would be all right, just to head back to town. He'd be in touch in the morning.' He shrugged. 'That's it.'

Marfa sighed. 'What time – here, I mean?'

'After midnight. I was going to bed. He rang me.'

'You came – he was waiting?'

He nodded, rubbing his stubbled, pointed chin. 'He was talking to Antipov, the commissionaire. Like I told you before.'

'He got straight in?'

'Yes.'

'What mood was he in?'

'Pleased with himself. He usually was. Why not? He had plenty of money, a big job. I was just a peasant.'

'But the tips were good.' She looked at her notebook, thumbing back through the pages. 'Did you see the limo waiting outside here when you picked Rawls up?'

'Where was it?' Noskov asked quietly.

'Antipov, the night porter, says on the other side of the street, perhaps forty metres away – over there,' she pointed, twisting in the seat.

'Maybe.'

'Did you notice it following you?'

'There was still a bit of traffic. I didn't notice anything specially.'

Marfa stared at him. Natural shiftiness, she decided. He'd say only what he had to. She nodded.

'You must have seen it come to a halt, out there – when you dropped Rawls off.'

'There – well, maybe. I didn't think about it much. Just wanted my bed.'

'And you didn't think it was odd, dropping him in the middle of the tundra?'

'He was paying. He got to say. He said he'd be all right, some-one was picking him up. Confidential meeting. That's what he called it. Out of sight, out of earshot. He wasn't worried. I don't think he thought he'd be kept waiting long.'

'He wasn't, was he?'

'I didn't know –!' Noskov whined. 'Do you think I'd get –?'

'Don't give yourself a coronary. Did you see him get into the limousine that followed you?'

'I didn't say it followed us.'

'Did you see him get into *any* limousine?'

'No. He was standing beside the road, the last I saw in the mirrors.'

Marfa flicked through her notes once more. Pondered, then asked: 'Was there anywhere else you took Rawls – anywhere unusual?'

'Like the knocking shops? No. He had a whore delivered. Not that night, though.'

'You picked her up?' He nodded. 'Name?'

'Vera – that's all I know.'

'Where did you pick her up?'

'Cocktail bar of the Sheraton. I don't know where she lives.'

Marfa scribbled. 'Anyone else you brought to see Rawls?' she asked with little enthusiasm.

'No – oh, only one of the doctors from the hospital. One of the Yankee doctors they have there.'

'Was Rawls ill?'

'No. Maybe he had the trots. I took him up there enough times!'

'That's the same joke as last time. My chief didn't laugh, either.'

'The word is he doesn't laugh at anything much.'

'Would you, policing this dump? Dealing with people like you?' Then she added: 'What was the name of this Yankee doctor?'

'Beats me.'

'I will, unless you remember.'

'Smith?'

'Try again. Why do you like being so obstructive?'

'Normal behaviour towards the cops – in this *dump*,' he retorted. 'His name was Schneider. Dr David Schneider. Is that it?' He pulled the cab forward to the head of the rank. 'I have got a business to run.'

'And I'd be bad for business? Yes, that's it.' Marfa wrapped her coat around her, tightened her scarf, and opened the door. The comfortable warmth vanished in a moment. 'Don't let me catch you on any yellow lines, Noskov!' He scowled as she shut the door, then mouthed an obscenity behind the window. She grinned and shook her head in mock reproof.

Another well-dressed tart, wrapped in expensive perfume, passed her without a glance. Taller than she, well made-up, but the face was hard and the eyes incapable of illusion; or disillusion. Suddenly, she felt better at the momentary proximity and the comparisons it suggested. She waved to Noskov and headed for the coffee shop of the hotel.

An American doctor called Schneider, and the black limousine that Noskov had evidently seen and wished to forget. Not because he knew anything, simply because it wasn't his business and he wasn't being paid to remember, only meekly threatened.

Vorontsyev wouldn't like it. If he found out . . .

. . . he'd have to. Schneider was the deputy director of the Addiction Unit. Why would Rawls want to see him? At his hotel, as if it was a house call? It was worth asking Schneider — but for that, she'd need Vorontsyev's permission.

'You're all going to catch something nasty in here!' Vorontsyev yelled at the top of his voice.

'For God's sake, Major —!' Teplov, the brothel's owner, tugged at his sleeve, his habitual unctuous expression replaced by one of — what? A sense of bad taste?

They were crowded in the narrow hallway of the old house, Teplov and his head girl and the two minders confronting Vorontsyev, Marfa, Dmitri, Lubin and the uniformed men behind them. Like two groups rushing in opposite directions, late for trains. The icy night air had hurried over and past them, as if intent upon a raid of its own.

'Don't blow the *whistle*, please, Major!' Vorontsyev had the instrument at his lips to taunt the brothel owner. The minders seemed perplexed, like the head girl who was carmined, heavily made-up, a mock-silk wrap dragged around her vast proportions.

Vice were usually so much more polite, that much was obvious. But then, they usually only dropped in for payment in cash or kind.

'Just make sure no one jumps out of the windows without their trousers, Teplov — it's brass monkey weather out there.' He leaned down towards the tiny, effete, bearded man whom it was hard to dislike; impossible to place in strict moral parentheses. Marfa evidently found it easier to summon contempt towards Sonya, the girls' shop steward and – Vice enjoyed the rumour – the tiny Teplov's demanding lover. 'We're not here to collect, little man, so just let us go about our business without interference, and we'll try to be as quiet as possible. OK?'

Sonya appeared inclined to debate, but Teplov said:

'You'll try not to upset the clients – or my girls, Major?'

Vorontsyev laughed. Lubin was grinning like a child in a toyshop. Dmitri appeared merely impatient.

'I'll try, Teplov – I'll try.' He could hear doors opening and closing upstairs. Anyone who took to the windows would be brought back inside by the uniformed men stationed around the house. 'OK, let's get on with it. You know what you're looking for – no *lingering*, *no* pilfering.' Teplov appeared relieved, as if Vorontsyev were some gentlemanly client inclined to sadism but prepared to pay to keep matters quiet.

The uniformed men began climbing the stairs. It was difficult to maintain gravitas. He heard someone squeal with pain outside somewhere, and raucous laughter. He grinned.

'None of the local bigwigs in tonight, Teplov? At least, I hope not . . .'

Teplov shook his bald head with fervent denial, then seemed to recollect something that contradicted the assurance – which he at once masked beneath compliance, fatalism. Sonya shrugged massively and turned away after visiting Marfa with a withering, superior glare.

'Hurry it up, we haven't got all night!' Dmitri bellowed, mounting the stairs to the first floor landing, where tousled, half-dressed girls were beginning to gather to watch the embarrassment of their clients and to taunt the police.

'What are you looking for, Major?' Teplov whispered, as if selling something on the black market. 'You know I keep my nose clean – and my girls,' he offered by way of ingratiation.

'None of your business – unless we find it.' He slapped the tiny man on one narrow shoulder, turned him around and hustled him towards his office at the rear of the ground floor. They passed the open doors of the two rooms off the hallway, garishly decorated, red-lit – why always red? – crammed with couches and sofas. Musak played softly. Then the kitchen, where an Iranian-looking man in an apron was slicing vegetables, undistracted.

Teplov's office was small and neat, like the man. A huge safe that might have been made in the Tsarist period, like the house itself, occupied one corner. His desk was against the wall beneath the window – which, in daylight, looked out over a weedstrewn, dilapidated graveyard and its moribund, stunted church. The rest of the room contained an old, rich Persian carpet and two armchairs, with a low table between them.

Teplov lit a cigarette and coughed at the smoke. Vorontsyev accepted the one he was offered, and the gold lighter, which he weighed in his hand like a grenade.

'You won't say keep it, will you?' he said. Teplov shook his head reproachfully, his brown eyes soulful, misunderstood. 'Good.'

'Have a seat, Major.'

'Thanks. Meanwhile, open the safe.' Teplov seemed puzzled for an instant, then realised he was not being asked for a bribe in a novel and indirect manner.

'There aren't any drugs here, Major. At least, not what you're looking for. One or two of the girls enjoy cannabis, and who can blame them after a busy evening . . . one or two of the clients *may*, unbeknown to me, be in possession. But not dealing.'

'You've heard, then?'

'That your last effort fell flat – yes, Major.'

'What else have you heard?'

Teplov was shielding the combination of the massive old safe from him. Then he reluctantly swung the heavy door open. Vorontsyev squatted on his haunches beside him, riffled the papers, flicked the heaps of notes in their elastic bands, found a photograph of a younger Teplov and a slim Sonya, but made no comment on them or the child the woman was holding; touched chequebooks, account books, ledgers – nothing. He wasn't disappointed because he had no real expectations. Something might come of interviewing the snatched clients – then again, something might not. He felt lassitude returning, his habitual lack of concern.

'Close the door.'

He returned to the chair.

'A drink, Major?'

'Why not? Scotch.'

Teplov poured the drinks, then sat behind his desk. The whisky was good, expensive.

'I heard you lost a man the other night. I don't play those games, or in that league.'

'You didn't, that's true. Perhaps you've become ambitious? People do, when the cops are so bloody useless.'

'Are you?' Teplov murmured.

Vorontsyev looked up from his tumbler, startled. His eyes narrowed with suspicion, even resentment.

'Watch it,' he muttered. Teplov shrugged the moment away. 'If there's nothing physical here, there's stuff inside your head. I ought to take you in and sweat you.'

Teplov appeared unnerved, then said: 'I make it my business to know nothing.'

'Why?'

'You need to ask, when one of your men got blown to pieces?'

'You've been threatened?' There were footsteps and voices above them, some protests from the hallway and outside the house. Floorboards creaked from the pressure of heavy boots and bullying excitement.

'No. I just keep away from it. It isn't here, your conduit or whatever it is you're looking for, Major.'

'You're a clever bastard.'

'You need to be, in this town. Perhaps you're not using your intelligence, Major – making waves?'

'The American who got himself killed – did he ever come here?'

'No. He'd use one of Kropotkin's girls, the high-class numbers who hang about the hotels. Special order, personal service.' He sighed. 'I had ambitions in that direction, once. Sonya persuaded me not to step out of my league.'

'And drugs would be –'

'Stepping out of my league in a big and very dangerous way.' He leaned forward. 'Just be careful, Major. You're tolerant as far as my business is concerned, and Vice asks no more than a reasonable slice –'

'Who?'

'You don't really want to know.' Vorontsyev tossed back the last of the Scotch. 'But everything I hear – and I have no names, no details, whatever you think – tells me this is big and organised.' He spread his hands. 'I don't think you realise how –'

His face became disappointed, as if he had stepped into a muddy ditch while negotiating a narrow path. The shouts were urgent, and from outside. At once, Dmitri was at the door, his face red with intense, exhilarated passion.

'– jumped out of the window, first floor!' he gasped. 'Arab-looking – he'd been waiting his chance to have it away!'

Vorontsyev saw knowledge cloud Teplov's features for an instant before weary indifference masked it. Cognition of something or no more than suspicion, perhaps. He joined Dmitri at the door.

'Which way was he heading?'

'Across the graveyard, past the church. We haven't got enough lights –!'

'Get the car started – I'll go after him. Meet me on the other side –' A collage of angry, nervous, outraged and guilty faces, the painted mockery of the girls' features, then they were out of the door, their shoes crunching on frozen snow.

Dmitri broke off and made for the car. Vorontsyev bent low, to catch a fleeing figure against the glow from the town. He could see nothing. His breath clouded around his face. A uniformed constable knelt beside him and he heard Lubin clumsily arrive. The church's stubby domes appeared like well-used pencils against the night-glow.

'He was definitely heading for the church, sir,' the constable explained. 'I didn't fire. You said –'

'It's OK. Come on, let's get after him.'

The tussocky, frozen ground was awkward, hampering. Vorontsyev's foot slipped on the rime of ice on a flat gravestone and he snapped: 'Constable, use your torch!'

The beam flicked ahead of them. There were black marks on the icy grass, the quarry's footsteps.

'What did he look like?'

'Dark overcoat, small. Arab, I think, sir.'

They reached the church and paused against the wall. Their breathing. Nothing else as Vorontsyev's heart quietened. He nodded.

'Keep that torch on the footprints.'

The wall of the church glistened with icy moss and stone. Their breathing and footsteps echoed like curtains rustling in a breeze. The footprints they were following had not halted with uncertainty, not once. Behind them, the engines of the two arrest wagons were starting up. Protests floated feebly after them. Why was this man running? Difficult to imagine a member of the town's executive committee, married or not, suddenly afraid that he couldn't bribe or bluster his way out of an arrest at Teplov's brothel. Or a policeman or a company executive – anyone, in reality, would be more concerned at their coitus having been interruptus than the round-up of the usual suspects.

He heard a car engine start; deep, big engine. A screech of tyres.

The churchyard led onto a narrow, twisting street of the cramped old town, little wider than an alley. He saw headlights spring out – where the hell was Dmitri?

'Quick!' he urged as they crunched down the weedstrewn gravel to the drunken gate. The big car was pulling away, tail-lights flaring. 'Shit!'

'– tyres?' he heard.

'Fat chance! Where's Dmitri?'

The big car – black Merc? – turned a narrow corner out of sight, its headlights flashing out like distress signals from gaps in the houses lining another narrow alley. Then his own car screeched into view, bucking towards them. He heard a dog barking. He was caught in the headlights as he crossed in front of the car, then dragged the door open as he reached the passenger side and the car halted. Lubin bundled himself into the rear but the constable was too slow. Dmitri screeched away, leaving him bemusedly watching their disappearance.

'Which way?'

'Left!'

The car banged against a dustbin or perhaps a low barrow left in the alleyway. There was no sign of the Merc's lights – it was a Merc, he confirmed. Dark coat, Merc, not wanting to be questioned – who? Why?

The old town pressed about them, narrow, shrunken houses, picket fences marking off plots of snow that sparkled in the headlights, in front of dachas and other low wooden buildings trapped within the loom of the surrounding high-rises. Russia's past flared in a series of half-images in the car's lights.

'Left again!'

He wouldn't have gone this way, it was too narrow, perhaps he wouldn't know it . . . must be heading for one of the well-lit, busy streets, to lose himself. This was quicker, if he'd guessed right. A terrified face in a dark doorway, headscarved and wrinkled. A dog skittering away from the headlights and the front wheels. They ran over something that made the car buck. Lubin was leaning forward between them. Dmitri wiped at the fugged windscreen.

'Next *right!*'

The car slewed into a twisting sidestreet, careering across unmarked snow – hadn't come this way, then, good – scraping its flank along a dilapidated fence that gave way and fell into the snow. A few scattered lights from the low bungalows and dachas, and from broken, still-inhabited houses –

– lights, traffic.

'F Street!' Dmitri exclaimed. 'Near 17th.'

'Wait!' Vorontsyev snapped.

The car nosed out of the old town like a hungry urchin dog. Vorontsyev craned forward in his seat, peering each way along F Street. Offices mostly, some blocks of apartments. Neater, quieter than most of the grid of streets and avenues of the artificial town. Pedestrians, homegoing traffic, mid-evening busyness. Black Merc? It should come out of –

He sighed.

'There he is,' he murmured triumphantly.

The black limousine turned out of Mockba Prospekt, a block

88

away from them, at once hurrying into the thin traffic, skidding then righting itself on the gritted thoroughfare. The driver, invisible behind the windscreen, accelerated towards them.

'Get out in front of him – no bloody chase, just stop him!' Vorontsyev yelled. He fastened his seatbelt and Lubin dropped back into the safety of the rear seat.

Dmitri accelerated violently out of the sidestreet and the Merc seemed to pause in stunned surprise. Dmitri slewed the car across the street, trying to corral the Merc onto the opposite pavement. Suddenly, the black limousine came on, seeming to hurtle directly at Vorontsyev. He tensed against the impact, leaning away from the door as much as he could. The Merc swerved, but was still coming on as Dmitri held it in a narrowing perspective, channelling it towards –

Collision. The door buckled inwards, against his thigh, tearing his trousers. The car shied away from the impact with the heavier Merc. Lubin was cursing in the rear, Dmitri's forehead was bleeding from impact with the windscreen, which was smeared but not shattered, he realised. Merc –?

It had collided with a brick-faced pillar, one of a row forming an archway over the pavement, making more elegant a row of discreet, expensive shops where gangsters purchased things alongside oil and gas executives. Spoons for cocaine sniffing, Burberry scarves, Gucci shoes, lace underwear, English cigarettes. He pushed at his buckled door. His thigh throbbed but wasn't bleeding.

'Bloody thing won't open!' he bellowed, enraged. The front of the Merc was rearranged, sunken. The windscreen was starred into opacity. He heaved again at the door and it gave. He thrust it open and climbed shakily into the icy night, then crossed gingerly to the limousine. 'Come on!' he yelled over his shoulder.

The heavy driver's door clicked smoothly open. The man was dead. He felt the disappointment envelop him for a moment. Then he pushed the light torso upright in the seat. Blood from the man's head and mouth was on his hand, darkening it in the light from the nearest streetlamp. He looked up. Lubin was waving on the traffic that had slowed to gawp. Dmitri, a bloodstained handkerchief held to his forehead, groaned beside Vorontsyev.

Vorontsyev switched off the engine. Put the automatic gearbox into park as smoothly as a car salesman. Then he studied the dead man's narrow, dark features. Arab, possibly Kazakh or Uzbek. Unshaven. The coat fitted him but didn't seem right. Cashmere, by the touch of it. He patted his hands around the man's pockets, withdrawing a wallet from the breast pocket of the overcoat. Burberry scarf, he realised. That didn't seem right, either, somehow – dirty fingernails, unwashed hair – the man didn't belong in the car or inside the coat . . .

He flicked open the wallet. Large denomination bills, in dollars, the *real* currency. Nothing Russian. Hundreds of dollars. The man's ID . . . He opened the folded piece of card.

'What is it?'

'It says he's a fitter – a *grease-monkey* – on one of the rigs. Iranian.' He stared at the overcoat, the man's dead, anonymous face. He searched the pockets again. An Iranian passport. The man came from somewhere he'd never heard of. An unskilled worker. Hundreds of dollars. The companies paid Iranians in roubles. He handed the wallet to Dmitri and reached across the body, keys in his hand, and unlocked the glove compartment. A large package, closed by an elastic band. Gold rings, he saw, on the unmanicured, dirty-nailed fingers. He tore open the package.

Passports. A dozen of them. American, Swiss . . . Austrian, one British . . . He shuffled them like cards, the street seeming empty and quiet. Entirely at a loss.

The man's dead face stared up at his sightlessly, but somehow mocking, despite the blood that stained it; knowing, almost smug.

He looked again at the passports. American, British, Swiss, Dutch . . . hundreds of dollars. A cashmere coat and gold rings. All in the possession of a minimum-wage gasfield worker from Iran.

'Get this car back to Forensic,' he said quietly, straightening up, closing the door on the dead man and offering the bundle of passports to Dmitri's uncomprehending expression. 'I want it taken apart, gone over inch by inch . . .' He turned back to the dead man, lolling against the side window. 'Who the *hell* are you?' he asked.

FIVE

Watching Ripples

The Vietnamese had telephoned twice more. Each time Lock had informed Vaughn Grainger, it had been like administering poison in dosages sufficient to make him ill without killing him or rendering him senseless. Nguyen Tran's mood had been sharklike beneath the deceptive calm of his tone. Grainger was terrified of the man – and silent, aggressive and enraged at the merest question or offer of help.

The old man was growing more ill before Lock's eyes – ill rather than drunk, despite the amount of alcohol he seemed intent on consuming. Billy's murder was a barrier to intrusion. What else could it be? Drunken grief explained everything . . . except that it didn't. It was Tran, and the fact that Vaughn couldn't find the courage to call the Vietnamese.

Lock stared from the panoramic windows of the huge lounge down at the glittering city. His hands were closed into fists in his pockets. Grainger's mood and the mystery surrounding him pressed palpably against his back like a mounting, undispersed charge of static electricity. There was nothing he could do, and he wanted nothing but to leave. He didn't even want to help, not *really* . . . because he sensed dark water, a whirlpool that would suck him down if he so much as reached out his hand to Grainger's assistance. During the day, Grainger's fear had communicated itself like a virus, so that even driving around Phoenix or out towards the Superstition Mountains still left everything unresolved. He wanted, more than anything, to walk away from it all. Everything had pressed close around him like the noon heat beyond the tinted windscreen and the air-conditioning.

He heard Grainger move to the cocktail bar, clumsily pour

himself another drink, then shuffle back to the leather chair in which he had sat hunched for most of the evening. The small noises scratched on his nerves like chalk on a blackboard. He rubbed his hand through his hair, tugging at it. He'd spoken to Faulkner in Washington that morning. The guy they'd arrested for trying to fence some of Beth's jewellery had named two small-timers. The police lieutenant had sounded falsely optimistic. The trail would lead no further than *I didn't know his name, he was just some guy in a bar.* They'd never find who'd murdered her.

The telephone blurted, shocking Grainger into attention and then a cowering pastiche of fear. Lock watched him almost with contempt, then hurried to the extension before the housekeeper or the butler answered it.

'Yes?' he snapped.

It was Tran, no mistake.

'Mr Grainger has not called me back, Mr Lock.'

'I told you, he's unwell. He can't come to the phone right now –'

'Then take the phone to Grainger, Mr Lock. That's my advice. Or perhaps I should come over in person?' It was an evident threat.

Grainger's features were flinty and drawn, as if he was very cold.

Lock's frustrations snapped like something stretched too far. 'Sure – why not?' he said, then thrust the phone towards the old man. 'Why not?' he repeated to Grainger, who crouched back from it as if from something that would brand or electrocute him. 'Talk to your Vietnamese friend, Vaughn, then maybe I can be on my way.'

He dropped the receiver into Grainger's lap, where it was inspected with one shivering hand, and turned away towards the door. He closed it behind him with an emphatic noise, intending –

– paused. He'd intended to walk out, to allow his frustrated anger to propel him, not even thinking of –

– picked up the receiver in the hall, very gently, very slowly.

He held his breath, held the mouthpiece away from his

lips, hand over it, heard his heart thudding. What the hell was he – ?

'– been *ill*,' he heard Grainger protesting, unaware that he was being overheard. 'My boy was *killed*. Scum killed my *son*,' he insisted.

'My old friend, my sincere sympathies. Do you think I would have intruded on your grief if matters were not urgent?'

Silence, for a long moment. Lock heard the housekeeper rattling crockery in the kitchen, the murmur of her voice and the butler's reply. Felt exposed and cheap hanging onto the hall telephone. The silence went on, broken only by the old man's ragged, slow breathing. Then:

'What's happening?'

'I do not understand, my friend. You must know why we have to talk. Why I have had to come personally to Phoenix?'

'Billy –' Grainger breathed, with a kind of appalled suspicion.

'It is now your problem, now that Billy . . . You understand that? I have given assurances – I was *given* assurances. I wish I could delay, but there are firm commitments to be met, and no sign of the red horse. I must have satisfactory answers, my friend.'

Menace floated like an oil-slick on the words, giving their rhythm an ominous calm. Then Grainger's breathing was the only sound; quicker, lighter.

'You *swear* to me you had nothing –!'

'Come, my friend, let us not indulge in fantasies!' Tran said quickly; so quickly that Lock knew he suspected an eaves-dropper. *You swear to me you had nothing . . . ?*

He felt nausea churn in his stomach, bit at the back of his throat. *You swear you had nothing . . .* Beth's composed, bluish features, staring up from the deep metal drawer in the police mortuary. No – *no*, he told himself.

'What of the red horse?' Tran asked. 'When can I expect delivery?'

'I don't *know*!' Grainger wailed. 'You know I don't know these things!'

'Then find out, my friend. Find out quickly. I am under a great deal of pressure. There are pledges to honour. I do not wish to lose face. You understand?' Grainger did not reply. 'You will find out – soon?'

Eventually, through agitated breathing: 'Yes, damn you, Tran – *yes*!'

The receiver was thrust down and Lock, startled into old cunning, put his down quickly. He had no doubt that Tran knew that he had been overheard. But had not been concerned.

He stood in the wide hall, staring at the paintings on the wall – American primitives and impressionists – his head whirling, his hands clenching and unclenching. Teeth noisy in his head, anger like a migraine at his temples. He glared at the telephone as if to blame it for his situation, wanting above everything not to have heard, not to guess, not to *know* . . .

Red horse. Delivery. Commitments. You swear to me you had nothing . . .

He blundered angrily into the lounge. Grainger was hunched forward on his chair, the extension still in his lap, his hand across his chest; his breathing stertorous until Lock's anger masked it.

'Vaughn – what the hell is going on here?' he yelled, rigid in front of Grainger. 'Who the hell is Tran – *what* is Tran? What the hell have you got to do with *horse*?'

Grainger was waving one hand feebly towards him, the other gripping the front of his slack shirt, twisting the green silk into a rag. His eyes were protuberant, his cheeks ashen. He seemed to be trying to ward someone off, someone he sensed behind Lock, someone stronger.

'Billy? Billy and *heroin*?' Lock bullied, leaning over Grainger, their faces almost touching. The old man's breath on Lock's mouth was moist and urgent. '*Red* horse? Coming out of – Jesus, Vaughn, *you*? You and Billy together?' He could not, *could not*, add the next terrible link . . . Beth's murder. There was a reason for her death and it was called heroin. He rubbed one hand across his damp forehead. He seemed to be burning with a fever.

'No!' Grainger groaned, his mouth crooked. 'Not Billy, not me –!' He winced with pain. Lock was unconcerned; the old man was faking. 'Nothing to do with it . . . Billy was going to

95

put everything right, he was – was looking into it, going to stop it – people in the corporation, we *didn't know* –!'

He attempted to rise to his feet, hand pressed flat against his chest, eyes wide, his other hand grabbing at Lock's shirt, twisting it into belief in his words, knuckles grinding against Lock's breastbone.

Then he fell; awkwardly, heavily, striking the carpet before Lock could grab at him. His hand was still pressed against his chest, his eyes stared sightlessly.

The police garage was icily cold, even at mid-morning. Vorontsyev wished he'd brought down his fur hat as he stamped his feet, his hands thrust deep into the pockets of his fur-lined parka. Forensic seemed dilatory and unenthusiastic amid the toylike disassembly of the Iranian's black Mercedes. He suspected the windscreen wipers, the radiator grille, the badge, maybe most of the car, would eventually disappear, cannibalised. For the moment, however, it lay around him like the shells of long-dead sea creatures thrown by waves onto a concrete, oil-stained beach.

A patrol car pulled out from its parking spot and growled up the ramp towards the street, its noise hardly distracting him. Lubin, limping exaggeratedly, shuffled around the chassis, then the front seats, the other two overalled detectives smoking as they dusted the windscreen and windows for prints. The setting might have been a backstreet garage and their task the respraying of a stolen vehicle.

Vorontsyev looked at his watch. Ten-thirty. A dozen hours since they'd raided Teplov's brothel and put this bird up into the air and towards their guns.

There were no drugs in the Merc – though that had been Dmitri's fond, concussed hope in the shocked, excited aftermath of the collision, before Vorontsyev had had him taken home. The passports meant nothing. He'd locked them in his desk drawer. The Iranian had no address in Novyy Urengoy, but neither did he stay at one of the R & R hostel blocks when enjoying his fortnightly breaks from the gasfield. He stayed at the Gogol, *in a suite* . . . three hundred dollars a night, hard currency only or credit card, preferably American. Vorontsyev had taken a photograph around the best hotels as a joke – and the joke had been on him.

'Anything yet?' he called out, impatient with cold.

Lubin looked up, his cheerful obsessiveness undiminished. And shook his head. Vorontsyev shrugged himself deeper into the parka, stamping his feet more militarily.

He'd had to send Marfa, with a junior detective she said she could trust, up to the gasfield to check the Iranian's – well, it was a *cover story* now, wasn't it? To check his background, length of employment, acquaintances . . . to check whether he was even *Iranian*, since it was what his passport alone asserted, and he had a dozen of them available . . .

. . . and one, only one, with a picture already in it. A Caucasian face, a Dutch name, and an innocuous occupation as an accountant. Who was *that* man, for God's sake?

Teplov had known little or nothing of the Iranian. Vorontsyev almost believed him. He rubbed his numb, weary face with his gloved hands as if to imitate the wash he had missed that morning, not having returned to his flat. He'd dozed in his swivel chair at the office. Teplov had said he thought the Iranian had had a racket, but he hadn't wanted to know and hadn't asked. The girl who'd served him knew him as a regular. She believed he was Iranian. He didn't want anything unpleasant or rough or back-to-front or upside down, so she had no complaints.

He'd paid in dollars, always welcome, with a satisfactory tip for the girl.

What would the post-mortem tell them, anything or nothing?

He yawned.

If the Iranian was into something, then he'd have known it was *drugs* the police were interested in, and if that wasn't his racket, why had he run? What panicked him if he *wasn't* linked to Hussain?

'Sir!' Lubin called, waving his hand urgently as he bent over a microscope balanced on a rickety folding table beside the wreckage of the dismembered limousine. 'Sir!'

He stamped over to Lubin's table. The other two had already lit new cigarettes and taken their relaxed places on the detached front seats of the Merc.

'What is it? Pond life?' Vorontsyev grumbled. 'A biology lesson?'

Lubin grinned. His good humour was – almost – infectious; would have been at a more reasonable temperature and after proper sleep.

'Fibres. From a coat. I can't swear to it, sir, I'd have to check it in the Lab –'

'He had a coat on. I saw that.'

'No. These fibres – foreign, like his cashmere, granted, but not his. Don't get too excited, sir, but I think that they'll match Rawls' overcoat. The one he died in.'

'What?'

'There's no blood, sir. Only his. Rawls didn't die in the car – if he was in it – nor was his body carried in the rear or the boot. But he sat in the passenger seat at some time, if these fibres match. Expensive wool mixture, colour, weave – they match, I'm sure.'

'Anything else?'

'Fingerprints. Perhaps we'll find Rawls' among them.'

'Or some of the local mafiosi, maybe?' He grimaced. 'OK, get back to the Lab with the prints and the fibres. Confirm Rawls was in the car and who else was with him if possible . . .' He rubbed his chin. 'I'll get out to the Grainger Hospital and check on the post-mortem. Or hold the pathologist's ballocks until he does finish!'

Lubin grinned. 'Is Dmitri coming in today, sir?'

'I told him not to – I don't suppose he'll listen. Good work, *if* it works. Call me when you have anything. On the mobile. And don't go yelling this all over headquarters.'

'Sir.' Lubin appeared offended. He added: 'You ought to check up on Dr Schneider while you're there –'

Vorontsyev glowered. 'I will!' he snapped.

Vorontsyev hadn't wanted – still didn't want – to think about Dr David Schneider. He hadn't told Dmitri what Marfa had found out from the taxi driver. Perhaps he should have let her talk to Schneider. It was sensitive, but a junior officer's blunder could be apologised into insignificance. Once *he* spoke to the deputy director of the Grainger Foundation Hospital Addiction Unit, about his connection with the dead Rawls, then he . . .

. . . might trip alarm bells, he admitted. Rawls' death was a warning. That much had been obvious. He'd been warned off, too, by Teplov's pleas of ignorance and veiled hints, by the murder of Hussain and the others in the block of flats. Alarm wires. He'd been blundering into them all the way along the path he'd been thrust on.

He stared at the Iranian's meatlike corpse on the stainless steel bench. The blood had gone, leaving only its smell, the organs had been removed, the breastbone and ribs parted as neatly as on a chicken served for lunch. The top of the head was missing. There was still the faint scent of bone heated by an electric saw, like the smell of teeth being drilled at the dentist.

All for nothing.

'He hadn't laboured much at all, and probably not recently,' the pathologist, Lensky, muttered, his voice gravelly, his grey eyes protruding above his glasses. He was wiping his hands on a towel. Beneath his robe, patchily stained, was the knot of a broad silk tie, vividly patterned. Lensky was well paid by the Foundation. 'The musculature is soft. The man's lifestyle was cushioned. You said a rig worker? What's the matter, Alexei — losing your touch?'

'That's what his papers say.'

'Expensive dental work. A neat, private-clinic scar where he'd had an appendectomy — sometime ago, by the look of it. He's been well off for a long while now, I imagine.' He sighed and scratched at his wiry grey beard, then adjusted his bifocals, at once studying Vorontsyev intently. 'I take it you haven't any idea who he is?'

Vorontsyev shook his head gloomily.

'There was alcohol in the stomach and the bloodstream. Not a very devout Moslem, was he?'

'I'd imagined not. Mr Al-Jani, from a village outside Tehran, is not at all what he seems. He stayed regularly at the Gogol, in a suite, he tipped generously, he threw parties, he met a great many people . . . all of whom, apparently, hadn't a name between them!' He snorted with a kind of weary disgust; or defeat. Lensky's expression indicated that he was unsure.

'Where will you look – for the real him?' he asked, gesturing towards the tidy, aseptic remains on the steel bench.

'Powder?' Vorontsyev suddenly blurted, staring down at the sightless eyes. 'Traces of anything on his fingers?'

'Explosives, you mean? No. Why?'

Vorontsyev was recalling the man's flight, his escape in the Merc, the sense he'd had of purposefulness rather than panic as the big German car had been coming at him.

'Just – like a double exposure on a snapshot. I keep remembering, seeing something *professional* . . . Never mind.'

'No,' Lensky murmured. 'You sleeping well?'

'Well enough.'

'I doubt that.'

'What about the bodies from the flat that blew up?' Vorontsyev asked hurriedly, as if resisting the pressure of something closing around him.

'Your young man, Lubin, was right. Fragments of rubber from a balloon, shards from a fragmentation grenade. They were murdered.'

'That nurse who was there?'

'I didn't know him. As I told you, he wasn't an addict. He must have been a friend – or a pusher. Or both.'

'I'll take the autopsy report, have a look at it.'

'As you wish. What's the matter with you, Alexei? We don't even play poker together any more. You're hiding yourself away –'

'Don't start, Ivan – not that tack again, please.'

'You used to be a good officer, Alexei. Too good. Just as I was once an idealistic doctor. Now . . .'

'Now *what*?'

'Something tells me this is looking as if it's too big for you. Forgive my bluntness, Alexei. If it made you happy hiding away, I'd say nothing. It doesn't. Me – I quite like the quiet life, the routine and the good pay in US dollars. But not you. You're sitting on your hands and you don't like it!'

Angrily, Vorontsyev growled: 'What are you – my mother or my priest?'

'Just your friend. Your oldest friend in this frontier town. As I said, forgive my intrusion into what is a private grief.'

'Grief?'

Lensky's eyes were wetly sad. Irony sat strangely on his short, dumpy, comfortable form.

'The town's got away from you, Alexei, and you can't forgive it or yourself.'

'Is that what you think?'

'It is. You've got a good team of people – not like the riff-raff in Vice or the dozens on the take in other departments. Lubin, for example. You should cherish him. And the girl – Marfa? Sharp as a knife, shines as brightly. And poor old Dmitri, the faithful borzoi . . . And you. The man who's lost his purpose –'

'Have you been saving this homily for just such an occasion?'

Lensky grinned through the hedge of his beard, his teeth displayed like white eggs in a nest.

'Maybe. But once you'd have been twitching like a bloodhound on a lead, badgering me for every detail, climbing up the walls because you couldn't solve a mystery! Now look at you!'

'You're a fine one to talk. How's the latest bimbo?'

'I don't need to be *just*, Alexei. Something in you does. That's the difference between us.'

'And if you're right? If I have this hunger for justice? What do I do – confronted with this town, which is just a microcosm of the whole damn country anyway?'

'You'd better pull the whole temple down, then, Samson – if that's what it takes.'

'You think I can?'

'Be a *middle-aged* idealist – before it's too late. You're fated to be a visionary of some kind, after all.'

'Am I?'

'Take my word for it.'

They stood in silence, for perhaps a minute, as if confronting one another, the Iranian between them like a wasted career, a spent life. And beyond him and the mortuary was Dmitri's daughter, Dmitri's ruined wife, the dead Hussain, the murdered Rawls . . . and the unspeakable, corrupt town.

101

'Jesus – you don't want much from me, do you?' Vorontsyev breathed.

'It's what you want – *really* want. After all.' Lensky smiled like a patriarch; then at once like a comfortable, lazy, clean-nosed, eye-on-the-pension friend who could be easily ignored.

'What do you know about Dr Schneider, Ivan?' Vorontsyev snapped out, grinning.

'Of the Addiction Unit? Not much. Young, idealistic, energetic – very Ivy League American. Or how I imagine such people to be. I quite like him. Pleasant company. Why?'

Vorontsyev shook his head.

'Nothing special. He was a friend of Rawls, the dead Grainger executive.'

'Perhaps they went to school together.'

'Perhaps. Where's that autopsy report on the dead nurse?'

'Oh, over on my desk – that table in the corner. One of those in that pile. Sort through them, will you? I'll just get changed – lunchtime, by my stomach's protests.'

Vorontsyev nodded and wandered across to the littered trestle table. Dismembered lives, just like the steel bench. A full ashtray, the remains of a sandwich meal, dozens of files. He flicked through one of the neater heaps, preoccupied with the chill of Lensky's analysis of his current self; the specious, indifferent, *lazy*, corrupt-by-omission minor bureaucrat he had become. Never put your head above the parapet, never volunteer, never *suspect*, *never* dig beneath the surface. Mottos to keep a man alive and sane in Novyy Urengoy. The place was full of steamrollers and crushers, waiting for the unwary.

He found Rawls' autopsy report. Bakunin must already have the GRU's copy . . . He spread the files under his long fingers. It's too late for ideals, he reminded himself. Lensky was whistling to himself as he re-entered the mortuary. The noise seemed like a warning from a bird rather than a tune. Hussain's dead face, the dead nurse's face, Rawls' face – the Iranian carved for inspection like a joint. His hand idly opened another file –

'Found it?' Lensky asked, slapping him on the shoulder.

'Who's this?' Vorontsyev asked in a quiet, halting voice.

'Who?' The pathologist adjusted his bifocals and studied the

102

photograph and the report. 'I remember. Cardiac arrest. Died in his hotel room, without even being on the job or full of drink. Congenital heart condition, almost certainly. Why? That was a week ago now. Ambulance got there too late. No suspicious circumstances.'

'Who was he?'

'Need glasses, Alexei? Yuri Maximovich Pomarov. See? From Kiev. A minor sub-contractor to the gasfield – to Grainger-Turgenev. It's all here.'

'Where's the body?'

'Flown home for burial, or so I understand. I don't *collect* them, Alexei!' He laughed uproariously. 'When I told you to light your inner flame again, Alexei, I did mean you to be selective in your enthusiasms! What can this man be to you? He died of a heart attack.'

'Maybe. But why was his picture in a completed *Dutch* passport, in the possession of Mr Al-Jani of Tehran? If he's from Kiev, why is he a Dutchman – and how does he come to know our jointed friend behind us?'

He stared at Vaughn Grainger. The old man, face masked, symbiotically existed with the machines and leads and drips that surrounded him. The nurses paused, checked, passed on – as if already imitating peasant women queuing past an open coffin containing the body of a national hero or dictator. Lock felt separated by more than glass from the faint rise and fall of the sheet over the old man's chest, from the hidden features and the neatly brushed hair. As distant as he had been as a child from the bodies of his parents.

He turned away from the window into the private room in the Grainger Wing of the Mountain Park Hospital, hands in his pockets, his features set in appalled, determined planes and creases.

He had ridden in the ambulance with Grainger, while the paramedics kept him alive. The old man had been cautioned not to move, talk or even think when he came round after his collapse. His heart had been damaged, they said. Lock had kept him warm and still until they arrived. But when he opened frightened, knowing eyes in the hurtling rear of the ambulance, he could not be prevented from protestation, as if he had merely been hypnotised during his heart attack. He continued his monologue directed at Lock the moment he regained consciousness.

He'd held Vaughn's hand and tried not to squeeze or crush it in his rage and fear at what the old man *had* to tell him; it had seemed more important than going on living. *Stay away from this, John-boy, for your own good . . . look what happened to Billy, your own sister – God's sake . . . nothing, do nothing . . .*

On and on, over and over. *Do nothing . . . people dangerous, ruthless, dangerous people . . .* The pieces shone in the lurid, hard lighting in the rear of the ambulance – shone in his mind like gold become bloodstained. People *within* Grainger Technologies were engaged in smuggling heroin – incredible to believe, certainly true, the old man's strain and desperation to convince him showed that. The paramedics hardly attended, except to attempt to quieten Grainger, who would not be silent until Lock promised not to act, to forget, leave it alone . . .

He hadn't, of course. He'd let them put Grainger out again, once he was certain of what he had heard, had his violent, horrified suspicions confirmed. Billy and Beth had been murdered by people inside Grainger Technologies because Billy had uncovered their racket.

He left the room adjoining Grainger's and entered the quiet, aseptic corridor. Helped himself to a paper cup and water from the dispenser. It was insipid, stale-seeming in his dry constricted throat. He threw the cup into a wastebasket, and thrust his hands into his pockets.

Beth had died to conceal evidence of a drug racket. A *Russian* drug racket. There'd been no names. He wondered if Vaughn even knew them – just what they'd done, what they were capable of doing. He had been unselfishly afraid, in the chaos and fear of his own heart attack, for Lock. He was touched, even indebted . . . feelings that his rage consumed every time Beth came to mind.

Billy told me, Billy was dealing with it, Billy . . .

. . . was dead. Like Beth.

Dead, Vaughn. To keep *him* quiet and just because *she* was in the house, just because she was *there* –!

He wiped viciously at his eyes, clearing them. A nurse paused as if to speak solicitously, but his features must have repelled her. She hurried away and out of sight around a turn in the corridor, with images of Beth and Billy flickering over her retreating form like pale flames.

Tran, the Vietnamese . . . He looked back at the door he had closed on Vaughn Grainger. The old man knew nothing more than he had desperately communicated. There was nothing to keep Lock in the hospital, in Phoenix. Vaughn would live or die according to the doctors' skills, not his presence or absence.

He glanced up as he heard noises along the corridor, only then realising he was leaning against the wall like someone in a queue. A gaggle of men in dark suits, women power-dressed, thrusting a nurse and a doctor ahead of them like a snowplough. Grainger Technologies executives. He recognised one or two of them, though none of them as much as glanced at him as they passed like a train, urgent and oblivious. The business would be taken care of. Since Beth's stock would have returned to Billy, it would now return to the company. To Vaughn, if he lived. There were other, treasured things in her will for himself. There was nothing to keep him here –

– except Tran. Nguyen Tran, staying at the Biltmore, less than a mile from the hospital. He glared around him. The Grainger executives were in a football huddle with doctors and nurses outside the door of Vaughn's room. There was a fierce, communal, sharklike concern about them, with a conflict of loyalties present on only one or two older faces. Otherwise, it was the beginning of a designer-clad acquisition of power within Grainger Technologies that was happening in the quiet corridor. It nauseated him.

The doctors wouldn't let the suits in.

Tran. He needed a telephone. Not to ring the Vietnamese, not just yet. First, he needed to know the man. He pushed himself away from the wall and along the corridor, away from Grainger and the crows at the banquet. More quiet corridors. He descended a flight of stairs and found a public phone. Visitors passed as he dialled the Washington number, with armfuls of flowers and an air of reluctance; like a funeral.

The duty man in the East Europe Office at State answered the phone.

'Lock – is that Ed?'

'Security identity code, please.' It was Ed. Lock gave his number and his password. 'Hi, John,' Ed said easily.

'You knew it was me, right?'

'It always pays to be security conscious,' Ed replied, imitating one of their seniors.

'Ed – I want you to check some files for me, and fax me copies of what you find, to . . .' He paused, then recollected Vaughn Grainger's fax number and gave it. 'Tonight. The subject is Vietnamese – no, don't ask why, just do this. It isn't top security, just top curiosity. OK?'

'OK, John. I go down to East Asia –'

'No, I don't think you do. The guy's name is Tran, Nguyen Tran, and I think you'll find a file under Special Immigrants. You remember? I'm guessing he came over sometime in the mid-'70s, and was set up in a business, probably without a name-change, though he'll be filed under both old and new identities, if he has changed. Got that?'

'This is Vietnam, right?' Ed made it sound like the War of Independence, a subject purely historical, somehow mythical. Da Nang equals Valley Forge. Unfortunately, it never had.

'Sure. But then, you majored in history, right?' Lock, despite the still-draining rage, accepted the office banter welcomingly. 'Tran. Tonight. I need to know everything about him, Ed.'

'OK, John. Will do.' He repeated the fax number, then added acutely: 'Be careful, uh?'

'How did you –? No, don't worry. Just background.'

'Did he know your sister's husband and father-in-law over there? They were in 'Nam, weren't they, both of them?'

Shocked, Lock stared at the receiver. 'Yes,' he said quietly. 'Yes, both of them. Thanks, Ed.'

He put down the receiver as if it burned his hand. It didn't mean anything, he told himself. It couldn't mean anything. Coincidence –

He smiled awkwardly at a child almost enrobed in a huge bouquet of flowers. The child smiled hesitantly back, though the father appeared truculently suspicious of him.

As Tran would be, when they met. Once he knew about Tran, he realised he would have to confront him. For Tran — alone — could lead him to Beth's murderers. Which was all that mattered to him, all that had ever mattered. Tran could bring them into focus, show him behind the nonsense that they were art or jewel thieves. Show him the truth.

When he knew who they were, he would kill them.

He breathed in deeply, grinning ferally in the direction of a young woman with a baby slung across her breasts like a papoose. It was a papoose, he realised. The woman was Apache. The Grainger Wing treated anyone, without question of income or insurance. Heroin was soiling that ideal just as surely as it had killed his sister.

He'd get back to Vaughn's house and wait for Ed's results. Tran was there in the files of State somewhere. If he was into heroin, he'd have had the capital of a wealthy man. Usually, wealthy Vietnamese had grown rich on the seed-corn that State and the Company had provided to those who had helped the US during the war.

The young Apache woman passed on up the gleaming, aseptic corridor, diminishing with distance. He nodded to himself, accepting the mood of dark elation which filled his body and thoughts. He wanted revenge for Beth — not justice, except in its most primitive form. They'd killed her, he'd kill them.

And Tran might have done it, or had it done . . . Tran, who was less than a mile away at that moment —

'This was his cot, his locker?' Marfa Tostyeva asked, sniffing as the warmer air unblocked her sinuses. Goludin, the young detective Vorontsyev had sent with her like a nursemaid, hovered beside her like an idiot, lumpen and unaware. The rig's assistant manager nodded, his beard sparkling with melted snow. 'And everything he possessed is still here?'

'We don't have pilfering up here,' the bearded man replied. His Russian was peremptory and acquired; he was Norwegian.

'Can I have the key?'

The Norwegian instead unlocked and opened the locker, then stood to one side. The dead Iranian was no one; unless the Norwegian's luxuriant beard hid emotions Marfa could not identify. She rummaged gently through the soiled clothes, the few possessions. It was a perfect cover story. Except for one silk shirt. She unfolded it and held it up.

'Liked dressing well, didn't he?' she murmured. The Norwegian inspected the shirt with seeming surprise.

'Up here?' he asked eventually after his fingers had identified the material. 'Why?'

'That's what I came to find out.'

'He wasn't anyone – wasn't paid well.'

'He had hundreds in dollars – credit cards, a cashmere coat.'

'Not up here he didn't. What's going on? The guy was lazy, unreliable. Should have been fired off the rig –' He hesitated, remembering something.

Marfa stood up, as if in his shadow. The Norwegian bulked over her.

'Well?'

'He was fired once, I think. Months ago. I'd have to check. It was reversed – the decision.'

'It wasn't *your* job?'

He shook his head. 'Personnel. Or his foreman. You want me to check?'

'Yes.' She thrust the shirt back into the locker. 'Pull the blanket back, Goludin. And the mattress.'

'Nothing here.' Goludin peered under the cot. There were five others in the cramped room. Bare walls, the minimum of comfort; a windowless segment of the accommodation block. 'Nothing under there, either.' He smiled like a dog expecting a pat.

She had told Vorontsyev the trip would, in all probability, be a waste of time. Seventy miles from town, out on the tundra where the last, sparse, dwarf trees straggled north, she felt isolated and uncomfortable. Rig 47. A man had worked here, but for the sake of establishing anonymity, a cover story. But why *here*? What he was really doing was focused on the town. Why would he be up here at all? When he was sacked, or about to be, why hadn't he just left and taken up residence in the Gogol, as he did when on R & R?

The wind banged against the accommodation block, making it seem flimsy, constructed of cardboard like an itinerant's shelter.

She shrugged.

'What the hell was he up to?' She studied the Norwegian assistant manager. 'Check his file for me, would you? Find out, if you can, who stopped the sacking and why. It's not difficult to get people, is it?'

'Any arsehole Third-World country has them queueing up. That includes Russia.' He grinned within the nest of his beard. 'Just a joke.'

'Not really.' She looked at the now unkempt cot, the small locker. In a gap in the wind, she felt certain she could hear the endless rush of gas through huge pipelines. 'Can you do that now?'

'Sure. There's no hurry, though. There's a blizzard on the way – you won't be out of here before tomorrow.'

She shivered. 'Hell.'

'We'll make you comfortable.'

'It's all that bloody *space* out there. I'd forgotten it.'

They left the dormitory, their boots sucking on the thermo-plastic tiles of the corridor. The wind struck at them as they left the accommodation block, snatching away the smell of the evening meal being prepared in the kitchens. Marfa ducked her head into the wind. There was heavier snow on it now and the low sun struggled against fast-moving cloud. She squinted around her. Gas flared from distant oil rigs as it was burned off. Rigs like Gulag watchtowers pressed along the horizon. Closer around them rose scattered buildings – administration, stores, vehicle sheds, accommodation. There were orderly rows of dilapidated trailers and caravans away to her right, where the overflow of workers bunked during their fortnights on site. A tracked crane lumbered out of the flying snow, startling her. The wind howled across the flat, empty tundra, making Rig 47, its flimsy buildings, skeletal towers and network of pipes raised about the tundra not merely inhospitable, but alien. She felt herself shaken

109

by utter dislocation. Isolated, of no significance. If it was agoraphobia, it seemed to *empty* her.

Then, in another moment, the doors of the administration block had slammed shut behind them and she could hear, in frozen ears, blaring music rather than the wind or piped gas. Marfa felt her whole frame shivering. Goludin's puffing relieved breathing at her shoulder seemed an inadequate commentary. Dear God in Heaven, it was *appalling* out there . . . The Norwegian was clambering up open stairs and she followed him as if fleeing the tundra outside.

He closed the door of his outer office behind them. Marfa, still icily cold, refused to hand him her parka or gloves and he smiled in superior amusement.

'Bring the file on Al-Jani through,' he asked the narrow-faced male secretary as he led them into his office.

Marfa slumped into a proffered chair, arms wrapped tightly around her. Goludin studied her in a not unkindly manner even if she felt it was somewhat patronising. God, what a bloody place . . . After a few moments, during which the secretary deposited the file and left, she raised her eyes and looked through the long window. The sun was lost except for a reddish smear along the flat horizon. The clouds rushed towards the rig's fragility in the last of the daylight. The window was wormed with wet.

'There's nothing here about his being fired,' the Norwegian offered, passing the file across his desk. 'I was back home on leave at the time,' he added. 'I heard about it later.'

'Who dealt with it?'

'Maxim – him outside – I expect. At least with the initial complaint. He'd have passed it on down, not up to Gustafsson, the manager. Maybe to Personnel. Perhaps he just forgot about it – it happens. We get a lot of people who don't come back, or get ill or injured, or can't stand the loneliness . . . If he wanted to work, maybe Maxim decided he couldn't be bothered to find a replacement roughneck.'

The telephone rang.

'Is it OK if I talk to Maxim?'

'Sure,' the Norwegian murmured, his hand over the mouthpiece. Then: 'What *kind* of fucking trouble have you got on that stretch of pipe?' He was nodding them out of the room.

Marfa opened the office door, glimpsing Maxim arranging his features carefully into blandness. Above his narrow, high-cheekboned face, his black eyes were suspiciously alert.

You know something, she thought with a pang of excitement. You know why we're here and what we want to know.

John Lock sat in the neat, aseptic emptiness of Vaughn Grainger's study, its large window overlooking the lights of Phoenix. He was staring at the silent fax machine. The house-keeper and the butler had retreated to their bungalow in the grounds and the maid was ensconced – probably with a man – in her flat over the garage. He was alone in the house. The barely tasted beer and the uneaten sandwiches that had been prepared for him sat beside his elbow.

The large house was silent, funereal, in the late night. It placed a deadness on his nerves, dulling his anger into a deep gloom. Tran filled his thoughts. There were no features he could employ to personify the object of his stifling rage, only a Vietnamese name.

The ample room contained two TV sets, the fax machine, a broad oak desk inlaid with green tooled leather, a typewriter, numerous telephone extensions, a VDU and keyboard. But the place seemed hardly used, as if a film of desert dust covered its surfaces. There were some photographs, measuring the passage of time. He avoided the one of Beth and Billy at their wedding. There were pictures of Vaughn, one of him in uniform which must have been taken in Vietnam, but the majority of the snap-shots, colour or monochrome, were of Billy Grainger. Lock him-self was in one of them, taken in the field in Afghanistan, he and Billy posed in front of a wrecked MiL helicopter gunship, laughing, ringed by cold and alien mountains.

His anger ate at him cancerously, as he cursed the fax machine's silence. The large second hand of the clock on the wall measured time in strained, faltering movements, and the slow ticking of the English longcase clock was as ominous as distant thunder.

111

Lightning flickered among the Superstition Mountains beyond the city, walking on the hilltops. He closed his eyes heavily on the image . . .

. . . then jerked awake at the signal from the fax machine. He stared at it, then at the clock on the wall; slowly realising that he had slept in the swivel chair for almost two hours. There was the faintest colouring along the horizon. It would be dawn in an hour. The page began sliding as smoothly as oil out of the machine, which chattered its satisfaction with itself.

He lifted it up and began reading, even as the pages continued to ease themselves into the room.

Tran *had* been a Special Immigrant, as he had guessed. Arrived in May '75, from a screening camp in the Philippines. *Flown* in on a CIA flight – he recognised the code-numbers of the flight. No *innocent civilians* had gotten themselves flown Stateside. Lock read on. Nguyen Tran, described as a retail trader in Saigon, had been born in a village to the north of the capital . . . Left Saigon in late April '75, as part of Operation Frequent Wind, the eighteen-hour airlift that had taken the remaining Americans and their most valuable Vietnamese allies from either the embassy roof or the Tan Son Nhut pick-up point. He'd have been flown in an H-46 out to a waiting ship.

He glanced ahead of himself, at the succeeding sheets. Copies of documents, mostly. He was disappointed. Tran had obviously been valuable – must have worked either for the Company, the Marines or Special Forces in some capacity or other. Tran was no simple, above-board retailer, he was a Company man or close enough to it.

He caught, as the fax stopped after the fourth sheet and whistled in self-satisfaction, a glimpsed snapshot in the corner of eyesight. Billy Grainger's features, grinning into strong sunlight. Billy had been airlifted out of Saigon during that same operation. He'd been CIA in Saigon for over a year when the final invasion came and the Viet Cong forces raced for the southern capital. As Billy had always said, laughing, every time they were in a tight spot in Afghanistan – or even when Grainger Technologies had looked like it might run into the buffers in the late '70s, after the oil-price hikes by the Arabs – he'd already been in the

112

tightest possible spot and gotten out alive. While he and his people were still on the embassy roof, waiting for the last helicopters, the Viet Cong were already looting the lower floors of the building. Billy could hear the childlike rapture of Charley and the occasional single, executioner's shot before the rotor noise drowned them. *So don't talk to me about tight spots*, he would always conclude after recounting the story.

Lock sniffed loudly in the again-quiet room.

Tran was set up, Stateside, with Company slush money, in a laundry business in Sausalito. Slowly, he had expanded the business into a chain of laundromats . . . Which is where, Lock realised, State lost interest in him, just as the Company would have. Tran fulfils the American dream, becomes a US citizen in 1981, and vanishes from official records. He glanced again at the other pages of the fax. Documents, including the green card, the citizenship, Tran's address – out of date by maybe three million dollars – and other trivia.

Tran, however unimportant he had become to State and Langley, had prospered – by means of heroin – on the West Coast. Red horse – Russian-derived heroin, made in Russia, *grown* in . . . ? Wherever the gasfield workers came from – the Moslem Triangle, for sure. It came up from there, was refined in Novyy Urengoy, and smuggled out by means of Grainger-Turgenev. Using the company's flights, maybe even using the company's people on the ground. And the executives Billy had discovered running the operation were in and out of there all the time. It was perfect. A frontier town thousands of miles from anyone who might care to stop them or investigate what was really going on.

Tran, however, was only the distributor on the Coast, or one of them. All he'd have would be names . . . but prominent names, *really* important –

– noise of a window breaking somewhere in the house.

Lock looked around the room, as if he expected to find he had broken a piece of porcelain. He strained to hear other noises beyond the heavy silence of the study. Nothing. The second hand of the clock moved jerkily as a crab's claw, limping the seconds away. Nothing –

– for almost a minute, then something creaked like old wood,

113

something else sounded as if snapped like a fragile bone. His hands were spread on the desk in front of his body, empty. Then the right one jerked out towards the small console and switched off the lights in the room. The darkness immediately brought rustling noises, like cloth breathing against skin. Gently, very slowly, he opened the top left-hand drawer of the oak desk and touched the Colt automatic Vaughn always kept there. Withdrew it and, as it caught the glow of the city dully, he slid the ammunition clip into the butt after scrabbling it from the same drawer. The noise as he eased a round into the chamber seemed betrayingly loud. He could hear his heartbeat.

And footsteps, soft and coming towards the study. From the lounge, the rustle of drapes being automatically drawn. Then a strip of light showed beneath the study door. He sat in the darkness, his heart loudening, a fine line of perspiration springing out on his forehead, the gun quivering in his grip. He could think only that it was Tran. Or his people. It wasn't accidental, casual – it was too like Beth's murder. He shivered. The footsteps paused outside the door – voices, whispering? He'd forgotten to put on the alarm system and remembered that Billy could not have done so at the Virginia house. He was as exposed as Billy and Beth had been.

Door handle being eased. He sensed the city behind him, beyond the window, outlining him, but could not move. Beth had been as helpless, asleep. Gleam of light, shadow beyond it. He saw the door open a few inches from where his less-helpless body had now placed him. He'd ducked behind the oak desk, his head peering over its rampart. The shadow bulked in the doorway, made neat by the foresight on the Colt. Made vulnerable. A gloved hand reached in beside the door, searching for the switch, its black fingers moving like a spider's legs. He squeezed the trigger and there was a scream and the black spider withdrew, hurt. Voices and groaning. Lock swallowed the saliva of excitement. A quarrel, then the inevitable returned fire, a gun gleaming in the doorway for a moment, fired blindly into the room. He fired back, twice, at the already retreating footsteps and the muttered curses speaking a foreign language that might have been Vietnamese.

114

A door slammed. The study reeked of explosives. There was a hole in the window behind him, a gouge in one of the upholstered chairs. Lock rose to his feet, shaking with exhilarated nerves. Then he stumbled to the door of the study and looked out into the corridor leading to the hall. A scuffed and disturbed Indian rug, a patch of blood on the pale wall near the door. The noise of feet on gravel coming through the open door as he reached the hall.

He thought he caught the voice of the butler, then lost all other sounds in the noise of a car engine. He ran onto the gravel drive which sloped up to the country road that wound past the house. Headlights moving off. His adrenalin pumped more fiercely than his heart, making his imagination wild, his body taut, invulnerable. He heaved open the door of the Toyota Vaughn had put at his disposal, fumbling in his pocket for the ignition key. He started the car, seeing the maid's bemused features at a curtained window above the garage just before he squealed the car around to face the slope and accelerated in a scream of gravel towards the road.

He reached it and turned out. Their car was already out of sight around a bend in the road as it descended the mountain. He knew, with utter certainty, that they were heading for the Biltmore Hotel and Tran. What was ridiculous, but which magnified in his thoughts even before he took the first bend with a scream of tyres, was the idea that the men ahead of him had killed Beth and Billy. Ridiculous . . . but compelling.

His heart jumped as he saw the glare of brakelights at another bend in the road, less than a quarter of a mile ahead of him. If they'd killed Beth, *if, if* . . .

He had to force himself to decelerate, keep his distance.

I don't like you, Vorontsyev thought as he smiled in imitation of David Schneider's open grin. But he wondered if it was because he mistrusted Americans in general, or because it was Schneider. Perhaps *innocent* Americans, especially if they're idealistic doctors, possess ready smiles and casual good manners, together with a supreme confidence, even when confronted with a senior police officer enquiring about a friend's murder?

115

He didn't know. Instead, he sipped the good Dutch coffee that Schneider had offered him. The American had asked him not to smoke out of deference to his intolerance, but it was no hardship and did not irritate Vorontsyev. It was the smile that did that, its readiness, breadth, warmth.

Or perhaps the spaciousness of the office created envious dislike, or perhaps the leather chair in which he sat or the rosewood desk . . . ?

He'd had to wait most of the afternoon to interview Schneider, but had spent that time investigating the Russian who had claimed to be a Dutchman on the false passport and who had died in the Gogol Hotel of a heart attack. A Dutch accountant. A *Russian*, from the Ukraine, who was a minor sub-contractor to the gasfield companies. He'd talked to Kiev. There was no Pomarov who owned or worked in an executive position for any such company. He'd faxed Kiev Central CID the photograph of the dead Pomarov and the more animated passport photograph.

By that time, Schneider had been free to see him and he had all but lost interest, absorbed by the identity of the dead man who had pretended – *or was about to pretend* – to be Dutch and who was, perhaps, not even Ukrainian Russian. He had died of a heart attack. Lensky was certain of that . . . *no, not poisoned, Alexei, I swear, nor bludgeoned or stabbed to death*. . . Laughing as he assured him.

Yet now Schneider, too, intrigued him. Another distorted impression in a hall of mirrors.

'I really am sorry I can't help you, Major. Jesus, I'd like to, Allan Rawls was a good friend, a college friend . . . But what can I tell you?' Variations on that theme had occupied them for the entire ten minutes of the interview.

Schneider raised his large, long-fingered hands, gesturing at the room and the Addiction Unit beyond it. Where Dmitri's daughter had been brought, OD'd and dead on arrival . . . Schneider was a busy, important man in the Foundation Hospital. His manner suggested he felt piqued by the unspoken suggestion that his idealistic nature might have any connection with something as sordid as murder. Even the murder of a friend.

And the man was well qualified, Lensky assured him, and could be making a great deal more money back in America. The Addiction Unit was lucky to have him, everyone said so.

Schneider had been in Novyy Urengoy for more than a year, a long tour of duty at the unglamorous end of the hospital's business. He lived in one of the largest company apartments in the most luxurious block. A succession of young women – nurses, a singer, a cocktail waitress, a businessman's daughter – Lensky knew most of the lubricious details – had preoccupied or distracted his leisure time. All partings had been amicable.

'So, Mr Rawls came to see *you*, and for no other reason did he attend the hospital during that week?' Vorontsyev summarised stiffly, as if reading from a notebook.

Schneider laughed. 'Sure – if you want to put it that way. He came to see me – out of friendship and because he was charged with writing a report on our work for the head of the Foundation, the older Mr Grainger. He takes a personal interest in the work of the Unit. And he demanded *good* briefings from people like Allan. That's why Allan was being so meticulous, Major – why he came up here so often!' His grin faded and his features adopted seriousness reluctantly but properly. 'As to what happened to him, what he was doing out on that road in the middle of the night, I have no idea.'

'I see. You visited him at the Gogol?'

'Sure. For a drink –' He looked ostentatiously at his gold watch. 'Is there anything else, Major? I guess I'm bushed. Time to go home, get some sleep.'

Vorontsyev put down his cup and stood up. 'Of course. Thanks for your help, Doctor –'

'Sorry I couldn't tell you anything helpful. It's a terrible business –'

'Thank you. I won't detain you any longer.'

He shook Schneider's cheerfully proffered hand, returned his ready smile, and went.

It was another ten minutes before Schneider left the hospital. Vorontsyev watched him cross the car park, his tall, angular frame leaning into the bitter wind, the sodium lighting catching

117

the blowing snow and the lanky, easily recognisable figure. Vorontsyev wiped the windscreen clear of the fug and switched on the wipers. They squeaked against the sprinkling of snow. He started the car's engine as Schneider reached and unlocked a small, dark BMW. Vorontsyev rubbed his stubbled chin and sensed himself as a creased, morose, awkward figure seated opposite Schneider in his warm, well-lit office. Then the doctor started the BMW's engine and he was merely a suspect being tailed and the authority of their encounter passed to himself.

The snow chains ground across the parking area. Schneider had more expensive studded tyres fitted to his car. The BMW pulled out of the hospital car park and turned towards Novyy Urengoy, which gloomed out of the snow like the wreckage of a metropolis, lights fitfully gleaming from a few of the tower blocks. The traffic was light. There weren't many cars in the town, despite its being awash with foreign currency and drug money and gangsters' profits. Cars were for show or shopping. To *go* anywhere you had to fly – for long hours if you wanted to arrive anywhere that pretended to civilization. He slotted in behind a light van which was fifty yards back from the German saloon. Schneider was going home, in all likelihood . . . well, it's not out of my way, is it?

He just wanted to be sure, to still the nagging toothache of doubt; quell the cynicism, he admitted, that could not accept someone so patently *good* as Schneider. Perhaps it was a national rather than an habitual failing in him.

The town closed around them, the caravans and dreary, decaying tin huts and wooden dachas growing as monstrously as the tower blocks and squat factories and shops. The smell of bread on the icy air from a bakery, its windows glowing out over the patient, immobile queue. Then he turned into the neon glare of Mockba Prospekt. Slowed quickly enough to cause the car to skid as the BMW pulled into the kerb. Schneider got out. Vorontsyev steered across to the far side of the prospekt and hauled on the brake. Schneider was paying a thin, stunted youth to watch his car while he entered the blaring lights of the McDonald's. Vorontsyev wound the window down so that he could make out the tall figure inside the restaurant, then wound

118

it back up and lit a cigarette. The youth sat proprietorially on the bonnet – probably as much to keep warm as for any reason of security.

The place was filled with people, as it was every day. The pavement was especially widened to accommodate the queues. Money rattled its gold chains and flaunted its foreign clothing at the bright windows. Outside, there was a hot potato stall with its own smaller, imitative queue. The faces were mostly darker or more peasantlike there. An ancient woman – he'd seen her before – was selling vegetables outside the restaurant.

Vorontsyev settled down to wait.

Rubbed his eyes and roused himself quick as an alarmed dog. The BMW was moving, the youth watching his source of heat and money retreating. Vorontsyev's engine fired a third time and he skidded out into the middle of the prospekt a hundred yards behind Schneider.

He wiped furiously at the fuggy windscreen, then settled to tailing the other car. Along the Mockba Prospekt, through two intersections, then into K Street. The tunnel of garish neon assaulted Vorontsyev as it always did; blatant, gaudy, tasteless. The BMW was moving easily on the cleared snow and new ice. The tail of the ZiL threatened to escape his control at every moment, despite the snow chains. Stripclub followed bar followed café followed cinema followed stripjoint along the street, their doors like dark mouths beneath the vulgar promise of their neon eyes.

The BMW turned into an alley and Vorontsyev slowed the ZiL until he was opposite the entrance. A sign for car parking, Patrons Only it insisted in green neon, for the Café Americain. He tossed his head. Even a Russian understood the allusion to *Casablanca* and Humphrey Bogart. This Café Americain, however, wasn't owned by a soldier of fortune trying to forget Ingrid Bergman but by a real-life, made-in-Russia gangster. Valery Panshin.

Vorontsyev hesitated, then turned into the alleyway and then the car park. He pulled into a parking space. Then locked the car and walked towards the entrance. A light over matt-black rear doors. The uniformed doorman recognised him. Had cause to. He'd narrowly evaded trial on two charges of malicious wounding with a knife. Vladimir – Vlad the Impaler as he liked to be known.

'Hold the door open, there's a good peasant,' Vorontsyev murmured, stamping his snow-laden boots on the carpet as the doorman did so.

The warmth of the place struck him and he removed his fur hat and gloves. The carpet was stained and lumped with snow. The cloakroom girl appeared offended as if by an unpleasant smell until she, too, recognised him. He moved towards the main bar and restaurant. There was a jazz group playing.

Perhaps that was why Schneider came, for the jazz? It was why Vorontsyev himself came and why Panshin could be forgiven some small things because he hosted the best jazz in western Siberia; even American and British bands, not just Russians or the more obscure French units.

He entered through the open doors and confronted a dinner-jacketed bouncer. One of Panshin's customer integration executives, or whatever he was calling them now. A hand was placed on his chest for a moment, before a waiter shook his head vehemently and mimed the taking of a warrant card from his pocket.

'Sorry,' the bouncer murmured.

'Accepted –' He was about to ask for the man's name, just for the pleasure of unsettling him, when he saw, seated in his usual place at the side of the small stage, Panshin himself.

And the tall figure of Dr David Schneider, about to seat himself at Panshin the gangster's private table.

SIX

Tidal Waters

Lock turned the Toyota off Camelback Road and the glare of
the desert sunrise slid off the windscreen as he entered the dawn
shadows between the buildings on 24th Street. Ahead of him,
the green Lincoln nosed into the grounds of the Arizona
Biltmore. The Lloyd Wright-inspired, blocklike building glinted
in the early sunlight. The car emerged into the sun once more.
He slowed and drew into the sidewalk, his chest tight with satisfied tension. They *were* Tran's men, the three shadowy heads
he had been able to see through the rear window of the Lincoln
– they were. The thought that they had to be Beth's murderers
shut out almost everything else except his awareness of his temperature, his nerves itching and jumping just beneath the damp
surface of his skin.

He eased the car forward to the hotel driveway. The green
Lincoln was dropping its nose, nuzzling into the underground
garage of the Biltmore. As it vanished, he moved forward, parking the Toyota beside a dry lawn already thirsty for the sprinklers
whose water caught the sunrise. He left the car and crunched
on gravel towards the entrance to the car park. His right hand
touched at the lump of the Colt in his jacket pocket as he walked.

He sidled down the slope, slid beside the automatic barrier,
and entered the garage. Cool and petrol-scented. Limousines
and smaller cars stretched away like racked groceries, neat as a
supermarket.

Silence. Hard striplighting. Then a muffled groan and the sigh
of the lift, as if it was shocked by evidence of pain. He saw
two black-sweatered figures beside the green Lincoln, fifty yards
away. Another man, clutching his one hand with the other, was
leaning against the bonnet, the other two men clustered around

him, arguing in high, trilling voices, arms waving, as if they had entered the garage to find their car stolen. Then the lift doors opened and another Asiatic in a white silk shirt and fawn slacks emerged, hurrying at once towards the Lincoln. His arms, too, semaphored distress and anger. Lock watched from behind the flank of a red Porsche as he moved closer. The silk-shirted man's voice was immediately authoritative, his arms offering superior signals that quelled the others. He seemed oblivious to the blood-stained wrapping around the injured man's hand.

Tran.

Two GM saloons, then a big estate car, then a European hatchback. He was twenty yards from them, his breathing calm. Tran – it had to be him – was gesturing angrily in denial. Berating them. Then the noise of his hand on the face of one of the intruders, who had dared truculence and excuse. Tran gestured towards the garage entrance – so violently that Lock ducked out of sight, suspecting he had been seen – and shouted what seemed like the same injunctions again and again. Lock cautiously raised his head.

The doors of the Lincoln were open, they were helping the wounded man into the back of the car. Then, nodding with furious, automaton energy, the driver and the third man got into the car. The engine fired. Tran had already turned his back on them, his broad features enraged. Lock's face assumed a similar mask in grotesque imitation as Tran walked towards the lift doors. The tyres of the Lincoln screeched and then the car heaved itself sullenly towards the daylight and the barrier.

Lock watched it as it passed him, then rose from his crouch and hurried towards Tran. The noise of the Lincoln surging to the top of the slope faded away. He saw and heard nothing but the small, compact Vietnamese and his diminishing distance from the lift. Tran reached it and pressed the button. The man's face was thoughtful, still angry. Lock was fifteen yards from him as the lift doors clunked open. Fifteen – running. He saw Tran's face turn towards the source of the echoing footfalls, saw his surprise and then his instinctive jab at the buttons inside the lift. Eight, six –

– doors beginning to close, Tran's face nakedly expressing

shock and the vulnerability of being unarmed and alone. He seemed to stare for a moment towards the sun-spilling entrance after the vanished Lincoln, as if to recall it. Two –

His arms blundered between the closing doors, springing them back. He lunged into the lift, thudding against the far wall. Tran began moving away from him. Lock thrust the gun against the man's ribs and jabbed over his shoulder at the Door Close button.

'Which *floor*?' he expelled like a winded breath. 'Floor?' He jabbed the gun into Tran's ribs. 'Come *on*!'

Tran, arms raised to the level of his shoulders, his eyes blackly calculating, then quiescent, reached out and pressed a button. The top floor, where the suites were located. Stupid not to know that, Lock told himself. He motioned Tran back against the wall of the compartment, leaning himself on the opposite wall, breathing heavily, his head hanging like that of a wounded bull. The gun was, he realised, remarkably steady in his hand. Tran's eyes flickered as if he was viewing a high-speed series of still pictures projected on a screen. He didn't know who Lock was, was trying to locate him in some mental file – and was afraid because of his anonymity. Until –

'Mr Tran?' he said.

'You are Lock?' Tran replied, his eyes now inspecting Lock like the fingers of a blind man, quickly and thoroughly. There was an imperceptible nod, as if he had satisfactorily answered his own question.

'You guessed it.'

'My – business is not with you, Mr Lock, nor yours with me.' Lock was shocked into attention at the prim, demarcating remark. Tran had regained an impassive composure that unsettled him.

'Your guys tried to kill me,' was all that he could find in reply. Even to himself, it rang hollow with complaint.

'My – guys?'

'The blackshirts in the green Lincoln – the ones you just sent away to find a doctor who won't ask questions about a gunshot wound.'

The lift stopped and the doors opened onto thick-piled carpet and the hot, airless scent of a hotel corridor. He gestured with the Colt, and Tran looked at his steady hand. The man's black eyes rose to his face, and slowly became unnerved.

'Out,' Lock said. 'Anyone else up here with you, Tran? I mean, people like those who burglarised the Grainger home –' Tran stared as the words choked off, and he saw the Vietnamese realise his assumption of a destructive recent past.

'I – am sorry concerning your family tragedy, Mr Lock. I know nothing of it.'

They had paused outside the door to Tran's suite. The Vietnamese, neat and small in his silk shirt and fawn slacks, had casually taken the keycard from his breast pocket. 'Inside,' he murmured. Tran shrugged and inserted the keycard. The lock buzzed and he pushed open the door.

'Please come in, Mr Lock.'

Lock nudged the door wide. There was no one concealed behind it, no one in the suite's large sitting room – or the bedroom or the bathroom. Tran wandered through the open windows to the balcony, the white net curtains stirred by the early morning breeze.

'Come back in here, Tran.' His voice lacked authority, as did the gun.

Tran re-entered the living room, gestured to two chairs on either side of a table, and seated himself. Angrily and impotently, Lock sat opposite him, the gun cradled in his lap.

'Why do you feel it necessary to interfere in my business affairs, Mr Lock?' Tran lit a cigarette in an ebony holder. 'Your distress at your family's murder is evident. I understand.' His voice was as bland as that of an analyst. 'But, as I said, those unfortunate events have nothing to do with me.'

'Vaughn – Grainger's in the hospital –' Tran nodded. 'You put him there. It's drugs, isn't that right? Red horse, I mean?'

'Shall I call room service for some coffee – tea?'

'No!' Lock snarled. Beyond the net curtains, the day was heating rapidly under the blank sky. 'They must have died because of the drugs,' he insisted. 'The people you deal with, Tran – inside Grainger Technologies –' There was the slightest flicker of surprise and satisfaction in the black, stonelike eyes. '– they wanted Billy silenced. They were covering up.'

'Ah, a cover-up. I see,' Tran murmured.

'You admit it?' Why was Tran at ease, suddenly more relaxed? 'What's happening here, Tran?'

The room's air-conditioning stirred the exhaled cigarette smoke.

Eventually, Tran asked: 'What did you expect to learn by coming here, Mr Lock – by following my people from the Grainger house?'

'I want to know the truth, Tran. I want to know who murdered my sister.'

'I don't know who killed your sister.' Were his eyes shaded with apprehensions of his own, for an instant?

'But you know names. You know who your suppliers are. Those names will do.'

'I do not think I can supply those names. It would endanger my investments, my business.' Tran glanced through the barely moving net curtains, down towards the gardens of the Biltmore and the peacocks' tails of the fountains and sprinklers scattered geometrically across the lawns. Patches of gravel were wet.

'I need those names, Tran. You'll give them to me. There are people inside Grainger Technologies, right, who supply you with heroin from Siberia . . . maybe it's even refined over there. It originates, I would guess, in the Moslem Triangle. The Russian mafia has to be involved, too, I imagine . . .' The numbers of people involved, the size of the operation, the power of each unknown person, retreated into the shadows of his imagination. Tran, sitting impassively, wasn't even frightened of a Colt. 'Am I right?' he insisted.

'I take delivery of an assured supply. There is no need for me to either know or speculate, Mr Lock.'

'You take an awful lot on trust, Tran.'

'It is sensible to do so.' Once more, the Vietnamese glanced down into the grounds of the hotel, like someone anxious for the arrival of the postman, or a plumber.

'Don't give me that garbage, Tran. You have the names. Don't worry, I won't be indiscreet. What you tell me won't be traced back to you.'

Tran smiled. 'Very reassuring.'

125

Again, he glanced towards the windows. The air coming in was hot now, the air-conditioning protesting against its intrusion more loudly. Tran lit another cigarette and stood up. The gun jerked out of Lock's lap uncertainly, almost convulsively. He realised the strained state of his nerves.

Tran sighed, cutting off the slight noise almost immediately. He sat down again, crossing his legs.

'You see, Mr Lock, however sympathetic I may be towards your tragedy, business ethics prevent me from being indiscreet. I am afraid I cannot help you. There is no benefit for me in doing so.'

'Then I have to kill you, right?'

'Then you would learn nothing.'

'Then tell me!' Lock raged, leaning forward on his chair, his facial muscles taut, his neck stretched like a child in a furious, blind temper. 'Tell me who's behind it, who *killed my sister*, damn you!'

Tran uncrossed his legs. He gripped the arms of the chair, as if to raise himself. Yet his attention was somehow beyond Lock.

'I do not know who killed your sister, Mr Lock.' Tran's voice was louder. 'If, as you suspect, they were killed by associates of mine – that their deaths had anything to do with the people with whom I deal – then I am sorry, I have nothing I can tell you. *I* do not know, Mr Lock.'

And then he realised he had his back to the door. Window, door, corridor, window . . . Tran had kept looking towards the windows, waiting for something, something he expected to *see* – just as he was talking loudly now, expecting someone to *hear* . . . Tran's people must have returned, Tran had seen their car or them out front.

Lock rose to his feet, brandishing the gun like a club. Tran flinched, but his eyes remained confident. They were close, almost there –

He turned away to the door. Opened it. The corridor was empty. He felt panic rising in him like choking water. Take Tran, get out –

He turned back to the Vietnamese. The man's body was disappearing into the bedroom of the suite. He heard the door lock.

126

The situation had reversed in an instant. There was not time to break down the door, turn Tran into a shield —

He looked out of the door. A shout. The sight of a raised hand. The figure of one of Tran's people, still dressed in black. Lock looked wildly around him.

FIRE EXIT.

He blundered through the doors and down the echoing stairs.

'You think he's covering something up,' Goludin remarked, his hands around the thick white coffee mug, his shoulders hunched against the palpable suspicion and dislike of the few gasfield workers with whom they were sharing the canteen.

'Yes, but I don't know what,' Marfa confirmed. 'It doesn't seem to lead us anywhere or even to make any sense.'

The canteen's high windows were thick with snow. The blizzard outside bullied against the flimsy buildings of the Rig 47 complex. The barracklike canteen was all but empty. There was rock music from loudspeakers, murmured voices, the deep distrust as obvious as the smells from the kitchen. Probably everyone in the room had something to hide, some fiddle, some shady past.

'Have you finished?' she asked with impatient enthusiasm, suddenly wrapping her long scarf across her throat, bunching her woollen hat in her gloved hands. Goludin appeared reluctant to move. 'I want to check all the supplies that have come in since the explosion in the flat.'

'You think someone else brought the drugs —' He was leaning forward and whispering now. '— up here in place of that guy Hussain?'

'The Major does. I do as I'm told.'

'Why up here?'

'I don't *know*. Just till things die down a bit, maybe. The Iranian worked here, he must have had something to do with the drugs —?' The statement ended interrogatively. She felt the gap between theory and instinct like a rush of cold air through an opened door. It *was* just theory. The wind howled in a short silence between pop songs. 'We can't find them in town, so maybe they're here. Who knows?'

127

'Where do we start?'

'You take the food store, I'll cover equipment and spares. OK?'

'It could be,' Goludin admitted. 'Hussain worked here, just like the Iranian. Doesn't seem they knew each other, though, does it?'

She rubbed her forehead. Hours of fruitless questioning came back like a headache. Al-Jani had no friends, no close acquaintances on the rig. Just another roughneck despised by the Russians and Ukrainians and Europeans, and ignored by his fellow Moslems, apparently. Hussain had friends here, though. A search of their quarters had revealed nothing, except resentment escaping like a leak of gas.

'Let's just check the latest shipment of supplies and hope this bloody weather improves by the morning.' She stood up. 'Come *on*, Goludin.'

She watched the men that watched their departure from the canteen. Sullen or merely weary, it was difficult to tell. Unkempt, bearded faces with split lips, red eyes, chilblained hands. There wasn't even energy for lust in their eyes and bodies. Just suspicion; dislike of the cops.

The blizzard tore the outer door from her grip and flung snow in their faces. The snow seemed so violent and solid she had the sensation of being trapped against the tunnel wall of a metro as a train hurtled past her only inches away. It blew through the garish floodlighting that illuminated the compound of the rig. She could see nothing, not even the other buildings.

Pointing, she shouted: 'I'll be over there! The equipment store – got that?' Goludin nodded. 'Whoever finishes first comes back here. We'll compare notes!' Goludin nodded once more, his face masked by his scarf and the hood of his parka.

She hesitated, then launched herself into the blizzard, sensing at once that she had already disappeared from Goludin's sight. The wind cut through her as if she was naked and the sense that she was invisible after her first two or three steps unnerved her. She was blundering through an endless series of heavy white curtains, trying as in a dream to thrust them aside. She thought she heard a door slam, the growl of distant machinery. She huddled her arms about herself, straitjacketed by the wind

128

and snow, trudging forward with her head down. The place was a bloody Gulag!

Cold – God, it was so bloody *cold* . . . She lurched into a wall, shocking herself upright and breathless, as if she had been attacked. Icebound metal under her gloved fingers. If she hadn't walked in a circle, this was the largest of the vehicle sheds. The equipment store, another large, hangarlike block, was next to it. She wiped the snow out of her eyes and mouth and moved along the wall until she encountered the corner.

A gap in the snow, momentary as it was, revealed the equipment store twenty yards away. Then it vanished like a snowy mirage. She rubbed her arms and body, hesitated, then plunged once more into the blizzard, hurrying towards what would be a welcome collision with the other building. Her hands, stretched out before her, found only cold rushing air, and a faint sense of panic began before she touched icy corrugated steel. She despised herself for her churning stomach and the feeling of alienation. The storm threatened her in a manner she could not explain, which could not be stilled by reason. The blizzard was like a shroud.

She felt her way along the building until she found the corrugated main door and the control panel beside it. The building sheltered her from the worst of the wind and flying snow, so that she could hear her own ragged breathing loud with relief. Silly bitch, she told herself. The Norwegian assistant manager of the rig had given her a passcard and she fed it into the slot and stabbed out her temporary number. The control box hummed and she pressed the Up button. The corrugated door groaned with its weight of ice, crackling like frozen clothing as it rolled up. She pressed Stop and ducked beneath it, lowering the door behind her. It clanged in the sudden, unexpected silence of the darkened building.

Marfa heard her own breathing, felt her breath cloud around her. She fumbled along the wall and threw the main light switch. Suspended striplights flickered on, greyly, dustily it seemed. Her breathing smoked in the icy air. Her body shivered with the aftershock of the blizzard, but gradually became calmer.

The store was huge, maybe seventy metres by fifty. The ribbed,

129

whalelike roof was all but lost above the suspended lighting. Half of the building was high rows of storage shelves, the remainder an open area of palleted crates and boxes. A line of forklift trucks stood against one wall like intent men in a urinal, their batteries being recharged overnight. The building was empty except for her intrusion. And baffling. What was she looking for? She should have brought the Norwegian with her. She fished inside her snow-covered clothing and pulled out a sheaf of photocopied dockets the assistant manager had supplied. She remembered the secretary, Maxim, bent over the photocopies, his dark eyes aware of her. He had been afraid of her, but there seemed no urgency to his apprehension. She couldn't see how he was connected with Al-Jani or with Hussain. Yet *both* of them had worked on Rig 47, had been billeted here in the compound . . . there had to be some connection between them, surely?

She began checking the invoices against the crates on the nearest pallets. Only luggage had come up on the flight from Tehran with Hussain — and halal meat and other Moslem food. Goludin would check that out. Spare tractor parts, valves, pumps, drill bits . . . She became absorbed, moving through the crates like a small, intent rodent, glancing occasionally at her watch. Nine-thirty, ten, ten-fifteen . . . The huge naves of storage shelving encompassed her. Silence, except for her footsteps, her breathing, her gradual frustration. And the wind baying outside the corrugated walls.

Opened crates she checked more carefully. The noise of bolts rattling to the floor and rolling away was like gunshots in the cavernous store. She didn't bother to retrieve them. Occasionally, the skittering noise of small, clawed feet. Some animal life that had wandered in off the tundra, lemmings or rats.

She yawned. Ten-forty. She'd wasted an hour and a half, almost. If the drugs were here, she wouldn't find them. If drugs were ever stored at the rig, they'd only stumble on any evidence by a miracle. Without a special reason for suspicion, it had been made clear to her that she wouldn't be allowed to access the computer. It would be easier to break Maxim — who knew something for certain but which might have nothing whatever to do with Al-Jani or Hussain.

130

In the silence after her yawn, the sound of footsteps, quick, hurried, furtive. She was startled fully awake. Then the noise of the wind increased and she lost their sound. Where? That way? She felt hot as she stood, completely still, between two great cliffs of shelving, crates stacked almost to the roof, their perspective stretching away to either end of the building. She could hear nothing but the wind, and shivered. Then hurried.

He was darkly dressed, small, thin-framed. She saw that much. His face was hidden by a balaclava, melting snow glistening on the wool and shining in droplets on his narrow shoulders. Then he hit her across the temple with something and she fell back, the great columns of the shelving like the pillars of a cathedral drunkenly tilting, then lurching. His masked face appeared above her own, then he struck her again across the head as she tried to roll away from him, kick out.

Then she felt herself, dimly and woozily, being dragged from the intersection where he had ambushed her, along the concrete floor, his hands beneath her armpits, her head filled with pain and sickeningly spinning. Then she blacked out —

— door being raised with a groaning clatter. Blank once more. Then the blast of the wind and the drenching of the driven snow woke her. She felt her hands seized. Blank again. Hands somewhere behind her, numb. Her coat was open, hands were pulling at her sweaters. Her terror at the prospect of rape. Then she blacked out again.

'Excuse me one moment, Val,' Vorontsyev murmured, taking the insistent mobile phone from his coat pocket. Panshin seemed amused, yet well aware of the tension between himself and Schneider; and of the latter's nerves. 'Vorontsyev.'

It was Lubin, almost breathless with excitement; his habitual manner.

'Sir, Rawls' fingerprints match! He was definitely in the Merc with the Iranian at some time. They're tied together, sir!'

Vorontsyev retained a casual, indifferent manner, smiling at Valery Panshin and his companions as he stood a matter of yards from their table.

131

'That sounds fine, Lubin. Good work. Just type up the report for me, will you? I'll be in touch.'

'But, sir —' Lubin began to protest, then said: 'You can't talk freely, right, sir?'

'Just so.'

'Do you need help, sir?'

'No. No problem. 'Bye, Lubin.' He cut the connection and returned affably to the three men around the table; Schneider, Panshin the jazz club owner *and* gangster, and Panshin's chief lieutenant, the small, neat, dangerous Dom Kasyan. His nickname among the small-fry, the parasites and the runners and hustlers was Mack the Knife . . . which, of course, was an interesting thought. Kasyan certainly had the skills to have despatched Rawls neatly and quietly — as did perhaps two hundred other people in Novyy Urengoy. 'Sorry about that,' he apologised mockingly. 'Pressure, pressure — a policeman's lot is not a happy one, with so many suspicious characters in the immediate neighbourhood.' He grinned.

Kasyan scowled, but Panshin shook his head. A waitress brought Vorontsyev the imported beer he had ordered. He placed a twenty-rouble note on her tray, to which she was on the point of objecting when Panshin waved her away. Vorontsyev's joke and custom was to pay in Russian currency. The club accepted only hard currencies or credit cards.

He sipped his beer. The house trio had just finished 'Stella by Starlight' and he applauded politely, as did one or two others in the room. Schneider seemed obligated to tap his big hands together for a moment or two. The man was discomfited yet somehow reliant upon Panshin's presence, the room; even on Kasyan.

'I didn't know you two knew each other. You come for the jazz, Dr Schneider?'

'Just the same as you do, Alexei,' Panshin intruded. Schneider flushed with relief. Panshin wreathed his smile in cigar smoke, his broad, open face pleasant, direct, concealing nothing.

'Of course. Who's up tonight?'

'Scandinavians.' The house trio bowed and departed the tiny stage. 'My booking manager tells me they're very good.'

132

'The club's filling up nicely, Val – people must have heard of them. But then, you pay only top rates.'

Panshin shrugged, holding his cigar beside his jowl.

'I like people to enjoy themselves, Alexei, you know that. Why else would I welcome the chief of detectives unless I was broadminded and public-spirited?'

'Especially as I'm not on the payroll.' He turned to Schneider at once and added: 'And how do *you* come to know Panshin the gangster, Dr Schneider? I'm quite jealous that you're also a table guest.'

'I – just through the music,' Schneider muttered. *Like hell it is, my young friend*, he thought.

'I see. One thing I wanted to ask you, Doctor. Lucky you're here. I forgot at the hospital.' Panshin's mouth flickered at the corner, just once. His eyes, creased in fat like those of a Mongolian, might have been a fraction narrower for a second. He suspected that Schneider was there to tell him what Vorontsyev had just revealed.

'Oh, yes?'

'Has your unit admitted any new cases in the past two days? I mean, people who have OD'd, or are sick on badly cut heroin . . . even into withdrawal because they –'

He was leaning forward across the table to Schneider, who could therefore not so much as glance at the two Russians.

'I don't recall any –'

'Even anyone begging at the door, perhaps?' Vorontsyev smiled, his hand over Schneider's wrist. The pulse jumped like the heartbeat of a captured bird. *I can check*, Vorontsyev's touch informed the American.

Panshin brushed a fat hand across his superbly cut grey hair and said: 'Do you have to turn my club into an annexe of police headquarters, Alexei? Dr Schneider is here to relax!'

'I thought he was dead beat and on his way home. Well, Dr Schneider – any new admissions, any *sense* that there are drugs on the street, suddenly?'

The Scandinavian drummer had begun putting his kit together and was making tiny tapping noises, like some forgotten prisoner, on the snare and the hi-hat. It seemed further to unnerve

133

Schneider, whose gaze Vorontsyev held, diminishing the presence of Panshin and his lieutenant.

'I was – was suspicious of two new admissions. I didn't run any tests, but they showed the usual reaction to new-cut heroin. Especially one of them, who'd been hanging on by means of methadone. You suspect that a new shipment has arrived?'

'We think one might have. Your information tends to confirm it.' The bass drum was tapping ominously. March to the scaffold, Vorontsyev thought. 'It's helpful, anyway.' The bass player had arrived on the stage and thrummed quickly through scales and chords. The sound, too emphatic, was threatening. Schneider, Rawls, Panshin. It was too neat, even as he thought it. 'Maybe I could send an officer up to interview any new admissions – tomorrow?'

'Sure.'

Panshin was not into drugs. Even Dmitri, at his most obsessive and dogged, had had to surrender to lack of evidence months ago. Extortion, protection, prostitution and gambling; most of the mafioso criminal pursuits, in which he had excellent, postgraduate qualifications, but not heroin. There wasn't a shred of evidence . . .

. . . nor was there against Schneider, or the dead man, Rawls. Then there was the Iranian with the cornucopia of false passports, who was linked to Rawls in some way. Yet nothing tangible connected them, beyond acquaintance . . .

. . . though he was certain that Schneider had come running to Panshin to inform him he'd been questioned by the police about Rawls.

He finished his beer and smiled. The pianist was running through scales, loosening his touch.

'You haven't branched out recently, have you, Val?' he asked meaningfully.

A momentary glare, difficult to recognise in the dim lighting of the club, then Panshin shrugged and laughed.

'Not me. Why should I, Alexei? You'd know where to come at once.'

Vorontsyev turned to Schneider. 'Did you bring your friend Allan Rawls to the Café Americain, Doctor?'

134

'I – I'm not sure. I think maybe we came once.' He glanced at Panshin. Kasyan was becoming contemptuously impatient.

'Your American friend who works for the gas company? You introduced him,' Panshin replied. 'I don't think he liked the singer.' Panshin laughed.

'She was good. I must have caught her on a different night.' He stood up. 'Enjoy the Scandinavians, Doctor.'

'You're not staying, Alexei?'

'No. I *am* tired. I think I'll have an early night. 'Bye, Valyosha.' The diminutive signifying friendship fell between them like a card thrown down on the table. Panshin stared at him, unblinking. 'Kasyan,' he nodded. The little man twitched at the sound of his name, as if being read a charge sheet.

He passed the bouncers and the manager hovering at the door, tramped almost blithely along the corridor and pushed his way out into blowing snow. The doorman was stamping his feet and clapping his hands for warmth.

Vorontsyev used his lighter to warm the lock of the car door, then opened it. He dragged the mobile phone from his pocket and dialled Lubin.

'Lubin, are you busy?'

At once: 'No, sir. What can I do?'

'I want surveillance on the Café Americain – from outside. Dr Schneider's BMW. I just want to know when he leaves and whether he's alone – and whether he goes home immediately. OK?'

'Yes, sir. I'll come right down.'

'Anything from Marfa?'

'Nothing.'

'I'm not surprised – it was a slim chance. The action's here.'

'Is Panshin involved? I thought he didn't do drugs.'

'So we thought. I'm not sure.'

'Why is Schneider there?'

'Claims he likes jazz. He showed not a flicker of interest. He knows Panshin well, apparently. I think he came by to tell Panshin I'd been asking questions about Rawls.'

'Why?'

'Why *would* Val Panshin be interested – quite.'

135

'We could turn Panshin over –'

'We could never organise a raid without Panshin being tipped off. He must have a dozen people in CID on retainers of one kind or another . . . But –' He paused, then murmured: 'We could check on Schneider's Addiction Unit. More drugs than anything else except swabs pass through a hospital.'

'The hospital, sir?'

'I'm suspicious of young, idealistic doctors who know gangsters. It's a personality failing of mine. Get down here as soon as you can. I'll hang on, parked on the street.'

He switched off the phone and started the engine, turning the car gingerly around and easing it into the alleyway. He parked on K Street beneath neon mammaries the nipples of which winked on and off, one red, one green. The outlined female form behind the giant breasts was nude and leering.

He dialled Dmitri's number, at once imagining the silent untidy rooms of the house, the noise of the television. Heard the set as the call was answered. Dmitri's voice was tired but sober.

'Dmitri – how's your head?'

'Alexei. OK. I'm coming in tomorrow, whatever. It's too quiet here.' After a moment, he added, 'Sorry. Is there something you want?'

'Panshin.'

'Yes?' Eager.

'He's friendly with Dr David Schneider, of the Addiction Unit – no, wait a minute. Tomorrow for that. When I spoke to Schneider, he admitted there's a new supply on the street, *possibly*, so that bastard who got blown up brought the stuff in after all. Can you get hold of your contact and check that?'

'I'll try. It shouldn't be difficult. Where the hell did it *go*?'

'You checked the manifest for that flight. What else was in store at the airport, just at the same time?'

'Christ, Alexei, you want Mr Memory, not me!'

'Get your notebook, jog *your* memory.'

He watched the play of neon over his hands and clothes as he waited for Dmitri to return to the phone. The impression was of disease.

'The freight hangars were stuffed to the roof with the usual – mostly to go up to the rigs by road or transport helicopter. Machine parts, pipe, pumps, the whole ragbag. I didn't bother to take special note of anything. Meat, restaurant supplies, vegetables. It smelt of cabbages in there, I remember. And whisky, needless to say. A crate got *accidentally* broken open. You wouldn't believe it was half-empty, would you?'

'I would. Anything else?'

'Just the whole town's diet and desires, crated up. What were you looking for?'

'Medical supplies.'

'Yes, of course there were. You think the hospital's something to do with it? Schneider?'

'I don't know. I think we should find out, don't you?'

'I'll get onto it. I'll get someone down to the airport. Check what supplies, when they were collected – and see if there's horse on the streets. Leave it with me.'

'I will. 'Night.'

He put the phone on the seat beside him and folded his arms across his chest, attempting to warm himself as he waited for Lubin's arrival. It was worth checking – oh, yes, it was certainly worth checking more closely on Dr Schneider.

Her head ached, but the throbbing she anticipated seemed muffled. There was a thong of cold tight around her temples, like whatever held her arms behind her back. She had no sensation in her fingers.

Marfa struggled with her thick, numbed senses, attempting to move, even *feel*, the body that seemed separated from her by a vast, blank distance. Something penetrated the numbness, near where her face, nose might be – something that stank of rotten meat, decayed vegetables . . . then that clarity whirled away, spinning in the darkness.

When near-consciousness returned for a moment, she had no idea when or how much later, she was vomiting, stretching her neck like a tortoise as she retched. She seemed to be shivering – *something* was shivering, anyway, a great way below the isolated, dim pinhole of light in which she was aware of herself.

137

Her body seemed to have been anaesthetised. The faint light winked like a distant star, then went out . . .

. . . conscious again, the noise of wind and rushing snow. She was certain of the sounds. Also knew that she could not move her arms, and that her upper torso was naked. There was a dim, orange light and she could see, actually see, for a moment. Her breasts and stomach looked white and dead, as if she were lying in a morgue. Her stomach churned. Corrugated tin rattled in the blizzard. She was no longer shivering. Though she could see, there was no other sensation, no feeling. Just the immensely slow and difficult realisation of her immediate surroundings.

Filth. She was covered in filth. She could smell it everywhere around her. She — stank. The dim light was retreating to a pin-hole again. She — had — been . . . left — to . . . freeze — to . . . death . . .

. . . garbage bin. Huge garbage bin. She was freezing to death at the bottom of an enormous garbage bin, half-buried in the rubbish, hands tied . . . her mind was at once exhausted by the effort of realisation. She opened her cracked lips to scream, but either no sound would come or she was unconscious again before a noise could emerge from her throat.

Vorontsyev lay in the dark, staring at the flicker of headlights passing along the street outside then glimmering and dying on the ceiling. The bedroom was cold, making the cigarette smoke acrid and sharp as a wood fire. The tip of the cigarette glowed —

— like my conscience, a fitful thing at best, he admitted, staring at the stub before grinding it out in the glass ashtray on the bedside cabinet.

It was late in the night and the old house was silent. His flat was on the first floor, comprising the best rooms of the Tsarist building. The window rattled with the passing of a truck. He could have had a more modern flat, more furniture and better carpets, even more rooms. He could have shared a fairly luxuri-ous modern block with senior officials, government people — like his chief, who had just left. He simply preferred this place, isolated among more modern blocks as if it had strayed out of the dilapidation of the old town and lost its bearings forever.

138

The roof leaked, the exterior needed repainting but the other tenants hadn't the money to spare – and he had nothing in common with them: a minor civil servant; the mistress of a prominent local businessman who was an ex-colonel in the KGB, and her new baby, in the smallest apartment at the back; and a young couple on the top floor above him. She danced in one of the clubs . . . danced? Took off her clothes, while he played the piano in pander relationship to her. Still, he liked jazz . . .

He favoured the place above anywhere else in the town. He listed its faults, and isolated himself from it now only because his chief had brought his official life into the house and somehow corrupted it. He had invaded his privacy.

An uncertain and corrupt man, he had shifted on his chair as if dodging the frequent assault of invisible projectiles, the entire ten minutes he was in the room. His fur hat had been clutched in his hands all the time, as if he were attempting to wring it dry of something, or strangle the small animal it had once been. *You are being careful, Alexei, aren't you?* Over and over, like a maiden aunt. Almost as if he must be sure he employed a prophylactic when dealing with the town. Not an unnecessary precaution, he thought, smiling despite his irritation. No real penetration, nothing *really* done, just playing at it . . . his relation to crime was sex wearing a condom. No one would feel a thing, just as long as he was wearing his indifference.

The chief of police for the district of Novyy Urengoy had come to ensure he wasn't treading on any toes, especially those of Bakunin. Perhaps someone had been unsettled by the raid on the brothel; hadn't been there, but expected to pay a call before too long and didn't want the police embarrassing him! The chief carried little messages like that. At times, it seemed his only function – his exchange for the kickbacks and the presents and the nice dacha and new car, and the jewellery displayed by his plump wife. It was difficult to despise him . . . he was a gentle, timid, sensitive man overwhelmed by the town, by Russia since the bad old days, and by his wife. His corruption saddened him as much as it did Vorontsyev.

And it wasn't much worse, he admitted, lighting another

cigarette, than bearing silent, ineffectual witness to the corruption of others. Being good, doing right, ought to be more than keeping your nose clean and not touching pitch!

As Lensky, the pathologist had remarked . . .

He sighed. His stomach rumbled from the cheese sandwich he had made and eaten on his return. And the beer. He felt no more than discomforted by his self-analysis tonight, no more than impatient with his insomnia. Almost reconciled. His chief's quiet desperation rendered Vorontsyev a certain complacency, a higher place in the moral pecking-order of Novyy Urengoy.

And besides, the gate had been left open – just enough. The drugs business had moved its epicentre, to Schneider and maybe even Val Panshin. Kasyan might have been Rawls' murderer, and he could continue to oversee the Rawls case because Rawls was now linked with Dr Schneider. There were drugs on the street, and Schneider might well be involved.

He continued to smoke, feeling sorry for his chief and agreeably indulgent of himself. The old house creaked around him in the wind, the occasional car passed, and once a child cried. Vera Silkova's new baby in the smallest apartment, or one of the civil servant's children – didn't the boy have earache or something? He sniffed, drew on the cigarette.

He was still awake, at two-thirty, when the telephone rang.

'Vorontsyev.'

The line was filled with distance.

'Sir, it's Goludin, sir –!' someone was shouting, his voice removed and faint. '*Goludin*, sir!'

'What is it, man? It's two-thirty in the morning!'

'– Marfa, sir,' he heard. 'We can't find her. She's *disappeared*, sir!'

'What?'

He felt very cold.

'– *blizzard*! She went out in it, sir, to check the store sheds. Hasn't come back. They've got search parties out, but there's no trace of her!' Goludin was hysterical.

'Find her!' he snapped. 'Do what you have to, but find her!'

He slapped the receiver down, hunched on the bed with sudden stomach cramps. Blizzard or not, it was enemy action, not

140

accident. She wasn't lost, she was gone. She'd been *removed*.

The reality of it emptied him of his complacency, leaving only a stark and raw fear in its place. Marfa, in all probability, was not simply missing, she was dead.

Noise. Penetrating, deafening. She seemed to be listening underwater. It was like the roar of a retreating tide. Her eyes opened, and she fuzzily saw a corrugated tin roof. She could not hear the wind, but could see the haziness of blown snow through her own grogginess. And cold. She was so cold. She stared up at the slanting tin roof and saw a shadow creeping across it like an eclipse of the sun.

Terror, like a dark wind, made the pinhole of light that was her awareness flicker like a candle flame. Then she saw the sides of the garbage bin and remembered where she was. And that she was smeared with filth. Her memory, as much as the present, reminded her of the rank smells of rotting meat and vegetables.

She fought against the failing light from the pinhole, against the dull dark which seemed to well up again. The noise was louder, as if her head had surfaced from water.

She knew the sound now . . .

. . . slowly – terrified. It was the noise of the grinding, crushing mechanism of a garbage truck. She had been dumped in the bin with this in mind. She would be – tipped – into the – crusher . . . buried on the tundra . . . she finished, as the thoughts whirled and blew like the snow coming in under the corrugated tin roof where the bins were stored. She moved her lips. She didn't seem to be gagged, but something filled her mouth so that she could make no sound. Her jaw was frozen like the huge, gaping mouth of a dead sturgeon she had once seen. She could not feel her hands, her limbs, her torso. There wasn't enough of her left alive to scream.

Darkness . . . *shadow*. Shadow of . . . the garbage truck moving under the tin roof, banging against the sides of the huge bin. She was aware that the bin was being jolted, then –

– tilted. Shifted on its base, angled. Tipped –

– blank once more. Awake. The bin seemed more angled, her body, to which she no longer belonged, had moved to the

141

circumference of the bin, was hard against its filthy metal. She was huddled against the side of the bin as it was hoisted at a steepening angle. She heard hydraulics soughing like the blizzard. She felt the dark coming on again, and tried to move in protest against it. The bin tilted more steeply, and she could see snow and darkness, the distant glow of dim lights. Still her mouth refused to scream.

Teeth. The maw of the truck. She was staring into the jaws of the garbage truck.

She seemed to scream. The organism had to scream, and did. She screamed again.

Perhaps it was only in her mind. The bin continued to move through its hydraulic arc, tilting her and the rubbish towards the truck. She was in a huge, foul cup tilted towards an enormous mouth and teeth.

Screamed. Screamed.

Something like a face —

— woollen mask, just eyes really, looking at her as the bin came level and she began to slide towards the grinding jaws of the truck. A face terrified in shock, above a body as unable to move as her own.

The maw. Blank —

He knew that they wouldn't wait much longer, that they'd be coming for him.

Lock stirred uneasily in the swivel chair, glancing once more out of the big windows of Vaughn Grainger's study down towards Phoenix. They would come soon . . . yet his dazed and ragged nerves would not move him from the chair, from the room or the house. He'd *had* to return to Vaughn's house, after losing the prize that Tran represented, despite the danger that they would suspect his hiding place. There had to be something for him to find, some explanation, some clue, some evidence to tell him what in hell was happening . . .

But there was nothing, nothing at all. Not in the safe or the filing cabinets or the desk drawers. No records, no details, no plans and no hints. He yawned with nerves and dull weariness. Grainger-Turgenev had become a conduit for heroin, and all he had to go on were Tran's threats and an old man's desperate, sick words in the rear of an ambulance rushing him to intensive care. There was nothing else, not even a suggestion of the corruption of Grainger Technologies.

There were only the photo albums, which now lay strewn on the big desk. Snapshots filed neatly in cellophane slips which unfolded under his hands like the images of an old What-The-Maid-Saw machine at the end of a seafront pier. Beth, Billy, himself, Vaughn, his parents in one or two, hundreds of others. Vaughn, in most of them, always a dominating, stern figure who seemed to be in uniform even when relaxing in shorts beside a pool or hunched over a smoking barbecue.

Lock glanced at his watch. Four in the afternoon, and still he remained there, his hands playing over the snapshot albums like those of an amateur conjurer. There was no rabbit out of their hat. Nothing to tell him what had happened in the past – and how it had led to Billy's murder. Beth's murder. He lit a cigarette and the smoke tasted stale on his tongue and raw in his throat.

He had told the butler not to report the burglary. Not yet, at least. The man had accepted his temporary authority with a shrug. The housekeeper had made him a sandwich lunch. Otherwise, they ignored him. At that moment, they were dutifully at the hospital, visiting Vaughn, whose condition was stable, according to the doctors.

He was alone in the house. The maid had retreated to her quarters above the garage. The poolman had come and gone, and the gardener was around back, hoeing at stubborn desert weeds among the flower borders.

He stared at the photographs as if willing the captured faces to speak, tell him what had happened. The sun burned in through the long windows. The air-conditioning purred. Tran's people had expected to find something – the drugs, just a lead to the drugs – what?

Which meant Tran knew very little. He'd stirred a hornets' nest for the sake of nothing. Tran would inform his contacts . . . if he knew who they were –

– Grainger's face staring up at him from a photograph. Tran had believed Grainger knew about the heroin, he'd gone straight

143

to what he thought was the top when his supplies didn't arrive. Why? If Tran *didn't* know who to contact, then Lock still had a little time, a small window through which he could squeeze in order to break into the case. From Washington. He had to get back. He had to know more about Tran, more about –

Turgenev. Pete Turgenev, of whom Vaughn had been so scared in that suite at the Jefferson Hotel. Scared almost to death, dominated and cowed by the Russian. *Grainger-Turgenev*. That had to be when it had happened, the corruption of Vaughn's company, Billy's company . . . when they went into Siberia and found Turgenev as a partner. Who in turn had found greedy men, men he could use . . . Had to be, surely?

Pete Turgenev knew. Whatever part he played, whatever he had done or ordered to be done, it had to be Turgenev who was behind it. Not just his people, but him. He had frightened Billy at the party, frightened Vaughn at the hotel. It was Turgenev against whom Vaughn had tried to warn him in the ambulance.

His hands closed into impotent fists, again and again. Then he drew deeply on the cigarette, expelling the stream of smoke towards the ceiling, his face stretched in pain and dull rage. He'd wasted a day, or almost a day, and alerted the enemy. Stupid . . .

He closed his eyes and at once saw Turgenev's face, with all the power and mass of a dense star controlling the orbits and motions of the other faces in his head – Vaughn, Billy, Tran and finally Beth.

He and Billy and Turgenev – Lock opened his eyes and stared down at one of the albums. There they were, the three of them, in Afghanistan. The big, real-life adventure for daring boys, the clean war – in its way – after the ethical mess of Vietnam. He and Billy working for the Company, supplying the *mujahideen* with Stinger missiles to shoot down MiL gunships in the mountains and around Kabul. He and Billy and Turgenev, after the announcement of the Soviet withdrawal, drawn together to negotiate the wind-down in weapons supplies, the safe passages, the prisoner exchanges. Companions-in-arms. The three of them, the *way* they were, dressed in headscarves and baggy trousers, unshaven, thin, laughing.

Drugs had been overflowingly abundant in Afghanistan. The

144

Russians had smuggling operations. The KGB and the army had been involved – just like the Company men who were doing the same. It had obviously been then that Turgenev had begun heroin smuggling. Lock slapped his forehead. It was *then* that he had acquired the capital to turn himself into an entrepreneur by the time Grainger Technologies arrived in Siberia! He grinned shakily. It fitted. It had to be so.

He stared at Turgenev in the snapshot.

Billy had left the CIA after Afghanistan, to run Grainger Technologies. Vaughn had wanted to spend his time exclusively with the Grainger Foundation, the charitable arm of the company. Lock had returned to the State Department. And then, under the skin like a tumour, it had begun. When Grainger-Turgenev had been established, it was gradually corrupted.

A snapshot of Vaughn Grainger, in uniform, lay beneath his hand. 'Nam. 1974 was the date on the reverse. Vaughn had re-enlisted, even though Grainger Technologies needed him, the company having limped along ever since the mid-'60s, when it had stumbled on Wall Street. It got by on handouts, small work, shuffling its loans. It looked as if the company would go under, and Vaughn seemed not to care, wrapping himself instead in the flag and heading for Vietnam. He'd eventually risen to command a Special Forces unit.

Then the oil-price hikes of the mid-'70s made companies like Grainger necessary once more in oil exploration. When Vaughn came back from 'Nam, with all a soldier's ruthlessness, he'd turned the company around inside a year. A series of night attacks and dawn raids had put Grainger near the top again, poised to go into Siberia when the Soviet Union collapsed. Vaughn, staring out from the photograph, posed in full uniform in front of a fuzzy C-130, medal ribbons vivid on his chest.

All that – just to end up in an intensive care facility, terrified and broken, an old man with the ground cut from beneath his feet, his son murdered, his daughter-in-law dead, too. Because of heroin. Red horse.

Lock got jerkily to his feet, aware of his vulnerability before the windows. Phoenix was hazy in its heat and smog. A distant, high aircraft winked like an early star. He needed to get back to Washington. Company records . . . he needed to check on Turgenev. He thought of Kauffman, Bob Kauffman whom he'd met in the bar of the Mayflower the day Beth was killed. Kauffman was still CIA, he could persuade him to let him see the files. There was material at State, too, he could use. He needed to know — *did* know. He wanted proof, before he went after Turgenev.

Before Turgenev came after him . . .

SEVEN

Free Enterprises

The wind howled across the concrete, whipping the snow into the open door of the helicopter, and over the stretcher onto which Marfa was gently strapped under a red blanket. Her face was the colour and texture of grey plasticine. His own face, if her staring confused gaze could focus on it, would be bitter, culpable. And she would see, in his squinting glance, the gleam of guilty relief. The doctors said she would recover. *Physically*, that is. He had no notion of how Marfa's psychology would cope with what had been done to her.

He supposed it would help that there had been no rape. There had been nothing sexual, no degradation or personal hatred in the attack. Its whole aim was to get rid of her, because she was police and asking questions about the dead Iranian.

Which meant she was very, very lucky to be alive.

He shivered in the blown snow, hurrying alongside the stretcher on its trolley, across the garishly lit apron in front of the terminal building where the helicopter from the rig had landed.

Her vision was clouded. Shadows flitted at its peripheries like ghosts, keeping pace with her, with the sense of movement that was so like her inexorable slide towards the maw of the garbage truck. Her hands had been tied behind her, she now understood. She still did not remember the hands that had grabbed her, or even the voice that had been screaming from the mouth-hole in a balaclava for the truck to stop tilting the garbage bin. She had been seen, just in time. She remembered the man's eyes. The same shocked eyes that had looked down at her, as she rustled and rattled like something for the oven in the crackling foil in which they had wrapped her.

Then it had been nothing but hands, rubbing, banging, pulling her like malevolent children playing with a cheap doll. After that, she had begun to burn, and scream . . .

Then figures around her, dark or light, but flickering like candle flames. Soothing noises, as if they were addressing a child or a simpleton. More burning and screaming . . . Then the wind and the cold and the rotor noise –

– now Vorontsyev, hurrying beside what must be a stretcher. She was . . . alive. Wind, snow, cold, then warmth striking her numbed cheeks like slaps. And a ceiling above her, Vorontsyev clearer, and something stinging on her cheeks. Tears?

Vorontsyev watched her crying helplessly. His guilt returned in a churning of his stomach. He bent over her, scuttling like a crab to keep up with the stretcher, as he patted her hand which lay beneath the blanket. Her face was less grey now, but somehow urgent, like the face of someone unable to speak who was desperate to communicate a great secret. She opened her mouth and at once her teeth began chattering. The tears continued to flow, beginning to embarrass him.

Then they were on the other side of the cramped terminal and the blue, revolving light on the ambulance was gleaming through the driven snow. He continued to pat her hand as she was shelved into the rear of the vehicle. Mid-morning gloom shrouded the town, all but obscuring it. He clambered into the ambulance and sat beside her, with the two paramedics and the doctor who had accompanied her – at his guilty, enraged demand – from Rig 47.

That same doctor had told him over the telephone that the heat from the decomposing rubbish had kept her alive. It had been that close. He looked back at Goludin's sombre, frightened face as the ambulance doors were shut. It hadn't been Goludin's fault, but his self-reproach had had to berate someone, put someone else in his own place.

Something was tugging at his arm. He looked down. Marfa's face was alive with an idiot's intent vacancy. Her voice, when she spoke, was no more than a crow's rough croaking.

'Moscow Centre,' he made out. He nodded comfortingly. The pale hand gripped his sleeve. The doctor made to interpose and

Vorontsyev's glance warned him. Whatever it was, it was urgent to Marfa.

'Send – picture . . . *Iranian*!' she shouted like someone deaf. 'MBRF – Dmitri Oberov – *Oberov*. Say you want ID that face, now!'

He nodded, understanding. Got up and banged open the doors of the ambulance, glaring at the paramedics and the doctor.

Oberov was an ex-lover. Vorontsyev knew the name, casually dropped by Marfa in a confidential moment, as something that was past and meaningless. A colonel in the SVR, the new Russian Intelligence. He'd survived the coups, had even prospered from them.

Goludin looked as hopeful as a dog expecting forgiveness.

'Get back to the office!' Vorontsyev snapped. 'Send a faxed picture of our dead Iranian to Moscow Centre, attention of Colonel Dmitri Oberov. *Most urgent*. ID immediately required. Got that?'

'Yes, sir!'

'Get on with it, then. I want an answer today!'

Goludin hurried towards Vorontsyev's car, after catching the keys as lightly as in a game. One could almost see his tail wagging. Vorontsyev climbed back into the ambulance, at once assuring Marfa that he had carried out her instructions.

'Let's go!' he snapped at the paramedics.

He was still angry as he joined the Dolly Madison Boulevard, after leaving Langley. Just as he was certain that he was being tailed. Tailed *away* from CIA headquarters? He was sure the Georgetown street had been empty of surveillance when he started the car, certain that he was not being tailed on the George Washington Parkway on the outward journey.

Almost certain . . . But the grey Lexus was there now, as he headed back towards Washington. Two cars and a big Mack truck behind him, but there, and maintaining exactly his own speed –

– accelerated, then dropped back, just to check. Beyond the spray thrown up by his tyres, the Lexus fulfilled the small test he had given it.

Then the Mack truck pulled out and began overtaking him.

149

The spray from its wheels blinded the windscreen. He flicked the wipers to rapid, and his anger was focused on the truck and the rain for a moment before it returned to Bob Kauffman. The guy had refused to help him . . . the files were either shredded or reclassified, he couldn't authorise access, sorry, fella, but this isn't any business of yours, is it?

Et cetera, et cetera . . . Lost your memory, John? Kauffman had grinned at his own joke. Why Pete Turgenev? You already know the guy . . . finally, Kauffman had said heavily, 'If you won't tell me why, I can't help you.'

Lock pulled out to overtake the truck. The windscreen cleared, becoming no more than a house window down which the rain slid. Then the truck, as if jousting with him in the driving rain, pulled out again and the windscreen was blind. In the rear view mirror, the Lexus maintained its distance, two cars behind him. He felt the nerves jump in his wrists as he gripped the steering wheel. He was still a dozen miles from Washington – should he lead them back to the apartment? Who in hell *were* they?

He recalled Kauffman's face as Lock left the Langley complex. Intense in expression, heavy and almost foreboding. He shook his head and slowed the car to let the truck pull away, to escape its blinding spray. The traffic was light. The fall-coloured trees beside the highway were drab and drenched, stretching away into the Virginia countryside. The truck seemed to tug the spray after its bulk and the windscreen lightened, as if a door had been opened from a darkened room. The Lexus was content to remain two cars behind.

It couldn't be a tail Kauffman had put on him. Not because of Turgenev . . . or Tran –? Kauffman's eyes had flinched at the name, then he had denied knowing the man. When he had gone to check the files, he had found Tran's shredded, Turgenev's reclassified, and suddenly there was no access. But Kauffman *had* known Tran; the name had brought an instant recognition and the sharpness of suspicion to his eyes.

Why?

The truck was too slow pulling ahead of him and he considered overtaking on the inside lane. The rain had begun before daylight. He had hardly slept after the flight from Phoenix. There had been no one tailing him there, or from the airport, he was certain. He moved into the inside lane.

In the *Washington Post* there was a rumour that Vaughn Grainger might be selling the family holding in the Grainger group, in the aftermath of the *recent tragedy*, as the columnist put it.

How much did Turgenev want that? How much did Turgenev already own, through dummy corporations, investors and banks which helped him circumvent the rules on foreign ownership? The wheel slipped angrily in his grip as he gestured his rage to the tyres. The car seemed to float for an instant, then recover itself. What – *exactly* – were the links between Grainger Technologies and Grainger-Turgenev?

He drew level with the Mack's huge rear tyres, the side window now blinded like the windscreen, the noise and weight and momentum of the truck sensible inside the car. The Lexus, wipers working vigorously, slipped into the inside lane a hundred yards behind him. The bulk of the truck was alongside now and Lock pressed his foot on the accelerator.

Who could Vaughn be selling to, if the rumour was true? He had to talk to Vaughn. He could see the rain-filled air brighten beyond the truck. Then the Mack seemed to lurch sideways towards him, a dark, vast bulk, looming inside the rain. He stepped on the brake pedal, but the truck continued to veer across the inside lane. Too late, he realised the Lexus had been a blind, distracting him –

– the truck was all purpose now. The brighter air disappeared as the truck's flank caused the door and wing panels of his car to scream in protest. Spray flooded the windscreen, extinguishing everything. The door buckled against his thigh and the window shattered. The Mack's noise was a rumble like that of a collapsing office block. His car left the road, dropped over the verge, careered downwards, the wipers waving frantically like drowning arms. The steering wheel bucked, trying to escape him. *The truck. The damn' fucking truck was trying to kill him.*

He glimpsed the Lexus in the rear view mirror, as it slowed, then his car lurched out of control, its head swinging like that of a wounded bull seeking its tormentors. It overturned, the roof

151

buckling inwards on impact as he hung helplessly upside down in the restraint of the seatbelt. The car slewed like a skater in slow motion. He saw dark, inverted pines, red-leaved birches, still at first then rushing towards him. The car's metal protested in a drawn-out cry as it collided with a slim birch, snapping it like matchwood. The car lurched a final time, onto its side, wheels spinning in the rain-filled air. His head revolved like the front wheel he could see.

Eventually, through the broken windscreen, he heard the rain. Heard his breathing. Saw his breath, clouding around him in puffs of distress and relief. His arm ached and his thigh seemed on fire. He moved his head gently, as if taking a priceless ornament from a high shelf with numb hands. Looked towards the road. An inverted image of the grey Lexus and two figures standing beside it, seventy or eighty yards away.

His hand fumbled with the seatbelt release and he tumbled sideways, hurting his hip on the steering wheel. He thrust at the door above him, to find it jammed. He gripped the doorframe through the shattered side window and heaved himself into the drenching rain. His head swam and he felt nauseous. He fell onto churned mud and torn grass. The noise of the traffic on the highway was very distant.

Lock staggered upright, leaning against the car. The wheels were slowing into stillness. No cars except the Lexus had stopped. The truck had disappeared. The two occupants of the grey car were coming down the slope as if following the crazed track his car had made. Groggily, in rising panic, he pushed himself away from the wreckage and staggered towards the trees. From behind him, he heard a shouted command to stay where he was, to come back.

He stumbled further into the crowding trees, slipping on pine debris and mud, his legs weak and treacherous, the panic in his chest making it difficult to breathe. They intended to kill him. He blundered on through the trees.

Vorontsyev shrugged at Dmitri, his features darkly angry. The mobile phone, clamped against his cheek, seemed like a weapon wielded by his caller – GRU Colonel Bakunin.

'No,' he announced once more. 'We're taking no interest whatsoever in the Rawls murder, Colonel. I can't imagine where you might have picked up that idea –'

'Are you waltzing me around, Vorontsyev? You think I'm *stupid*?' Bakunin bellowed into the phone with unmasked, brutish authority.

'Nothing of the kind,' Vorontsyev murmured.

Dmitri was gesturing innocence with spread hands and arms, hunched in his overcoat. Beyond the window, cloud hurtled raggedly across the face of the moon. It had stopped snowing. Dmitri was shaking his head, as if accused of a schoolboy theft.

'You have no interest in the Rawls business. It's a GRU matter. I made that clear. Do you want me to make it clearer still?' Vorontsyev scowled at Dmitri. Goludin, who seemed to anticipate that the anger was directed at himself, seemed to cower in his chair like a small marmoset that had already suffered cruelty at his hands.

'No. It's already *very* clear, Colonel.'

'Then keep your nose *out*. Understood?'

'Understood.'

The phone clicked in his ear like a pistol shot. He closed the mouthpiece and thrust the instrument into his pocket. His littered desk, inconclusive and shapeless in image of his investigation, enraged him. He banged his fist onto the scattered files and papers.

'How the hell did Bakunin find out we were still interested in Rawls?' he barked. 'How do I find myself being ballocked by that *ox*? I told you to be careful, Dmitri.'

'I was careful – sir.' Dmitri added the respect for Goludin's sake. 'I combed a couple of the files, that's all. Rawls' previous visits, stuff *we* had here, nothing else . . .' He grimaced. 'How on earth did the GRU find out?'

'You mean, apart from whoever they have inside CID who would have told them?' Vorontsyev threw his large hands up as if juggling with something explosive. 'I tell you something, both of you – this isn't funny. It's sinister. The GRU's the bureaucracy of Russia, same as always. More powerful now, perhaps. But that bruiser on the other end of the line has just told us that we're not wrong – apart from telling us he's somehow involved. He's not being a bureaucrat any more, but an interested party. Do I make myself clear?' he added, staring at Goludin, before growling: 'You're in it up to your neck, sonny. I hope you realise that?'

Dmitri appeared pained on behalf of the young detective. Goludin was silent for some moments, before he nodded and said:

'Yes, sir – and thanks.'

It was a small comfort. Not a restorative by any means, but the scanty kind of reassurance that was available to Vorontsyev. Another of the few reasonably honest young officers on whom he could depend. Up to a point.

'OK – then off you go. You haven't got time to go home and shave and shower, get yourself down to the hospital and relieve the man on guard outside Marfa's room. I'm making you responsible for her safety. Understand?'

'Yes, sir,' Goludin replied, apparently grateful that what might have been regarded as his dereliction up at the rig was not to be mentioned again. He exited noisily, inflated with the renewed trust Vorontsyev had in him.

Dmitri grinned at Vorontsyev's smile and said, once the door was closed: 'Like Lubin, he's a good lad.'

'You sound like his mother.'

'Don't you need some children you can trust, Alexei? I do my best.'

'I – know. Sorry. But how did that shit *know*?'

'Any one of a dozen ways. *We'd* better be more careful than ever – if we're . . . ?' The question faded into silence.

'We are,' Vorontsyev replied. Dmitri seemed both unnerved and excited. 'Oh, no, we're not putting Mr Rawls on the back burner. He's connected with the drugs, through Schneider and through our dead Iranian, Mr Al-Jani. He's ours.'

'What about Marfa's theory?'

'That her old boyfriend in Moscow Centre will be able to identify the Iranian – give him a name and a rank? Maybe. She was convinced. She insisted we did it, until the doctors smothered her in the best of expensive, charitable care. She thinks he's definitely professional.'

Vorontsyev lit another cigarette and blew smoke at the dark square of his office window, where the moon was emerging like a dazed prisoner from behind rags of cloud.

'So are the mafiosi, the *biznizmen*, Alexei. And if you think Bakunin's somehow close to this, then it has to be for money, not politics – and that probably means the drug connection. Have you thought about that?'

Vorontsyev rubbed his face. His eyes looked bleakly at Dmitri.

'We've retreated about as far as we can go. Onto the last beach. Feel the cold water round your balls, Dmitri? What do we do? Ignore *everything*? We're the cops, for God's sake.'

'We are.' Dmitri was nodding, his smile embracingly under-standing, compassionate, like that on the face of an ikon. 'So, what's next?'

'If the Iranian was a professional, why was he here – other than the drugs? Maybe he collected Tehran's ten per cent, or worked for a minister or mullah who grows the poppy? Let's see if Marfa's friend in high places has an answer. Unless he's too busy keeping his own arse doused while setting fire to other people's trousers – which is about all those Moscow Centre bastards are good for these days.'

'I heard that's all they'd ever done. What about Kiev? That dead guy you were interested in?'

'The man with his picture in the Dutch passport?' Dmitri nodded. 'He doesn't exist. Kiev are still checking. But there's nobody of his name and description working for any such com-pany in the Ukraine.' Vorontsyev shrugged.

'Then why was he here? Is that drugs, too?' Dmitri's private war seemed to be expanding too rapidly for even his comfort. He was puzzled, unsure. 'Some other mafia business?' He seemed almost hopeful of an affirmative.

'Protection, prozzies, smuggling, currency fiddles, arms deals, murder – take your pick. They're trawling missing persons for me now. We must wait and see, old friend – wait and see.'

'And Schneider – the American doctor?'

155

'He's hanging there like meat, Dmitri – all the muscle and gristle softened, the flavour just right . . . We only need one thing, one link with Panshin other than association.'

'So, Val Panshin's decided to go into the drugs business?'

'Beats the profits from a Siberian jazz club and a sideline in pimping and contraband. He must have been tempted.'

'Their team seems to be putting extra players on the field all the time, Alexei . . .' He was troubled, then he blurted into the silence he had created: 'Can we cope with this, Alexei? I mean, have we got the resources – ?'

'– and the resolve? We'd better have. Hadn't we?'

Eventually, in a room that seemed to have become hotter and where the light seemed dimmer, Dmitri nodded.

'Yes. We'd better have,' he murmured.

'Turgenev's back, by the way,' Vorontsyev remarked. 'The social column of *Novyy Urengoy Pravda* will no doubt inform you of that fact in its next issue. I saw his private jet at the airport when they flew Marfa in.'

'Pyotr Leonidovich Turgenev, the town's richest man . . .' Dmitri's face narrowed. 'Oh, no. Not him, Alexei. He's out of our league. Even if it is Grainger-Turgenev that may be involved, we don't want *anything* to do with Turgenev himself.'

Vorontsyev grinned. 'Just joking. If Turgenev were involved – ?' He shrugged. 'He doesn't need to be. Even if people like Rawls and Schneider are part of it, they're just salaried monkeys. Turgenev owns the world – at least, locally. He can make billions just being legitimate.' He grinned. 'Forget about Turgenev. We're not going to have to worry about finding him under one of the stones we turn over –'

He turned his head, as if alarmed, at the ringing of the fax machine in a corner of the office. Then the high, singing tone warned of a transmission. Dmitri, too, turned to watch the grey-looking paper slide out of the fax machine's slitted mouth. One page, then a second . . . the impression of a smeared monochrome photograph. Then the peremptory, whistled announcement that the transmission had ended.

Vorontsyev tore the sheets from the machine and smoothed them on the desk as Dmitri got up and stood at his shoulder.

Eventually, Vorontsyev murmured: 'Clever girl. She was right. This boy's been everywhere in his short life.'

The smudgy photograph from an SVR file was of the man who had died in the Mercedes. But his name was not Al-Jani, as his passport had declared. It was fake like the others he had been carrying. His real name was Vahaji, Mostafa Vahaji.

'Rank of major in Intelligence – Office for the Protection of the Islamic Revolution,' Dmitri muttered excitedly. 'Their elite foreign intelligence department. Mostafa Vahaji . . . hello.'

'And goodbye, Mr Al-Jani, gasfield worker. Look at his record. Bright lad, travelling far and fast.'

The file was brief. Vahaji, whose life had ended in a Siberian gas town, had been sighted by the old KGB, over the years, in Egypt, the Gulf, then London, Paris and Moscow. There were unconfirmed rumours of activities in the central Asian republics, post 1989. And most recently he had been posted to Washington.

'Until April last year,' Vorontsyev read aloud. 'Then nothing. Suspected recall *either for disciplinary hearings or special assignment*. Then suddenly he turns up here as a roughneck on a rig, someone who's supposed to be barely literate, with no qualifications . . . ? Until last year, Moscow Centre was rating him four star. Likely to reach the top or very near it. What happened?'

'Damn,' Dmitri muttered with impotent, nervous anger. 'What if *this* was his special assignment? Us – *here?* Oh, ballocks, that bloody big picture again!' He seemed anguished, as if a joke had turned into the drowning of a friend. 'Why couldn't it have remained small?' he wailed.

There was a bleakness in his eyes. Major Vahaji's real identity had snatched away his illusions, his comforts, just as the drugs had snatched away his family. Vorontsyev, watching the moon once more smothered with cloud, felt their inadequacy, too. The thing was growing like a rampant tumour, spreading, infecting, killing. It was too big.

'It hasn't!' he snapped. 'It's what it is, no bigger, no smaller. Right?'

'You're worried, too.'

'You're bloody right, old friend. But we can't do anything else but go on with it. If only one of us knew, we could hide it from the other. But we both know. We can't lose face – can we? We're landed with it, and that's that!'

Dmitri said after a long silence: 'He's just someone who helped kill my daughter. Something to be stepped on.'

Bob Kauffman owned an apartment overlooking the Potomac in the Watergate complex on the Rock Creek and Potomac Parkway. In the wet afternoon, the cars swished through the falling rain and the river was dull and chill under low cloud. Lights were already springing out in the complex and its surrounding hotels. Office buildings blazed with light, as if it were already evening. Headlights sprang out across the Theodore Roosevelt Bridge.

Lock sat in the hire car and watched the frontage of the Watergate complex, or studied the rain-puckered water of the Potomac. His thigh and knee hurt, as did his bruised hip. And he seemed still to possess the chill of his flight as he sat, engine running, heater on, hunched towards the steering wheel.

He had, somehow, evaded the two men in the Lexus – or they had given up. Eventually, after more than an hour, he had stumbled onto a minor road and hitched a ride back into the city. From his apartment, after he had showered and two bourbons had begun to calm him, he had called the police to report the accident. No, he didn't think he could prefer charges . . . no, he didn't know the number of the truck, maybe it was green, or blue . . . no, fine, I'll have the wreck towed away, sure . . . A third bourbon had allowed him to begin to form a resolution.

His two pursuers had been Caucasian, not Vietnamese. Not that that ruled out Tran, nor did it rule in Turgenev . . . but Bob Kauffman's unhelpfulness and suspicion kept returning to him, flashing on a huge screen in his imagination, so that he could minutely inspect the expression. And the earliest embodiment on Kauffman's face was the recognition of Tran's name. Kauffman had served with the Company in 'Nam. He could have known Tran then . . .

There was only Kauffman. For the moment. Turgenev had

checked out of his hotel and flown back to Russia in his own jet. He was temporarily out of the game. Perhaps he had left orders concerning Lock and it had been his people in the grey Lexus and one of his men driving the truck . . . but Kauffman knew Tran and that link was much more direct than any cloudier speculations concerning Pete Turgenev and the way in which he had frightened both Vaughn Grainger and his dead son. So, he had to talk to Kauffman.

Almost as important were his memories of his apartment. It had been as if he had occupied a hotel room in a new and strange city. He had showered, poured himself a drink, then another, called the police, changed his clothes — all as if the place had been rented for the afternoon and he was engaged on business that had nothing to do with the place as his home. He had neglected even to switch on the hi-fi, play some music. It was a recognition of something that was cold, even icy; as if he had passed from one stage of his life to another with only an amnesiac interlude that blotted out all sense of change.

He had refused to check the answerphone, as if it was nothing more than a learning tape for a foreign language, spoken in a tongue which he would never require, not now. That part of him, and of his life, was finished with, meaningless. He had glanced into the small study, seen the scattered stave paper, the various printed scores of that obscure opera on which he had fitfully worked — and the music's paged deadness had been too akin to his ordinary life; an unperformed work, grown musty with lack of use.

He knew he had changed. He just hadn't seen it in the mirror in the bathroom or the cheval mirror in his bedroom or the mirrored wall in the hallway. Only seen it now, sitting in the rented Chrysler in the downpour, watching the lights across the Theodore Roosevelt Bridge as if assessing the worth of a double string of glowing pearls. Cars hissed and susurrated past him, sounding like waves on a beach. A tide raging but going out, leaving him stranded. He was changed. His apartment had been nothing more than the bones or carapace of someone else, a chrysalis he no longer needed.

Sea change. Into a past self. The boy who had fought other

159

boys who insulted or teased his sister, the young man who had fought the Russians – helped to fight them – with the same innocence as the boy had done. The field agent given an assignment. That was who he was. His mission was to find and deal with Beth's murderers, who had tried to kill him, twice.

And he had no other avenue to explore outside of Kauffman . . . whose proximity to Tran and Vaughn and maybe Billy in 'Nam tormented him now like something he was attempting to remember in a half-waking dream. He had to go down that mean avenue, whatever he might find at the end of it –

He looked at his watch. It was almost five in the afternoon, and the light was beginning to drain away above the cloud, darkening the rain. It made the river glitter with reflected light from the bridge and maybe fifty buildings along the parkway. Kauffman probably left his office early these days. He was just serving out his time. He hoped Kauffman wasn't on his way to the Mayflower or some other bar . . . because he was impatient now; however reluctant something deep in him was about facing the worst, he wanted to *begin*. His body was shivery with anticipatory nerves, not fear.

Turgenev – awful, dark irony – was almost his creation. His and Billy's. He'd pointed Billy in Turgenev's direction, he'd checked the man and his companies out . . .

He shut out the creeping guilt that clung like seaweed to the memory.

Watched a Ford pull off the parkway towards the Watergate complex. As its cloudy windows passed beside a streetlamp, he recognised Kauffman. Lock swallowed. The car moved through an archway towards the entrance to the underground garage. He knew the apartment number. He would give Kauffman ten relaxing minutes that would make him comfortable, off guard. He flicked off the wipers now that he had recognised Kauffman. Rain streamed between himself and the scene, all but blanking it out, like the dead screen of a TV. The minutes passed precisely in his head.

He got out of the car into the downpour, shrugging his rain-coat across his shoulders, bending his head as he scuttled towards the Watergate complex. The pistol, in the raincoat pocket, bumped ominously against his thigh as he hurried.

Vorontsyev yawned, with impatience as much as sleeplessness, as he leaned on the counter of the hospital's reception desk. The plump, heavily made-up woman, her skin crow-walked beneath the orange foundation, studied the photograph from the forged passport he had found in the dead Iranian's glove compartment.

'Did anyone enquire after him or visit him – even come with him in the ambulance after he had his heart attack?' His forefinger tapped the enlarged snapshot.

'I don't know, Major – when exactly was this?' There was at least a minimal, ingrained respect for his rank and office in her manner.

'I gave you the date. He was admitted to Emergency, he was in Intensive Care – then he died. Try to be helpful.' He could have consulted someone in hospital records. But Bakunin seemed already aware of his every move in the direction of Rawls, and the Iranian was linked to Rawls. Better the oblique approach – even if it didn't seem to be leading anywhere.

The hospital foyer whispered with the voices of the central heating and the occasional nurse or doctor. The warmth and luxury numbed.

She squinted again at the photograph, her nose creased with assumed concentration. She'd been on the day shift, changed two days ago to nights and didn't enjoy the change. She'd been on duty when the dead man had been admitted; she'd have supervised the form-filling.

'I think there were two of them who came with him in the ambulance – or in a car following the ambulance.' She shrugged. Her grey eyes looked up. 'I didn't take much notice.' Her white uniform was tight on her plump body. 'They seemed concerned about him, of course.'

'They evidently knew him.'

'I think they said they were friends of his.'

'Staying at the Gogol, like him?' Dmitri was on his way to the hotel now to question the porter, the night staff, anyone who

161

would know who was booked in at the same time as the dead man.

'I don't know, Major. They sat in the foyer – over there – for a while, then went away. One of them came back the next day, but the patient was dead by then.' She nodded. 'I remember telling the one who came back his friend was dead. He seemed upset.'

Vorontsyev sighed. 'And that's all you can remember?'

'That's all there was.'

'Thanks.' He put the photograph back in his wallet and turned away. 'Goodnight.' He walked towards the lifts. He ought, to assuage any remaining guilt, to look in on Marfa. Tell her she was a clever girl, that they'd identified the Iranian as an intelligence officer.

His mobile phone peremptorily summoned his attention as he waited for the lift. In an instinctive, anxious hurry, he went out of the sliding glass doors into the icy wind, where the stars seemed to wobble and dance. Whatever the call, security needed to be paranoid because of Bakunin's suspicions.

He answered the call. The moon was a cold knifecut in the black, starry sky. Beyond the town, the rigs glowed like enemy campfires surrounding Novyy Urengoy. He crunched on the ice of the car park as if maintaining a hopeless patrol, awaiting an attack.

The line crackled with distance.

'Major? Inspector Vlad Botchkov, Kiev Militia. Your office told me your mobile phone number – eventually.' There was what might have been a laugh, or just an exasperated exhalation of air. 'Lazy bastards, your people.'

'Isn't that what you Ukrainians always say about Russians, Inspector?' There was a kind of shallow camaraderie. 'You're bad tempered because you're on the graveyard shift, is that it?'

'Too true. Major, your enquiry was dumped on me by Criminal Investigation. They couldn't be bothered with it.'

'I'm sorry –'

'That's all right. Missing Persons was the right place to come, as it turns out.'

'Oh.' He felt a tickle of excitement. 'You've identified the man in the photograph.'

162

'He wasn't very well when it was taken, was he?'

'Sorry again. He died of a heart attack.'

'You had him on a false passport, is that right? That's the other picture of him?'

'He was calling himself a supplier to one of the gas rigs. Name of Pomarov at his hotel and on his papers. But there was a *Dutch* passport with his photograph, in someone else's possession.' An Iranian intelligence officer.

'I'll fax you the details – but he was neither Dutch nor a businessman. He's from Kiev, all right. At least, his family is. He moved back a year or so ago. His only daughter reported him missing fairly recently. He's a widower and she and he didn't get on. Nearly three weeks ago now, she called at his house, only to find the place locked up and deserted. She went back a couple of times, tried calling. But eventually she reported it. No trace of him anywhere. Now he's dead.'

'Yes.' While his daughter had been looking for him, he had been a thousand miles away, in another country. 'What's his real name?'

'His name actually is Pomarov. That's why we didn't have too much of a problem.'

'Who was he – what was he?'

'A redundant research scientist. There's a lot of them about. Like so many of them, now the arms race is over, there was no job for him any more. He was bitter about it, his daughter said. Pride hurt, I suppose. He worked at Semipalatinsk at one time. Anyway, the girl said he was depressed, which was why she was worried. And that's about it. Any help?'

Carefully, having recovered his breath, Vorontsyev said: 'Doesn't seem to be. I can't see how that background fits in with my problems. Looks like a dead end. Thanks, anyway, Botchkov – I owe you.'

Vorontsyev switched off the phone, newly aware of the wind's howl, the distressed moon and stars. He felt cold, icily chilled to his marrow. Semipalatinsk, where they –

He cut off the thought, even as it threatened to grow like a nightmarish weed in a speeded-up film sequence, flowering hideously. He hurried back into the hospital foyer, his feet

163

uncertain on the icy tarmac. The receptionist he had questioned hardly remarked his return. He pressed for the lift. Mostafa Vahaji, alias Al-Jani, of the Office for the Protection of the Islamic Revolution in Tehran . . . and a scientist from Semipalatinsk who was to leave Novyy Urengoy on a Dutch passport. With *others*. The lift doors opened and he pressed for the floor of Marfa's ward. He shivered. Vahaji had a permanent suite at the Gogol Hotel, Pomarov had booked in there, with *friends*. He had travelled from Kiev under the *cover* of a connection with Grainger-Turgenev.

It wasn't just drugs. It was some kind of trade in people — scientists. It was smuggling knowledge, maybe exchanging intellect for heroin, who could say? Dangerous knowledge; the knowledge of men who had worked in Semipalatinsk.

The lift doors opened and he hurried into the aseptic, hot corridor. He pushed open the door of the ward, and the duty nurse looked up, recognised him, and returned to the report he was writing.

Vorontsyev saw Marfa sitting up in bed, her nightlight on, arms folded across her breasts, glowering at the foot of her bed. Then she saw him and her features brightened. It was as if he were her father, come to take her home. Yet, as he neared the bed, her eyes seemed pale and cold, retaining the terror she must have felt. She looked older, fragile. Her hands were pale on the coverlet, and her freckles looked like liver spots, as if she was made up for the part of a much older woman.

'Where's Goludin? I told him — '

'Gone to the toilet.' She peeled back the coverlet, revealing a gun. 'He left me this. He'll be back — '

Vorontsyev heard the doors open and the breathy hurry of someone approaching them.

'Sorry, sir — ' Goludin began apologetically, but Vorontsyev waved him into his chair at the bedside and sat down himself on Marfa's other side.

'You all right now?' he asked awkwardly.

Marfa shivered. 'I think so . . .' She nodded. 'Have to be. They say I have to stay in for at least two days, for observation. Nothing's fallen off — so far.' The attempted humour was leaden, false. Her eyes were wide with remembered fears and her skin more ashen than when he had entered. He felt deeply guilty, profoundly angry.

'Good. I've some interesting news.' Goludin leaned forward. 'Your Moscow Centre boyfriend came up with Al-Jani's real name and rank. You were right – clever girl.'

'Intelligence?' She asked the question reluctantly, as if she were being made to relive something she wished profoundly to forget.

'Yes.' He withdrew the faxed sheets from an inside pocket and handed them to her. Goludin scraped his chair forward in order to look over her shoulder and she held the pages so that he could read them. Like two children with a romantic story, an adventure . . . which it wasn't. Pomarov. Semipalatinsk. It was appalling. He wouldn't tell either of these two, perhaps not even Dmitri, of his growing concern. Not at the moment. 'Interesting?' he asked with forced lightness.

'You think he's connected with the heroin, sir?' Goludin asked eagerly.

Marfa snorted derisively. 'Obviously,' she mocked.

They could continue down that road – at least for the time being. As they resumed reading, Vorontsyev looked around the four-bed ward. Two of the beds were empty. The one opposite Marfa contained a resigned old lady – her skin was yellow and her body shrunken – yet she seemed somehow overwhelmed by the warmth, the clean sheets, the silence. Unsettled, he looked away from the old woman who emanated worlds and experiences he could not define.

He turned back to the ridiculously young-looking Goludin, with his eager, dumb dog's expression, and the ill, frightened Marfa who looked up and, as if catching the shadow of his interest in the old woman, nodded towards her.

'She's dying of cancer yet she *likes* it here. Never been so warm and well fed before. Poor old soul.' She sniffed, and seemed more herself, recovered from her recent experiences, if only for a moment. Her compassion was instant and embracing. 'It's warmer than my flat, too,' she added.

Vorontsyev smiled, then said quietly: 'Listen to me, both of you.' It might be endangering them once more, but he was able to shrug that idea aside as his own speculations made all other elements and risks of the investigation minimal. 'Dr Schneider. I want to know for certain whether or not the heroin comes through this place.' He was whispering, as if the nurse or the old woman had been planted in order to spy on them. He felt his nerves ripple. 'Schneider, as Goludin already knows, is friendly with Val Panshin. Who may once upon a time not have dealt in drugs, but now I'm not so sure. I'm going back to have a word with that old pimp Teplov at his knocking shop. He knows more than he's letting on; meanwhile, I want you two . . . are you up to it?' She wanted to confess that she was not, but couldn't allow such weakness or lack of duty and enthusiasm in herself to be admitted. She nodded slowly, her eyes big. 'Good.' He was setting them up, like two inquisitive chimpanzees, with a stick with which to poke at a termites' nest. 'A shipment of medical supplies – remarkably – came off that flight from Tehran, the one carrying our dead friend Hussain. Tehran is, as you know, the epicentre of advanced medical research . . . so, what was in the consignment?'

'How do you know all this?'

'Dogged Dmitri turned it up, and checked it out. Medical supplies, the crates said – but not off a US or Moscow flight but one from Tehran. Keep your eyes and ears open, and see what you can learn, or what you can find. You sure you can do it, Marfa?'

'Yes, sir.'

'Good. The crates arrived here, in this building, two days ago. Usual manner of collection, by hospital truck. See if you can find out what was in them. And be *careful*.'

He stood up.

'Watch out for each other this time,' he warned Goludin, who appeared gloomy in an instant. Vorontsyev was aware of the old, dying woman at the edge of eyesight. 'Be *extra* careful.'

He nodded to both of them and left quickly, as if a sudden bout of nausea or the temperature of the place threatened him. In the corridor and the lift, he felt stifled by his own suspicions. He blundered across the foyer and out into the wind.

166

The moon was down, the stars more unsettled in the cloud rags and the wind.

A scientist named Pomarov. A place called Semipalatinsk.

The heroin was becoming as insubstantial and unimportant as black-market cigarettes or denims. Dear *God*, what in hell could he do about it?

EIGHT

A Little Knowledge

'I'd like these registration forms,' Dmitri Gorov murmured, yawning. Unlike Vorontsyev, he did need sleep; at least he could occasionally find it, sometimes without the help of the bottle. He tapped his finger on the creased papers, hardly larger than rouble notes. 'You admit they left suddenly, booking out together, at exactly the same time.'

The assistant manager of the Gogol Hotel nodded. Night duty dragged at his eyelids and he had smeared, dark marks beneath his pale eyes. Blond eyelashes, a receding hairline, a stiff approximation of aloofness borrowed from hotel staff in the West.

'They paid their bills – at least, their bills were paid. There seemed nothing suspicious about them.'

'Who paid their bills? Suite 12, by any chance?' The night manager appeared startled, his eyes open for a moment in admission before they became officially blank once more.

'That's hotel business.'

Beside Dmitri, Lubin grinned at the manager across the reception counter. Obviously, his anger at being dragged from bed and wife and child had evaporated, Dmitri realised.

'Thanks for the information,' Lubin said.

'I said nothing.'

'Were these two collected, these friends of Mr Pomarov? What transport did they have?'

The night manager clicked his fingers by way of reply and a man in a porter's uniform ambled towards the hotel desk.

'Ask Antipov here. He's the member of staff who summons taxis.'

There was a gust of icy air and the noise of the wind and warm laughter as a sleek individual and a high-class hooker entered the lobby. They headed for the lifts. Dmitri watched them with what might have been a child's puzzlement.

The night manager said: 'These officers want to ask you some questions.' He smirked, unsettling the porter. Dmitri remembered the name, *Antipov*. The man Marfa had interviewed over the telephone, at the beginning of this business.

'We know all about you, Antipov,' he snapped. 'Quite the little whoremaster, aren't you?'

The night manager avoided any complicity or embarrassment by moving to the other end of the long counter and fiddling with a sheaf of receipts. Antipov's face crumpled into abjection, solicitation, worldly cunning.

'It's not harming anyone. It's a public service, more or less.'

'Christ!' Lubin laughed. The porter winced at the noise. 'You'll be telling us you're saving us work next!'

'I might be.'

'We're not interested – at the moment – in your part-time job. Nor are we interested in the dead American. It's about the companions of the guy who had the heart attack. Remember him? I hope he wasn't a client of yours, didn't ask you for a girl too frisky for his heart condition?' Antipov scowled, his eyes ferreting after something he might have mislaid amid the pattern of the thick carpeting of the lobby. Lubin sniggered. Antipov rubbed his long nose and chin with a dirty-nailed hand, shaking his head continually.

'I didn't have anything to do with him,' he finally protested.

'The other two. Friends of his, we presume.' Antipov shrugged. 'They were together, weren't they?'

'Dunno. I saw him with them, yes – but they didn't seem friends. Not close or anything. They didn't arrive together. They met up here.'

Dmitri recalled Vorontsyev's insistent warning to *tread carefully*, and said casually: 'Did you ever see them with the American – you know which American? Or with anyone local?' Suite 12, the Iranian, had paid their hotel bill. The porter shook his head, his eyes darkening and filling with slow, bland cunning.

'No.'

'He's lying,' Lubin offered.

169

'I'm not –!'

'You are,' Dmitri affirmed.

'Look, I don't know what it is you want to know, do I?' Antipov whined. 'Tell me what you want to know.'

'Did you ever see all or any of them with Mr Al-Jani? You know, one of your best clients,' Dmitri added, guessing –

– correctly. Antipov blanched.

'Maybe,' he admitted slowly, 'just a nod and a wink, sort of thing. I didn't know what they had to do with one another – honestly.'

'Good. Now – when they left, did anyone collect them? When they left in a hurry?'

'Hurry?'

'This is like pulling hen's teeth, sir!' Lubin growled, understanding what was required of him. 'Let me take the little shit outside and kick some sense out of him!' The assistant manager seemed to have discerned a smell from the drains. 'Come on, you –!' Lubin roared, grabbing for Antipov's collar.

'I didn't *see*!' the porter roared back. 'I saw them go out, get into a taxi. They were in a hurry, yes, but I don't think there was anyone with them!'

'Not Mr Al-Jani?'

'Why do you keep on about him? I didn't know him! Just the occasional girl, always blondes –'

'All right. Calm down. Stop whingeing. Go on, sod off – for the moment.' Dmitri, still grinning, turned to Lubin. 'Let's take these registration forms back to the office. Our beloved, insomniac chief should be back by now. After he's been to Teplov's knocking shop.'

'Where do you think these two disappeared to? Have they disappeared?'

'God knows. They must have been on false papers, like Pomarov, mustn't they? It's too coincidental otherwise. But why the hell were they here, anyway, and associated with Major Vahaji of Iranian Intelligence? Mr Al-Jani, as was, with a fistful of false passports? I hope our revered leader's come up with more than we have!'

*   *   *

170

'I want you to tell me about 'Nam,' Lock announced, as Kauffman handed him a bourbon. 'I want to know about Tran, how he fits in, what he *was* over there.'

Kauffman sat opposite him in a second leather armchair. His features had retained surprise, as if photographed with that expression, for some moments after he had answered the door to Lock. Now, there was a specious bonhomie that had no effect in stilling the quick, sharp eyes. He raised his glass in salute, then swallowed at his martini.

'You waited outside all afternoon just to ask me about a Vietnamese? I told you, John, the files aren't available or they no longer exist. I'm sorry, but that's the truth.'

'Is it, Bob? Is it really?' Kauffman's eyes narrowed, then he was at once expansive, warm.

'John, what can I tell you? I *understand* – you need to do something. What happened was awful. But I just don't see what this guy Tran has to do with anything.'

'You said this morning you couldn't help me unless I told you why. Does that mean you *can* help me, Bob?' His raincoat lay across his lap as he sat hunched in the chair, and he was angrily aware of the gun in the pocket. 'I got run off the road by a truck on my way back from Langley, Bob. I mean, *run* off the Dolly Madison, it was no accident.' Kauffman was shocked and disbelieving. It was the latter reaction in his eyes that convinced Lock he had nothing to do with the attempt on his life . . . but there was worry, too, deeper in his expression, like someone catching an old, dangerous scent. 'Someone ordered that, Bob. I think it was Tran.'

'*Tran?* The guy's in Calif –' Realising his error, he swallowed at his drink. 'The guy went west, years ago.'

'You remember. Why?' Lock hunched intently forward. The draped raincoat let the gun's weight nestle against his calf. 'Why do you remember one special status immigrant, Bob?'

'I remember the name, that's all. *You* reminded me I knew the name. There isn't anything else to it, John – on my life.'

'Now I know it's important, Bob,' Lock murmured.

They sat facing one another, Lock suppressing his excitement, while Kauffman studied him, weighing the danger he represented. He evidently regarded him as a threat. Which probably meant what he knew was old, he was no longer involved . . . but he knew something, that was all that mattered at the moment.

'It's *not* important,' Kauffman said eventually in a level, almost schoolmasterish tone. 'It hasn't been important for a very long time. Believe me. Whatever you think happened to your sister and Billy Grainger, it had nothing to do with Tran or Vietnam. That's ancient history and it's – it's better left buried.'

'Like My Lai, Bob?'

'Don't be smart. You weren't over there – count yourself a lucky man.'

'Who is Tran, Bob?'

'Tran is *nobody*.'

'He tried to kill me – in Phoenix. I can't be sure about today, but there, I'm sure. I met him. He believed I was a threat.' He said nothing of the heroin, of Vaughn's fear of Tran, of the red horse. How much did Kauffman know? 'You want to know why I would threaten him? Because of some connection between himself and Vaughn Grainger.' He paused abruptly.

Kauffman's features were paler under the downlighters of the bright, modern apartment, he was certain of it. His eyes narrower. Beyond the blinds, the rain continued to slide down the windows and car headlights flashed on the darkening air outside.

'What connection with Vaughn? I told you, Tran wouldn't have had anything to do with Billy and your sister.'

'How can you know that, Bob?' Lock felt angry tension stiffen in his jaw.

Kauffman raised his hands in a gesture of calm. 'I just know it. There's no connection.'

'Then why did Tran ring Vaughn and threaten him? I *heard* him, Bob. I *have* to know all about Tran.'

'There's nothing I can tell you, John. Really, there isn't.'

'Tell me about Vietnam. Tran worked for the Company, that's kind of obvious by his special immigrant status. He was bankrolled by the Company after he got here.'

'OK – my memory's hazy, it was a long time ago, but all I recollect is Tran was a messenger boy. We used these guys all

172

the time, running errands, informing, setting traps . . . you know the kind of thing that went on then. He was no more important than that. Someone just looked after him when we got out. That's it, all of it, as far as I can tell you, John.' There was the faintest trace of special, insistent pleading in his last sentence. But there didn't seem to be much more behind it than a man backing away from a past the Company now regarded as unsavoury.

'He worked for Vaughn's Special Forces unit, right?'

'I wouldn't know.'

Lock remained silent. Kauffman was only in the slightest degree edgy.

'Another drink, fella?' Kauffman asked. Lock shook his head.

Kauffman made himself another martini, his back to Lock. There was no mirror on the wall that would reveal his features. Then he returned to his seat, raised his glass, and settled himself.

'I ought to see about dinner,' Kauffman announced eventually. 'You eaten yet?' Lock shook his head once more. There was no invitation in the question; rather the opposite. He sensed himself as he appeared to Kauffman, someone thrashing about in the dark, begging for information like scraps of food. Someone stumbling about, banging into the furniture of the past and unable to recognise any single item for what it was. 'I – have a dinner date,' Kauffman added, which was evidently a lie.

Lock looked up. 'I've been trying to recollect Vaughn's stories about 'Nam. He didn't talk often, and Billy only ever talked about his own time there . . .'

'Yes?' The nervousness of a cat unexpectedly stroked.

'His group worked up against the Ho Chi Minh Trail, at first . . .'

'Did they? Maybe you're right. Like I said, ancient history, John.' An effortful shrug of Kauffman's large frame which failed to convey ease.

'Then, later, in Military Zones Two and Three, further south . . .' It was only now, facing Kauffman, that he could recollect with any clarity. The modern apartment, with its tubular steel and smoked glass, had the anonymity that rendered memory easy. It was like a debriefing room. He debouched

Vaughn Grainger's past, as he knew it, as if he were the one undergoing interrogation. 'Further south,' he repeated. 'But they were always near the Cambodian border. Tran was from just outside Saigon. What use was he to Vaughn – what local or specialist knowledge would he have?'

'You're worrying at a rabbit that's already dead, John. Died of natural causes.' Kauffman grinned, as if Lock's recollections were childish dreams that could be safely indulged.

'I remember something else –'

'What?'

'Vaughn talked, once or twice, about some scheme for putting people back on the land . . . I remember – yes, I remember one afternoon, by the pool, a bright, hot day, and he was angry about that movie, *Apocalypse Now. It wasn't all like that*, he said. Really angry. *We did good things, we tried*. What did he call it? I can't remember the *name* he gave the project!' His sudden outburst of rage seemed to unsettle Kauffman. He stirred in his chair. The gun dropped from the raincoat pocket onto the pale, thick carpet, lying there between them.

'What in hell –?' Kauffman began. Lock snatched up the pistol, embarrassed. 'What is this, fella?' Kauffman barked angrily, frightened. Lock held the pistol in his hands, cradling it and staring at it as if he had outraged hospitality. 'What in hell do you need a gun for?' Kauffman hissed.

Lock looked up. There was perspiration along Kauffman's hairline and his forehead was coldly pale. He almost gestured with the pistol, to signal harmlessness – then he turned the gun on Kauffman. In his head, something echoed away like a stone down a deep well. Anger surged in him like nausea, filling his throat.

He growled: 'You know something, Kauffman. Stop being an asshole and tell me about Tran and Vaughn and Vietnam!'

'I know nothing!' Kauffman shouted back at him.

'You *know*, dammit!' Lock raged. 'You know the connection between Vaughn Grainger and Tran!' The pistol waggled dangerously in his hand, as if animate. The truth about Beth's murder was in the room with them. 'Tell me, Kauffman, or by God I'll blow your head off!'

174

The threat was real. Kauffman believed it, his features venom-ously afraid.

Then, in a quieter voice, Lock said: 'Tell me, Kauffman. Tell me all of it. About the drugs . . . everything. I want to know because nothing else matters now. Not you, not me. Tell me . . .'

Vorontsyev stood looking at the onion domes of the church, sombrely heavy against the hard glow from the town. The wind cried in an empty place, which might almost have been inside him, and he thrust his hands deeper into his pockets and hunched into the hood of the parka.

After some time, when his irresolution and fear had subsided, he turned from the church and trod carefully along the path to the door of the brothel. Two scientists were missing – they had to be people who were to use other fake passports, they were at the Gogol with Pomarov – and he hoped to God they were still in Novyy Urengoy . . . hiding out in a place like Teplov's brothel, which Mostafa Vahaji had used.

There was a grubby light at one of the windows, behind thin curtains. It was an hour before dawn, early or late enough for Teplov to feel vulnerable; invaded and violated by his arrival.

He ignored the doorbell and banged on the wood, yelling out Teplov's name. A light went on somewhere far back in the hall. The stained glass panel of the door threw liver spots of light over his face and hands. He felt icily cold in the wind.

The door opened on a safety chain. Sonya, eyes bleared with sleep, had the magnificence and size of a ruined monument as she stared suspiciously at him. Then, when she snarlingly spoke, she was just an ageing whore and even the soft glow from behind her was too much betraying light.

'You – what do you want *now*?'

He pushed past her. The stuff of her vast wrap rustled against the parka. 'Just a chat – another talk.'

'Why don't you leave him alone, Major – he doesn't know anything,' Sonya protested, her slippers flapping heavily behind him as he moved down the hall towards the stairs. 'You know him, Major.' Her voice was rough, coarse, yet neither whining

175

nor pleading. Sonya was dealing in statements of fact. 'He walks a fine line, but he walks it. People like Panshin leave him – '

He turned on her and her face told him she sensed her own indiscretion.

'Val Panshin – what's Panshin to our mutual friend? To the *respectable*, tightrope-walking Misha?' He grinned.

'Nothing, Major. I was just going to say he doesn't move in such circles, not Misha. They leave him alone. You know all this!' she concluded.

'What is it, love?' Teplov called from the top of the stairs. Vorontsyev looked up and Teplov saw him. 'Oh – yes, Major? To what do we owe the –?' He was galloping down the stairs, his silk dressing-gown flowing about him.

'It's not a friendly visit,' Sonya warned, folding her arms across her huge breasts. She stood at the foot of the stairs, protecting Teplov.

'I'm not going to beat him up, Sonya – or arrest him. At least, not yet. You can stay, if you want. Make us some coffee. Come on, Misha – along to your office, I think.' He put his arm around the man's narrow shoulders, almost hugging him to his side. 'Let's talk about Val Panshin, for one thing.'

'Nothing to do with him,' Teplov protested in a tired, uninflected voice, unlocking the door of his office. Sonya hesitated, then made for the kitchen. 'Come in, Major.' The church gloomed in the darkness beyond the window before Teplov switched on the light. 'What is it now?'

Teplov sat down, pulling his thin dressing-gown closely around him. He lit a cigarette. Vorontsyev helped himself from the box and they smoked in silence for some moments. The office seemed almost warm to him.

'Have you ever been asked – by Mr Al-Jani, our late lamented Iranian friend – to put people up here overnight? Or for longer?' He studied Teplov through the smoke he exhaled. He had – but hadn't complied, Vorontsyev guessed.

'Never.'

'But you were asked – he asked you if you would?'

A long silence, into which Sonya galleoned with a cafetière and two china cups and saucers, a sugar bowl and a milk jug.

176

The mockery was evident, as was the taste that had acquired the china. She poured Vorontsyev's coffee, murmuring:

'People don't ask people like *us* to do things like that, Major. They just come here for a good time.'

'Good coffee,' he replied, then added: 'You won't be mentioned, or this place. I just want to know.' He hesitated, then added: 'No raids for two months, I guarantee. Just so long as you don't take too much advantage. No under-age girls –' Teplov looked affronted, Sonya malevolent. '– no drugs, no S-M beyond the usual whips and scorpions. No raids for two months . . . Really good coffee.'

'You only bully us because we're *not* connected!' Sonya observed caustically. 'Why don't you raid Panshin?'

'He's really under your skin, Sonya – why?'

'Because he's a fat bastard!'

'Have you had trouble with him – Misha, have you?'

'If we had, what would you do?' Sonya challenged, arms folded, positioned behind the chair like a bodyguard.

Vorontsyev adopted a gloomy expression. 'Not much, that's true,' he admitted. 'But enough to look after you two.'

Sonya appeared sceptical, but Teplov's pinched, chilly features seemed warmed, as if by the idea of heat rather than an actual fire.

'Well?' he added. 'Do you want to talk about Panshin, or not? The bastard's into drugs, correct?' Teplov nodded involuntarily before Sonya's arm descended warningly on his thin shoulder. 'What's the connection between Panshin and the Iranian – exactly?'

'There isn't one,' Sonya replied quickly.

'There must be. Why else was Al-Jani here? He was Iranian Intelligence, by the way.' Teplov was startled. 'It's true. No tricks. He has to have been the main supplier, right?'

Teplov said slowly, carefully: 'From what we heard. *Overheard* . . . the heroin you're interested in came in under his supervision.' He glanced up at Sonya's clouded features. His hand touched hers as it lay on his shoulder. 'We mind our own business. Even the Iranian understood that. He didn't abuse it.' He puffed furiously at his cigarette. Sonya's grip remained firm, but relaxed. She'd squeeze his shoulder if she thought him too compliant. 'Panshin became interested about a year or so ago – I think.'

'The Iranian hooked him?'

'I think so.'

'And the American doctor, Schneider, was connected – and the hospital?'

They were genuinely puzzled, without knowledge. Vorontsyev was disappointed.

'We don't know about that.'

'OK. Did the Iranian ask you to put up people who didn't come for the fun and games – any time?'

'Once.'

'When?'

'Four, five months ago. I – we – said no. Pushers with the heat underneath them, were they?'

'No. Nothing like. Did it seem *important* to the Iranian? Really important?'

Sonya said. 'He tried to make it casual, nothing much. It didn't fool me – or Misha,' she added. Teplov looked glum and guilty.

'But he didn't explain?'

'No. He left it at that.'

'Would he have asked Panshin?'

'I doubt it. He didn't like Panshin. He thought he was a greedy bully – the girls he used all had tales of his mockery of Panshin with his haircut, cigars, rings and big gut!' He smiled, shrugging at Sonya's withering contempt. Vorontsyev grinned.

'Poor old Val – he couldn't bear it if he knew we didn't think well of him!' He spread his hands. 'OK. Four or five months ago, there were people the Iranian wanted to hide. Not more recently?'

Teplov screwed up his narrow face, but the effort at memory seemed no more than politic. 'I don't remember.'

'He might have been in a panic. A couple of weeks ago? Was he here? Did he have to do something in a hurry – come down from the rig unexpectedly?'

'All right, so you know already!' Sonya snapped. 'It wasn't

178

four or five months ago, it was the week before last! We said no.'

'Good. How many people, for how long?'

'Two, he said. For a couple of days, till he got something else sorted out – what's the matter now?'

Vorontsyev had stood up.

'Thanks,' he said. 'That's all I wanted to know.' He yawned. 'Thanks for the coffee, Sonya. No raids for a couple of months – even if you weren't going to volunteer the information! I'll keep my side of the bargain.' Sonya's expression was dismissive, and relieved. Teplov smiled weakly. They didn't want to know more, hadn't wanted to at the time. Like himself, he reflected dully. 'I'll see myself out,' he muttered. 'Take care, both of you.'

'Why, Major? You're not going to *do* something, are you?' Sonya snapped.

Pained, he replied: 'I think I may have to, Sonya. Tell me one more thing. Any idea who the Iranian would have used to hide these people? You say it wouldn't have been Panshin. Who else?'

'There are Iranians and other wogs all over town, Major, or hadn't you noticed?'

He shut the door behind him. Any decrepit flat anywhere in the town. One of the dachas outside, a hut, a shed . . . ? The wind howled and the sky was lit only by the lights from the town and the menacing breaths of flame from the rigs. Ice sparkled on the onion domes and crosses of the church.

He had to involve Dmitri. Didn't want to, but it was necessary, now. The two men who had been with Pomarov had disappeared, Vahaji was dead. Rawls –? Connected or not, he was dead . . . he had to find those scientists –

She had waited until the end of the night; just before dawn when the nursing shifts changed and while the corridors were still only anticipatory of the smells of the first meal of the hospital day. Yet her vulnerability did not diminish. It was partly reaction from the way she had nearly died up at the rig, but also her own bodily weakness, however much despised, and the sense of herself in slippers, pyjamas, dressing-gown. The hospital

179

clothing refused to become a disguise, a declaration of harmlessness.

And then there was Goludin, ten paces behind her, his hand furtively inside his jacket, hovering near the butt of his pistol. There was an element of farce in the situation that Marfa could not help feeling was the prelude to error or discovery. People had already died, *she* had almost died, on this same journey. She halted at a turn of the long, aseptic corridor and Goludin caught up with her.

'Is this it?' she whispered hoarsely.

Goludin's face was solemnly certain. 'Yes. The door's at the end of this hallway. I double-checked,' he all but pleaded. It would be the easiest of things, to ask him to die protecting her, such was his guilt at what had happened at the rig. She shrugged his sentiments aside.

'Right, let's have a look at the locks.'

He remained beside her now. The silence pressed behind them as palpably as if the corridor were being bricked up, entrapping them. She reached the door and began at once to study the lock. The warning notice, in Russian and English, forbade entry to any but authorised personnel. Otherwise, it was simply a general storeroom.

'Stiff plastic should do it,' Goludin offered.

'Do it, then.'

He seemed reluctant to damage his credit card from a German bank, but began to insert it beside the lock. Marfa listened behind them and heard only the heating pipes grumbling and the sough of the air-conditioning and dust extractors. The Foundation Hospital wasn't even cluttered and rat-infested and unsafe *below* ground level – God certainly blessed America. She sniffed, and was afraid of the sudden volume of the noise in the oppressive silence. The lock's click was quieter. Goludin, beaming and red-faced, opened the door for her like an escort. She switched on the lights – and shuddered.

It was nothing like the hangarlike shed where she had been caught, knocked unconscious and dragged to the garbage bins . . . but the shelving and the orderliness made it seem like a doll's house image of the other place.

180

'All right?' he whispered, his breath tickling her cold ear.

'Yes,' she snapped back sternly.

'I just thought –'

'Keep *quiet.*'

'Yes.'

'You're sure this storeroom is the most likely?' She pushed the door quietly to behind her, leaning back against it. Reaching out, she touched Goludin's hand for the reassurance of the cold barrel of the pistol he was holding.

'It's the least used. Look over there – linen, bandages, toilet paper. Reserve supplies –' More doubtfully, he added: 'I thought it seemed the most likely, if it wasn't used very much.'

'Let's get on with it – you take that side. Go *on.*'

She began to pace along the farthest shelving on the left-hand side, as if measuring the ground for planting. She could hear Goludin's footsteps, as deliberate as her own, and his breathing, artificially steady. Toilet paper, sanitary towels, swabs, bedlinen, bandages . . . almost immediately, it seemed a ridiculous waste of time to be investigating this storeroom. No drugs, just the mundane. Disinfectant, cleaning fluid, toilet paper . . . She turned on her heel, almost losing her slipper in her impatience, and began the next valley of shelves.

'Anything?' she called out in a hoarse whisper.

'Nothing yet.' His disappointment was as evident as her own, mingled with a growing embarrassment.

She completed the second defile of shelves, already inatten- tive, her nerves beginning to mount, her sense of time exagger- ated, the seconds hurrying much more quickly than her breathing. Nothing, nothing –

'Goludin!' she snapped angrily. Bloody waste of time. The shelves were closing in, claustrophobically. 'This is –' She glanced upwards, feeling hot and constricted, trapped by futility and anger. The downlighters in the low ceiling were like the eyes of infra-red cameras – were there cameras? She hadn't even checked.

He appeared at the end of the rows of shelves which enclosed her.

'You all right?' he asked.

181

She must have looked ridiculous, standing there, like someone in a drought area amazed at rain falling on her face. She continued to stare at the downlighters and the top shelves. Then she pointed.

'Up there.' Her throat was tight.

'What?'

'The top shelves. No one ever looks *up* in a storeroom. They're difficult to reach, too.'

'Yes?'

She shook his arm, gripping it with both hands.

'The bloody shelves are full of boxes! Climb up and have a look!'

He nodded eagerly as a puppy and handed her the pistol. Then he gripped the shelving and shook it. Dust rose slowly.

'Solid enough,' he muttered and began climbing, grunting as he did so. His feet scrabbled past her, then stilled. He was raised above the top shelves like someone looking carefully over a parapet.

'Well?'

'Lots of boxes – Medical Supplies they – *all* of them say. Just that.'

'Country of origin?' she snapped. 'Brandnames? There must be brandnames.'

'USA, it says on this one – and that one. Looks like most of them are Yankee –'

'And?'

'And what?' He seemed breathless, impatient and disappointed.

'Who manufactured them?'

'Doesn't say.'

'It must!'

'Well, it doesn't! Do you want to climb up and have a look? It just says General Medical Supplies on plain cardboard boxes, except *USA*. Otherwise, they're anonymous. Wait –' He grunted, leaning out across the top shelf to which he clung. She heard the scrape of cardboard on dusty metal. 'This one says Grainger Foundation, Phoenix, Arizona – what you'd expect, isn't it?'

182

'Vorontsyev says the delivery came from Tehran, not Phoenix. Come down from there. You've wasted our time –'

'Sod that! I'm opening one while I'm up here. No one will know.' She heard grunting and ripping, the screamlike tear of masking tape being tugged free.

'Come on, we haven't got time –!'

'Bugger off, Marfa! I've said I'm sorry – said nothing else, ever since you were brought here. But you're not my superior officer, so bugger you!'

She wanted to laugh at his ridiculous, pompous protestation. 'Hurry up!' she barked in lieu of amusement.

'It wouldn't say Heroin, a Present from Iran on the boxes, would it?' His breathing was ragged, the tearing noises somehow more desperate. 'Oh, bugger this –!' he growled. The box continued its struggle against his efforts, seeming to back away from him along the top shelf with gritty, grumbling steps. 'There!'

Silence. Eventually, maddened, she barked: 'Well?'

'Catch,' he replied and his hand dropped a package. Brown paper tied with string, as unadorned as some of her Christmas presents as a child. Those had usually been knitted mittens, a repainted doll, a scarf or balaclava.

'Have you –?' She cleared her throat. 'Do you know what it tastes like, heroin?'

Unwrapped, the parcel contained a cellophane block of compressed whiteness which could as easily have been soap powder or talcum as –

'Yes,' Goludin breathed, reaching the floor.

She watched him as she might have watched a careful parent lighting a candle for her, so that she would avoid all hurt. He opened a penknife, slit the package at one corner, dipped in his finger as if into sherbet, placed the powder on his tongue, tasted – and spat.

'Yes!' he sighed orgasmically. She felt her cheeks hot with excitement and admiration. Goludin's whole face was a beaming grin. 'Yes!'

'What about the rest of it – is there more?'

'If we get a warrant, *now*, we can search the whole place from top to bottom, with this as evidence. Come on – !'

Marfa clutched the cellophane package against her breasts like a long-desired baby or some other cherished dream.

'Come on!'

Then he paused and caught her hand. She, too, heard the footsteps coming along the corridor.

Lock could not have planned it. It had been nothing like his anticipation. The conclusion of a waggled pistol and enraged threat – the collapse of Kauffman before his gaze. Nor had he anticipated how committed he would be on the other side of a singular accidental moment when the pistol slipped from his raincoat pocket. It had been like some desperate hand in a high-rolling card game, that had changed the whole atmosphere of the apartment and their relationship.

Yet even that was not quite all of it. There was Kauffman's insistent, abstracted *confession*. His unburdening.

Yes, Tran had been recruited . . . Tran had been a shopkeeper outside Saigon, attached himself to Vaughn's group, *or so I was told*, but his family had come from a border area and his local knowledge was vital . . . he was on Vaughn's staff, unofficially but importantly . . .

Kauffman talked to an exact spot on the pale rug, where the last of his second martini had been spilt and was now drying. The rain ran down the windows, the headlights flowed like pale mercury against the open blinds and the tyres swished like stiff skirts outside on the parkway. Kauffman had had little to do with Vaughn's Special Forces group, but he knew the story; or could now reassemble it into a narrative. Lock sat opposite him, watching the man's bent, middle-aged, sagging shoulders, feeling himself filled with a creeping, pitying horror at the confirmation of all his most appalled speculations.

I just ran into Tran from time to time, or news of Grainger's project . . . Tran had undertaken trips to Saigon, to My Tho and Vung Tou on the Mekong Delta. *Tran was a good friend, that much was obvious to a blind man – the kind of passes the guy had, the protection he was given* . . .

Lock rubbed his forehead insistently as he listened, as if to ease a headache; in reality it was because the nightmare threat-

184

ened to burst out of his head, so great was the pressure inside. Kauffman's hands were together, reminiscent of prayer.

Why was Tran important? Lock wasn't certain he had even voiced the question, but Kauffman seemed to answer him almost at once.

Putting people back on the land . . . *Project ReGreen, you wouldn't remember it, you weren't there* . . . Right in the border areas. Resettlement, providing an economic and human bulwark against Charley, the Viet Cong. Lock had vaguely heard of it. A naive and noble ideal, to turn the south into a prosperous agrarian region and bolster it against the north. Making capitalism on the hoof, what the Communists in Vietnam were doing now – ironic, that. *They replanted fields, gave grants, machinery,* repopulated abandoned villages, grew a new harvest, a new hope . . .

That's what Vaughn had been angry about when he saw Coppola's vision of Vietnam and had had to endure the scorpion of Robert Duvall's line about the smell of napalm on the morning breeze . . . but that couldn't *really* have been it all, could it? Lock felt concussed and nauseous, as if he had survived a car accident . . . only to realise that the accident was happening again and again, as it would in a nightmare.

The trial scheme for *Project ReGreen* had been established under Vaughn Grainger's command only for a matter of a year and some months before the Pentagon decided that large-scale resettlement would be impossible. Kissinger's apparent diplomatic successes suspended the resettlement programme before it had really gotten started . . . Lock nodded.

It was the original trial scheme, Kauffman said, *that Vaughn used*. It had been set up in the Da Dung river area of the central plateau, a sparsely populated region of scattered tea plantations. It was nothing like the main rice-growing areas of the crowded, chaotic delta and the Cambodian border. *And it was easy, man, it was so easy* . . . Lock flinched and swallowed.

The CIA's own airline, variously nicknamed Gremlin Airlines, Poltergeist Pan Am or Thin Air, had flown in the supplies, machinery, equipment, money – for camouflage, build-on-site greenhouses and warehouses, silos . . . *The flights came into Vung*

Tou on the coast, Tran was overseer for their shipment upcountry to Tho Da Dung. . . . Lock swallowed painfully. It was like watching the slow, painful death of a beloved older relative. Kauffman's words were changing Vaughn Grainger's identity, it was becoming its own opposite. The granite, frontiersman image that had always somehow accompanied Vaughn Grainger was gone.

I clerked the docketing out at Vung Tou for a few months, that's why I had to be bought off . . . Kauffman did not look up for sympathy, or to assess reaction, even at that point . . . *The money was good, it was a lot of money. I turned my back.* . . . The project and the trial sites were finally abandoned in 1973, late in the year. Vaughn and whoever else – *Tran* – had had almost eighteen months before the trial project was closed down. Two, three harvests?

He realised that he was sweating. The rain on his hair had long dried, but his collar was again damp, his forehead chilly. ReGreen, Thin Air and its C-130s and medium haul Boeings, a couple of Starlifters . . . He remembered the rumours that the CIA was smuggling heroin in Afghanistan, to offset the costs of the Stinger missiles and the other weaponry. In that war, everyone had wanted to deny it and believed the denial. The *mujahideen* had grown heroin, the Russians had used it, bought it, smuggled it . . .

Kauffman's narrative continued.

They had harvested the heroin at Da Dung, the heroin the Special Forces and their Vietnamese allies like Tran had grown, and the CIA's airline had flown it Stateside. Kauffman and people like him had assisted, or turned their backs, for the right price. Vaughn and Tran . . . *no wonder Vaughn had turned around the fortunes of Grainger Technologies in the '70s, he had the money from the Vietnamese heroin to invest* . . . *maybe that was why he had done it?*

It didn't matter. He had done it. And had gone on doing it . . . Vaughn had claimed he and Billy were trying to stop it, but they had been the ones behind it. And . . . been killed for it.

He stood up. Kauffman, still contained by the aura of prison or the confessional, did not look up or pause in his rambling narrative. Lock stumbled to the door and let himself out of the apartment. His stomach lurched with sickness.

Beth had been killed because of Vaughn and Billy, not for any other reason on earth . . . The rain lashed against his hot face, chilling him. Ran into his collar, his eyes, soaked him. He blundered across the parkway, amid the glare of headlights and the noise of tyres, towards the hire car.

He had to see Vaughn, make *him* tell him . . . and, if it was true, then he would kill Turgenev. He had to see Vaughn.

The dawn was leaking into the eastern horizon like a lighter stain as Vorontsyev stopped his car beside the crumbling, leaning picket fence that marked the boundary of Dmitri's dacha. The leafless trees drooped under their weight of snow. A solitary bird croaked and hopped amid the skeletal branches. There was a bird table, but it had not been supplied that early in the morning. There was a light on in a side room; probably the bathroom.

Vorontsyev got out of the car and shut the door quietly. The town was a silent glow a couple of miles away, like the scene of a nuclear meltdown, and the flames from the rigs were less real in the growing light. He pushed open the gate and stumped up the trodden but uncleared path to the low wooden home. House. It had ceased to be a home when the daughter had overdosed. Now, he was about to heap a greater burden on Dmitri's broad, drooping shoulders. It could not be avoided. He couldn't carry it alone, and he couldn't act alone.

He rang the bell. It sounded echoingly in the house, as if there were no rugs or furniture inside.

The door was opened by Dmitri, dressed in trousers and a greyish vest. There was shaving lather on his right cheek and chin, the left already scraped clean. Their breaths mingled.

'Alexei! I've only been home an hour or so – couldn't sleep – come in.' He gestured Vorontsyev inside. The narrow, pine-walled hall opened into the large sitting room. Dmitri, waving the razor, said: 'Won't be a minute, Alexei – is it important?' He did not wait for a reply. 'Sit down,' he called, 'I'll make some coffee when I've finished.'

187

As Vorontsyev sat himself on the sofa, amid the scattered newspapers and the plastic plate stained with Dmitri's last meal in the house, Dmitri called out:

'Lubin and I got the registration forms for the other two — they're on the table there . . . Probably not their real names —' Vorontsyev heard the splash of water, then the doglike splutterings of a wet animal as Dmitri towelled himself. 'What did you find out?' he heard in a muffled voice.

Vorontsyev picked up the forms from the Gogol. He noted the names and the professions neatly filled out. The addresses — some place in Georgia, another in Byeloruss. His hand, he realised, was quivering. Dmitri re-entered the room, towel in one hand, shaving soap lingering on an earlobe. His eyes looked as if he habitually wore spectacles, his shoulders sagged like his paunch; he seemed dogged and ineffectual.

'Pomarov. It was his real name, apparently. I had a call from Kiev . . .' His voice tailed off.

'Good. What else — who was he?'

'Make some coffee, old friend.'

Dmitri looked anxiously quizzical, and then shrugged compliantly, vanishing into the kitchen. A noise of drawers and implements, and eventually the boiling of water and the smell of coffee. Vorontsyev looked at the registration forms as if willing them to reveal their subjects' whereabouts, or to render themselves meaningless. *Both* men dealt with the gas companies, the forms claimed. With Grainger-Turgenev.

'Learn anything at Misha's knocking shop?' Dmitri asked, handing him a brown mug. 'I take it there weren't any unexpected guests?'

'No.'

'Don't be so gloomy, Alexei. I've combed quickly through the routine passenger manifests the airlines deliver to headquarters — left Lubin to go through them more carefully — and there's been no one on a Western passport on any flight to Tehran or points south. I take it that's where they would be heading, whoever they are? Maybe they were just in town to pick up supplies, and returned to wherever they came from . . . ?' He studied Vorontsyev. 'What's the matter? They can't be important, can they? Stands to reason. Just couriers?' Vorontsyev shook his head. 'What, then?'

'They – unless I'm wrong, and I wish to God I was, they're nuclear scientists.'

'What?' Dmitri breathed after an interminable, oppressive silence.

'Pomarov, the dead one, worked at Semipalatinsk. He suddenly and mysteriously disappeared from Kiev, left no message, didn't even say goodbye to his only daughter. Our Iranian friend had his Dutch passport ready for him, and a job –'

'– in Tehran. Jesus . . . you're certain about this?'

Vorontsyev nodded. 'There's a trade in brains. In scientists who've worked on advanced nuclear research, on lasers maybe . . . on bombs, weapons. On *the* Bomb, Dmitri . . . It's almost too terrifying to think about, isn't it?' He looked up at Dmitri, as if he felt himself exaggerating. Selling the means of making the Bomb to the fundamentalists, the unstable regimes, the expansionists. 'Christ, every tinpot dictator, every ethnic or religious psychopath – could end up having his own bomb. Doesn't that frighten you, old friend?'

In the silence, he sipped his coffee, watching Dmitri absorb the information and its implications. Eventually, Dmitri said:

'Did they get out *before* Vahaji got himself killed? Are they still *here*?'

'Let's hope so.'

'Then we'd better find them, Alexei. We'll need the whole team for this, and quickly.' There was no shock, no creeping sense of disaster. Just the practical, the narrow perspective of immediate action. 'Don't look as if you've stumbled on something *unique*, Alexei, like the secret of the universe – that it will end tomorrow, at precisely three in the afternoon! Come on – you know we'll sell anything these days for hard currency. They took a dozen of these people off a plane in Moscow last year.'

It was true. A hamperful of nuclear and biological warfare scientists on their way out of Cheremetievo airport, bound for Iraq and Pakistan. Bought and sold as simply as any other export, any other product of Russian origin! There were as many poorly paid and redundant scientists in the Russian Federation as there were tanks for sale.

'Agreed,' he replied heavily. 'Were they paying for them in heroin – was that it?'

'That might be too neat. Right, what time? I'll get the people we can trust organised.'

'Ten. My office.' He stood up. 'Thanks, Dmitri.'

'For what? Not being terrified at the prospect? Come on, Alexei, it's not the end of life as we know it – not yet!' There was almost a grin on his shabby, worn face. Nothing was real for Dmitri, nothing except the people who killed his daughter and rendered his wife a vegetable. This was little more than a *distraction*, incredible though that seemed.

For himself, he had no distractions, there was no lessening of his fear. Anyone who wanted it, who could *pay* – cash or kind – would have their own nuclear arsenal, their own nuclear threat, in five years or less. Russia was selling these people the means of her own destruction. It was a suicide note. Dmitri sensed his foreboding and added with deliberate cheerfulness:

'We'll find the buggers, don't worry. We're getting close, Alexei, I can feel it. These scientists could be the way in. We're nearly there!'

'Yes, they've just reported back. It's been taken care of . . . No, I wouldn't have ordered it if it hadn't been necessary. They were getting close to the other business, not the heroin . . . Good. No, without him, the others won't make a move. Why did he wake up? I've no idea, but he did. Sadly for him. I did warn him off, I took the investigation out of his hands – he should have realised, gone back to sleep . . . yes, all right, I underestimated him. But it's been taken care of. What? Yes, I'll call you when I hear the result. Don't worry – all right, you're not worried. My people know what to do. You think *no* GRU training sticks? Yes, I'll call you just as soon as –'

The call was ended abruptly. GRU Colonel Bakunin put down his receiver with a grimace. Bastard . . . The sky had lightened now. His people had a tail on Vorontsyev, and the policeman was doing exactly what was required of him to become a victim.

190

Stupid bastard. He was so *ineffectual*, like a daydreamer; an intellectual, a moral posturer who never actually *did* anything. Until now —

— and without him, his team would subside like an old wall being knocked down.

Vorontsyev locked the car and warily crossed the rutted, ungritted row of parking spaces outside his apartment house. He could smell petrol fumes on the cold air as a delivery van pulled away onto the street, into the noise of traffic heading into the town or out towards the rigs. He had picked his way across the treacherous surface of the investigation just as warily. Always the intellectual — had been for years, he mocked himself. Tut-tutting the state of the world from some ethical pinnacle made only of sculptured ice.

Dmitri's commonsense and eagerness had upbraided him, justly so. He did not feel resolve, merely less depressed, shaking his head at vices as if they were follies.

Most of the still-curtained windows in the large, dilapidated old house were lit. Shadows hurried across one, then another as his neighbours stumbled towards their jobs or their children's schools. Against a rear curtain, no doubt Vera Silkova was holding up her new baby — the one that kept him company during his sleepless nights, voicing simpler protests than his own through the bedroom wall. He smiled. His eyes were gritty with tiredness, but his body, though cumbersome, was satisfied, lacking any edge of nerves. Dmitri's plain man's attitude had done that much for him. The men they sought could well still be in the town . . . it was a simple manhunt. If one forgot that they were nuclear scientists being sold to Iran.

He unlocked the front door and entered the house. Isolated amid the newer blocks and shops, it was as if it had become lost in its present unfamiliar surroundings, a building suffering from senile dementia or amnesia. He had nothing in common with his neighbours, despite his momentary lapses into fellow feeling. They liked him living there; the police didn't bother them, they felt safer from thieves.

He closed the door behind him, hearing the noises from other

191

apartments, as innocuous and unsuspicious as ever; the way ordinary people registered their lives. He always felt, coming off duty, as if he had arrived with a search warrant. He climbed the stairs towards his own door on the first floor. On the ground floor behind him, Otzman the civil servant's door slammed as he hurried to work. Vorontsyev yawned and fished out his key. It was after eight. He'd try for an hour's sleep, then shower and shave before the ten o'clock briefing.

'Major?' He winced, hearing the voice of Otzman's wife, Nadya. His key was in the lock and he half-turned it as she called out: 'The gas fitters said they'd repaired the leak you'd reported. They didn't —'

He had turned the key in the lock —

— was blown backwards, upended, then crushed against the landing wall by the fragmenting door. He understood that much. Understood, too, that there had been a bomb, that walls were crumbling, that his body was hurt, badly hurt . . . and that he was beginning to scream.

Then, nothing —

PART TWO

Capital

'The capitalist class of a country cannot,
as a whole, overreach itself.'
                    Karl Marx: *Das Kapital*

NINE

Bad Old Ways

He returned to the Georgetown street in the evening gloom, the rain hardly diminished against the windscreen by the action of the wipers. He pulled the car into the kerb and switched off the engine. The tape's relentless Dylan ceased at the same moment and his thoughts returned like angry hornets to fill the silence. The image of Kauffman, hunched in his confessional chair, clutching an untasted drink, was very vivid; and profoundly enervating. He sat in imitation in the hire car, watching his aimless hands fiddle at the circumference of the steering wheel. The rain blinded the windscreen like a waterfall. Not at all like tears.

Nothing else matters now, not you or me. . . . He'd said something like that to Kauffman, simply in order to threaten him – but the words had gained weight, come like a rock to crush him. Nothing mattered – not now.

Except Turgenev, except the certainty that the pattern had repeated itself in Afghanistan and later in Siberia. Billy, just like Vaughn, had grabbed the easy dollar, the easy lie. Found heroin, sketched a supply route, put everything in place, made money.

Been killed. Deservedly.

Not Beth, though –

John Lock removed his hands from the steering wheel so that they might gently hold his head while it raged with the unborn life of what he had learned from Kauffman. It hurt like a migraine. It assaulted his present and his past, turning them inside out. He had been placed in a moral vacuum by Kauffman's story and the pressure suit of his past had not protected him.

Lock groaned, pressing his head against the windscreen, which was mercifully cold. Billy, Vaughn, the Company . . . all reduced to a multiple murder because of money in a Virginia mansion outside of which the Flag flew and inside of which the elite of Washington had assembled the previous evening, to toast his sister's birthday. While Billy had been fingered in the library by Pete Turgenev because . . . ? Why? Siphoning off more than his share? A double-cross, a wrong deal, a too-late fit of conscience?

And an innocent bystander had been killed along with the perpetrator. His sister.

He got out of the car, forgetting to lock the door he slammed in rage. He stamped up the steps of the apartment house and let himself in. His rage carried itself into the hall ahead of the smell of the rain and the fallen, sodden leaves and his wet clothing. He mounted the staircase blindly, head hanging, swinging from side to side. Someone was going to pay, someone was going to answer – it was all he could think with any clarity amid the whirling, upthrown images of things spoiled or past redemption. He threw back his own door and clomped down the hallway towards the living room.

The girl was lying on the big sofa, her body twisted around so that one arm lay underneath it and the other was drooped to the carpet, as if she had been fending someone off. Her face confirmed that. Her very young, stranger's face. The blue eyes, heavily made up, were wide and terrified, staring directly at him as he entered the room. One of his ties – he immediately recognised the vivid pattern as that of a present he had received from Beth last Christmas – was tight around her slim throat.

He had strangled her, the body declared. In his apartment, with one of his ties. Her skirt was around her waist and she was wearing no underclothing. He had strangled her in a violent, sadistic rape after the drinks left half-emptied on the coffee table. In their struggle, which must have been very brief, she had overturned the standard lamp and rucked up the Chinese rug. But he had been too strong for her, and had raped and killed her. All of it was evident – *so* evident – to his heightened senses, that he at once listened to the street outside, waiting for the noise of police sirens. The slowing swish of a car –

– he touched the net curtains, but the car turned into a drive-

196

way across the street. He recognised it as that of a neighbour. Not yet, not quite yet –

He turned back to the girl's body. A teenage hooker, maybe even a schoolgirl, someone of no account to them, who could merely fulfil the part of a raped and murdered body. Like Beth, a bystander . . . They knew he was getting close and had to be stopped.

Something inside him was thinking beyond the panic the body inspired. It moved him to the bedroom and the safe under the floorboards, where he removed the fake passports that had been religiously renewed ever since his days with the Company. His hands started to fill a sports bag, when he found the pistol . . . only to replace it in the bedroom drawer because it would be found on him at any airport in the United States. Instead, he was prompted to gather his toilet bag, other things . . . crumbs of a life, like the photograph of Beth in a silver frame.

By the time he returned to the apartment's living room, he could hear the loudening noise of a siren. There was no time left.

Lock looked at the girl and the rage boiled inside him. But he also knew that the apartment had been taken from him, that he would never return here. Turgenev had taken Beth first, and now the rest of his ordinary life. Leaving him only with a past self he thought he would never again need; the man who knew how to kill people, how to deceive, how to escape, how to survive.

Turgenev . . . Vaughn Grainger had to tell him it was Turgenev, that he was behind everything, including the murder of this girl. When he heard it from Vaughn, he could –

He dragged himself away from the room and the girl's body, ran through the hallway, slamming the door of the apartment behind him. The siren's noise was audible on the landing.

Dmitri Gorov was shaken from an exhausted sleep by the telephone's peremptory insistence. He shrugged awake, sensing himself still clothed. His mouth was dry and tasted awful. He glowered at the dial of the clock as it came into focus. He must have fallen asleep about an hour ago, after Alexei had left. He

197

groaned and picked up the receiver. Goludin's excited, somehow boyish voice.

'– found it, sir! We've found – Marfa and me, we've got a bag of the stuff, heroin!'

'Calm down!' he growled. 'Where, how? Take it slowly.' Dmitri felt his own excitement. The cramped, dull room seemed warmer.

'One of the storerooms in the hospital.' His voice suddenly became a hoarse, theatrical whisper. 'Calling from there now. It's in my pocket, the evidence!' Then, after a pause: 'What do we do now?'

'Don't leave Marfa,' he ordered. 'I'll come over.' He rubbed his cheeks, then his weary, gritty eyes. 'I'll come over now. Stay with her till I get there – no one suspects?'

'No. We thought –' The voice was now an exhilarated chortle. '– someone was going to stumble right into us, but no one did. Footsteps outside the door, they just went on down the –'

'Never mind. Just try to act normally. Routinely. And – well done.'

He put down the receiver, after balancing it in his hand for a moment, wondering whether to call Vorontsyev.

'Leave him to rest,' he muttered as he got off the bed as heavily as an invalid. Then, like a fierce bout of indigestion, the enormity of what Goludin had told him struck his stomach, doubling him over. 'Jesus –!' But the exclamation was exultant. His hands clenched into fists as the tension eased and he straightened up. He wanted to punch them like an athlete signalling success. 'Got you! *Got* you!' he exhaled, grinning, rubbing his hands together as he hurried to the bathroom.

He flung cold water against the sleepy numbness of his face, towelled himself vigorously, then studied his features for a moment in the mirror, aware of the house's perpetual silence. A weary, ageing, defeated man stared back at him, belying the excitement that still wrenched at his stomach.

He dismissed the image and hurried from the bathroom, rubbing down his ragged dark hair, tugging on his overcoat. He almost failed to hear the telephone, even exclaimed against its noise as he turned back down the hall.

'Yes?' he snapped impatiently.

'Dmitri? It's Lubin. There's a report just in –' His voice was awed, as at news of a bereavement or the loss of a lifetime's savings. 'It's the chief, an explosion at his flat. The place is wrecked!'

'Is he alive?'

'I don't know, I've been trying to find out. The report's only just come in, from a patrol car. Half the house has caved in, a young woman and a child are dead for sure, but I –'

'Meet me there!' Dmitri snapped. *'Now!'*

He put down the receiver and turned, disorientated. He felt dizzy and sick. He put his hands gently to his face, as if to assure himself of his identity. His forehead was icily damp with perspiration, and he was once more aware of the house as silent and empty. Alexei, Alexei . . . They'd got to him because they were too close. Much too close to be left alive.

He stood in the doorway of his house, staring at the snow. They *had killed* Alexei.

Goludin reached the door of the ward, to find Dr David Schneider coming away from Marfa's bed. He had almost challenged the doctor before the realisation that Marfa was unharmed and was vigorously shaking her head beyond Schneider's shoulder to stop him. His cheeks flushed, and his eyes became shifty, unwilling to meet Schneider's careful inspection of him.

'I – thought you were guarding your colleague?' Schneider remarked. There was a nervousness about the American, but Goludin was aware only of his own embarrassed guilt. 'I found her bed empty and the sister unaware of your location,' Schneider added stiffly, as if imitating a formality of manner he did not feel. 'I've –' He attempted a reassuring smile. 'I've warned the young woman to stay in bed, for her own sake. OK?'

'Oh – what? Yes, yes –' Marfa was still shaking her head as if in warning. What excuse had she given, what if *he* was asked where they'd been? 'Sorry about that.' Schneider's Russian was schoolroom correct, carefully enunciated. Yet Goludin was

199

aware that his own replies made him seem the user of an unfamiliar language.

Schneider, he was certain, suspected something. Then the doctor nodded dismissively, and moved past him. Goludin hurried to the bed, blurting:

'What did you say?'

'That I went to the toilet while you must have wandered off for something to eat!' she replied excitedly. 'Well?'

'Dmitri's on his way here now – we just have to sit tight!' He was grinning in imitation of her now, the tension radiating from both of them in the aftermath of their discovery. 'Bloody hell! We've done it, Marfa – we've actually done it!'

Schneider paused in the corridor to glance back through the windows set in the ward's fire doors. He saw the young detective bending over the woman in the bed. It was as if they were children hugging a secret to themselves and congratulating themselves on their knowledge. The realisation was an icy trickle in the small of his back. He hurried to the lifts.

He'd kept an eye on them, suspecting they had been deliberately secreted into the hospital, arrivals in some Trojan horse. Yet they'd done nothing, seemed to know nothing, have little or no suspicion; a rather intense young woman and a clodhopping detective. They had gradually ceased to represent any danger.

Now –?

He thrust through the lift doors even as they began to open and clattered along the corridor in the basement towards the storeroom. He passed a nurse whose arms were laden with fresh linen and who nodded respectfully. He felt his returned smile was sickly.

He inspected the lock. There appeared to be no damage, no signs that it had been forced. He unlocked it and let himself inside, relocking the door before switching on the lights. At once, it seemed, he saw the small, spilt patch of white powder on the floor, though in fact it must have been some seconds later. He moved slowly towards it, his heart thudding in his chest, his side feeling winded. He bent awkwardly down like an old man, wetting his finger, touching the powder, tasting –

– spitting it out. It was the horse. His body was bathed in

sweat. He glanced wildly up at the shelving, then rose to his feet, clambering and scrabbling to the top of the shelves as if to escape rising water. Found the opened box, touched it again and again in disbelief and the wish that he was wrong; the fervent wish that . . .

He slid rather than climbed to the floor. Rested his head against the cold metal of the shelving. Banged his fist limply against a shelf, as images of the woman in the bed and the stupid young male detective appeared in his head, like mocking masks. How could *they* have found it, those *amateurs*, those morons . . . ? The older cop suspected him, he knew . . . One of the packets was missing, they had evidence now. Hard evidence. They'd come looking for him with a warrant.

He sniffed. He had to tell Panshin. Now that Rawls was dead, only Panshin could get him out from under, help him climb out of the deep mire he was in —

'Calm down, Panshin!' Bakunin barked, his hand clenching in a strangling motion on the desk. 'It's been taken care of! The head has been chopped off the chicken, you're just watching the body die.' He listened. 'They can be dealt with easily. Just tell the American doctor to calm down. What's the matter with these people, haven't they anything resembling guts?' They were all grasping and pathetic, like Rawls, who had been too greedy and whose removal had brought the others back into line. An *example* had been made and had had its effect. Now, because some of the shipment awaiting transport on from Novyy Urengoy had been stumbled on by a moronic detective second-grade and a woman, the panic had broken out again like a revisiting epidemic. Schneider and Panshin — what poor straw-men they both were. Greed was their only confidence; otherwise, they were negative, empty, grubby creatures. In-vertebrates.

'Tell Schneider to watch them, see who visits them. And reassure him, Panshin. Tell him everything has been dealt with, that everything is now *OK*. Do you understand? The head has been cut off the chicken. Tell him that!'

Bakunin thrust down the receiver, the fingers of his other

hand drumming on the desk. The morning was sullen, skulking like a reluctant worker beyond his office windows. Hiding behind cloud.

What *was* the matter with these people? he asked himself again. Did they . . . ? He inspected the idea that had sprung into consciousness. Handled it like a priceless vase. Did they want *another* example? Is that what they needed?

It might, anyway, be sensible to remove Schneider, even if it was no longer necessary.

The shadows of the mountains shrank like curled, dried leaves in the Arizona sunrise as the flight from Baltimore dropped out of a cloudless desert sky towards Phoenix. Lock watched the landscape brighten into aridity, become hard, unforgiving; a reflection, he realised, of the man who observed it from the Boeing's high, small window.

Ahead and to port, reservoirs gleamed as small as puddles after a shower, and Phoenix glinted through the haze of distance. He felt his tension return and stirred in his seat to ease its slow, certain grip on his stomach.

He had abandoned the hire car, taken the airline shuttle bus from downtown up Interstate 95 to Baltimore-Washington airport in Maryland. The red-eye to Phoenix and Tucson had not been under surveillance, his false identity had not been challenged at the gate – despite the first reports on CNN of the Georgetown murder and the proclamation of his identity and background and an old, State Department photograph of him that had appeared on the portable TV being watched by the black woman working at the newsstand. He had made the aircraft carrying only the shreds of calm and resolve with him, his past as intangible and lost as old, flaking skin shed by his body.

As the Boeing had lifted into the Maryland night sky and pushed through rain into starlight, all the people he had been had seemed like figures, far out to sea, drowning. The orphaned child with the elder sister who organised his life and eased his grief; the college student and basketball player, the *cum laude* graduate; the CIA field agent who had *enjoyed* his bitter little war; the State Department expert on the new, chaotic Russian

Federation; the occasional, uncommitted lover, the dutiful, accomplished partygoer and dinner guest, the music buff. They were all out there, in the deep, drowning. As others watched the inflight movie or tried to sleep, he watched his past slip beneath the waves, unable to save any of those people he had been –

– except one. Except for the trained, artificial person he had been for a few short years when he had worked for the CIA. That younger man was the only person he had ever been who could – *now* – hope to survive; the one who had packed the sports bag, collected the money and the false papers and had been able to ignore the dead girl lying in his apartment.

As America, deep in night, slid beneath the aircraft, he came to a gradual, reluctant accommodation with John Lock, field agent – a man who had killed people, arranged death, employed cunning and ruthlessness; who had survived Afghanistan. That man was all he was allowed and all he wanted to be; because he was the only one who could get close enough to Turgenev to kill him.

He had drowsed for a time after accepting that fact. The lights of Oklahoma City, after all the other cities, and then a brief, almost dreamless sleep. He had woken only when they served breakfast, feeling stale but alert, tense more than tired. Hardly fearful, hardly at all.

Phoenix's desert and glass towers and the giant cactuses. The low, purple hills, the tiny shadows, windscreens on the highway glinting like semaphore, then the aircraft was making its final approach to Sky Harbor airport. The mountains suddenly surrounded the city and were taller than the flightpath. He had to hear from Vaughn Grainger's lips that Turgenev had ordered Billy's death, that Tran was not the main man, that it was Turgenev behind the heroin smuggling. Vaughn had to tell him that Turgenev now wanted the whole pie for himself.

The wheels touched the runway, skipped then settled and the turbines whined in deceleration. Turgenev had gotten greedy and decided to take the whole shooting match away from Vaughn and Billy. When he heard it from Vaughn's lips, then however long it took and by whatever means, he would avenge Beth's

203

murder. Avenge even the teenage hooker dead in his apartment.

The aircraft slowed, then turned off the runway towards the blinding mirror of the terminal building. Sunlight flooded the cabin. People stirred as if from hibernation. He shook himself and stared abstractedly through the window until the plane's flank met the tunnel in a kiss and the passenger door was opened. He waited. The other passengers could disembark first, in case they were waiting for him, the Phoenix cops or the Bureau.

Eventually, he walked off the aircraft, smiling conventionally at the conventional smile of the stewardess, the sports bag in his left hand, his right hand aware that he was unarmed. Would they guess he had come to Phoenix? How could they?

The first cop seemed unaware of him, talking to a man in a loud check jacket and a straw hat. A family passed him, the man and woman bulbous in shell suits, children and suitcases towed behind them. He had no luggage to collect and headed for the cab rank, walking towards the blinding desert sunlight as if towards a searchlight. Another indifferent cop. He felt the sweat as a thin, damp line along his collar and forehead. Then he was out into the hard sunlight, his eyes squeezed narrow against its glare. The heat of the morning was already intense. He felt exposed in his grey suit and tie amid the splashes of bright shirts and colourful shorts and print frocks. He bent hurriedly into the driver's window of the first cab and murmured:

'Mountain Park Hospital, fast as you can make it.' The driver's shrug invited him into the rear of the cab. He looked around him. No one seemed interested in him, no one at all.

He sat back in the plastic bench seat, the sports bag beside him, hot from his moments in the sun. He rubbed his unshaven face, feeling as trapped in his clothing as he did in the interior of the battered Chrysler. The cab driver's Latino eyes studied him indifferently in the mirror. Lock turned his head and looked back along McDowell, then studied the cars that turned after the cab onto 7th Avenue. It didn't seem as if anyone was tailing them, but he was suddenly too weary to be certain.

The hospital gleamed like polished desert rock in the morning sun. He paid the driver, then glanced at the few cars that had turned into the driveway behind the cab. None of them seemed suspicious, no one stayed behind a tinted windscreen. He entered the air-conditioned foyer gratefully, his steps increasingly leaden as he headed for the Grainger Wing. As if he had come, unarmed, to challenge a lord in his castle, not to interrogate one old man concerning his twenty-year criminality. Lock took the lift to the top floor.

A panoramic window looking over the park towards the New River mountains. Cactus and the flash of a hummingbird against the glass, come to sip at the provided liquor containers. He realised that the duty nurse recognised him.

'Mr Grainger is very much better, Mr Lock,' she announced. 'We thought you'd returned to Washington – ?'

'Uh, yes. But I –' He shrugged. 'There isn't anyone else, no other family. I felt –'

'We understand, Mr Lock. I'm sure Mr Grainger will appreciate your visit.' She got up. 'I'll just see if he's awake, and prepare him.'

She entered Vaughn's room, leaving Lock alone in the corridor. A moment later she returned, beckoning him through the door.

'I'll leave you two alone together, Mr Lock. Try not to tire him.' Lock nodded and the door closed behind him.

He was immediately aware of his familiarity to the nurse, aware of his name and the photograph on CNN. The woman would be on the day shift, she would have had time to watch the news. He shivered. Vaughn Grainger, he realised as he became accustomed to the shadowy, blinded room, was watching him with fierce eyes. He moved slowly to the bed.

'Uh – hi, Vaughn. How are you?' he murmured awkwardly. Involuntarily, he glanced at the heart monitor, which bleeped softly, regularly, and at the tubes that connected the old man to the monitors and the medication. 'Vaughn – ?' The old man was staring at him, but the fierceness in his eyes was lifeless, as if he had died or been paralysed in a moment of rage.

Grainger raised his hand and indicated a chair beside the bed. Lock offered to take his hand, but it was withdrawn to the languor of the smooth white sheets. He sat down. The room seemed hot despite the purr of the air-conditioning. A bird sang outside the window.

'I – had to come back,' Lock announced, rubbing at his damp, prickling forehead.

'Why?'

Lock tried to reassure himself that he possessed sufficient time. He had glanced almost subliminally at the newspaper headlines as he passed the airport newsstand. He hadn't made the front page. The Washington PD would not necessarily assume he'd come back here. Rather the opposite. There was time –

'Vaughn –' He cleared his throat, leaning towards the old man's sculpted, arrogant features propped against the plump white pillows; an invalid pope or king. 'Vaughn, I know some things,' he began. 'I've been told some things. Reasons why Billy and Beth were killed . . .' His words failed against the old man's pleading and contempt. Lock was staring at two faces, Vaughn in the past and present, both there in the room.

'What things?' It was the Vaughn he had always known who triumphed, as if there was no right on earth that allowed anyone to question his actions. 'What's gotten into you, John?'

It was a trick. The heart monitor bumped its green, charted line more quickly and more irregularly across the screen and he could hear Vaughn's stertorous breathing. It was nothing but an old man acting a part too young for him; unsustainable illusion.

'Vaughn,' he pressed more confidently, 'you know what things. Things about Tran, about you and 'Nam . . . Billy, too. Those things –'

The liver-spotted right hand gripped his wrist like the talon of a hunting bird. Vaughn's eyes blazed.

'What in hell made you *ask*? Why in hell did you want to know?'

He shook the old man's grip away.

'They killed my sister!' It was an enraged whisper. Vaughn seemed more distant, shrunken, his face that of a stranger. 'You think I could forget that? You think it's something *to* forget?'

Grainger's head moved from side to side amid the pillows in what might have been distress rather than denial. His hand now patted the bed impotently. The heart monitor was like a radio

206

picking up a distant and elusive signal. Then Grainger gestured at his mouth, then at the oxygen mask hanging over the head of the bed. Lock passed it to him. The room seemed filled with greedy sucking noises . . . which gradually calmed. Eventually, he removed the mask. The monitor had settled like his chest into regularity. Another trick? At any moment, just by calling or pressing his bell, Grainger could end the conversation. He would have to leave.

The old man's eyes glittered wetly.

'You shouldn't have looked, John-Boy. You shouldn't have turned over the stones. There's only ugliness there.' His breathing was loud and tired.

'I had to – don't you understand?' Lock pleaded in his turn.

Grainger nodded reluctantly.

'Yes – but it's done you no good, John . . . You can't do anything. Nothing. This is a grown-ups' game, not an adventure. You won't get called into the house for peanut butter and a bath just as the game gets interesting, John.' His hand was patting Lock's now. 'They won't let you.'

'Vaughn, my bridges have all been burned behind me. They saw to it. A dead girl in my apartment, the cops tipped off. I know how they play!'

The revelation surprised Grainger. His skin became more pallid. The monitor bumped like the index of a failing economy.

'You can't do anything.'

'There's nothing else I want to do,' Lock replied.

Grainger studied his features as he might have done that of some surgeon or priest newly arrived at his bedside, offering life and hope. To Lock, the regularity of the heart monitor was now clocklike, marking time he could not afford.

'They'll kill you, John. I can't let that happen . . . not after everything.' He was suddenly weeping uncontrollably, silently, the tears running down the pale, leathery old skin of his cheeks, darkening the collar of his pyjama jacket. 'John-Boy, I just *can't* tell you –! You can't do anything except get yourself killed, and I can't let you do that.'

Silence, then, into which the hum of machines entered quietly. Then the noises of the distant hospital routine. Vaughn's breathing, his own, the soft blipping of the heart monitor.

Eventually, he said gently: 'You have to tell me, Vaughn. You just have to.'

Another silence, before: 'How much do you know?'

'I know about you and Tran — I know how you turned the company around in the '70s. With heroin.' He glanced at the monitor, but there was no quickening of its trace. 'I don't know if Billy was involved way back —' Grainger shook his head.

'He wasn't,' he growled defiantly. Lock nodded, attempting a smile.

'I know how you brought the drugs in. I know why you did it. A guy called Kauffman in the CIA —' It was evident that Grainger recognised the name. '— he told me all he knew, which was most of it.'

Each phrase, each nugget of accusation, prompted a small jerk of Grainger's head. There was pain in his eyes, together with defiance. Rather than guilt, there was the sense of a gambler who had lost; no self-revulsion, just a flinty admission that the game was over and he had been beaten. Guilt was for the little guys, the no-accounts. The realisation hardened Lock and enabled him to say curtly:

'But it went on, changed into a new inning, right? The game wasn't over when you turned the company around, when you were riding high. Why, Vaughn? Was it too hard or too easy to stop?'

Grainger's gnarled hands closed into fists on the sheet. The accusations demeaned him. Lock was contemptuous of him, morally superior. Grainger's features sharpened, became cold as in death.

'You'll never know,' he replied. 'Will you, John-Boy? You'll never know.' The dismissive chuckle rattled in his throat. The heart monitor was steady as if by an effort of will.

'One thing I do know, Vaughn — and it's a fact — Pete Turgenev's the main man. Not *you*.'

It was true, then. The blanched skin, the pinpricks of pink on the cheekbones, the glare in his eyes — and the hands, working with the cotton of the sheet as if it was something that writhed in his grip and fought him.

208

Lock said: 'It's a long time since you headed the whole thing up – isn't it, Vaughn? Neither you nor Billy has been in control. *Pete*'s the studio boss – uh?'

Grainger did not reply. His glittering, pale eyes moved furiously, seeking escape, justification, perhaps even continued silence. Lock was aware of the warm room, the heat of tension that seemed to enclose them, the bed, the dazzling frame given to the blinds by the desert morning outside the steady, almost monotonous blips of the heart monitor, charting Grainger's life like a seabed.

'What happened, Vaughn?' Lock asked eventually, in a soothing voice, trying a change of mood. At once, the old man's eyes softened, became calmer and less focused. 'When did it all start going wrong?'

Another silence, the heart monitor like a ticking watch marking Lock's sense of time wasted, making his body jump with nerves.

'A long time ago,' the old man offered to the ceiling, as if Lock was a priest from a faith still disavowed. 'Somehow Turgenev knew about Vietnam . . . the guy *was* KGB, wasn't he? He'd know those things, or make it his business to find out. He came with an offer – to Billy. Billy almost threw him out. I –' The voice faltered. 'I had to – to put Billy straight on a few things . . .' The hands worked at the cotton sheet again, this time in furious smoothing motions. Lock sensed Billy's outrage, and was thankful for it. 'Billy *liked* being a *multi*-millionaire,' Vaughn Grainger offered to the room by way of justification.

'Heroin smuggled via Siberia, right?'

'Right. We went ahead. We wanted to get into Siberia, open it up. It gave us the funds when the banks weren't lending to expand. Heroin was a loan, no more than a wise investment. 'Tran and other people had the network, from back then. We just activated it.' Then, contemptuously: 'The CIA used heroin as another currency – we did the same, John-Boy!' There was no special pleading in the rage, merely an informative tone. This is the way the world dances, boy, and you'd better get used to it. Perhaps he'd told Billy in the same manner?

'I understand,' he soothed.

209

There was a bright gleam of disdain in Grainger's stare.

'Not you, John-Boy – not you. You think the world works another way. It doesn't.'

'What happened that made Billy's death necessary?'

Grainger swallowed; an ugly, guttural noise. Then he said: 'Turgenev wanted to take over – just like that. He had a plan all ready to present to us here in Phoenix. Last week, was it . . . ?' The old man seemed terrified at the vagueness of memory rather than at the recalled events.

'Yes, last week,' Lock confirmed, feeling nauseous.

'Billy was stalling him, trying to bring in big new investors, interest the banks in rescheduling the company debt . . . Turgenev knew he had the arm on us, he knew we couldn't stand up to his dummy corporation trying to buy us out – or we'd all go down the tubes and into jail for a thousand years apiece!' The hands were strangling something on the bed again, the head was raised slightly from the pillows, the neck muscles ropelike, the eyes staring.

Lock snapped: 'So you knew he must have killed Beth and Billy, right from the beginning!'

'I swear to God, no!' His head turned to stare at Lock, appalled that he could have been so misjudged, so blackened. 'I knew hardly anything, almost nothing at all . . . Billy explained here, last week, the week before. I was involved only with the Foundation –' It sounded so much like plea-bargaining that Lock was revolted by it. 'It was only then I found out that Turgenev and some other people, the Russian mafia over here, in our country, wanted to move in and move us out. I swear to you, John, I didn't know . . .' What had begun as a protestation became, even as he spoke, a recognition of weakness and self-contempt. He lay back on the pillow, releasing Lock's hand, and stared defiantly at the ceiling, where the blind's shadow was thrown like the white bars of a cage imprisoning darkness. Then he announced: 'The asshole government, the banks, the big corporations – no one realises the Russian mafia's here, organised, in big numbers. They'll wake up to it too late to do anything about it.'

'You knew he'd killed them, though?' Lock prompted, their

210

breathing audible in the room, almost masking the heart monitor as it returned to calm. It hurried once more as the question was asked.

Grainger shook his head. 'I didn't know. Maybe I – I didn't believe it. Maybe I underestimated . . . I didn't know, not right off.'

'But eventually . . . ?'

'No one wanted Beth killed, John.'

'Turgenev did.'

'His goons killed her.'

'His orders. You know that, Vaughn.'

After a long time: 'I know it.'

Lock sat back in his chair, drained. The old man seemed calm, empty, waiting to die rather than recover. There was nothing more he could learn – and there was nothing more he could do, or wished to do, for Vaughn Grainger. The room was intolerably warm, as if the air-conditioning had failed. It was finished now – or begun. Perhaps that was the reality. Had he wanted Grainger to deny everything, turn him around so that he could go back to Washington and to being who he had been – until last week? He shook his head. No, he hadn't wanted that. But hadn't expected this *emptiness* either, this vacuum inside himself.

Grainger startled him. Still staring at the narrow ribs of sunlight thrown on the ceiling, he said:

'You take care, John. You take good care.'

There was a sense of concern and even pride in the voice. Perhaps, most weirdly, a sense of recognition, as if they were united now, the same kind of people.

He stood up. Accepting everything else, he could not permit the chasm between himself and Grainger to be bridged. He turned away, hearing the old man murmur:

'Take care, John. Good luck –'

Then he was through the door and the nurse looked up in a moment of concern, then a longer instant of bright optimism.

'You didn't tire him too much?' she chided.

'What –? Oh, no. Thank you, sister. I have something to do now, you'll excuse me –?'

211

'He shouldn't be using you to run business errands for him, Mr Lock. The doctors prescribed *complete* rest –'

He turned on her angrily. 'I think he's easy in his mind, nurse. I really do!'

He turned away from her and down the corridor, her little puffs of offended professionalism sounding like the noises of a small engine. He waited for the lift without glancing back at her, then descended to the foyer of the Grainger Wing. Its emblem, name, motto, all offended; paint on a skull, white on a whore. Conscience money. He strode towards the entrance, the sports bag swinging at his side like a weapon. The doors sighed back, allowing him into the heat and light.

He stood, half-blinded, on the marble steps, his fingers dabbling in his breast pocket for his sunglasses. He saw no police vehicles, no one watching him, as his eyes adjusted to the glare. As he slipped on the glasses, there was a faint noise near his head like an angered insect. Nothing else for an instant, but even before he could raise his hand to waft it aside, the glass of the doors behind him shattered.

He heard a scream, drawn out and low, as adrenalin surged through his body and he fell, then rolled across the steps. Gunshot, silenced weapon. More shattering glass, then he saw marble chip and fly up from the impact of a third shot, beside his head. He heard it whine away in ricochet.

Heard, too, the noise of police sirens –

Pyotr Leonidovich Turgenev scanned the sheet he had removed from his secure fax, nodding in self-compliment. The takeover of Grainger Technologies by his dummy corporation in America was meeting with little in the way of resistance. Grainger-Turgenev would become, apparently but not in reality, an entirely separate and autonomous company, the dummy corporation buying out the Grainger shareholding. He placed the fax sheet on his broad walnut desk and walked to the wall-length windows of his study. Elsewhere in the office suite, even late in the evening, his secretaries and assistants continued to monitor his business interests, share purchases, currency dealing.

The security lights mounted along the eaves of the hunting lodge cast purple-tinged shadows on the snow that stretched away from the window towards the belt of trees which encircled the estate. There was a faint, livid glow away to the south where Novyy Urengoy lay like a pool of brackish water, festering and vile. He detested the place and its concerns – even those which involved him. Novyy Urengoy was people like Panshin, the American Schneider – like Rawls before him a craven, greedy, spineless thing – and even Bakunin, the peasant GRU colonel. He disliked their necessity in the scheme of things, their satellite status around his star.

The hunting lodge had once belonged to a half-mad prince from the last century. He had built it in the middle of Siberia's desolation, far from plentiful game and wildfowl, had dug lakes, planted trees, had imported deer, bear, fox and duck to kill at his leisure.

There was, he admitted, something admirable about the scale of the thing and the wealth necessary to create a hunting estate in a barren wilderness at the edge of the arctic tundra. He enjoyed the house – more than the New York apartment, less than the villa in Antibes, and perhaps to the same degree as the ranch in Montana. Moscow and Petersburg he loathed equally.

He rubbed his long forefinger up and down the aquiline curve of his nose, staring out at the snow. A secretary entered after knocking, explained the urgency of some papers. He gestured they be placed on his desk and dismissed the woman with another wave of his hand. He was content – no, it was *necessary* – to brood for a few minutes longer. Lock, the subject of his mood, was little more than an itch. He was all but less than nothing. And yet ... he was still out there, even after the frame-up involving the dead hooker in his apartment. The police had been only moments too slow, but Lock had blundered through the closing trap, and was now in Phoenix. What did he expect to learn? Turgenev knew what he could be told by Grainger, but he wondered how much Lock desired those truths. Did he really want to bring his world crashing down?

Turgenev smiled in puzzlement. He disliked not really knowing Lock. In Afghanistan, he seemed always in Billy's shadow, a somehow formless, immature figure; dull, conventional, almost prim, a maiden aunt in a war zone. He smiled again. That had been true . . . the man had had the necessary courage, he had absorbed his training well, he'd survived a few tight situations. But he hadn't been real, somehow, not quite *there*.

Did his ignorance threaten to cause him to underestimate Lock? He didn't think so – he simply liked certainty.

But then, he was certain of his people and Tran's people. They would eliminate Lock . . .

He snapped his fingers to summon his attention to the desk and its papers. Lock was a dead man. The local problem of Vorontsyev had been settled –

He paused for a moment. He *had* underestimated Vorontsyev. The policeman he had thought ineffectual, almost a dilettante or intellectual, morose and solitary, hanging on for his pension, had surprised him by persisting; by getting as close as he had done before he had been stopped.

Therefore, *had* he underestimated Lock?

He resolved the question by sitting in the leather swivel chair behind the desk, his back to the window, and taking up the sheaf of papers the secretary had brought in.

No, he had not underestimated the man. Lock was about to go under for the third time – not waving but drowning.

His hand grabbed instinctively for the sports bag he had dropped, scrabbling like a crab across the marble steps, as the police sirens loudened and he tensed against the next bullet. Then Lock rolled across the mosaic inlay towards the shattered open doors of the hospital. Something puckered the marble near him and buzzed angrily away. Then he was on patterned carpet, his body colliding with a woman stretched prone and terrified in the foyer. He got to his knees and scuttled away from the door. The carpet was littered with frightened bodies as if there had been an air raid.

There was blood on one bright print frock, then he was on his feet and blundering past a nurse in uniform and a doctor kneeling over someone else in shock. His heart thudded against his ribs, the tempo of his panic. He fled past the lifts, hardly aware of his direction, allowing the survival mechanisms to dictate to him. He plunged down steps into an empty, soughing corridor that smelt aseptic and safe.

Whether they were Tran's people or belonged to Turgenev no longer mattered. All that was important was that he was still acting like a slow-moving target, open to surprise, easy to kill —

— stairs ascending again. He glanced back along the corridor. Two distant white-coated figures, neither of them in pursuit of him. He clambered up the stairs, his breathing loud and ragged, his legs heavy. He emerged into a smaller, more cramped foyer. Accident and Emergency. A man was bleeding onto thermoplastic tiles from a head wound, there was another man with a bandaged arm. A harried, untidy nurse belied the orderly calm of the Grainger Wing before the first shot. He blundered through the stiffly opening doors into the hard, varnished sunlight and onto the dusty concrete of a car park. He could immediately hear the police sirens, and glanced wildly around him. The staff car park, ranks of cars and 4WDs glinting with chrome and glass.

A woman standing beside one small Nissan sedan was struggling into a white coat. He ran towards her. At once, her face was startled and determined.

'Keys!' he snapped. 'I don't have time to explain, give me the car keys!'

She was frightened, but not sufficiently. He saw her raise the keys to throw them out into the car park. He snatched at her wrist, smelling her perfume and fear at once, his face close to hers. Her eyes were wide, panicked at the prospect of violence. He wanted to shake his head, but thrust her away, keeping hold of the keys.

'I just want your car!' he shouted at her like a plea, and unlocked the door. Her fear changed into outraged anger. She was looking around for help; then she began moving towards him as he threw the sports bag into the back of the car. A baby seat, empty, for which he was thankful.

'Hey —!' she began, but he glowered at her.

'Lady — *doctor* —! Just keep away from the car!' He climbed in and fumbled the key into the ignition. It fired first time. The

215

woman was banging the driver's window. He waved her away, snarling: 'Get away from the car!'

He let off the brake and the car surged forward, brushing her aside. The tyres squealed on the hot concrete as he headed the car wildly towards the barrier of the car park, which swung up at his approach. The woman, waving her arms in furious anger, diminished in the mirror. The Nissan bumped out onto a narrow road. He turned . . .

. . . north. Towards the mountains and the desert beyond them. Out of Phoenix.

Away from the airport – there were other airports. He accelerated away from the traffic lights, turning onto Black Canyon Highway – Interstate 17. Flagstaff was a hundred and forty miles north. It had an airport, flights out of Arizona. Far enough to begin with. He studied the mirror. He was sweating profusely but his temperature and heartbeat were returning to normal. There was a sense of exhilaration nudging aside the shock of the unexpected attack.

The cactuses lined the road now like crosses. There didn't seem to be a car in the mirrors, intent on pursuit or on matching his speed. With luck, he had perhaps thirty minutes before the police put up a helicopter to monitor the I-17 and the other roads out of the city. The doctor would describe her car, describe him. He would, in a half-hour at most, be identified as John Lock, fugitive. Less if they asked the nurse outside Grainger's room.

The suburbs straggled away on either side of the highway. As if dousing green and gold fires, crop-spraying hoses fountained great peacocks' tails of water that rainbowed in the sun. An aircraft dropped towards Sky Harbor airport. The mountains opened. Cholla, prickly pear and saguaro cactus populated a dusty expanse as the road began to climb towards the New River mountains and into the Sonoran desert. Sun City, nibbling at farmland, lay behind him in the mirrors, as ordered as a trailer park, the planted fields seemly and neat. Phoenix was little more than a mirage in the morning heat.

He began scanning the high desert air, paling to colourlessness, for the first signs of a police helicopter. He realised he

216

had to get rid of the car but shivered at the thought, the desert suddenly more real, pressing around the air-conditioned box of the Nissan. He had to have another car, and quickly.

TEN

A Form of Escape

'Good, good,' Turgenev murmured, adding: 'That's fine, Ivan – and thank Takis for me.' He settled back in the leather swivel chair, watching the smoke rise from the Cuban cigar resting in the onyx ashtray. 'I'll leave the detail with you – sure, I'll be there for the signing of the new contracts. How hot is Athens at this time of the year? Good . . .' He chuckled companionably with the caller, the CEO of Grainger-Turgenev in Greece. 'OK, talk to you soon.'

He put down the telephone, picked up the cigar and puffed contentedly at it. He was aware of himself in the gilt mirror on one wall, exuding what the English would call complacency. He smiled at his image, and was tempted to wink at himself. The Athens operation was an unqualified success. The Greek government scheme, seventy per cent financed by the European Commission in Brussels, to bring Russian natural gas to Athens via a pipeline from Bulgaria, had become hopelessly behind schedule. To avoid the penalty clause in the original contract, Russian contractors had been offered a bigger share of the project. It was worth, conservatively, as much as six per cent of the total cost, perhaps fifty million dollars, to Grainger-Turgenev. *His* company.

Besides which, he reminded himself, Greece was his own judas gate into the billions of dollars that could be siphoned off from the EC over the next few years. Greece alone would receive twenty billion écus over five years . . . the opportunities for profits were enormous.

He put down the cigar and rubbed his eyes. He slipped on half-glasses to study the sheaf of reports that had been left on his desk. In a week's time, he expected a delegation of senior politicians from the republics of Central Asia – Kazakhstan, Turkmenistan, Uzbekistan and Azerbaijan – at the hunting lodge. A crucial meeting. The gasfields and oilfields that clustered around the Caspian Sea had been called *the new Gulf*. Western Siberia's output was gradually falling . . . He had to take advantage of the opening up of the Asian fields. To wrest the potential huge profits from the pipeline work, the terminal construction on the Black Sea, in conjunction with Chevron and other US and European companies, was a prize almost beggaring belief.

And within his grasp. He closed his hand on the desk, as if merely flexing it, opened and closed it again and again as he read the reports. Grainger Technologies, which would be his within days, a couple of weeks at most, was crucial to his strategy. Billy should have stood aside – Turgenev sucked his teeth as he recalled Billy on that last evening, at his Maryland home, sweating, guilty, defiant and washed up . . . Billy should have sold out to him, or at least agreed that the Central Asian project was the future – *their* mutual future – for the next twenty-five years. But Billy hadn't seen it, wouldn't agree . . . poor Billy.

He finished reading. The planning had been exact, even to the removal of Billy Grainger and the acquisition of the company. Finance, cooperation, funding, strategy – and murder. Meticulously considered and arranged. Billy's death was business by other means, he smiled to himself, consciously misquoting Clausewitz.

Against all of which Lock was merely a hornet buzzing outside the window of his study . . . a harmless nuisance, like a beggar in the street.

His hand passed over the sheaf of papers, brushing away a small grey beetle of cigar ash. The sister's death, of course, had been unavoidable. If Billy's murder had not been disguised as violent robbery, he would not have been as easy to kill for some time after that night. Beth had, unfortunately, therefore been endangered along with Billy. And Billy's bout of Protestant morality regarding the heroin had sealed his fate as much as the necessity to direct Grainger Technologies towards the rewards of the new oil power region of Central Asia. He had to have

219

control of Grainger by the time the delegation arrived. He had to be able to offer them a package, a unitary capability that would outweigh other consortia.

Eventually, there would be no need for the fuel of heroin to power his empire – but that time was not yet. Just as one day, the smuggling of nuclear scientists and technicians to Iran and Iraq would prove unnecessary. At present, however, it gave him presence and leverage in the Middle East, dealing with those governments the West kept at arm's length.

He looked at his watch. Nearly midnight. The woman had arrived earlier in the evening and now awaited him like the denizen of a harem. He grinned. Time for bed . . . He bent and picked up the faxed sheet from the floor where it had curled itself into a tube. It referred to Lock's escape from the Mountain Park Hospital. Lock had spoken with Grainger. He knew it all now. That had been what had enraged him, but now he contemplated it calmly. Lock was the subject of a manhunt across the continental United States. He was a plague carrier, a leper and outcast with nowhere to go. If and when he was arrested – if Turgenev's own people were beaten in the race by the police – who would believe him? He was a sex murderer; a teenage heroin addict, playing at prostitution to feed her habit, had died. Lock had killed her. There were even witnesses. Lock would *never* get out from under . . .

. . . even though his death would be simpler and more satisfying.

He placed the fax on his desk and barely paused to consider it further. Tran's people, working in harness with his own men, would prevent Lock ever leaving Arizona. They had a car registration, a description, a possible sighting on the Interstate 17, heading north into the desert.

Turgenev was whistling softly to himself as he switched out the lights in his study. For a moment he watched the pale glow of security lights and snow reflected into the darkened room. Then he finally closed and locked the door behind him and began climbing the wide staircase with its elaborately carved banister towards his bedroom.

*   *   *

220

It was a place called Bumble Bee, west of the I-17, which he had left at Rock Springs. The Sonoran dust blew through it on the slight breeze, and the wooden stores, hotel and handful of houses seemed almost desiccated by the sun. Even the image of Colonel Sanders seemed more aged and leather-skinned above the diner. There was a garage and petrol station next to the Kentucky Fried Chicken parlour and a large sign above a low building that claimed it was the General Store and that it possessed Jeeps for Hire. It was what he had been seeking and he felt the relief rumble though him like the subterranean approach of a subway train.

The traffic was little more than a duo of pick-up trucks and a dusty Oldsmobile. Figures in stetsons and denims added to the sense of timelessness as if the place had been bypassed by the years as surely as it had been by the interstate highway. There were hills like broken teeth in red-sand gums to the west and south; omnipresent saguaro cactus, and yucca and pine and oak woodland darkened the slopes of the mountains to the north.

His body was quivering with released tension as he climbed stiffly out of the car into the baking, suffocating heat and the gritty dust. The breeze was like the breath of a furnace. Even so, he shivered. The sight of a TV aerial was sufficient. This was a town, however fossilised; there would be newspapers, TV, radio, any of which could be broadcasting and detailing a description of him and the Nissan. He had drawn the car into a narrow space in the shadow of a dilapidated trailer parked behind the garage. It might go unregarded for two or three hours. A repair truck masked it from the main street of the town. He pulled out the sports bag and locked the Nissan. Then he dropped the keys and dustily kicked them beneath the car.

Lock crossed to the store, his assumed nonchalance threadbare even to himself. He nodded to an old man perched on a hard chair on a wooden verandah. The sidewalk creaked beneath his shoes – city shoes, city suit. He cleared his throat and entered the cooler, musty air of the store. It was a little before noon and he was tired: dragged down, too, by the revelations in that hot, quiet room in the hospital and by the sense of what dimly lay ahead of him.

221

'Good morning.'

The storekeeper, in a tartan shirt and denims – his stomach spilt the pattern of the shirt over his belt – studied him, then asked:

'How come you parked all the way over there?'

'I – er, I didn't want to be in anyone's way, block anyone,' he replied lamely. 'I want to hire a jeep, do some desert sightseeing . . .'

'We got jeeps. You from Phoenix?'

'Visiting. My – er, my wife's been taken into hospital. Appendicitis. She's OK, but I didn't want to hang around, kicking my heels for the next –'

'I'm not your father, boy – you don't need to explain. You want a jeep, I can hire you a jeep. You got desert clothes, boots?' There was an increased eagerness – and innocence – in the inspection now being carried out. There was no suspicion of him except as a stranger. A lofty, dismissive contempt. 'Everything you're gonna need is right over there,' the storekeeper said, the foretaste of profit gleaming in his eye. His hand caressed his greying beard as if he were milking something. Lock was thankful for the safety implicit in the man's attention to business, to fleecing the city-feller who walked in out of the sun looking for a vicarious, safe experience in the Sonoran desert.

'You got to take out insurance – I got the forms right here,' he continued, following Lock to the counter set in front of a window looking out over the forecourt and the petrol pumps. There were hunting rifles and handguns, desert boots, denims, thick shirts, knives. Lock controlled his breathing. The place had the excitement of an Aladdin's cave. 'You want a hunting licence, feller?'

'I might as well.'

'You shoot good enough not to harm yourself nor anybody else out there?' Lock nodded. The storekeeper produced the hire forms, the insurance docket, the hunting licence. Lock produced his passport. At once, the storekeeper looked up, surprised. 'You planning on leaving the country with my stuff?' he asked.

'I thought it might help,' Lock offered, a new bout of tension seizing his head like a migraine.

'You city boys,' the storekeeper sniffed. 'OK – you go pick out

222

some clothes and a rifle, I'll use this here passport for the details. Like you say, it saves time.' He donned wire spectacles and studied the passport which, to Lock at least, looked suspiciously unused. *James Laurence* was the name on it, a resident of Baltimore. He was in advertising. 'You here on vacation?' he heard from the storekeeper.

'My wife's folks live in Phoenix – retired out here.'

'Uh-huh.'

Lock selected two shirts and a pair of denims from the shelves, tried on a pair of boots. Then he inspected a glass case of handguns. There was a Smith & Wesson 459, a gun he had handled in the field. The rifles were racked on the wall beside the window.

'You got an address in Baltimore – make that Phoenix?'

Lock supplied a fictitious number on Camelback Road. The storekeeper scribbled. Lock would have liked the M-16, but as a civilian he knew he ought to choose something that approximated to a hunting weapon. He reached out, tentatively touching each of the rifles in turn. It was as if he were making some bargain, signing something irrevocable, were he to buy one of them.

There was a Ruger single-shot carbine, looking as if it belonged in Bumble Bee and not the world beyond it. It was accurate, though. At too close a range. He chose another Ruger, the Mini-14, on which a telescopic sight could be mounted and its magazine could hold up to thirty rounds. A ten-round magazine would make it lighter. He ignored the shotguns.

'You done shopping, feller?'

'Yes.'

Lock indicated the Ruger, and a scope from the glass case. Then the Smith & Wesson pistol. Then a knife. He dumped the shirts and denims and the boots beside the weapons.

'You're sure aiming to do some serious hunting,' the man observed mockingly, a greedy glint in his eye. He had difficulty preventing his hands from rubbing themselves together in congratulation. A truck pulled up outside and Lock flinched. An arm, throwing. Newspapers landed on the stoop near the old man in the hard chair. 'You want a paper?'

223

'No.'

The storekeeper shrugged. 'I'll bring 'em in later. Food, feller – 'cross the street. Not old Colonel Sanders but the café next to it. Sell you anything you want – say, you'll need camping equipment, right?' His grin broadened into what might have been carnivorous appetite.

It was another fifteen minutes before Lock was shown out to the jeep he had contracted to hire. His face was on the front page of the Phoenix newspaper lying on the sidewalk near the dozing old man's boots. He shivered again. His suit was in the sports bag. The storekeeper had allowed him to change his clothing behind a rudimentary curtain at one dim end of the store. His photograph, supplied by the Washington PD, was there for the man to recognise, in all probability, only moments after he cut the rough string holding the bundle of newspapers together. Then he would phone the cops in Phoenix . . . He felt his whole body become sacklike, all his determination slumped in him like a great weight dragging him down. He barely heard the storekeeper's words of advice and warning as he took a map from the man's hand with a vague, numb grip. The storekeeper studied him, then shrugged. The jeep was insured, you've paid for the equipment, I don't have any problem if you get lost and die out there, his look said.

Lock started the jeep and pulled away from the store along the town's one street. He sensed the storekeeper watching his departure. He would buy food later. All that was important now was to get out of Bumble Bee before an alarm was raised. He was hungry and his throat was dry. He headed north, accelerating involuntarily towards the I-17.

The weight in his stomach increased and his shoulders slumped. His knuckles were white, gripping the wheel.

Serious hunting. It had been said mockingly. It might easily come to that.

Serious hunting . . . ?

The pistol and the rifle were a joke, part of an elaborate charade. Lock pulled the jeep off the highway just north of Cordes Junction, onto a dirt road that wound drily towards tree-

224

sloped mountains. He parked beneath a paloverde, startling a mourning dove from its branches. He watched the bird circle, then flutter back to rest; returning as surely as his thoughts to the same perch. It was no good, there was no point in running. He couldn't fly away from it . . . He switched off the engine and at once the desert silence encroached, pressing against his ears like a depth of water.

The song of a cactus wren pierced the quiet, slitting it like a blade, relieving the pressure of the desert; though not the weight of his thoughts. Nowhere to run . . . the one inescapable fact being the girl's body on the sofa of his apartment. There was evidence, eye-witness accounts, a continental manhunt . . . He raised his head, eyes closed tightly, to the sky. Opened them and saw chollas, barrel cactus, buckthorn – felt dust on the faint breeze. It settled on his hands. He let his head drop forward onto the steering wheel.

He was hungry. He had bought food at one of the service stations at Cordes Junction – where they would remember him, have his description for anyone who asked – but a pervading sense of nausea prevented him from reaching for the food. It was akin to despair, the sense of failure that enveloped him.

Pete Turgenev was seven thousand miles away and more, safe in Siberia, while he was on the run from his people, Tran, and the police. Those brute facts had pursued him along the highway like a desert wind, however fast he drove, however hard he gripped the wheel and tried to retain a hold on his imagination. But they had overtaken him the moment he stopped to buy food, spare cans of petrol, water. Pete Turgenev was safe while he was surely, inexorably, being run to earth. Impotence, fruit-less, pointless rage, were all he had left. His picture was in maybe fifty newspapers in a dozen states already. There was no way out of it.

The wren poured out its strange, rasping song, largely unnoticed, punctuating the passage of a blank, dead time. The faces of Beth, Kauffman, Billy, Vaughn, the dead girl, all circled in his mind, Turgenev's most of all. They were moving as slowly as distant comets, too distant to have any significance . . . The wren's song, the faces, the hard rustle of the cactus and the

225

paloverde, the wren's song, the breeze, the whirr of rotors, the wren, the breeze, the whirr of rotors . . . wren, no breeze, then only the rotors. Appalled into consciousness, he looked up. The helicopter passed low over him, throwing up a cloud of dust that masked him from it and it from him. The paloverde's leaves rattled like tin as the rotor noise diminished with distance. Then the black insect turned and came back towards him, certain.

Jetranger, but not a police helicopter. He flinched against the momentary sense of relief. This was Tran, or Turgenev's people – they wanted him dead. He fumbled with the ignition key and the engine roared to life, the noise drowned suddenly by the helicopter's passage. Its shadow flicked coldly over him. He stared through the upflung dust as the wheels of the jeep spun in the roadside dirt. Red dust settled on his wrists and forearms. The small Bell spun on its axis as lightly as a dancer and came back at him, nosing forward like a hound, its pace an insidious, threatening crawl through the dusty air.

The jeep strained, then leapt free of the wheelspin. A head leaned out of the open door of the helicopter, white hands poked a black stick in his direction, as if they were about to stir him and the jeep like an antheap. The first shot glanced off the flank of the jeep, whining away into the desert. He bucked onto the dirt road, across it, plunging the jeep into cactus and brush, which flicked wildly at him like grabbing, frail hands; whipping the windscreen and slashing at his face.

The shadow of the helicopter was above him as he swerved to avoid a giant cholla cactus which seemed to leap into the path of the vehicle, waving its stiff, needled arms to halt his flight. The shadow slipped aside for a moment, then reasserted itself like a cloak. The driving mirrors were filled with dust . . . not just his, he realised, or that thrown up by the Jetranger. There was another vehicle, perhaps a hundred yards or so behind him, churning its way through its own dust.

He felt very cold. The jeep lurched against a prickly pear and the wheel almost escaped from his sweating hands. His temperature jumped, jumped again as two more shots from the helicopter careened off the bonnet of the jeep. In the mirror, the other vehicle's dustcloud continued to pursue him.

Lock looked up. The dust that surrounded the jeep was made as murky as a sandstorm by the hovering helicopter, its down-draught ploughing at the red desert. It was becoming more diffi-cult for the marksman to aim accurately. He had to keep moving, had to help create the dust-screen. The jeep stumbled and tore its way through the thickly scattered sagebrush and cactus, crushing low hedgehog cactuses, swinging to avoid the chollas and the scattered, isolated paloverdes. The mountains appeared more distant. The windscreen shattered near his hand, shower-ing it with needles of glass. Flecks of blood mingled with the thick red dust on the backs of his hands. The dust storm behind seemed to be closing.

He swung the wheel again, then again, as he drove into a blind alley of tree chollas that had gathered like senile spectators to stare at an arroyo where there must once have been water. The jeep tumbled into the dry watercourse, wheels spinning, driveshaft screaming before the tyres bit again. Narrow gully, the tree chollas leering over him, the dusty cloud over his head spinning wildly as if caught by a small tornado . . . Only then, as the helicopter tilted crazily across his vision, did he realise that the jeep was mounting the other bank of the arroyo before he could turn the wheel. The vehicle was failing to make it, was falling back slowly, turning onto its side as slowly as a large animal that had been anaesthetised.

The scream of the driveshaft again, then the tear of the offside wheels, the mad spinning of the other two. He switched off the ignition as the jeep subsided with great, slow dignity, coming to rest at the bottom of the arroyo. So slowly that he was aware of no impact, no jolt. The sky seemed to spin across his vision for a second or so — that was the only disorientation. The tree chollas appeared cool, their needled flesh like thick bunches of strange fruit. He scrabbled from the driver's seat, grabbing at the Ruger Mini-14 which had been flung loose from the rear of the vehicle. The Smith & Wesson pistol was thrust into his belt. He seemed to swim through dust into the shadow of one of the chollas. Bullets plucked up dust around the jeep. Within the noise of the rotors he heard the gunshots and the approaching vehicle. Through the distressed shadows of the cholla's branches, he could see the occupants of the Jetranger. There were three of them.

He recognised Tran. Peering between the pilot and the marksman. Then their faces vanished behind the updrawn red dust. Lock crouched against the low wall of the arroyo, hunching into himself, feeling the vehicle's approach through the earth like an echo of a distant tremor. He could hear its engine. Jeep, some other 4WD. Two men, three — ? He clutched the rifle against his cheek as if the metal would cool its burning. It would be finished here.

The vehicle stopped. He listened to its engine idling, to a masked and incomprehensible exchange by radio or R/T. Now he was still, the desert's afternoon temperature seemed choking, unbearable, as close around him as a straitjacket. He was pinioned there by the heat of the place until they came for him. He heard the door of the vehicle slam shut. The helicopter, as if to gain a better vantage or to distance itself imperiously from the necessary, unpleasant violence, slipped higher in the sky, manoeuvring gently on the other side of the stricken jeep so that it could locate him; then just watch.

Inevitable —

— he turned onto his stomach quickly, wrenching his muscles, and fired the Ruger as a figure leapt into the arroyo, dropping the six or seven feet to — become a deadweight, even as it fell, so that it sprawled, grey-suited, on the red dust. An M-16 held in one unmoving hand. A voice called out as Lock rose into a crouch and began running, away from the man's body. He sensed rather than heard the Jetranger shuffle closer, as if angry at having lost sight of him. There was shouting behind him, but caution, too. They'd climb nervously down into the arroyo, now.

The Jetranger loomed above him. Shots plucked at the ground around him. The helicopter leaned like a drunk, like someone peering down into a well, so that the marksman, suspended in webbing, could lean further out, take more certain aim. Lock watched the slow, careful increase of the helicopter's angle. He could see the marksman's mouth, stretched into a rictuslike grin. He was Caucasian, like the pilot. Tran's face was that of a child between two adults manoeuvring to kill him. He raised the rifle without thinking and fired once, twice – four, six, seven . . . The marksman hung in the webbing like a doll, the perspex of the helicopter's windows was starred like a spider's web. He could see neither face; only that of the marksman, who still seemed to be grinning at him, his hands moving with the tilt of the machine . . .

. . . which was slowly sagging, as if the helicopter had lost its tight grip on the air. The Bell turned, nose drooping, leaning tiredly on the desert air, tilting towards the dust it was throwing up around Lock.

Lock was blindly thrusting a new magazine into the Ruger as he continued to stare with utter, rapt fascination at the slow death of the machine. It fell towards him, but it no longer possessed the slightest suggestion of danger. It was harmless, a dead man hung from its open doorway, arms jigging senselessly in imitation of a scarecrow. The Jetranger toppled towards the arroyo, its rotor blades whirling like a dazzling, sun-catching dish as it drove towards him –

– broken spell. He moved leaden legs very slowly, clumping as through deep water, away from the last plunge of the helicopter. Then he flung himself flat, the Ruger stretched out at the end of his arm.

The helicopter ploughed into the bank of the arroyo, churning dust, rock, gouts of dry, dead soil over him. The noise ground in his teeth and bones, the earth shook under his body in a frenzy . . . The screaming of metal, the breaking of the machine. The slow fall of the level of noise into eventual silence; perhaps minutes later, he could not tell. He kept his hands pressed over his ears for a long time after the noises seemed to have stopped. Then he fumbled for the Ruger and turned onto his back before sitting upright amid the rubble of soil and dust and broken tree chollas.

The sword of a broken rotor blade thrust up from the dry bed of the arroyo. Another was plunged into the bank. The helicopter was smeared with dust, cactus, darker soil. The windows were entirely obscured. There was no one else there, it seemed, except for himself, no other spectator. Cautiously, he rose to his feet and walked unsteadily towards the machine.

229

The marksman had been caught in the rotor blades. The smearing on the fuselage and shattered windows was not entirely cactus juice and damper soil. The corpse was headless, almost shredded; what remained of it was still suspended in the soiled webbing from which it had been hanging in order to kill Lock.

Lock vomited. Retched until his throat ached. Then shivered with a sudden chill, as if the still-high sun had set. The pilot's door was hanging open. The pilot was strapped stiffly into his seat, staring sightlessly at the spider's web Lock's shots had created over his window. Lock leaned over the body – a hole in the chest, another in the left temple – and saw Tran's small form, broken-necked, lying against the bulkhead. One arm lay underneath him, the other was stretched out as if to ward something off. There was no doubt the Vietnamese was dead.

Startled, Lock straightened at the noise of a door slamming in the desert silence. Then an engine fired, wheels spun, and the 4WD careered away. Its dust rose like the smoke of a fire beyond the rim of the arroyo.

One of them had already died. They hadn't been paid enough to hang around after Tran's death, or without back-up from the Jetranger. The surviving foot-soldiers had fled.

Lock walked away from the wreckage, towards the shade of the remaining tree chollas. He sat down in the inviting shadows, cradling the rifle on his knees, his head hanging forward with new, drained weariness. He closed his eyes, trying not to imagine the first flies humming around the bodies in the helicopter.

It was a long time later, by the sun's declination, that he was awoken by the noise of a light aircraft passing low to the west of the arroyo. He stood up, adrift on sudden nerves, and located the plane, descending towards some hidden desert airstrip three or four miles away from his position. It was obviously not engaged in any search for him. It dropped to cactus height as he scrambled clear of the arroyo. The airstrip was due west. His head ached and he felt dizzy. The dirt road he had been on must lead to it.

He looked at the overturned jeep and shook his head. To right it alone was probably beyond him. He would have to walk. He heard a mourning dove, then a cactus wren. The flies around the wreckage were a constant, distant murmur, like that of a small, muffled motor.

He thought of calling Faulkner in Washington. But he had seen a newspaper at the service station. The girl had been a hooker and an addict and he had picked her up. His hire car had been seen cruising the district. Turgenev had him in a box, and the lid had been nailed down tight.

Despite what he had done here . . .

. . . he had done nothing but alleviate the immediate pursuit. Given himself a breathing space, maybe a few hours, some of which time he had already wasted by falling into exhausted sleep.

There was nothing else he could do. Turgenev had burned all the bridges behind him. There was nothing left for him here –

Water, he must take water. Eat something. He should make the airstrip before nightfall.

Igor Trechikov, chief of police for Novyy Urengoy, stared down at Vorontsyev, who was propped against plump pillows in the hospital bed. A sense of sadness assailed him. His chief of detectives' arm was in heavy plaster, his forehead was bandaged and, beneath the sheet, his broken ribs were strapped. There was bruising on his jaw, scorch marks on his cheeks.

Trechikov shifted uncomfortably from foot to foot. Vorontsyev's people – Dmitri Gorov, the female detective Marfa, just herself released from the hospital, and Goludin – were arranged around the bed like a ceremonial bodyguard.

Vorontsyev's eyes glared blearily at him, and he fumbled to find the sense of outrage that he had felt on receiving his instructions from Bakunin. That anger would now serve to maintain his dignity and authority during his reprimand of Vorontsyev. Looking at the younger man now, he seemed accused of dereliction.

'I – I've been kept informed of your condition, Alexei,' was all he could immediately find to say. The girl scowled contemptuously. Vorontsyev blinked once, a remote, detached gesture. There was not, it was claimed by the medical staff, any brain damage. Concussion, yes, but that was supposed to have passed. 'Terrorists, of course –' He quailed. Until Bakunin's phone call, he had been able to believe that embracing fiction, even act upon it. House-to-house searches, arrests, interrogations all designed to unearth the terrorist cell.

Bakunin, without the slightest explanation, had ordered him to suspend Vorontsyev and his team. Thereby dynamiting the fiction, as surely as those far too powerful even to suspect had dynamited Vorontsyev's flat.

Vorontsyev's lips opened like an oyster shell.

'Vera Silkova's dead – together with her baby,' he announced in a faint, dull voice.

Trechikov was bemused, then he recalled the two fatalities of the explosion. A young woman, someone's mistress, and a baby. The flat behind Vorontsyev's. The explosive had been hidden in the TV set and radio-detonated. Vorontsyev had delayed on the landing outside his door, talking to a neighbour. The – terrorists had claimed they were gas fitters. Perhaps they'd got the timing wrong, or been hurried into the detonation. Whatever, they were ten seconds too early – though not for the young woman, who had been sitting at a table on the other side of the wall between her flat and Vorontsyev's television. She and the baby had been killed instantly.

'Terrible business –' Trechikov began, shuffling his feet afresh as the echo of Bakunin's hard, demanding tones returned to him. 'I –' He faltered once more.

Vorontsyev's unplastered hand moved on the bedclothes.

'I know it upsets you, Chief. She wasn't *important*.'

The tone was sympathetic, the intent icy. Dmitri Gorov appeared embarrassed, while the young detective and the woman wandered away from the bed to the other end of the spacious private room. At least he had been able to insist on that quality of treatment for his chief of detectives when neither rank nor money could demand it.

Trechikov nodded Gorov away from the bed and sat on the chair Goludin had vacated. Dmitri, after studying Vorontsyev for a moment, nodded the other two outside and closed the door behind them. Trechikov relaxed until his gaze returned to

232

the pitiless stare with which Vorontsyev regarded him. The room was too warm for Trechikov in his fur boots and greatcoat, but he felt that to shed the coat would be to divest himself of some last lingering authority. Vorontsyev continued to look at him as if he were a beggar who smelt of vodka and dirt.

'By next week they'll have you as good as new —' he began, but Vorontsyev interrupted him, the free hand gripping Trechikov's wrist.

'*Listen*, Igor Vassilyevich,' he hissed, painfully hoisting himself higher against the pillows. 'Listen to me. I can *smell* their scent on you like your wife would smell another woman's perfume! I know you've come to tell me to lay off — suspend me?' He studied Trechikov's face, the glare in his eyes a source of heat that drove the man back. 'Right. That's the crux of it. Someone's given you your orders.'

'No, Alexei —! I came to see how you were, it's my first free hour since the . . . Look, you'll have to take some leave, the investigations are in the hands of the GRU — I just want to make sure you get well.' *Stay well, stay alive*, the panic in the voice announced unambiguously. Vorontsyev retained his fierce grip.

'Vera Silkova's *dead*, Igor. Don't you understand? They almost killed Marfa up on that rig, now they've managed it in the case of an innocent bystander.' He was whispering, yet Trechikov was held as by some ancient mariner. 'They don't care. There were people in the other flats when they tried to blow me to smithereens. They killed Vera Silkova and her baby just to get at me, to make *sure* of me!' He swallowed. The bruised lips were opening and closing like the pastiche of a healthy mouth. 'I don't care about Rawls, about the Iranian, anyone else who died because of them. But don't tell me it's *all right*, Igor, don't tell me that!'

He released Trechikov's wrist. The older man rubbed it immediately, as if it had been burned. Vorontsyev lay back once more, seeming to subside into the pillows.

'I — all right, Alexei, all right . . . I won't say that, not in the way you meant. I tried to keep you away from it, Alexei. You should have listened to me — obeyed my order.'

'Maybe,' Vorontsyev admitted grudgingly after a silence. 'What do you *know*, Igor?'

'Nothing!' Trechikov at once protested. It was true – thank God, it was true.

'Who called you, who told you to come?'

Trechikov shook his head vehemently.

'I'm here to place you on leave, Major,' he said, fumbling for formality as for a defensive weapon.

Vorontsyev's lips grinned. The eyes remained hard as flint. Trechikov had never suspected this stubbornness before.

'Bakunin?' Trechikov was astounded, so that his expression confessed even as he attempted to control it. 'I thought so. It had to be him. And who is *he* answerable to?'

'How the hell would I know that?' Trechikov burst out.

'You might have a guess.'

'I don't know!'

'Calm down, Igor – careful of your angina.'

'I do have angina –' Trechikov protested at the mockery.

'And a pension and a dacha and a greedy wife, Igor. I know.'

'It's easy for you, Alexei –'

'Yours is the easy way, Igor,' Vorontsyev sighed, his eyes filled with pain. He seemed wearied by the argument, or by whatever process of reason had preceded his observations. Trechikov felt nettled at being upbraided, but no sense of superior authority seemed to hand. 'I tried it. I know.'

'Look, Alexei, just keep your head down, man!' Trechikov protested.

'I might have done – *before*!' Vorontsyev snapped. 'I'd have got tired, we'd have got nowhere, everything would have settled down. But they couldn't wait, could they, Igor? They couldn't wait for that to happen! Doesn't it irk you – just a little – that they don't give a *fuck* for any normal kind of behaviour? They don't even behave like your average crook! Their *first* response is explosives.'

'Look, Alexei, I understand your outrage, I really do. But it will only get you –'

'– killed? I know that, too.'

'Well, then?'

234

'I don't have any choice. Not now. I've found things out.'

Trechikov flinched away, as if Vorontsyev had announced he had a communicable disease. He was, Trechikov admitted to himself, afraid. Alexei even knew that he wouldn't report this conversation; knew his weaknesses, his self-pity, his fear, and the shreds of decent normality he attempted to keep wrapped about him in the coldest wind.

'I – there's nothing . . . ?' Vorontsyev shook his head. Trechikov leaned forward, his forehead damp. 'You're on leave. Read that as suspension. Your team will be reassigned.'

'When?'

'At once. For *their* safety, Alexei. Think of them, won't you – whatever you decide.'

'I'll try.'

'Be careful – very careful, Alexei.'

'Yes,' Vorontsyev replied tiredly. There was a tinge of regret in his voice, as if he felt himself coerced on his intended path.

Trechikov was very afraid. In a few moments, he might be able to consider Vorontsyev pig-headed, criminally stupid. But not quite at that moment. He stood up, nodded brusquely, and walked to the door. When he looked back, Vorontsyev had deliberately shut his eyes. Trechikov left, and felt himself walking through a small cloud of censure from Vorontsyev's team, who had now been joined by another detective he recognised as Lubin. They parted for him, but he sensed their hostility, as if he had entered a puritanical courtroom, his criminality already plain in his demeanour. They were fools, blindly stupid, all of them.

Vorontsyev opened his eyes as he heard the door open. Dmitri, Marfa, Goludin and Lubin crowded into the room, half-afraid of their visit yet deeply curious. Dmitri perched himself on the chair vacated by Trechikov and Marfa sat on the other side of the bed. The two young men remained near the door, as if guarding it against violent intruders. In a sense, that was exactly what they intended.

'What did the old man want – another warning-off?'

'Just that, Dmitri. He meant for my good. Like he means to reassign all of you for your own good.'

235

'No –!'

'Maybe it's best, Dmitri – no, listen to me. The old man's terrified. Bakunin's been at him. And there has to be someone else behind Bakunin. Drugs, nuclear physicists, technicians – it's too clever by half for that ape Bakunin. Do you understand me? All of you?' He stared at each of them. One by one, they nodded like sullen children. 'OK. I want you to realise how dangerous it is. There is *no* safety net, none at all. We've been abandoned – that was the message and it wasn't in code. *I* am on my own. Is that clear?'

He looked at each of them carefully . . . Goludin seemed doubtful, anxious; Marfa had a clarity of enthusiasm that might be innocence or trust; Lubin attempted to appear grave. Dmitri – was Dmitri; there was nothing else to do but go on with it. He had no right to take anyone except Dmitri with him.

'Look,' he said tiredly, 'I'm putting a sticking plaster on a cancer – that's all I can do. It won't count for anything, it won't really help. I've been put in this position. My head's above the parapet – yours aren't.' Dmitri's look excepted him. He rubbed his loose jowl and the stubble of his beard rasped in the quiet of the room. 'I'm trying to give someone who's dying pink medicine that will do them no good at all. I refuse to let you become as futile. You understand – really understand?'

He realised pain and pleading had both appeared in his expression. He was asking them for their help, even their protection; behaving like a demagogue, filling their heads with an ideology that was alien to them.

'Don't answer – just go,' he said.

Marfa burst out: 'Whatever you say about sticking plasters – *sir* – we know more than that!' She glowered at the two younger men as if dragooning them into her cause. 'That heroin – the boxes it came in, they had Grainger Foundation, Phoenix, Arizona stamped on them. The hospital's involved, of course – but we can all guess who *must* be behind it . . .' Her confidence faded. Perhaps it was anxiety that quietened her and made her next words uncertain. 'Can't we?'

Goludin seemed on the point of panic, but Lubin smiled

gravely at him, then he appeared to draw calm from their numbers.

'Can we?' Vorontsyev asked with forced lightness.

'Turgenev,' Dmitri offered after a hot silence. 'It has to be him. Grainger-Turgenev is the ideal conduit, we've known that since Schneider and Rawls came into the picture. Flights in and out all the time, money no object, power to –'

'Control Bakunin and the chief,' Vorontsyev finished. 'I should have left it on Bakunin's doorstep, shouldn't I?'

'As you said, he doesn't have the brains. Or the power, really. Only Turgenev has that.'

'Now you see why I asked you to leave – all of you?' He looked at Dmitri, who shook his head in a minimal gesture. Then Dmitri said:

'Here's the rundown. I have a score to settle and, anyway, we're friends. Lubin and Goludin think they're on an awfully big adventure, the sort that makes cop movies – the idiots – and Marfa would follow you, like a dog, wherever you went.' The woman blushed furiously, her eyes hot, and filled with admission. 'OK? Anyone been misrepresented? No? Good. The next question is – what do we do now?'

'It isn't that easy,' Vorontsyev protested.

'It is, if you'll just keep quiet, Alexei.'

Vorontsyev was embarrassed at their gauche, crystal enthusiasm, their blindness to reality. And relieved and grateful not to be alone. He said quietly:

'You *want* to do this?' In turn, after looking almost furtively at each other, they each nodded. 'Very well,' he sighed. 'And thanks.'

Then their enthusiasm burst out in a cacophony of suggestions.

'We know there are a couple of scientists around –'

'Check the use of his private jet –'

'Pull Schneider in, he must know who's –'

'Panshin's another key to it –'

Vorontsyev held up his hand and they eventually fell silent.

'This town is Turgenev's web. Step on it anywhere, and he'll know about it. *If* he's behind it . . .'

237

There was no doubt. Not any longer. No one else possessed the immunity from ordinary existence that would allow them to have the chief of detectives blown up in his own home and be entirely careless of any response. He had masked the suspicion from himself during the days he had lain in that bed, terrified, only gradually certain of his own survival.

There was so much money to be made, there was influence to be gained in the Middle East and the Moslem Triangle. Above all, there was great cunning and intelligence on display, and enormous power. Only Turgenev had power enough to control the police, Bakunin and the GRU, the American hospital, and executives of Grainger-Turgenev. Only Turgenev could have had him ordered to death with such impunity . . .

. . . the thought that had brought him sweating awake during the long last few nights. The gradual colouring of a silhouette, the growing accuracy of a photofit. Eventually, he had seen Turgenev's features clearly. He had been in no doubt for twenty-four hours now. All roads led to the hunting lodge on the tundra.

'All right,' he said, clearing his throat, 'let's get to work. Get some more chairs, coffee and food. Just remember –' He looked at his plastered arm and strapped ribs as he had done so frequently and impotently. '– one mistake is one too many. Just one.'

John Lock sat in the KLM first class lounge at Toronto International, waiting for his flight to Amsterdam. He had bought the ticket with the credit card showing the last of his identities. With the last of his strength, too, it now seemed. His nerves were itchily weary, easily alarmed; his hand, picking up the bourbon, shook each time he stretched it towards the low table. He had little sense of whether it was night or day outside the windowless lounge, no sense whatsoever of his waiting fellow passengers; of the girl who served the drinks. He remained stale and unwashed and exhausted within the aftershave and the smooth cheeks and the new shirt and jacket. The denims had cleaned up sufficiently. The new sports bag at his feet was all but empty. Two paperbacks, another shirt, some underwear – all bought at Toronto International.

He looked at his watch once more, blinking the dial into focus. Another hour before his flight.

He'd found the airstrip – yesterday, today? – almost four miles from the arroyo. The single-engined Cessna he had seen landing was used for crop-spraying, mail deliveries, grocery flights, the occasional passenger. For the right steep price, the pilot had flown him to Reno, Nevada. He had intended to find another plane to take him south, anonymously, to Mexico. And had known at once they would anticipate his choice. Yankees on the run *always* fled to Mexico, as if it was the only border they had ever heard of.

So, he had headed north. First from Reno to Sacramento in a twelve-seater jet, then from Sacramento to Vancouver, and finally Vancouver to Toronto on Air Canada. No big airports, no security checks until he reached Canada. He'd slept overnight in an airport hotel in Vancouver, then flown to Toronto . . . so it was yesterday or the day before that he'd killed Tran, he realised with a jolt. The realisation was no more than a muffled, distant explosion.

It was unreal now. As was the girl's dead body in his apartment. Only the beginning of it – Beth – and the end he envisaged – Turgenev – were real to him. Beth and Turgenev. What Turgenev had begun, he would end.

There was nothing else he could possibly do, even imagine. Nothing whatsoever.

ELEVEN

Incidence of Arson

John Lock stood in the fur-lined boots he had purchased at Moscow's Cheremetievo airport, hunched in his new overcoat against the evening wind and blowing snow, and stared at the ruin of the house. The traffic of Novyy Urengoy passed behind him, hissing and grinding through gritted slush, headlights flaring, brakelights eager. His cheeks were numb with the icy cold. His whole head ached with it, despite the fur hat he wore.

It had taken him almost two days from Toronto to reach this place, and someone had blown it away. Curtains flapped like soaked rags at glassless windows, there was charred paintwork and stucco, a half-collapsed roof, no lights. The janitor of a newish block of flats along the street had told him that *terrorists had tried to kill a cop*. He knew the only cop who lived in the Tsarist, ramshackle house; Vorontsyev, the *honest cop* he had told Beth about, the evening before she was murdered. He could remember the interior of the house, the rooms of Vorontsyev's apartment on the first floor. He'd accepted the Russian's invitation to dinner, then to listen to jazz records in his apartment. Had warmed to the man almost at once, after the incident in the hotel bar had been cleared up. Now, he simply stared at the blind empty windowframes like open mouths, lightless like all the other windows. The place had been taped off by the police, but he had already seen dim figures, shabby as rats, moving amid the rubble. One of them had carried off a scorched-looking microwave cooker, two others had loaded a damaged washing machine onto a wheelbarrow and disappeared into the sleet.

Turgenev . . . Lock shivered. His whole being was cold. Turgenev could strike at Vorontsyev without a qualm or hesitation. Even the janitor somehow hadn't believed the terrorist story, shrugging morosely and cynically after its relation. And a young woman and a baby had died, and another woman had been injured by falling masonry. Lock shook his head. He knew the town well enough to know there were no terrorists . . . only gangsters, the *biznizmen*; the Russian mafia. And he knew that Vorontsyev had been concerned about heroin – he had said as much, that evening he had invited him back to the prim, airless, lonely apartment. Heroin angered him; there was something about it killing his inspector's daughter, wasn't there? However hopeless, even ludicrous it seemed, he wanted to enlist Vorontsyev's help. He *had* to have the policeman's aid. He was the only man in Novyy Urengoy he could trust.

To get Turgenev – to have the remotest chance of killing him – required help. The help of a man he hardly knew.

Ridiculous.

But no other way lay open to him. No other way at all.

Drugs, Vorontsyev, an attempted murder . . . Turgenev. He sensed himself forestalled, anticipated – though he knew it was all but impossible. Turgenev might already know he was in Novyy Urengoy, but it must be coincidental that Vorontsyev had become a target. Nevertheless, he shivered once more; he was not the other player in a chess game, he was a mere piece on the board.

He moved closer to the ruined house, scuffing a scorched floorboard with his boot, shuffling his feet amid ashes and shattered brick and stucco. The snow was already lying; it was white on his shoulders.

The cop had been *taken to the American hospital*, so the janitor next door informed him, turning away from a tenant grousing about the absence of a glazier to replace shattered windows *and the snow coming in and her baby sick* . . . Could he risk the hospital, the Grainger Foundation Hospital? It had to be tied in to the drugs somehow, it would be too easy for it not to be. Vorontsyev was still alive, surely he'd be under surveillance? Under *guard*?

What else could he do? Walk away? Go back out to the airport? He'd be snowed in anyway, he told himself with a self-deprecating grin. Might as well spend the time where it's warm and quiet –

He had no plan, beyond talking to Vorontsyev, beyond the attempt to enlist the policeman's aid. Vorontsyev, as they listened to his jazz records and drank his vodka weeks before, had been someone afraid of awakening his own moral ardour. However, his inspector's tragedy was eating at him, making him pursue the drug smugglers. He had intended feeding Vorontsyev everything he knew, then turning on him like a trapdoor spider and demanding his help. Giving him Turgenev, of all people, on a plate – and enlisting his help in killing the man.

Badly injured, yes . . . the janitor had informed him. He had spat as much out of habit as dislike.

What possible help could Vorontsyev be to him now? He was on his own . . .

Christ, but it was cold, so damn *cold*.

'Very well. No, just have him watched for the moment . . . you have someone on him? Good. Keep me informed.'

Turgenev put down the telephone, the forefinger of his left hand brushing back and forth across his lips, as if he had only recently shaved off a moustache. He studied the telephone as if he expected it to continue to inform him of Lock's whereabouts and intent. Intent? Obvious, of course. He had wondered about the man during the last three days, since his people had let him get away in the Arizona desert. He'd thought that the sister's death had been avenged when Lock had killed Tran, but he'd been traced to Reno, then Sacramento, finally Vancouver. There, in the mêlée of the international airport, descriptions of him were futile; and he'd changed to another identity, new papers. They had no name for him.

Now, he was in Novyy Urengoy. Bakunin's people, alerted by himself almost on a whim and certainly not from anxiety, had identified the American disembarking from the Moscow flight two hours ago. Last plane in. A blizzard continuing perhaps three or four days was sweeping down on the region from the arctic; the first real storm of winter. No one would be able to get in or out, certainly not Lock. The blizzard would imprison him in Novyy Urengoy. Turgenev was satisfied.

He glanced down the columns of figures he had received

detailing his currency speculations against the French franc and the measure of his profit. Given such gains in so brief a period, the profits from heroin – now that he was poised to acquire Grainger Technologies – seemed meagre, begrudged. He smiled, then continued plucking his lower lip between finger and thumb, removing his half-glasses.

Grainger Technologies and the other companies he had acquired in the US – and those he was moving against now – would render him immense power and wealth. The two thousand and more émigrés from Russia who comprised the *biznizmen* engaged in organised crime in the United States were small beer, fleas. People like himself – perhaps at first only himself – were making far greater inroads . . . He was content.

His thoughts returned to John Lock with a mild, nostalgic regret. Novyy Urengoy was the best possible place to have Lock situated. *His* town. He must consider how best to rid himself of the American, then set Bakunin on him like a savage dog. Lock was alone – of that he was utterly certain. There would be no loose ends. He had fled America as the subject of a murder charge. His death in Russia would not be reported. He would simply have vanished, which was perhaps suitable for someone so *unformed* as Lock, someone who left so little impression on people and things. Sad? Well, perhaps, for nevertheless the American was likeable . . . But he was unimportant.

In the end, it was a simple matter, only the death of a single individual.

'Yes?'

It was the American doctor, Schneider – the one with the Jewish name. Bakunin tasted contempt as ready as raw onion in his mouth.

'My routine report,' he heard Schneider offer in a humiliated, angrily self-pitying tone. 'Vorontsyev has been visited by the overweight officer and by the girl. They didn't stay long.'

'Which one of them is guarding him now?' The chief of police had refused to enforce any order keeping Vorontsyev's people away from the Foundation Hospital; Bakunin could not openly demand it. Unless someone like Schneider could administer a lethal dose of something, by needle or via his food, Vorontsyev was safe in his bed.

'His name's Goludin, I think. He seems very innocent – and innocuous.' Then, Schneider added quickly: 'Why can't one of *your* men make these reports, Colonel?'

'One of them is,' Bakunin snapped back. 'Goodbye, Doctor.'

He put down the receiver and rubbed his ear where perspiration made it itch, then he picked up his cigarette and drew deeply on it, blowing the blue smoke at the ceiling of his office. Schneider was shit-scared, that much was obvious, but entirely malleable because of his involvement with the heroin. He could be extradited to a country that would crucify him – his own – or he could die as a foreigner just like his friend Rawls in a distant country. Either way, his cooperation was ensured, almost genetically guaranteed. Bakunin grinned to himself, coughing on the amusement and cigarette smoke.

Vorontsyev . . . ? Turgenev seemed unduly hesitant, if not reluctant, in Vorontsyev's case. Was he waiting for him to leave hospital? All he wanted for the moment was surveillance on the man's team – the woman, fat Dmitri, Goludin and the young forensic officer Lubin. All of whom had been ordered back to normal duties by the police chief . . . and all of whom appeared to be engaged on other cases – a rape, small-scale extortion, an overdose, a knife wounding. The usual scum on the surface of crimes committed by the rabble. If they had been given any orders by Vorontsyev, then they didn't appear to be carrying them out.

Bakunin rubbed his chin with the fingers holding the cigarette. The smoke curled into his eyes, making him blink.

It didn't seem suspicious; it was difficult to believe that after what had happened to their chief of detectives, they were left with sufficient nerve to continue their investigations. They'd run their cart into a brick wall, the donkey was injured, they were dazed. End of journey . . . though Bakunin would prefer that they were eliminated altogether; one by one or at the same time, it didn't matter. Who, after all, would have the temerity to ask questions about their deaths? He had to press that matter with Turgenev. The problem had not been solved, simply postponed.

Vorontsyev . . . ? For the moment, Turgenev appeared to be preoccupied by the American, Lock. Bakunin looked down at the file that had been faxed to him by somebody Turgenev employed in America. Lock was a State Department official . . . Bakunin did not recall having encountered him in Novyy Urengoy, despite the American's frequent visits to the region. A bland, good-looking, too-young face looked up at him from the fax. A bland record, too. He didn't appear dangerous, though Turgenev stressed that point particularly. He had made this Lock a priority, one that overrode even Vorontsyev.

Very well – so be it, Prince Turgenev, he remarked mockingly to himself. Yours is the say-so, the authority. If you want Lock killed, so be it.

His accent and manner appeared as effective as his passport. He was an American in an American-funded, American-run hospital, and if he wanted to talk to an injured Russian, so what? The nurse on duty simply pointed along the corridor to the door of Vorontsyev's room and dismissed him from her mind.

He hesitated for a moment with his hand on the doorknob. A wave of weary defeat came over him and he wanted to surrender to it. It was as if he were a parent summoned to this place because of an accident to his child. He anticipated the scarring, the brokenness, the incapacity that lay beyond the door. His desire for revenge which had brought him here in the drugged, heightened state it induced – a state in which anything and everything was possible – now deserted him momentarily, leaving him drained, incapable, anxious. What help could this Russian policeman give him, having barely managed to survive a bomb attack? What help would he want or dare to give to someone he hardly knew?

He pushed open the door. The man's one arm was in heavy plaster but the other scrabbled beneath the sheet. His forehead was bandaged; eyes glittered abnormally bright, watching him. Lock raised one hand defensively and closed the door behind him.

'I – er, they said I could see you, you were OK for visitors,' Lock stumbled out. The man in the bed, so disappointingly immobile, was surprised at his accent, the words in English. Relaxed by his evident innocuousness.

'Who are you?' Vorontsyev seemed to hesitate on the edge of recognition. 'You're American?'

Lock nodded. 'We've met.'

Suddenly, Vorontsyev's eyes were brightly suspicious.

'I remember – Lock.' The hand rustled beneath the sheet. Then: 'You're State Department – American government . . .' The hidden hand had a firm grip now on what had to be a gun. Had he imagined the tiny click of a safety catch being moved?

'Sure,' he said tiredly. The man entirely disappointed him; cancelled everything in an instant. Uninvited, he slumped onto a chair beside the bed, his head held in his hands. He was so tired, his body at last admitted, having nothing of the drug of revenge to stimulate it.

'Why are you here?'

'My family are – were – connected with this place, the people who run it. My sister married into this . . . She's dead.' Lock obviously disconcerted the Russian.

Vorontsyev saw bent shoulders, a stubbled face, stained pouchy eyes; a man defeated, inadequate. It was as if he was interrogating some petty criminal, someone small, motiveless, opportunistic. Lock, the man he had invited to his flat – the flat Turgenev had had blown up, killing Vera Silkova and her baby – given drink and confidences to, warmed towards; forgotten within days. The man had seemed as anonymous and trusty as a counsellor, a doctor. 'But why are you here, John Lock?'

Lock hesitated for some time. The warmth of the room was somnolent despite Vorontsyev's tension. Then he said: 'I knew I could trust you. I even told my sister about you.' He smiled bleakly. 'My sister . . . She was murdered.'

'In America?'

'Yes.'

'But not by an American?'

'Not by an American. Not on American orders.'

246

Vorontsyev shifted in the bed, as if Lock's bleak, aged gaze disconcerted him. He rested the gun in his lap.

'Have we –?' he began, clearing his throat. 'Have we anything in common?'

'I don't know.'

It was a simple matter of trust; an extremely complex matter. He couldn't read the American's mind or his recent experiences in his face. To pretend to do so would be to delude himself. This man *knew* Turgenev, had been close to him, he recalled. Lock had told him that, as they had eaten a Chinese meal from one of the new take-away shops in the town and drunk foreign beer.

He'd liked the American, then. Only weeks earlier . . . 'Someone has to begin,' he said. 'You?' He waited, then added: 'If there's something you want from me?'

'Are you in any condition to supply it?' Lock replied. The American seemed baffled and defeated by his being injured and in hospital.

'You wanted my help, then?' Vorontsyev said softly.

'Maybe.'

'Because of a single evening's conversation? You trusted me to help you?'

Eventually, Lock replied: 'You were my only hope – I knew no one else.'

Lock glanced around the hospital room, towards the double-glazed window. Snow flew in the glare of sodium lighting thrown up from one of the car parks and a gas rig flared like a fading distress signal out on the tundra. Then he looked intently at Vorontsyev, realising that the decision to tell the Russian why he was there was . . . well, it was no big deal, was it? He'd walked into this place of his own free will.

He struggled to remember Vorontsyev's remarks on the heroin problem in Novyy Urengoy, his concern, his anger; there was his inspector, too, the one whose daughter had overdosed.

'It's about the drugs,' he said. Vorontsyev flinched in surprise. 'I know a lot about it – now. I didn't, when we talked. I wasn't even very interested. It was your problem, not mine . . . But it is mine, now –' His voice was choked off by memory gripping his throat tightly. He cleared it and continued. Vorontsyev was

247

watching him as if he were telling the most compulsive tale ever created. 'It's Grainger-Turgenev. The whole place is a conduit –'

'Don't say anything more, just for the moment,' Vorontsyev said. Lock looked at him suspiciously. 'This place is a staging post. A warehouse –'

'Jesus, they contaminated everything, didn't they?'

'Who is they?'

'Pete Turgenev – my dead brother-in-law, his father.' He sat back on the chair and rubbed his face as if roughly washing away a great deal of grime.

'How big is the – business?'

'Millions of dollars. The whole of Grainger-Turgenev's been built on the profits.' Vorontsyev's eyes gleamed, then grew alarmed as they heard a knock on the door, which opened at once.

'Dmitri.'

'Who's your visitor, Alexei?' Dmitri Gorov was holding out a package of sandwiches towards Vorontsyev. Two bottles of beer were tucked into the crook of his arm.

'An American – a friend. Someone who has good reason to be here. The same drugs that killed your daughter, Dmitri, were most probably responsible for his sister's death. Not through a needle, maybe, but just as directly.'

Dmitri's features, clouded with pain, became at once conspiratorial. 'This the American you took home, the diplomat, by any chance?'

'Yes.'

'What does he want?'

'I think he wants to kill Turgenev.'

The only sound was the inspector's surprised breathing. The silence that followed was heavy, stormy. Lock's Russian had come back fluently, naturally. He'd stumbled over simple phrases at the airport in Moscow. Now that he'd burned his bridges behind him, he had become, in a strange and somehow comforting way, almost as Russian as the two policemen. As if he had changed his identity. Eventually, Vorontsyev said:

'And he wants us to help him do it, old friend. Turgenev, as we were forced to realise for ourselves, is the kingpin.' Dmitri

248

was nodding and frowning. The sandwich remained unre-
gardedly held out towards Vorontsyev. 'It's much bigger than
we ever imagined –'

'You're taking a lot on trust, Alexei, from the mouth of a
Yankee who just walked through the door and introduced
himself.'

'Look –' Lock began, but was interrupted by Vorontsyev.

'We haven't time to go through all that, Dmitri. The hour's
too late.'

The door opened and each of them turned to it. To his great
surprise, Lock recognised the doctor.

'Dave – Dave Schneider,' he said, getting up from the chair.
The expressions of mistrust on the faces of the two Russians
startled him.

'John – what are you . . . ?'

Lock knew that it was all somehow wrong, that Schneider was
wary of him just as the two Russians seemed afraid of Schneider;
alarmed at his having seen Lock in their company.

Lock and Schneider shook hands. Vorontsyev kept his free
hand firmly around the butt of the gun. The safety was still
pushed to Off. It would make a noise, of course, but if necessary
he would shoot Schneider . . . if Lock would stop placing himself
in the line of fire. Something bleeped and Schneider removed
his pager from his pocket.

'Back in just a minute, John – you can tell me how the hell
I find you here, and in the chief of detectives' room!'

The door closed behind him.

'Quick, Dmitri – get Lock out of here. Back to your place!'

'What –?' Lock was bemused.

'He's part of it, Lock. Get moving! Who's in the car with you,
Dmitri?'

'Goludin – why?'

'Take him with you – lie low at home until I can think our
way out of this mess! Get moving!' Lock turned to him as he
said: 'Get either Marfa or Lubin over here to watch my door!'

'What is going on here –?' Lock began.

'I'm saving your life, Lock! Just be satisfied.' Dmitri was
already at the door, checking the corridor. 'Now Schneider

knows you're in town, the GRU and Turgenev himself will know inside another ten minutes! I would imagine their only idea will be to kill you.'

'Clear,' Dmitri said, drawing back from the door, glaring at Lock. 'And they'll bloody well know you've talked to us! What the hell did you come here for, Yank?'

Lock hesitated between their evident enmity and their panic. He stared at the injured Vorontsyev, the man's body tense and enraged as if it struggled in chains rather than plaster and sheets. Then he nodded. 'OK – what about you?' Vorontsyev seemed relieved that his question was appropriate.

'Just go with Dmitri. I'm safe for the moment, but you're not. Go on, get moving!'

Dmitri dragged him by the arm and he gave in to the hard urgency of his grip, following him through the door. His disappointment was already insinuating itself. One injured man in bed, another fat man suspicious of him – and he'd heard only three other names . . .

He hurried after Dmitri, whose coat was flying around him, aware he was unarmed.

'No, Schneider called me only a moment ago – it must be less than ten minutes since he saw the American in Vorontsyev's room.'

'That may already be too long,' Turgenev's voice replied, and Bakunin scowled at the receiver he momentarily held away from his cheek. 'What measures have you instigated?' The cold formality was deliberately aloof.

'You'd better decide their outcome, don't you think?' Bakunin sneered, swilling the remainder of his coffee in the mug he held in his free hand.

'Very well. Bring matters to a conclusion immediately.'

Was there someone in the room with him?

'You're certain?'

'Yes.'

'You want the American eliminated?'

'Yes.'

'What about the others?'

'Anyone in the vicinity –' There was someone with him.

'Vorontsyev?'

'Later. Thank you for letting me know. Just make sure it's successful.'

Turgenev switched off the phone and placed it on his desk, which he then walked behind as if it would provide him with a barrier. The blizzard, still gathering strength, flung the snow across the large window of the study, through the glare of the security lights. He sat down and smiled apologetically at his visitor, who had remained all but oblivious of the call.

'I'm sorry for the interruption, Hamid. You were saying . . . ?'

The Iranian, dark-featured, as compact as a coiled snake, adjusted his tinted designer spectacles. He was unshaven rather than bearded and his shirt collar was buttoned beneath the jacket of the grey silk suit.

'My friend, I was simply relaying the impatience of Tehran in the matter of the consignment that is overdue.' He smiled, placing his fingers together in a steeple; a mullah of the Office for the Protection of the Iranian Revolution rather than an agent or case officer. Hamid was as ruthless, cunning and effective as the best of the KGB had ever been – like himself, he observed. But there was something chillingly *sincere* in his abuse of power, his acts of espionage, suppression, torture. Hamid, like so many Iranian intelligence officers, believed the ideology. Faith, of course, in his case. It was all for Allah and Islam, the killing, the imprisonments, the exterminations.

It made Hamid and his kind, including the dead Vahaji, more difficult to deal with. His thoughts returned to the image of the coiled snake. To disappoint these people was as risky as thrusting one's hand into a sack containing a cobra.

'I understand the impatience. Hamid my friend, I do not seek to make excuses. The heart attack of one of those people delayed matters – but it was the lack of security, the indiscreet nature of your own officer's behaviour that has meant greater care, slower progress.' He shrugged and spread his hands in the air in front of him. 'I have successfully added to the little stock of people you expect to take delivery of. There are now six *key* people in Novyy Urengoy –'

'Here?' Hamid asked greedily.

251

Turgenev shook his head. He detested dealing with Hamid and Iran precisely because of their sincerity, their hungry urgency.

'No, not here. But safe.'

'Then I would like to take delivery of them at once, if they are *top* people?'

'I give you my word they are. Your weapons programme will be accelerated by perhaps as much as a year.' He grinned disarmingly. Charm rarely worked with the Iranians – only results satisfied, gained influence. And even though Turgenev felt himself poised to move beyond the influence in the Islamic world that Iran could supply, and was all but ready to play a much larger game, he could not afford to dissatisfy. Which irked like a wasp sting. Hamid's eyes glittered. He touched his chin with a rasping sound. The wind outside was a low, distant moan, as of an animal dying in great, lonely pain. 'I *do* deliver what I promise, Hamid – I always have.'

'Agreed. Then, at once.'

'You've seen the weather, Hamid – where can you take them in a storm like this promises to be?'

The Iranian's eyes gleamed with anger.

'I do not know – and do not ask – what difficulties there have been, or how much jeopardy has arisen as a result of Vahaji's death and the police investigation –' Turgenev kept his features expressionless. Hamid possessed more background than he had supposed. '– but I must ensure that these people are not discovered. They are safe only in Tehran. Your not entertaining them here tells me as much.'

Turgenev began an expansive, soothing gesture, but merely placed his hands on the desk, fingers spread.

'If planes can't fly, you can't move them, Hamid my friend.'

'A plane must fly – as soon as possible.' He scowled over Turgenev's shoulder at the blizzard.

'That I can't guarantee.'

'There are guarantees on both sides, my friend. This is one of yours. There has already been too much delay.'

Despite everything, Turgenev admitted with a sense of weakness he loathed, he still required the goodwill of Iran and Pakistan. Especially, he needed to counter growing Chinese

252

influence in Islamabad that was already leaking through to Tehran. *He* must remain pivotal in the assistance given to nuclear weapons programmes in both countries for the foreseeable future. And he needed the drugs that came as payment to ease the spread of his influence in America. The heroin was the bluntest of instruments, and perhaps the most effective. Much remained dependent on Tehran and people like Hamid in the Office for the Protection of the Islamic Revolution.

'I'll arrange for detailed weather forecasts, maps, satellite information. Hamid, I will do what I can – '

'Then I am certain that it will be sufficient.' Hamid smiled. Turgenev was unable to entirely resist the image of a snake's mouth opening as it struck. He stilled his body which wanted to squirm in his subordination to the Iranian. He had to please them, as a servant would have pleased a master, or a whore a client. They were a strand of the web, but angering Tehran would set the whole of the web quivering with suspicion of his lack of cooperation, with rumour and doubt. Then, as if to brand him with the mark of a bondman, Hamid said softly: 'The woman is here, the one I requested?'

'Of course, Hamid. She is waiting in your room, I imagine.'

The Iranian stood up. He was little more than five feet in height, slightly built. His hand was cool and dry – like scales on a . . . Turgenev shut away the recurrent image and shook Hamid's hand firmly.

'I will say goodnight, my friend. You will arrange for the meteorological details?'

'Of course. A pleasant night to you.'

When the Iranian had left, Turgenev went to the sideboard and poured himself a large – vodka, he decided, and threw the liquor to the back of his throat where it burned satisfyingly. A Russian drink, he told himself, to rid his mouth of the taste of the Iranian and his own humiliation. He poured another vodka and turned to the window.

Damn the blizzard – damn Hamid equally.

And Lock . . .

. . . Bakunin had better make no mistake there.

*　　　*　　　*

253

The car remained parked where it had lurched against the snow-laden fence surrounding the dacha, its outline little more than a huddled white shape. The room was still cold, despite the log fire Dmitri had lit and the oil stove on a sheet of newspaper in the middle of the old rug. Their wet footprints had dried to vague reminders on the polished wooden floor.

Lock was chilled to the bone by a coldness that seemed part of the house and its recent history rather than an accident of the blizzard. They ate in virtual silence on a bare table at one end of the long room; baked beans, sausages, potato. Lock was hungry almost to viciousness. The younger man, Goludin, who had driven the car from the hospital along treacherous roads out of Novyy Urengoy, seemed morose and depressed, wary of Lock as if warned he carried infection. He was a lugubrious blank sheet of paper that had absorbed the ink of Dmitri's mood. Which burst out again as he said heavily, fork emphasising his meaning:

'You've brought us the news we didn't want to hear, American! How *powerful* our leading citizen is! Did we really need to know that? I ask you, does it help us? Turgenev was out of our league *before* you came . . . now? God alone knows!'

Lock spread his hands defensively.

'I needed your help. You think I'd have asked for it if I wasn't desperate?' he replied. 'A handful of half-assed detectives in a hick town. This place needs Wyatt Earp and his brothers, not you guys.'

'The only American we've got is you, Lock – and you don't seem up to all that much, even if you do speak good Russian!' Dmitri spat back, potato flicking onto his chin as he spoke.

'That makes two of us, man, two of us.'

The ensuing silence was lengthy, tightening around them like a drying shroud.

'So I'm not Schwarzenegger,' Lock murmured eventually. 'And you're not Alexander Nevski. Given those shortcomings, what do we do about our mutual problem?'

'Alexei – Major Vorontsyev – issues the orders. I told you, we're hamstrung. Now you're here and you've been seen to be here, it's just a matter of time before –'

'Then we'd better take the fight to them, hadn't we?'

Goludin said woefully: 'How *can* we get to Turgenev? It's impossible.'

Dmitri nodded vigorously, wiping his chin. 'Out of the mouths of babes,' he pronounced. 'You heard him.'

'So, we wait until the hospital patient makes up his mind what to do?' Lock snorted. 'You have to have leads, man! People you can lean on, a way of opening this thing up!' He hesitated. Uncommunicative as Dmitri Gorov had been, the smuggling of the scientists the Russians had stumbled on was more unnerving than the heroin. Turgenev paid for the heroin with the brains of men and women who had worked on the Soviet nuclear programme. He controlled Novyy Urengoy, and his means of doing so was the GRU. Turgenev was a tsar in this place, an autocrat . . . and he would be protecting himself against the discovery of a crime that even Moscow couldn't ignore. 'OK, you tell me what we can do,' he concluded, sighing.

Dmitri seemed satisfied, but without response. Goludin pushed his plate away and got up from the table. His boots squeaked on the polished floor as he walked towards one of the windows. His shadow moved across the wall, thrown by the firelight and the lamps. Dmitri ruminatively picked his teeth with a match. Lock stared at his own hands, clasped as if in prayer on the table.

'There's got to be some way,' he announced as if cheated. 'Some road we can open up to get to him. You must have evidence –'

'Have you?'

'It'll all be buried deep by now,' Lock admitted.

'Your case is just like ours, Lock. Powerless. You can't even go home, if all you say about yourself is true.'

'It's true.'

'And you still think there's something we can do?'

Goludin's shadow moved on the wall, slowly and comfortably like that of a parent, enlarged and authoritative. Lock heard the young man say:

'Shall I feed the rabbit, Dmitri?' It dissolved all sense of comfort the shadow had offered.

255

'What? Yes, if you like. There's some stuff in the –'

There was a noise that Lock was slow to identify. Goludin's bulky shadow on the wall behind Dmitri seemed to enlarge further, but that was no more than a trick of the light, or –

– Lock turned in his chair as Dmitri began to get to his feet. Goludin was skating across the floor towards them, his arms raised, his face distorted by agony. Then the rug tripped him and he blundered heavily to the floor. The bullet had spent itself against the wall above the fireplace. The shattered window was crazed as if with frost. Goludin lay still on the floor at Dmitri's feet. An instant later the windows shattered inwards at the insistence of a hail of bullets. Icy air flooded in as Lock crouched to the floor.

Dmitri, his face pressed close to Lock, his hand on Goludin's collar as if he intended dragging him upright and back to life, shouted:

'Put the lamps out! I'll douse the fire!'

Lock nodded, crawling away from Goludin's body across the polished floor, his hands sensing splinters. He pulled one lamp, then a second to the floor, fumbling with their unfamiliar switches. He heard the log fire roar aqueously, then sizzle into a dim glow. The room was in darkness. Snowlight seeped in, the noise of the wind and the rustle of the distressed curtains masking everything. Then Dmitri was beside him, lumping across the floor on all fours like an arthritic old hound. His breathing was ragged.

'No bloody time *left*!' he cried in a shouted whisper. 'Have you got a gun?' Lock shook his head. 'You useless bastard!' Dmitri's rage had all the anger of a man helpless against a storm or an earthquake. Which had obviously been visited on him by Lock. Then he crawled away and Lock heard scrabbling noises before he lumbered back on his haunches and pressed something metallic and cold into Lock's hand.

'Makarov 9mm,' he instructed, 'eight rounds. Here – spare clip. Can you use it?'

'I can use it.'

'They're heavily armed – that was an assault rifle hole in Goludin, poor bastard.'

'Is the place surrounded?'

'I'm just about to check. *You* watch the front of the house. We're cut off from the car.' He crawled away, eventually into another room. His eyes had been big with fear and anger, but there was the beginning of the trust of mutual risk. Then he heard Dmitri's mobile phone punctuating the wind, like a failing distress signal.

'Alexei –! Get out of there now! I don't care *how*, just get out! What? Is Marfa there? Good – now get out. Where? Yes –!'

Lock raised his head slowly until his eyes were level with the windowsill. He could hear Dmitri as he collided softly with some item of furniture. He could see nothing through the curtain of blown snow, hear nothing other than the wind. He shivered in the icy temperature, aware of the body on the floor just a few feet behind him. He squinted. The hazy light from the town outlined the igloo that their car had become, and there were other, more distant shapes similar in size. But there was no sign of movement, people. Military intelligence troops. Lock shivered once more, then was startled by the noises of Dmitri's return.

'I can't see a damn thing out there!' Dmitri whispered. 'You?' Lock shook his head. 'There won't be just one or two of them, Lock, they'll have come by the busload!' Talk was keeping his desperation at some slight distance, that much was evident. 'A barracks outing, and that bastard Bakunin in charge! Because of *you* –!'

'Calm down, man!' Lock shouted back in a hoarse whisper. 'For Christ's sake, let's think of some way to get out of here, not how to do their job for them!'

Heavy, dragged breaths for a time, then, with barely suppressed anger still evident in the voice: 'OK – OK. Any ideas?'

Then a sudden movement removed any lingering caution as he fired and the moving white bundle seemed to hunch into itself before falling into the snow beyond the garden fence. Rifle fire flickered like a row of candles in the blizzard. Lock and Dmitri lay together on the floor, their bodies shuddering with the impact of the bullets into the wooden walls, the floor.

Gradually, the noise was replaced by the sound of the wind. And Lock heard, with a rage that was like fierce excitement:

257

'You stupid bastard!'

'Sure. I counted six separate locations – what about you?'

'Five.'

'It's six . . . and maybe the same out back. At least as many strung out around the house. That's a dozen and more. This guy Bakunin – he doesn't take prisoners, right?' Dmitri shook his head. 'Then they'll be changing positions now, having given themselves away – take someone out, if you can. From the other window –'

Lock raised his head beside the window. A flicker of fire and the impact of a bullet against the far wall, the sound of a ricochet. He fired at the spot where the muzzle flash had originated but the two bullets disappeared silently into the snow. Ducked back as more gun flashes leapt out. The bullets hummed like insects in the room. Dmitri fired once and cursed a miss. Their reply was fourfold and the big man crouched beneath the window like some catatonic mental patient.

'You all right?'

'Yes – you?'

'OK.' Two lost animals calling to one another. 'You think they'll close in?'

'I don't know!'

'How do we get out?'

'God knows.'

Lock, lying on his stomach, could smell old polish on the floor, old cooking in the furniture, mustiness.

'I should watch the back of the house,' Dmitri offered reluctantly.

'Sure. Do that.'

'I can't call anyone . . . It'd be risking their lives, too.'

'Sure. Watch the back –'

Something, entering through the shattered window, burst near the fireplace. The room exploded in a blinding, white phosphorus light. Lock slapped at shards of flame on his clothes. The skin on his hands burned. Dmitri was exposed as by a flashbulb. The explosion filled Lock's eyesight, making him unable to see the fire it had started.

'Incendiary grenade –!' he heard Dmitri shout. Goludin's

258

clothes were smouldering, so was the rug, Lock realised as his eyesight returned. There were other fires, dotted over the room, flaring up quickly. The curtains near him were ablaze.

'No choice!' he shouted. 'Back door!' Then: 'What's out back?'

'Garden – a shed, vegetable plot –' He sounded like someone from a realtor's office. 'Fence, low enough to climb over – OK?'

'It's all there is – get going!'

The room was being greedily consumed by the fire. Two shots, as if poked in their direction to stir them into movement. They'd be waiting out there –

'I'll go through the door, you try a window.' Lock swallowed saliva, and at once his mouth was dust-dry. They crawled side by side to the kitchen door, Lock following Dmitri through it.

'You'll see the shed, off to your right.'

'OK. Watch yourself –'

The fire crackled behind them, stirred to a rage by the wind.

'Christ, the bloody rabbit!' Dmitri cried. Lock was stunned – the girl's, he realised. The four-legged icon wrapped in fur, every feeding-time a devotion for the lost daughter. He couldn't say *damn the rabbit* . . . Dmitri awkwardly pulled on the overcoat he had dragged from the table. Lock felt his own thrown against him and he struggled into it. Then Dmitri lifted the rabbit's cage down from a work surface and cradled it to his chest.

The fire was garishly orange, blocking the open door to the living room. Smoke roiled and billowed, making Lock choke. He stared at the kitchen door. 'The church in the old town, can you find it?'

'Yes –'

'Rendezvous there if we lose contact – OK? Alexei will make for it, too!' The rabbit's eyes were preternaturally large, hypnotised in terror by the light of the fire as it crouched in its cage.

He hesitated only for a moment, then slipped to the door and reached up to silently unlock it. Gripped the handle, then flung it wide, his whole body protesting at the imminence of pain. He flung himself to the right side of the door, rolling along the narrow, snow-covered verandah, bullets slapping into the wooden wall just above him, throwing up puffs of snow near his face. *A bloody rabbit*, was all he could cogently think, *a bloody rabbit, for Christ's sake!*

Rolled off the verandah into deep snow which masked him, whitening his overcoat into camouflage. He swallowed icy snow and looked up, attempting to locate the shed. Flame burst through the roof of the wooden dacha and from the windows at the rear of the house, outlining him. He climbed to his feet and ran in a crouch, stumbling through the snow as through deep, tidal water. Shots. Felt nothing. Numb with cold and shock, he wouldn't even sense the bullet that crippled or killed him –

– breath bullied from his body by collision with the wall of the shed. Snow fell from the roof, covering his head and shoulders. Impact like that of a bullet, halting him. His cheek against the rough wood. Still alive, unhurt. Just winded.

Firing, away on the other side of the house. Dmitri and *his daughter's bloody rabbit* – pointless. Pointless without the rabbit? He dragged air into reluctant lungs. Ice in his throat, his cheeks numb as the blizzard dried the melted snow on his face, caked it with more snow. Two shots impacted into the opposite wall of the shed, smashed glass. He saw a child's swing skeletal against the pale sheen of the snow, oranged by the fire. The whole of the dacha was now ablaze.

The church in the old town. He remembered it from his previous visit – a lifetime ago. Onion-domed, neglected, black with grime. Shots again from the far side of the garden, perhaps pistol shots, perhaps Dmitri . . .

He knelt in the snow, recollecting the surroundings of the dacha, aware of his shadow thrown by flames on the wall of the shed. The haze of the town's lights was dim, almost invisible. *That way – ?*

That way. He crawled into a bush which shed its weight of snow on him. Crawled into and through its snagging, scratching thorns and found the fence. Rickety, low, decayed –

– turned at the noise and fired, giving away his position, killing the greatcoated man who was blundering at him, rifle aimed. The soldier seemed to dive over him, still attacking as he died, then the body was still in the deep snow, arms splayed as if he had drowned and the body was floating.

Lock flung himself against the fence and it gave outwards, then collapsed. He fell sideways and ludicrously into a snowdrift, hearing a voice cry out:

'Over here! Across the lane – in the trees, here!' He did not even pause to consider some kind of trap, it had to be Dmitri calling to him. He blundered through the snow, which suddenly dipped and spilt him into what must be the lane. He struggled free of the drift and climbed the bank of the buried lane. A few lumbering steps more and the depth of snow diminished, surrendering to the dark barrier of the firs.

He could see nothing.

'Dmitri?' he called.

'Over here!' It was him.

He gripped the man's sleeve as he might have done a lifebelt, breathing stertorously, hearing the gasps of Dmitri's exhausted breaths. Head hanging, he found himself staring into the wide, black, terrified eyes of the rabbit, its cage half-filled with snow. The eyes reflected two tiny, burning dachas.

There was silence inside the trees, hardly any wind, little blown snow.

'How did you –?' he began.

'It's my place. They don't know it, didn't know the lane was there, probably – no time now. Come on, this way. Quickly!'

Vorontsyev switched off the mobile phone, then stared at it as if he had received news of a bereavement, puzzled and shocked rather than endangered. Marfa seemed more alarmed than himself at the raised, urgent tone of Dmitri's voice.

'What is it – what's wrong?' she asked, moving closer to the bed, glancing back more than once towards the door. 'Dmitri sounded as if he was in trouble.'

'He was,' he said, pushing back the bedclothes. His legs looked pale and weak as he stared at them. The hospital robe that tied at the back was rucked to his thighs. 'We have to get out of here – check the corridor.'

'Now?'

'Yes, *now*!' he snapped at her uncomprehending expression. She looked bovine, simple. 'For God's sake, check the corridor, then get me my clothes!'

She scowled at him, then crossed to the door. Looking out, she saw nothing, not even the duty nurse or another patient. Was that suspicious? She turned back into the room, to find Vorontsyev struggling to twist the shiftlike robe around so that he could untie the knots. His plastered arm flailed as if he were beset by bees or dogs. He appeared so comical she burst into laughter. His reddening face glowered at her.

'Get me my bloody clothes!'

'What's *wrong*?' she yelled back at him.

'They want to finish it tonight, by the look of it!' he ranted, sweat breaking out on his forehead, the fingers of his left hand merely tightening the knots in the ties of the robe. 'For God's sake –!'

'Don't waste time dressing,' she said levelly, calming a surge of fear that was as sudden as nausea. 'Just get your boots and a coat on –'

'I'm bloody dressing *now*!' he bellowed.

It seemed like a domestic quarrel that had ascended to some insane boiling point, like some of her parents' rows.

'Then let *me*,' she said, pushing him towards the bed. Then she dragged his clothes from the wardrobe. 'Sit down – sir.'

His gun was in his hand, as if to ward her off, but aimed at the door. She bent down and put on his socks. Then she reached for the knots of the robe and he sat staring stupidly at her. It was risible rather than erotic and she bent her head to avoid his noticing her smirking expression. She was aware of the door behind her and of the skin itching on her back in anticipation of someone entering. She undid the knots with quick, nervous fingers, then said:

'Take it off – sir.' Her voice was as clogged as if she were undressing him in sexual foreplay, but the fear was becoming uppermost now. Dmitri's voice had been panicky, over the edge. 'Is – is Dmitri in immediate danger?'

'Quiet – I'm listening for noises in the corridor!' he snapped in a hoarse whisper. 'Yes,' he added. 'I'm certain.'

He shuffled his loins into the jockey shorts she held out like a mother dressing an infant. He seemed unaware of her, but before she could experience pique, what he had said jolted her and she felt very cold.

'Trousers,' she said hurriedly.

He stood up and climbed into them as she held them. Then the shirt, then she zipped the trousers, buckled the belt. *Off to school* . . . He thrust his feet into his boots and she laced them, her fingers cold and anxious.

'Come on!' he snapped.

'I'm hurrying as fast as I – '

'Sorry.'

She helped him into his overcoat, and held out his fur hat after she had buttoned the coat loosely across his padded, immobile arm. He shook his head.

'Painkillers – that drawer,' he said, pointing with the pistol. Then he moved to the door and opened it softly.

Vorontsyev looked out. Empty. Good. He waved the pistol in his left hand, to bring Marfa to the door behind him. 'We'll use the big lift, the one they use for moving people about on stretchers . . . come on.'

He went through the door and Marfa followed him, watching beyond his shoulder, expecting at any instant the arrival of armed men, and aware of his broken arm and the stifled grunts of pain as she had dressed him. His condition made her fearful for her own safety rather than his, even though the sensation shamed her. He was too vulnerable, too weak and injured to be of help.

She tried to outface the thought of death, squash the memories of her experiences on the rig – the attack, the semi-consciousness, the smells of rubbish, the maw of the garbage truck towards which she had slid helplessly . . . He turned, and his expression made her realise she had stopped and was leaning limply against the corridor wall. He hurried back to her, shuffling like a hunchbacked grotesque, something from a movie.

'Come on!' he said urgently. 'It's all right, we'll make it!'

Vorontsyev realised that the calm with which she had dressed him had been all she possessed to help her confront the situation. Her ordeal at the rig had been too recent. He threw his left arm around her shoulders, to drag her into an embrace of encouragement and to move her towards the lifts. They really had to hurry –

TWELVE

Modest Offices

The two men hurried behind him along the corridor, as if they were in pursuit or taking him on a journey he had no wish to make. His panic mounted as he reached the door of Vorontsyev's room. His hand refused to reach for the handle. Then one of Bakunin's men, the one in the leather topcoat, elbowed him aside and jerked open the door, throwing it wide onto –

– bedclothes pulled back, signs of urgency. A glass of water had spilt onto the carpet. David Schneider felt a great relief overwhelm him, then a sense of danger as the two GRU men glared at each other, the bed, then him.

'Where are they? *You* were responsible for keeping them under surveillance!' one of them bellowed at him. His companion in the leather coat moved towards Schneider, the Makarov pistol gripped like a small club in his fist.

'Who warned them, Yank? *Who?*'

'Not me! They were your orders, *you* two were told to take care of him – he was here only minutes ago!' he blurted it all out, the words like flailing hands attempting to counter an assault.

'The lift!' one of them snapped. 'They can't have got far, the cop's injured – come on!'

They passed Schneider, the one in the leather coat growling: 'We won't find them in this storm, if they're already outside.'

'Get some back-up!' the other shouted back at him as they stood before the lift doors. 'It's being used, look –!'

'Stairs –!' Schneider heard, and then they were running along the corridor to the staircase.

He slumped against the wall, wiping the back of his hand across his wet, loose lips. God –

*   *   *

265

'Where's your car?' Vorontsyev's breath whistled between pursed lips that registered the pain in his arm and ribs.

'The car park – not far from the main doors.'

'OK.'

'Where then?'

'Teplov's knocking shop. I told Dmitri the church, but he'll know what I meant. Teplov will be discreet.' He tried to grin, but his lips were as wet as his forehead. Groaning in a short-breathed manner, he cried: 'These bloody ribs!'

She moved involuntarily towards him but he merely glared her away. The lift door opened. Icy cold drowned the compartment, snatching away their breath. Vorontsyev shivered uncontrollably.

'Come on,' she urged, and he leaned the least of his weight against her, no more than a gesture.

The underground delivery and emergency area stretched away around them like a cavern of concrete. The blizzard hurled itself down the ramp and through the echoing stanchions. He stumbled ahead of Marfa, doubled up as if against the full force of the wind rather than to nurse his arm and ribs, and she followed like a servant. The security man in his booth, its windows fugged and cosy, seemed oblivious of them as they climbed the icy ramp –

– to be struck by the wind and its burden of hurled snow, made breathless and blind by it. Vorontsyev staggered against her, knocking the breath from Marfa's lungs. She felt drowned in rushing air. Then her breath caught. Sodium lamps flared like distant gas rigs in the bellow of the storm, showing the snow as impenetrable, solid.

'All – right?' she screamed against his cheek.

'Yes!' he bellowed back, a thin, small noise.

'This way. Over *here*!'

He merely nodded, his head slow like that of an ailing donkey, as she guided him towards the car park. Their boots clumped through six or seven inches of snow and, as the wind numbed her to the bone, she was further chilled by the thought of an iced car, the failure of the engine, the condition of the road. She was afraid of awakening the pain in his ribs as she touched at

266

his elbow, moving them like two ridiculous, lost blind people across the indeterminate white expanse of the car park. She looked up once, twice, a dozen times to orientate herself by the dim, masked lights of the main hospital block. There was no noise but the wind, no images that were not fluid and white, except the occasional whitened lumps of cars, shapeless as cows asleep in a field. She began to yearn for the warmth that even the distanced, almost obscured hospital lights dimly promised.

Then she lurched in a cuffingly stronger surge of wind into her own car, her numb gloved hand smearing the snow on the windscreen. She rubbed at it furiously as if to uncover a familiar, buried face. Vorontsyev was crouching beside the lock, flicking at a cigarette lighter, which refused to ignite in the storm.

'Try it,' he said.

The key turned like a lever lifting a great weight, then she pulled the door open, climbed in and unlocked the passenger door. Vorontsyev collapsed gingerly into the seat and shut the door. The blizzard seemed hardly diminished by the metal of the car; it drummed and plucked on it, making it a sounding box. The windscreen fugged. Marfa turned the key in the ignition. The engine coughed and refused. Twice, three, four – coughed and accepted at the fifth attempt. The engine sounded very small, like that of a distant lawnmower. She heard Vorontsyev's laboured breathing before she gently pressed the accelerator. She had left the handbrake off when parking. The back of the car squealed and shimmied itself like the rear of a cat about to strike, before it moved out of its parking place, clambering over thick snow covering rutted ice. The car struggled, danced drunkenly, slipped and mocked its way towards the exit. In the headlights came the occasional whitened shape of another car and the flying snow.

The streetlights . . . ? Two of them – another two as she turned onto the road towards the invisible town. Another two coming slowly out of the storm as she passed the second two – then a fourth pair, a fifth, measuring out their tortoise journey across the treacherous, cleared but filling road. The snowploughs could do no more than bail desperately, like men in a sinking dinghy. And all the time, Vorontsyev's breathing . . .

267

. . . maddening her. A snowplough surged forward like a liner, flung snow enough to bury them, moved away behind them. The car skidded across the road, then furiously back as if eager to make amends. Her wrists ached . . . arms . . . eyes . . . Eventually, her ears dulled to his breathing and winces of pain.

A hundred pairs of streetlamps, two hundred – phantasms of shops and cafés like blank screens to either side, and finally, after perhaps an hour or more, the semi-darkness of the old town, then the dome and cross of the church against the town's bleary light. She drew the car close against dilapidated fencing, behind another vehicle – a customer, in this weather? The libido – *pigs*! Exhausted mockery and contempt whirled slow as planets in her mind.

She looked across at Vorontsyev, who was struggling from a doze.

'Are we – here?'

She nodded.

'Yes,' she sighed, releasing the steering wheel with difficulty, as if she had captured it long ago as a prize. 'Yes. The knocking shop – do you think you're ready for it, sir?' Then she began giggling with relief, aware that he was looking uncomprehendingly at her, helpless to prevent the giggle from becoming a roar of laughter.

'OK now?' he asked in the eventual quiet.

Catching her breath, she said: 'Yes. Can you climb out unaided or shall I – ?'

'Help me, please,' he said with ungentle abruptness.

She got out of the car, rounded it through the snowdrift, and struggled his weight upright. He leaned gratefully on the roof while she locked the car, then dumbly followed her beside the churchyard, across the lane and along the side path to the brothel. The old house seemed shrunken by the blizzard, its walls stippled and sheened with ice. The light above the front door fell weakly onto the snow-covered, trodden steps. Vorontsyev slumped against the stone of the porch as she rang the bell.

Dmitri tugged back the door as if startled from sleep, his features widening into shocked relief, then narrowing at once to solicitation as he admitted Vorontsyev's condition.

'You look like my mother!' Vorontsyev growled.

Dmitri closed the door behind them. Vorontsyev raised his head and found himself confronted by Sonya's bulk. She was dressed in an expanse of red sweater and trousers that seemed like those of a badly stuffed teddy bear. Her face was a hard, heavily made-up mask. Teplov, in dark slacks and jacket that hung from his small frame, stared out from behind her as if slung from her matronly back, his eyes tired and pessimistic. Vorontsyev laughed barkingly, the noise almost at once becoming a cough of pain.

'What do you want, Major – a reduction for a party booking? We don't have any girls to accommodate *her*, by the way –'

Sonya and Marfa glowered at each other.

'Why, Major – why?' Teplov moaned, complaining to an invisible and higher authority. Sonya appeared violently pleased at Vorontsyev's injured helplessness.

'Because there's nowhere else –' he began, but Dmitri interrupted.

'I told them it was surveillance, Alexei.'

Vorontsyev shook his head. 'Misha won't have swallowed that – will you, Misha?' Teplov appeared to wish he had been able to digest the fiction; devoutly so. 'It's Turgenev, Misha. He and Bakunin are after us.' Fear, cunning, hopelessness pursued each other across Teplov's thin features, animating the corpselike skin. He shrugged. 'See, Dmitri? Misha knows it's too dangerous to tell anyone. They'd bump him off, too.'

'You are a *shit*!' Sonya bellowed, striking Vorontsyev across the face, causing him to stagger against Dmitri, cry out with renewed pain. Sonya announced at once: 'Get him upstairs, into a bed. Come on, you stupid policewoman, help me!'

She walked Vorontsyev to the staircase, and began half-lifting him up each step. Three of Teplov's girls watched Sonya and Marfa, prepared either to giggle or commiserate.

'Where's Lock?' Vorontsyev called back to Dmitri, climbing the stairs behind them together with Teplov.

'Along the corridor – nice room. Lubin's with him.'

Sonya knocked loudly on the door, demanding it be opened. Lubin's bright look faded as he saw Vorontsyev, who snapped:

'I'm not dying – just need a rest. Painkillers . . .' he added in a mumbling voice to Marfa.

Lock's face was appalled. Vorontsyev was thrust onto a bed by Sonya's large, strong hands. The pillows were scented, clean, utterly soft, enveloping, and the big bed was welcoming, so welcoming and embracing . . .

. . . blinked awake.

'What – ?' He attempted to move, then squealed with pain. 'Oh, Christ!'

'Before you ask, Alexei, you've been asleep for less than five minutes,' he heard Dmitri announce. 'Sonya's brought coffee. There'll be sandwiches . . .'

They helped him into a sitting position.

The room was cheaply opulent, an image from a collection of titillating studies of brothels of the last century. Sonya's idea of style, taste, sophistication. But it was warm, clean, subtly lit and the scents were pleasant. Mirrors heavily gilded, the bed a four-poster, the carpet imitating Persian or Afghan rugs. Red flock wallpaper, of course. Dmitri's daughter's rabbit was chewing on green leaves, hunched in its cage on a nineteenth-century German sideboard with a bulbous, serpentine front. He felt safe, strangely.

He looked at each of them in turn.

'Where's Goludin?'

'Dead, Alexei – that's why I warned you to get out of the hospital.'

'Oh my God – tell me the rest of it,' he said, feeling utterly weary; no longer safe.

'Yes, be ready to move them when I give the order,' Turgenev repeated, wrinkling his features into an expression of distaste that mocked him from the bedroom mirror. Panshin in his damned jazz club was the personification of corruption in miniature; he was sleazy, squalid. 'Yes, check for surveillance, if you have any sense. And try not to sound too relieved – you should have no trouble from the police.' He paused, then pressed the console beside the bed, accepting the incoming call he had kept waiting. 'Yes?'

He stared at the ceiling as he resumed his position against the pillows, avoiding the mirror.

'Bakunin –'

'Yes? Is it over?'

'Gorov and the American – got away.' The voice was an abashed, anxious murmur.

'You incompetent bloody fool, Bakunin,' Turgenev's voice strained for control. His hand, truer to his mood, clenched and unclenched on the counterpane. 'What happened?' He listened. 'Then find them. What of Vorontsyev – you *what*?' Perspiration sprang from his hairline. The pillows enveloped rather than embraced. The armpits of his silk pyjamas seemed clammy. Events in Novyy Urengoy could not possess such self-volition, could not possibly orbit beyond his control. He was quivering with rage. It was as if everything was denying his authority. 'Yes?' he snapped, every emotion concealed by the fiction of busy irritation. Finally: 'Then they are hiding somewhere – they are together. Find them and finish them. Make sure you're successful this time.'

He put down the receiver and rubbed his temples as soothingly as a masseuse might have done. His head ached, as if he had entered a cold place from a warm room. The blizzard murmured beyond the double-glazing and the heavy drapes. He was deeply enraged. Challenged by a handful of petty, ignorant men who had decided upon self-destruction, on useless heroics. Nevertheless, *successfully* defied, every moment they remained alive. He inspected his fingers as if they had dabbled in dirt. Inferior, weak, unreliable individuals – Panshin, Bakunin, Vorontsyev and his crew . . . all no more than dogshit on one of his shoes, but now walked into the house, onto priceless rugs, offensive and unignorable.

Angrily, he got up from the bed and crossed to the bathroom in search of aspirin.

'I *know* there are five of us, Lock, I know that –' Vorontsyev's exasperation made his voice high, strained. 'I know Turgenev as well as you do, only not under such elegant and sophisticated circumstances! I understand better than you do how easily he could rid himself of us.' His anger faded and he lay back against the pillows. But Lock would not let him rest.

'Then what exactly can we do to even things up a little? *You* know the town, the quality of the opposition. What do we do? We can't stay here forever.'

'I know that, too,' Vorontsyev sighed, waving his good hand feebly. The painkillers made him feel tired, made clear thinking difficult. 'It's still a question of survival, not revenge, Lock — however much you want it to be the other way around.' He paused. Lock's intent gaze disconcerted him; he could see the American had little interest in survival, none in escape. Lock had come for Turgenev and his new and untrusted companions were mechanisms whose only purpose was to place him in a position from which he could destroy his enemy. 'It can't be done,' he said, 'what you want. We can't help you with it, no one can. There's no way you can get close to Turgenev.'

Lock glowered at him, and said: 'Then I'll find the way for myself. Thanks for your help.' He looked meaningfully at Dmitri, then stood up.

'Sit down, Lock . . . there is one way. It won't come out neatly, you killing Turgenev at high noon on the main street —' He grinned and the mocking laughter in his chest was punished by the searing pain of his ribs. He coughed. 'Forget the drugs for the moment.' Dmitri appeared betrayed, let down. 'It's the scientists we should concentrate on.'

'Why?' Lock asked bluntly.

Vorontsyev gestured at the scattered papers on the bed and the other furniture, at Lubin and Marfa crouched on the floor, sorting the files Lubin had snatched from headquarters on Dmitri's orders.

'There's everything in those files we have on the heroin. Even on Turgenev — our suspicions, *all* suspicions, are in the heads in this room. But there's no proof and there never will be. He kills people, remember, to keep his secrets.' He shivered. 'You were once CIA, you claim . . . OK. There are CIA people in Georgia, protecting Shevardnadze, in Moscow around Yeltsin, the FBI is all over Moscow and Petersburg advising the local

272

militia, gathering material on the mafia to help clean them up in America, let alone in Russia – '

'I know all that!' Lock protested.

'Then use what you know!' Vorontsyev snarled. 'Instead of imagining you're in a cowboy movie, *think*!' He coughed again. Marfa's empathetic wince made him angrier. 'If we can nail down some proof, some actual evidence, regarding the trade in nuclear physicists and technicians with Iran or any other Moslem country, the CIA and the FBI will crawl all over Novyy Urengoy! Can't you bloody well see that, Lock? That it's not a one-man crusade against the forces of darkness? We need to find one of those very valuable human commodities, just one, and get him away from here.'

'To Moscow?' Dmitri asked in surprise.

'Anywhere, now we've got Lock to help us. He speaks American, he's State Department – '

'I'm wanted for murder,' Lock said quietly.

'A little local difficulty. Give them this and you'll give them Turgenev. You'll get a citation, shake hands with your President. Be on the front cover of *Time*, I shouldn't wonder!'

He waved his good arm and lay back once more, exhausted.

Lock continued to study his face, even when the Russian closed his eyes. Unexpectedly, he felt less alienated and alone in the room, less aware of four pairs of strangers' eyes watching him. He rubbed his hands through his hair, aware, in an unwelcoming way, of the worm of survival wriggling in the pit of his stomach. And of Turgenev, remote and enfortressed and secure, and the smallness of their numbers, their utter powerlessness.

The shuffling of papers from the two younger ones kneeling on the carpet, the quiet scrape of pencils and of Dmitri scratching himself. Vorontsyev's breathing and the ticking of an ornate, last-century clock on the marble mantelpiece . . .

'OK – all right,' he announced eventually. 'I agree with your analysis. Washington – and maybe Moscow – would move heaven and earth to stop top Russian scientists being smuggled out. Drugs – ' He swallowed angrily. 'Drugs are passé, yesterday's problem. Too *ordinary* to get excited about.'

'You really agree the Yankees will want to know?' Dmitri

273

interjected, rubbing his loose jowls, looking tired, almost drunk. He got up and poured himself some more coffee from the percolator Sonya had replenished. 'Well, Mr Lock?'

Lock looked at his watch. It was after one. The blizzard roared around the old house, rattling the ill-fitting windowframes. He had a sense of urgency, but lack of sleep and agreement with Vorontsyev distanced it, made it comfortable like the rabbit in its cage. He shook himself.

'Yes, I do – how much time do we have?' he asked, turning back to Vorontsyev.

'As long as we stay hidden,' Dmitri muttered.

They had heard the creak and growl of half-track vehicles passing the house; the GRU had to be turning the whole town on its head in an effort to find them.

'That long?' Lock replied cynically. 'OK, Major – what now?'

Vorontsyev opened his grey eyes, then leaned forward, hand pressed against his ribs, and said to Lubin:

'Anything – anything at all?'

'We've been over and over the stuff here, racked our brains, sir. Just can't narrow it down –'

'They have to be somewhere!'

'Obviously, Lock. Turgenev owns the whole town, or most of it. What he doesn't own he has in his other pocket. They could be anywhere – *not* the hotels, though. That's how we stumbled on them in the first place. Not out at his place either, that would be stupid of him. Somewhere close, somewhere safe.'

'Panshin's club – Panshin's apartment?' Dmitri asked.

'Who's Panshin?'

'The jazz club.' Lock nodded. 'He's into the heroin business, we're certain of that now. That's a recent venture. He could be dragooned into this, too . . . ? I'm not sure.'

'They're as locked in as we are, anyway,' Dmitri observed. 'They won't be going anywhere in this – and it's set to last another two days at least. If we can stay alive, we might have forty-eight hours!' He smiled pessimistically.

Vorontsyev shook his head carefully. Lubin was afraid and Marfa was rubbing her upper arms vigorously as if cold.

'You see, Lock? We're really as desperate as you,' Vorontsyev murmured. 'OK, Panshin for one – where else?'

'Turgenev has offices all over town,' Marfa offered, Lubin nodding in agreement as he sifted a sheaf of papers. 'Companies he owns or part-owns. Warehouses – even out at the airport he's got cargo hangars. Shops, industrial units.'

Vorontsyev laughed, puzzling Lock.

'You see, Lock, it's the geological record of a capitalist,' he explained. 'Even Tsar Peter had to start somewhere, in quite a small way. Importing luxury items, especially food and booze. Then fashion for a time, wasn't it, Dmitri?' Gorov nodded, himself smiling in recollection. 'Import-export. Just like today, only smaller. Different cargoes, different profits. Gradually, he acquired gas leases, and the money to exploit them. Then more quickly, he grew and *grew*.' He stared at the ceiling. 'So, we have dozens of small to medium companies, all with offices, still connected to Turgenev, little bits of his empire all over town. Give Mr Lock the list. Let *him* choose which one we hit first!'

'That'll just draw attention to us!' Lubin protested.

'Sorry, youngster.'

Lock took the handwritten sheet, glancing down the considerable list of companies. Turgenev's recent past, his last six or seven years. Toes in the water, no more than that. Food importing, frocks, drink, just as Vorontsyev described. He looked up.

'He was creating a dozen covers, wasn't he?'

'I imagine so. Every means he could to gain constant access to the airport, to flights in and out.'

'And these companies are still in business – legitimately?'

Vorontsyev looked at Marfa, who nodded.

'Apparently.'

'Then he won't use any of them, will he? Not for this, not at *this* moment in time.' He handed the sheet abruptly to Marfa, who scowled at his condescension. 'Find one that isn't trading any longer, one with large enough premises. That's where they'll be.'

'Sir?' Marfa asked.

275

Vorontsyev nodded.

'Humour Mr Lock, Marfa,' he said, carefully excluding all excitement from his voice.

The dress shop was on 9th Street, three blocks from the elegance and triple mark-up of K Street. Its grille-protected windows were dark and empty, like a number of the shops on either side of it. Small, dingy emporia that seemed to have been early casualties of the rising tide of affluence in Novyy Urengoy, patronised now by the dependents of rig workers, the unemployed and old, the disabled and the remaining locals. The car, slewed onto the opposite pavement, was alone in the snow-filled street. The few sodium lamps merely tinted the blizzard.

Vorontsyev imagined rather than saw the flicker of torchlight behind the dark blank of the shop window, the cloudy pupil of glass left free of ice and driven snow. The car's heater protested loudly at its forced labour, and Lubin was reflectively silent in the driver's seat. Lock had tried to insist he stay at Teplov's, but he had outmanoeuvred the American, leaving Marfa on the pretence that Sonya wasn't to be trusted not to call someone to inform on their whereabouts. Dmitri and Lock had entered the empty shop. There was an apartment, cramped and uninhabited, it appeared, above the shop and owned by the earliest manifestation of a Turgenev property company. Turgenev had bobbed on down the street on the surge of money brought into the town, to own the leases and a claim on the profits of a dozen of the smartest, most expensive boutiques and stores, bars and nightclubs. Yet he had kept this place untenanted, unearning, when he might as easily have sold it to one of the Iranians or Turks or Pakistanis who supplied their own communities – at least rented it to one. Vorontsyev felt a tickle of excitement in his chest, like the beginnings of a cough. Lock was smart; more into the covert than he was, the secretly criminal, the world of mirrors and disguises. Places where things *didn't* happen. He and his people had watched only the inhabited places, the movements and motives of crowds.

He saw a torch flash light against the upstairs window, then sensed that a curtain was drawn across the glass. He lit a cigarette and listened to the storm and Lubin's efforts to control his breathing. The boy was all right – just.

Ten minutes later, he saw Dmitri and Lock emerge from the narrow alleyway leading to the rear of the shop and lump their way across the treacherous street. The snowploughs hadn't cleared it for hours and traffic had consequently avoided it.

The blizzard whirled snow in on him as Dmitri opened the door and clambered into the front passenger seat. Then Lock repeated the shower as he slid in beside Vorontsyev. The American was grinning.

'It's a place waiting for someone to arrive!' Lock exhaled, self-satisfaction wreathing his chilled features. 'Tell him, Dmitri, tell the man!'

'Nothing there – the place is empty,' Dmitri began, turning round in his seat. Vorontsyev felt his own impatient excitement mount. 'Hasn't been used for much at all, by the look of it, for some time. Dust everywhere in the upstairs flat. But, food, a couple of fan heaters, drink. The electricity supply's on, so is the gas. Camp beds stacked at the back of the shop, too.'

Vorontsyev gripped Lock's arm.

'You could smell cigarette smoke, Major – I swear it. Maybe four, even five people, judging by the supplies and the camp beds. We just have to stake this out!'

'Where are they *now*?'

'Alexei, it doesn't matter – they must be coming here!' Dmitri insisted. 'As Lock says, all we have to do is to wait for them to arrive.'

'Who? Bakunin and a division of armour? We can't sit around on the street in daylight, Dmitri!'

'Maybe they'll come tonight?' Lock suggested seductively. 'Any minute now – uh? Think about it.'

Both Dmitri and the American were reckless at the ease with which they had uncovered the safe house – for it had to be that – and he felt almost shamed at his own cautious reluctance; as if he refused to join in some childish game that might prove dangerous. Nevertheless, he continued shaking his head.

'An hour – no more. *One* hour. Lubin, move the car down the street.'

277

The engine clattered noisily as Lubin pressed the accelerator. The snow chains on the tyres ground and creaked and the ZiL rolled away from the deeply rutted kerb, skidding into the middle of the road. Lubin righted it and drove cautiously down the centre of the street to the junction with gaudier L Street. The occasional lurching truck, one or two cars, shop windows holding a subdued glare, a couple of all-night cafés optimistically still ablaze.

'Park here,' Vorontsyev instructed.

Lubin dragged on the handbrake and, at Vorontsyev's nod, switched off the engine. The blizzard was suddenly louder inside the car, shaking it like a riotous crowd. L Street was obscured, then revealed, obscured again; darker 9th Street seemed like a narrow tunnel.

'Right, gentlemen, I said an hour, and an hour is what I meant.' He looked at his watch. 'We leave at three, at the latest –'

The mobile phone in his pocket trilled. All four of them were startled, as if by a sudden searchlight thrown on them. Lock tugged it from Vorontsyev's coat pocket and switched it on.

It was evident to Lock that it was Marfa's voice, despite the hoarse, urgent whisper she employed like a bad actress.

'They're here, Alexei – sir. GRU. They want to search the place from top to bottom –' There was another, harsher female voice beyond Marfa, urging the girl to get out. 'They're here –!'

'For God's sake, Sonya – shut up!' Marfa snarled, pressing her face close to the mask of make-up worn by the older, heavier woman.

They were standing against the bedroom door, Sonya's large, plump white hand still gripping the porcelain doorknob. Sonya's eyes were wild with concern, almost oblivious to Marfa except as a presence. There was spittle on the carmined lips.

'Get out, leave us alone!' Sonya repeated. 'They mustn't find you here!'

'Which way?' Marfa demanded, the mobile phone pressed against the side of her face like a dark poultice. She heard Vorontsyev gabbling reassurance. 'No, don't come here!' she snapped at him. 'The place must be surrounded. I'll get out –

278

where are you? Yes, 9th and L – I'll find you. Yes!' She closed the connection and thrust Dmitri's phone into her pocket, tugging her scarf tightly around her face.

Then she was adrift, bereft of volition. She felt panic begin to spread like a blush across her features. Sonya was contemptuous for an instant, then simply afraid again. Only the rabbit, browsing leaves in its cage, seemed oblivious of threat. Marfa forced herself to the window and lifted the edge of the drawn curtain, which smelt of old velvet and old dust. Headlights glared through the blizzard outside and she heard the sound of raised voices and the clump of boots on rutted snow. Dark figures hurried. Behind her, Sonya was clearing coffee cups with clumsy hands. Marfa knelt and began shuffling the scattered papers into an untidy bundle, then stared wildly about her for a place of concealment – for the papers, herself? God –

Sonya was staring at her, but her attention was directed beyond the door, her head cocked to one side like that of a large, predatory animal. Marfa opened the heavy old wardrobe to push the bundle of papers into it. Garish slips and housecoats, boots, underclothes. A spangled, ribboned basque lay like an abandoned piece of armour on the floor of the wardrobe. Then Sonya was behind her, her hands gripping her shoulders, her lips against Marfa's cheek.

'Quick – get your clothes off! Come on – put the papers in the *bed*!'

She was tugging at the scarf, the long dark coat, even the glasses Marfa had not removed. Marfa tried to push her hands away, then experienced a moment of terrified betrayal as the woman held her wrists with one big hand and slapped her face. The spectacles flew off.

'Get *away* –!'

'Get your clothes off, put on a housecoat – *here*!' Sonya replied. 'I hope to God Teplov doesn't give the whole bloody game away! Come on!'

Marfa took off the coat, then her sweaters, lastly her denims. Sonya bundled them into the wardrobe. Closing the door, she snapped:

'Don't get into the bed, it's too obvious! Christ, why can't you

279

women wear some make-up – who'd fancy you in a month of Sundays?'

She pushed Marfa down on the bed. Marfa was chilly in the flimsy housecoat which reeked of cheap scent and barely covered her white knees. Sonya seemed no less distraught than when she had entered the room to warn her.

'Can you smoke a cigarette without coughing?' she asked. Marfa nodded doubtfully. 'Here!' She thrust a cigarette at her. 'And stop shivering!'

In a mockery of stately ease, Sonya sat in one of the velvet-upholstered chairs, lighting another cigarette.

There were noises along the corridor, then the door was flung back and two GRU soldiers, greatcoated, wet-shouldered and grinning, appeared at the threshold.

'Didn't your mother teach you to knock?' Sonya snapped. 'What is this, another raid?'

'Shut up, Grandma!' the more pimply of the two young men mocked. The other snickered, nudging his companion and announcing:

'Don't fancy yours, Sasha!'

'Mother Fat and her daughter, Miss Thin – bloody hell, you don't go to any trouble for the customers, do you?'

A voice, sharp with authority, called from a distance, and the two soldiers snapped to half-attention before Sonya's mocking laughter made them shambling figures of uncertain contempt once more. Quickly, they opened the wardrobe, drawers in an old chest, glanced beneath the bed.

'Expecting to find your older brother here, boys?' Sonya observed, exhaling smoke theatrically at the ceiling and crossing her legs.

The two young men scowled. One of them, onion on his breath, stared affrontingly at Marfa, his body hovering very close to her. She forced herself not to flinch, to present no more than patient indifference.

Tired of his lack of authority, the youth with acne snapped to his companion: 'Let's go before you catch something!'

'Not even the flu, boys,' Sonya shot after them as they slammed the door.

Sonya's features crumbled into a clownish expression of exaggerated defeat and anxiety. Then she said hoarsely:

'Now, get your clothes on and get ready to leave as soon as they do.' She was listening to the clump of retreating boots. Marfa tried to control the shiver that possessed her, rubbing her arms furiously and hunching into herself. She could *taste* the onion that had been on the soldier's leering breath! 'Come on, they won't be back – just a couple of tarts, they'll report. Not that anyone but a *kid* would say that about you!' she snorted, relieving her nerves. 'Snap out of it! Sod off and don't come back!'

Vorontsyev stared at the phone in his hand, listening to the noise of the disconnected call. Then he and the others were startled as the blizzard buffeted a shapeless staggering lump against the side of the ZiL. Then the drunk or addict or whatever he was slouched on, bent against the flying snow and the force of the wind, towards the lights of an empty, hopeful café. A snowplough ground across the next intersection, its warning light dim through the storm.

'What's happening?' Dmitri blurted, turning back to Vorontsyev.

'The GRU are there.'

'Teplov?'

'No, he wouldn't. Just bad luck –'

'What about Marfa?' Lubin all but wailed.

'She told us not to go back there!' Vorontsyev warned as Lubin turned the key and the engine coughed.

Lock remained silent as he watched the snowplough disappear and the huddled lump of the man retreat up L Street. The girl was none of his affair, however her vulnerability nagged at him. If they caught her, she'd talk, as would any of them in time, but there was little or nothing to tell. Only the location of the ZiL.

Lubin and Vorontsyev were staring at each other in challenge. Then the young man in the driving seat turned away, swallowing loudly. Dmitri's large hands rested on the back of his seat. Then he flapped his fingers in acquiescence and shrugged his

281

shoulders. Lubin's breathing was the sole noise of dissent.

'We hang on?' Lock asked.

Vorontsyev nodded. 'We hang on —' he began gloomily.

'Hello, what's that?' Dmitri was looking past Vorontsyev. Then he opened the door and began clambering out of the car. 'There's a car on 9th — parked. I'll just go and have a look.' He shut the door quickly on any reply.

The wind cut through his bulky clothing and the snow blinded him for a moment, until he read the direction of the wind and turned his gaze aside. He staggered like the drunk against the wall of wind and snow, as if feeling his way blindly along its solidity. Heard his teeth chattering and pulled his scarf across his mouth. His boots floundered through the drifted snow against shop fronts, grilles, steel doors. Signs in Arabic, Farsi, Turkish, pigeon-English, Russian, Ukrainian. Smells, even in that temperature and force of wind, mostly the scent of the poor and the crowd, what they ate and drank.

He realised his mistake even as he imitated the figure who had faltered against the car. Lurching against the black, snow-roofed car, he identified it as German. BMW. The thin, pale face of the driver stared into his and he recognised Dom Kasyan, Val Panshin's hit man; small and neat as ever in a dark overcoat and black driving gloves. The face twitched with recognition and the decision to act. The door of the car began to open. Dmitri pulled himself away as if from a magnetic field, stumbling back across the pavement and against a darkened shop window protected by an ice-cold metal grille. Kasyan's face was alert, threatening, even as his lips moved close to the mouthpiece of the carphone. A white wrist rested on the steering wheel. Something gleamed as it was held in the black driving glove.

Dmitri struggled with his clothes, opening his overcoat and reaching for the pistol in the shoulder holster. Kasyan put down the phone. It was only seconds since —

— the BMW's engine fired, the door slammed, and the car screeched and ripped its way on snow tyres across the ruts and into the middle of 9th Street. Dmitri's gun wavered in front of him, as if held by someone else. His heart was pounding.

'Oh — bugger it, *bugger*!' he bellowed at the flying snow, waving his arms as if he had been stranded in the storm by the accelerating BMW.

He turned and blundered back towards the ZiL, the wind behind him pushing him like a rock down a mountainside. Lubin and Lock were already standing beside the car, guns drawn. He looked back, stumbling, and saw the BMW turn out of sight.

'What is it?' Lock shouted.

Ignoring him, Dmitri reached the car and leaned into it, his breath coming in great sobs.

'Kasyan – that little shit Kasyan!' he shouted. 'I recognised him and he recognised *me*! Oh, shit, Alexei, it's all cocked up –!'

'What's the matter?' Lock demanded.

Vorontsyev snapped: 'Panshin's right hand. Panshin's got the scientists all right, Kasyan must have been scouting the place – they won't bloody well come now!'

'Lubin, let's move it, uh?' Lock ordered. 'They know where we are now. Come on, fella, move it!' He bundled Lubin back into the driver's seat and climbed in beside Vorontsyev. 'How far is this guy Panshin from here?'

'What?'

'Speed, man, speed. Did the guy use a phone?' Dmitri, slamming his door, grunted in the affirmative. 'OK, so Panshin knows. But he has to talk to Turgenev now. There have to be new arrangements, another safe house. Panshin must have them at his place – jazz club, you said?' Vorontsyev nodded. 'Then let's hit it before they can get those people out of there. Hit it *now* – or forget it!'

'Four of us –?' Dmitri began.

'What about Marfa?' Lubin asked urgently. 'She'll expect us to be here.'

Marfa had obviously escaped; had necessarily escaped, for Lubin's equanimity, his ability to function. Perhaps each of them assumed the same, Lock realised, even himself. The reminder of their numbers jolted him. He shook his head.

'Hit it now, or forget it,' he repeated. His hands were clenched into fists in his gloves, resting on the thighs of his denims. Come on, Vorontsyev, he thought, willing the policeman to agree. He

283

looked at the Russians in turn. 'We need *one* guy, just one. It was *your* idea – one guy to show to Moscow, to the CIA or the FBI. Only one.'

'Lubin – take us to Panshin's . . .' He smiled, though he was leaning back in the rear seat to ease his ribs and arm. 'I feel like some late jazz.'

'What about Marfa?'

'I can't call her – it might kill her!' Vorontsyev snapped.

The scullery door of the old house was slammed shut behind her. She stood shivering in the wind, her scarf flying away from her face so that she had to release her shaking body and grab at it. The cold she blamed as much on the ridiculous, humiliating housecoat – her throat and cheeks still reeked of the cheap scent – as on her fear or the storm. The door being banged shut was Sonya's final ejaculation of angry relief.

She looked at her watch. Almost two-thirty in the morning. The blizzard and the darkness oppressed her. Her own escape sharpened her sense of Goludin's death. He'd been casually, finally erased, like some mistake. She saw his earnest, affably willing features and experienced a lurching sense of loss that momentarily dizzied her.

She shook her head to clear it and sniffed loudly; then reached into her pocket and removed Dmitri's phone, at once dialling Vorontsyev with clumsy, gloved fingers. Then she waited, hearing nothing but the wind. The looming church was the only other building she could distinguish. Come on, come on, she muttered in her thoughts, stamping her feet.

'Alexei – I'm all right!' she blurted, at once embarrassed at her released nerves.

'What happened?' she heard in a voice from which all emotion was excluded, to her disappointment.

She told him in a babble of disconnected sentences, concluding:

'They didn't fancy me!' And giggled with tension.

'Where are you now?'

'Outside the brothel. You?'

'We're –' It was as if he had paused to consult the others,

284

then he added: 'We're on our way to Val Panshin's club. We think the people we want are hidden on the premises.'

'I'll join you,' she said quickly. 'Be there in fifteen minutes at most.' She switched off the phone at once and thrust it decisively back into the pocket of her coat. In the other pocket, she gripped the pistol. The file of papers was held under her arm.

She stepped out into the full force of the wind and the hurled snow, which stung hard against her face. Her boots plunged into heaped snow as she walked lumberingly towards the church's dark, empty, decayed bulk and the lane where the car had been parked –

– aware that someone might have been left to keep the car under surveillance. It had a police numberplate, even if it was caked and hidden with frozen, dirty snow. She gripped the gun more tightly as she reached the broken fence that bordered the lane alongside the church. The deep impressions of the ZiL's tyres were all but hidden. Maybe they hadn't noticed the smaller car, her car . . . ?

There was no one near it. She warmed the lock with the petrol-fuelled handwarmer she kept for the purpose, pressing it against the icy metal, then inserted the key. Tugged the door open with a crack of ice and climbed into the driving seat. The storm's noise hardly diminished inside the car. She could hear her own breathing though, and saw it cloud the inside of the windscreen. She thrust the ignition key towards the dashboard –

– hands, a stiff arm, around her throat. Heard someone else breathing, close against her face, closer than the soldier with acne, smelt the scent of his clothes and old sweat . . . Her head was being dragged back by the arm locked around her throat, dragged upwards to be snapped away from her body, the breath squeezed out of her. His fierce breathing beside her, his bulk leaning over the seat from the rear of the car where he had concealed himself . . . others?

Couldn't breathe now, not at all, not even through her nose which was running, not through her mouth, clogged with saliva and terror . . . Sensed his success, the imminence of it, through his frame and stiff arm. The windscreen was blind but the snow was darkening, darkening –

285

– body a long way below her now, not part of her, head spinning but in darkness, just little flashing lights like red and green stars flickering in the blackness . . . Body further away, much too far to help, that slow-moving arm more distant than his arm around her throat, *much too distant . . .*

The shot deafened her, so that she hardly heard his roar of pain. Hardly felt his arm release its grip, or saw it waft in slow motion away from her, sliding like a defeated snake back over her seat into the rear of the car. She turned to watch the white hand as if it belonged to a waving friend. And *her* hand – really her finger – squeezed the trigger once more. The pistol exploded, illuminating his face and blinding her . . . There had been a great deal of blood from the first head wound.

She turned away from the dead man, her whole body shaking in the seat, her thoughts repeating that she had not noticed the wetness of recently melted snow on the door, *should have noticed it was wet, should have . . .*

She started the engine out of panic, and the car squealed and wriggled down the lane, thrown from rut to rut, drift to drift. She winced in anticipation of firing from behind her. The last air bubbled out of the dead man's lungs. She felt sick, so desperately sick – she had to stop . . .

. . . She threw the door open and vomited into the snow.

When she closed the door again, the shivering would not stop. She was icily cold. She wiped her chin with the back of her glove. Gripped the wheel hard enough to still her arms, then slowly, deliberately accelerated. The car appeared much bigger, overwhelming her as it seemed to turn out of the lane towards the new town of its own volition. She clung to it as if vainly to restrain it from bolting.

They'd left only one man. Probably didn't know it was hers, hadn't given it much of a priority. The watcher had decided to be clever, hide *in* the car, or just be more comfortable than pressed against the wall of the church. She didn't want to think about him. She could smell the blood but could not bring herself to stop the car again in order to bundle the body into the snow. Not yet, anyway, not just yet –

*　　　*　　　*

286

They sat in the car, the engine and the heater off, where Lubin had parked it on K Street, one block from the entrance to Panshin's club. The Café Americain was closed and lightless. Panshin's car was parked at the rear, as was the BMW driven by Kasyan. There were two other cars, small and Russian – but no transport in which half a dozen people could be easily smuggled to another location. Lubin was watching the rear of the club, eager to erase any sense of insubordination his concern for Marfa might have evoked.

'You think they're still inside?' Vorontsyev asked.

'Maybe – maybe not. Panshin's in there, for sure. Let's ask him, uh? How many other guys would be around at this hour?'

'Three, perhaps four. The place has been closed for about an hour. In this weather, and with what he's been hiding in the attic, he might not even have opened.' He shrugged. 'There could be more than four. Extra guards. Lock, we won't know what we're walking into –'

'Doesn't matter.' Lock's expression was bleak and introspective; dangerous to himself and those in his immediate vicinity, Vorontsyev concluded. 'It's the only shot we have. We have to take it, both of you know that.'

Dmitri sighed, but he was nodding, however reluctantly and with however much reservation.

'We'll need Marfa – she can watch our backs.'

'We need to go in *now*,' Lock said levelly. There was, once more, the sense of an actor rehearsing a role that did not quite suit, one that required another voice, a stranger's mentality. Vorontsyev remembered Lock's CIA background. This was a field agent resurrected; bad old habits, recovered instincts. 'Kasyan's been back maybe twenty minutes now. They'll have called for back-up. We don't have much time.'

'If she walks in blind, she could get herself killed!'

'Then *call* her!'

Vorontsyev handed the phone to Dmitri, who dialled his own number.

'Yes?' Marfa sounded distant, removed.

'All right?'

'Dmitri –!' she burst out.

'What is it?'

'*Nothing!*' she snapped back. 'Nothing.'

'We're going in to Panshin's now. When you get here, wait outside, watch our backs. We don't know who's in there or how many. We may be coming out in a hurry — be ready for us.' Dmitri snapped off the phone.

'OK?' he asked.

Vorontsyev nodded. The click as Lock slid a round into the breech of the Makarov was startling, bell-like in clarity. Dmitri exhaled noisily.

'OK.'

Lock opened the door and got out, shutting it softly behind him. Vorontsyev looked darkly at Dmitri and murmured:

'Don't let anything he does get you killed, old friend. Remember that. We watch out for each other, not for him. Understand?'

Dmitri's expression was a conflict of acceptance and disappointment, good sense struggling with some bright new loyalty that embraced the American. Then he said:

'Understood — sir.'

Vorontsyev snapped: 'Lock is dangerous to everyone around him, whichever flag they're carrying. Just remember that! All he wants — *still* wants — is Turgenev dead. He's humouring us. Don't let him humour you into your pine box!'

THIRTEEN

Members and Outsiders

'Very *well*, Hamid — very well!' His exasperation was like a broken bone thrust through the surface of their conversation; the polite mincing game he was forced to play kept tearing like ricepaper. 'I will personally supervise your departure on *my* aircraft.' There it was again, that note of pressure in his voice, that admission of the Iranian's superiority.

It is *temporary*, he reminded himself, merely a negotiating ploy. He was weary of the storm and his own narrowed focus, forced upon him by Hamid — above all he was weary of the small, neat, efficient Iranian. This is *temporary*. He repeated the mantra, comforting himself.

'Good, good — my friend, I realise I am trespassing on your patience and time.' He shrugged. 'I myself have people I must please, even if that is not your situation. Thank you for helping me.'

Turgenev grinned and rubbed his hand through his thick fair hair. The apology was sufficiently generous for him to accept it; it smoothed him like a woman's hand.

'Accepted.' He raised his hands. 'We continue to need each other, Hamid — it's best that we work closely together.' Even as other, more important matters piled up, he added to himself. Deals, negotiations, reports, analyses were stacked in his mind as blatantly as would have been billions of dollars heaped in neat piles on the desk in front of him. Those matters were worth such sums, but he had to superintend the boarding of half a dozen nuclear scientists and technicians onto his private jet for the flight to Tehran, like some damned steward in an airline uniform. He continued levelly, his voice pleasant: 'The weather window is forecast to appear around eight, soon after full

289

daylight. It could last two hours, or twenty minutes –' The Iranian's features darkened with annoyance. '– they can't be more accurate, I'm afraid.'

'I understand,' Hamid said slowly.

'Good.'

'They are prepared?' He made them sound like meals that would be served on the aircraft.

Turgenev nodded. 'They are. Safely hidden but fully briefed. They know what is happening to them, and they have been handsomely down-paid.' One or two of the early people had panicked at the last moment. A few had tried to back out, even to leave Iran or wherever, disgruntled and homesick. *Pour encourager les autres*, they had not been allowed to return. 'It's not like the early days any longer, Hamid. Moscow treats them like dirt now. They *want* to work for you!' He laughed.

'What time shall we be leaving?'

'Six, Hamid, not before.' It was as if he heard the blizzard more clearly for an instant, bellowing about the hunting lodge. A window rattled somewhere. The snow had drifted to first floor level outside the heavy curtains of the vast, panelled sitting room. The storm seemed intent on burying his home. He smiled, toasted the strict Moslem with his whisky, then swallowed the last of the drink. He felt almost at ease, despite the Iranian's presence – until he remembered Bakunin and the business of Lock and Vorontsyev.

He wished to hear of a successful conclusion to that fiasco before he left for the airport.

'Is there something wrong?' Hamid enquired with fastidious politeness.

'No – nothing,' he replied evenly, without emotion. 'Nothing.'

Vorontsyev listened, head cocked to one side. Dmitri's noises at the front door were barely audible, even in the sheltered car park behind the Café Americain. Lock stood beside him, softly stamping his feet against the cold or his own tense impatience. Lubin, features pinched with cold beneath the fur hat, waited with what might have been reluctance for his next order.

Dmitri's yelling and buffeting of the front door was suddenly carried to them clearly by a freak of the wind and Vorontsyev nodded to both his companions. At once, Lock moved clumsily forward, as if released from some huge restraint. His borrowed pistol was gripped in one gloved hand, stiffly at his side. Vorontsyev's own gun was in his left hand. He'd had Dmitri *strap him more tightly together* – paradoxically the recollection of Dmitri's description caused him to smile – so that it was difficult to swallow the icy air as he breathed. He was on the edge of grogginess because of the painkillers.

He stumbled once and Lubin caught his arm to steady him. Then they were in the shelter of the porch, trampling on drifted snow. Lock banged on the rear door of the club, which masqueraded as its members' entrance. Other punters used the door on K Street.

'Open up – GRU!' Lock bellowed in Russian, startling his companions. 'Come on, you lazy shits, the Colonel's here and wants to talk to Panshin! Open up, you bastards! He wants to know how you managed to cock it all up!'

Lubin was smirking in open admiration of the American, even as the door opened and a face Vorontsyev recognised as belonging to one of the bouncers inspected them, then began protesting.

'Keep the fucking noise down! You want to – ?'

Lock struck him across the bridge of the nose with the barrel of the Makarov and thrust the door against him as he screamed in pain. The bouncer was shovelled back into the corridor like a sack of something. Lock bent over him and withdrew the pistol from the waistband of his trousers, then at once stood up. His movements were jerky, adrenalin-filled, under only the most effortful restraint. His eyes were as wide as a cat's on seeing a small rodent break from cover.

'Where?' he snapped.

'That way!' Vorontsyev replied, pointing down the corridor. They would have to cross the floor of the club, through the tables, to reach the offices. The corridor remained empty. A smell from the lavatories and stale cigarette smoke. Inside, away from the storm, they could hear raised voices as Dmitri argued with whoever had opened the front door to an apparent drunk.

Aggressive and indifferent, he was demanding a drink. 'Hurry! I don't want Dmitri out there for too long.'

They whirled their way between the tables, neatly stacked with their upturned chairs, across the width of the club towards a velvet curtain that masked the corridor to Panshin's offices and the stairs to the accommodation above the club. The first shot surprised them, biting at one of the chairs Lubin was negotiating, leaving a white, bonelike scar even in the dimness of the room's poor light.

Lock, crouching behind a table, fired twice towards the curtains. Vorontsyev, squinting after the muzzle flashes, saw no one. There had been no cry.

He stood beside Lock, who quietly growled: 'It was wearing a uniform. How many of them, Vorontsyev?' His demand for information was intent.

'I don't know. How many would Bakunin spare to –?'

'Alexei?' The cry of a father as Dmitri came hurtling into the club from the corridor leading to the front entrance. His gun was waving wildly, his head moving like that of a threatened prey-animal. Two shots from within the velvet curtain and Dmitri ducked back as Lock returned fire.

'Dmitri?' he yelled.

'All right!'

'Lubin?'

'Yes!'

'Watch the stage!' Lock called out, then scuttled away between the tables, on all fours like a quick dog. Vorontsyev flinched as shots were directed towards the sound of his voice. His ribs were like hot needles thrust into his side and chest, and his arm, immobilised though it was, shrieked in concert with his torso. 'There –!' he heard Lock call, and was blinded by the muzzle flashes.

Someone tumbled back, making a poor stage exit, a dim shadow disappearing. The club reeked of explosives. He watched as Lock clambered swiftly up onto the low, narrow stage where the musicians performed, saw him scuttle towards the side of the stage, then disappear.

There were no orders, he realised, no noises of command and

disposition – and he began to fear they were too late. Kasyan had called Panshin or someone else from the car, the moment he had recognised Dmitri. There had been time, too *much* time, for them to move the scientists. Dmitri appeared beside him, breathing like a beached whale.

'You were right,' he gasped, 'he'll have us all dead before morning at this rate! Are they here, Alexei?'

Vorontsyev shook his head. 'I doubt it.'

'Shit! Where are they?'

Two shots directed at them whined overhead. Dmitri returned fire, as did Lubin. Then Vorontsyev heard Lubin scrabbling to a new position. Two more shots from behind the curtains, then they parted violently as a figure was thrown through them, dragging them aside. A uniformed greatcoat, the dim patch of a white face, then Lock's figure appeared, his arm raised and waving them forward.

They hurried towards him. His face was twisted with angry disappointment.

'There aren't enough of these GRU guys!' It was as if he wanted more killing. 'They've gone!' He studied their faces and realised they had reached the same conclusion. Lubin joined them, his face shiny with perspiration and excitement. 'Where would Panshin be?'

'Upstairs, or in one of the –'

Vorontsyev fired twice, almost resting the gun on Lock's shoulder. Kasyan's slight figure ducked back into the doorway from which it had emerged. Lock whirled round on the empty corridor. A smell of dust and explosives mixed with their tension.

'Panshin!' Lock bellowed. 'I'm here for you, man! I want *you!*' He looked at them. 'Dmitri, watch the corridor while we check upstairs. You, Major, stay with him. Come on, kid.'

Lubin hurried behind Lock up the flight of narrow stairs to the apartments and changing rooms above the club. Lock thrust out his hand at the head of the stairs, pushing it into Lubin's chest to halt him. Then he glanced slowly, carefully around the corner, along the landing. Blank doors of veneered board, the smell of cigar smoke and expensive, over-employed aftershave. He grinned, turning to Lubin.

293

'Don't get in my way. Keep behind me. OK?'

Lubin nodded.

How many of them were there? He knew, with a sick, enveloping disappointment, that Turgenev had moved the scientists. That would have taken the majority of the GRU men away, too. But Panshin and Turgenev would have guessed that he and Vorontsyev would come here, so how many had they left as a protection force? The ground floor was silent. Whatever Kasyan was planning, it wasn't immediate. But there weren't enough people with him to take any risks . . . how many does that leave up here, with the man with the aftershave and the cigar?

'What does Panshin look like?'

'What?' Lubin was surprised. 'Short, round, grey hair. Lots of rings, bracelets — '

'OK, let's find him.'

The place was turning like a coin between Turgenev's fingers; a safe house was becoming a trap. If they hadn't left more than a handful of soldiers, then Turgenev wanted him and his team inside before anything happened. He kicked at one flimsy door and it flew open. He flinched back, but had not been in any firing line. The room was dark, smelt of food and cigarettes. He reached beside the door and switched on the light. A table, four half-empty plates, cutlery, glasses, an ashtray. His disappointment was as heavy as a stone in his stomach.

Then he quickly kicked at another door.

'Panshin, get out here!' he roared.

'Watch —!' was all Lubin had time to cry out.

Lock dropped to one knee, gun stiff-armed before him, the trigger squeezed three times as the magazine of the Kalashnikov was sprayed along the walls and ceiling of the corridor and the soldier staggered backwards under the impact of his shots. Then the finger slackened on the trigger as the man fell. The corridor was filled with smoke and plaster dust. Lock looked round towards Lubin.

The young man was sitting against the wall, inspecting his fingers as he took them from his temple, a kind of bleak wonder in his eyes. His hand was shaking violently. Then he saw Lock and grinned shakily, even held up his hand. Flesh wound.

Lock nodded. Heavy, hurrying footsteps on the stairs. Lubin whirled round, gun ready, as Dmitri lumbered into sight, blurting:

'All right – Christ!' Plaster dust settled in a fine down on his wet shoulders. Vorontsyev paused at the head of the stairs, doubled up as he fought for breath. 'Where's Panshin?'

Lock indicated the door from which the soldier had emerged, waggling his gun at it. Then he lunged forward towards the open door and the upturned boots of the dead soldier. He crouched beside the doorway. In the pool of light offered by a standard lamp and a desk light, Panshin sat like an effigy, a caricature of a gangland boss. His plump, beringed hands were clearly in view on the leather top of the desk. His eyes watched Lock watching him without expression. There was no fear, Lock realised, getting to his feet.

He kicked the door wide, but Kasyan was not directly behind it, instead to one side. Lock fired the Makarov as he held it close against his side. His stomach felt the heat of the barrel, the two shots. Kasyan collapsed against the far wall of the study and slid gently into a sitting position, his features retaining their surprise, even their cleverness for a moment. There was a second door to the room. Kasyan must have used a flight of stairs that linked the study to the ground floor. Panshin's hands had barely moved on the desk before Lock turned to him.

Slowly, Panshin's round face, which seemed designed to express no range of emotions beyond confidence and a cunning superiority, slid into the discovery of fear. His eyes flickered beyond Lock as the others filled the doorway, then came back to the American; the stranger, the threat. Lock crossed the room to the desk, rounded it and stood beside Panshin.

He leaned his face towards the Russian.

'I hear you're the main man, Panshin,' he announced. 'You're into heroin and people-smuggling, the real big time.' The Makarov was out of sight at Lock's side. 'Cut me a deal,' he added mockingly.

A clock that ticked in unison with his breathing had begun in Lock's head. Panshin was unnerved, but not in disarray, even though his eyes strayed to the slight, dead form of Kasyan sitting like a dosser against the wall. Reserves of confidence, yes; untouchability, too. The familiar presence of Vorontsyev and the others diminished the threat of Lock, for they had always been containable, dismissible. And the GRU were looking after him now and there weren't enough dead bodies visible to Panshin to make him really afraid.

'You're American,' Panshin managed in innocence, as he glanced at the small carriage clock on his desk.

Lock swept the clock to the floor. Panshin flinched.

'Let's take him, Lock,' Vorontsyev suggested, not moving from the doorway.

'Too much excess baggage!' Lock snapped back. 'Well, fat man? What's the deal? Where have they taken your guests?'

'I don't think I know what you're –' Panshin began. Then Lock struck him across the temple with the barrel of the gun. He heard Lubin's indrawn, shocked breath.

He dragged Panshin upright in his chair, perching himself on the edge of the desk, the gun pressed against the man's cheek. Blood seeped from the expensive grey coiffure, down one rounded jowl to the white collar of the silk shirt.

'OK, here's my deal, Panshin. I don't give shit about you. You're just something I have to go through to get to Turgenev. I *want* to know where he's stashed the guys he dumped on you. Five, six nuclear physicists, technicians, whatever. Where were they taken – and when does he plan to send them on their way?'

'I – don't know . . .'

'You can do better than that. A whole lot better.'

'I don't know –!'

Their shadows against the wall loomed together over the desk. Lock's body blocked Panshin's view of the others. He heard the whispered instructions as Vorontsyev sent Lubin and Dmitri downstairs. Lock knew he was becoming the room's only reality for Panshin, he saw it in the man's eyes. They flicked again to Kasyan, whom Lock allowed him to see, then to Lock's shoulder, which blocked the reassurance that the sight of an injured and exhausted Vorontsyev would have given.

Panshin shrugged. It was a costly effort.

'I don't know what happens next. The GRU came here and took away some people I was asked to – to look after for a day or so. I asked no questions.'

'Someone as cautious as you, Panshin? You'd have needed to know the whole game-plan. That skin of yours is too well filled not to have been looked after over the years.' He smiled. 'Once more, here's the deal. Where and when? Your gain is you get to survive.'

Panshin began shaking his head, but a second blow with the barrel of the gun snapped his head back, making it appear loose and doll-like. The man cried out with pain. He fumbled a silk handkerchief from his pocket and pressed it with the greatest solicitation against his cheek. The wet, pained eyes regarded Lock with impotent hatred. Lock forced casual, indifferent satisfaction into his expression. It wasn't difficult, he realised.

He said quietly: 'Pete Turgenev had my sister killed, Panshin. After that, why should I care what happens to you, what happens here?' He raised the gun and Panshin flinched away, hands waving feebly as he began to drown in the danger to himself.

'No –!'

Vorontsyev lurched forward out of an apathy of fascination and revulsion towards the desk and the cameo of Lock's control of Panshin. He experienced a pang of empathetic fear for the club owner, even as he reminded himself of the gangster's background. Panshin's features greeted him with relief as he lunged against the desk.

'Leave it!' Lock snarled.

'Sod you, Yank!' Vorontsyev growled back. Then he banged the fist of his free hand on the desk and said urgently: 'Val, it's all going down the tubes and I don't know if I can keep this American from killing you! Just tell us what we want to know.'

'What in hell are you doing playing around with this, Vorontsyev?' Panshin demanded. 'This isn't how it's done!'

The remark was ludicrous. Vorontsyev felt diminished, as if he had been making a fraudulent insurance claim.

'Well, damn you, Val – it's how *he* does it!'

Panshin's features creased into sulky folds; uncertainty now dominated his horizon.

'See, *Val*,' Lock said, 'the rules have been changed. Guys like him –' He tossed his head in Vorontsyev's direction. '– didn't have the motive to go up against Turgenev. It was all *getting by* and *making a rouble* and *losers are assholes* and *keep your nose clean*. The cops and the bad guys played to the same script. Don't tell me about it, Val – my country invented those rules!' He leaned forward. 'It isn't about superpowers and systems, Val – it's about whether or not I kill you. And the *rules* don't apply. Do we deal?'

He was on the point of raising the gun, but there was no remaining need. Panshin believed him.

'I don't know where . . . I swear it – but he's going to get them out today, this morning. Airport. There's a break in the weather coming . . . his plane . . .'

There was nothing more. Panshin slowly subsided onto his desk, his folded arms cradling his head. The coiffured grey hair was glossy in the light of the desk lamp; he seemed to continue to exude power and money, even in decline.

Lock was staring at him.

'There's nothing more!' Vorontsyev stormed. 'That's all he knows, all we need to know.' It was as if Panshin was an actor resting after a performance of sincerity. 'Let's get out of here.'

'Him?'

Vorontsyev snatched Panshin's head off the desk by jerking at the thick hair. He turned the man's terrified, bemused features towards Lock. 'Tell him you won't ring Turgenev, Val – tell him you'll be signing the order for your own execution if you so much as lift the phone.' He shook Panshin like a rat. 'Tell him, Val, and he'll let you live!'

'It's true,' Panshin muttered, too submerged in the moment and the most distant consequences to give his assertion any authority. 'It's true.'

When Vorontsyev let go of his hair, Panshin let his head decline onto his arms once more. Vorontsyev nodded to Lock, who got up from the desk obediently and followed him to the door.

The phone in Vorontsyev's pocket trilled.

'Yes?'

'A friend at headquarters gave me your number.' It was Bakunin. 'I know where you are. I'm calling from just down the street. In my night-glasses, I can make out the head of your girl detective, sitting in her car. So can one of my marksmen through his nightscope. Will you come out or shall I give the order to fire?'

Turgenev whirled round in triumph, erasing the expression from his features. The Iranian had not knocked, simply emerged into the study as if by right. The phone in his hand seemed to Turgenev to betray something.

'Yes,' he said carefully, 'I quite agree. Put that into operation right away, would you.' He cut off the connection to Bakunin and put down the receiver. 'Hamid – I'm sorry, but I do have other concerns.'

'Of course, my friend. I simply came to collect the files on our passengers to Tehran. I hope that is in order?'

Turgenev plucked up from the desk a thick wodge of files, bound with red ribbon.

'Appropriate, I think – the colour of celebration?'

'Perhaps. Thank you.'

And now, get out, Turgenev thought. *Get out and allow me to attend to more important matters.*

He admitted tiredness, the erosion that bouts of unaccustomed excitement, much like sudden debaucheries, had brought on. The punctuations of Bakunin's reports, on which he had insisted, had dragged at his reserves. That Vorontsyev and more especially Lock were trapped in Panshin's club was a line drawn beneath the whole business – but instead of being able to turn freely to the matter of Grainger Technologies or his other American interests, he must attend to this medium-ranking officer in Iranian Intelligence. It demeaned him; the man's presence was no longer tolerable.

'If you'll excuse me, Hamid, there are things I must attend to.' He ushered the small Iranian to the door.

'Of course. My apologies.'

Then he was gone, at least for the moment.

Turgenev carried a sheaf of faxed reports to the desk, a whisky in his other hand. Putting both down, he fumbled in his pocket for his half-glasses and sat down. There were at least a dozen urgent phone calls, faxes –

He plucked off his glasses and stared at the blank of the window behind the desk, turning his chair with a slight squeak. His gaze travelled past the paintings and porcelain that invaded even the one room that was intended as a workplace, a puritanical domain. The storm continued to fling the snow across the window, almost horizontally in the glare of the security lights. Around eight, they continued to predict.

Very well, he would believe them. It would be little more than a diversion, now that Bakunin was on the point of eliminating all immediate risk. Lock, the anxious, eager-to-please boy, the young man never-quite-there, the *stereotype*, would soon be bagged rubbish to be carted away. He smiled, almost sadly, with recollection. It had been Billy Grainger who had described Lock as *the best and worst kind of American – the Peace Corps boy with a handgun*. They had agreed, over the vodka and caviar in the rude hut in the Afghan mountains, while Lock patrolled outside on guard, that *the world had killed a lot of Americans just like him in a lot of foreign wars*.

Which is just what this encounter was. Billy had even added that *America had killed a lot of Americans like Lock*.

Turgenev shook his head, again with some proximity to sadness.

Then he replaced his glasses and checked the most urgent faxes and retyped phone messages. Yes, he decided, he would sell his small holding in that Far East satellite TV corporation to Murdoch . . . no, he would not sell that much sterling at the moment . . . yes, he would take that offered stake in the Kuwaiti exploration company seeking to nuzzle into the trough of the Asian republics' oilfields . . . no, not that, yes, that was OK . . .

'Then torch the place yourself – before they do it for you!' Lock shouted, rounding on Vorontsyev.

They were collected like the dispirited remnants of an audience for a concert that would never begin, amid the stacked tables of the club's auditorium. Dmitri was to one side, on

Vorontsyev's instructions, and Lock's raised voice angered him because it might alarm Marfa, make her next movement precipitate and suspicious.

'– still, that's it,' he encouraged, as if he could actually see her sitting in her car outside on K Street. 'No, there's no order to fire . . . all you have to do is to slide down slowly, *slowly* in the seat, or bend down as if looking for something, and get out of the car . . .' Why she hadn't seen them arrive, Dmitri had no idea. He was sweating profusely, on her behalf rather than his own. 'OK – no, begin when I tell you . . . What?' He held Vorontsyev's phone close to his lips. He hoped that Marfa was holding her phone below the sightline offered by the windscreen as she had been instructed to do. She seemed consumed by guilt that she had noticed nothing through the rushing blizzard.

'OK. All you have to do is to get away from the car. No, I don't know in which direction they have you in sight, I'd guess from the front, in this weather, to see you at all. Just remember they can't see anything properly, nightscopes or not, through the snow. OK – yes, in your own time, but *slowly* . . .'

Lubin was still dabbing at his temple. The blood had already dried to a crust. Perhaps it was a nervous reaction because Marfa was in danger. Dmitri nodded to Vorontsyev.

'Is that what they'll do, Lock – really? Why not storm the place, call on us to surrender?'

'Listen, Vorontsyev, what would you do? *Not* as a cop, not even as GRU – but as a gangster? Have *fun* setting the place on fire and shooting the rats as they come out . . . wouldn't you?'

Vorontsyev nodded with great reluctance. 'Perhaps.'

'Good!'

'And afterwards?'

'We don't have any choice, you know that. The airport.'

'And how do we get there?' Vorontsyev stormed. 'We can do roadblocks in this country like no one else on earth! You don't think someone like Bakunin has forgotten all those old habits, do you? I'm pretty easily identified, in case you hadn't noticed!'

'OK, OK – I can get through on my fake passport. Gas company executive. You – you go in the trunk of a car or the back of a truck, well hidden. Look, just get there, OK?' he ended in exasperation, waving his arms as if against a sudden swarm of midges.

'Separate exits?' Lock nodded. 'K Street is – ?' Vorontsyev glanced at Dmitri, who held up the mobile phone, shrugging pessimistically. God, she had to be all right –

'They're all around us, if they have any organisation,' Lock pronounced. 'But we're dots in a blinding snowstorm. They're the best odds we can get, Alexei.'

The trilling of a phone.

'*Yes?*' Dmitri's voice.

'Is she – ?' Vorontsyev began, but Dmitri waved him to silence. He listened intently, then began nodding like a Russian doll; the layers and enclosures of the doll were exposed one by one, so that the final impression was of a furious, small figure rocking violently to and fro. Marfa was all right.

'OK – *OK*. She says sorry. She can't see anyone, apart from one truck on the street. They must be in the buildings.'

Lock crossed to Dmitri and snatched the phone, in the same moment gesturing to Lubin to begin dousing the furniture with the petrol he had found stored in the basement, next to the racks of house wine.

'Listen to me, Marfa,' he said overbearingly. 'It's up to you to help us out of here – don't argue, just listen! OK, that's better ... Now, describe the cover out there, the streetlighting, everything!'

'Wait!' Vorontsyev ordered, turning to where Panshin was sitting hunched on one of the club chairs, his temple still bleeding and covered by his stained silk handkerchief. 'There's Panshin's BMW outside. Got the keys, Val?' Lock's flippant exhilaration was infectious.

'Not all of us,' Lock warned. 'We need to split up. We're too easily spotted together. Marfa – hold on.' He studied Panshin thoughtfully. Then he said: 'Lubin, go look out the rear. Carefully. If they're not around, then OK, you and Dmitri can get the Major out in the BMW. Move it.'

Lubin put down the petrol can and scuttled away and along the corridor to the rear door. Lock seemed puzzled for a moment, then he began studying Vorontsyev and Dmitri, examining them as carefully as a doctor reluctantly confirming a pessimistic diagnosis.

'We're it, Lock, the whole army,' Vorontsyev murmured.

'I know it. Marfa —'

'Yes?'

'Any movement?'

'N-no,' the girl replied with urgent uncertainty. A girl scout, he thought disparagingly.

'OK, hold on there — I'll get back to you.' The girl seemed unresponsive to the joke; perhaps she didn't understand it.

'Yes,' she replied gloomily.

Lubin reappeared, his face excited as a child's.

'I can't see anyone out there — no fresh footprints, tyre tracks —'

'They have to be out there somewhere —'

'Lock, we're wasting time!' Dmitri barked, joining them. 'Either we move now or we don't move!'

'OK. The Major can't move quickly, anyway. Take him in the BMW.'

'Call Marfa in.'

'*I'll* take care of Marfa!' Lock replied.

'You mean, she's part of the distraction. I won't have her put in more danger —'

'Vorontsyev, she's all the way into this thing! She's no passenger. I'll take *care* of her!'

Vorontsyev nodded reluctantly. Lubin appeared about to protest, then Lock snapped at him:

'Torch the place!'

'What about him?' Dmitri asked, nodding at Panshin. Then he understood. 'You can't,' he whispered hoarsely. 'He'll just blunder out of one door or the other and they'll —'

'— be *distracted*,' Lock completed. 'Let's hope so.' He turned to Lubin. 'Go ahead, do it!'

Flame spurted at once from the place where Lubin had thrown the bundle of paper napkins he had lit. Panshin's face was filled with firelit horror.

'Get moving!' Lock growled to Vorontsyev. 'Forget him!' He urged them towards the rear door. Dmitri had snatched

Panshin's keys from his hand. The fat club owner seemed uncertain, but Lock knew he would follow him to the front door.

The flames roared up towards the club's low ceiling. The smoke was already thick, choking. Panshin's features crawled with terror, and with concern at the fate of his club.

Vorontsyev nodded at Lock and disappeared along the corridor towards the rear door, Dmitri beside him like an overcoated nurse. There was no time to consider their chances – nor his own. He began moving swiftly towards the club's street entrance, half-attentive for the noise of shooting, or a car engine from the rear. He heard Panshin labouring after him, heavy-footed, dazed.

Lock crouched against the tinted glass, dark enough at night to conceal him even from nightscopes. He visualised the street as best he could. The storm flung its weight of snow across the blurred light of the streetlamps and neon that dimly summoned to shops and clubs and bars he could no longer see across the street.

Time to go. Panshin? He watched the man as he might have done an insect . . . Something stopped him from thrusting Panshin through the door. The corridor was lit by the fire, and the smoke wrapped itself more thickly about them. Nevertheless, the moment of utter detachment in which he could have used Panshin as a shield had passed and he couldn't recover it.

'You're on your own, pal!' he snapped and pushed the door wide. 'Live long, uh?'

Then Lock was through the door, slipping on the drift of snow heaped in the porch and on the steps – skidded, was deafened by the wind, then lurched against the smoked-glass windows of the club, his hand smearing the snow. The glass shattered near his hand, fell inwards from the impact of the first shot. They could see nothing more than moving blurs, shadows – but hadn't missed by more than inches. He scuttled to the corner of the alleyway, and heard the roar of a car engine, saw the muzzle flashes of two guns, high up as if suspended in the storm. Window vantages overlooking the club car park. The BMW's brakelights wobbled on and off as if in uncertainty, but they were retreating into the storm's murk, heading away from K

Street. A last violent glare of the brakes, then it was gone.

Now *you*, he urged himself. More glass shattered somewhere close. He skidded his way across the alleyway, dropped behind the cover of Marfa's parked car, already assuming the lumped lack of identity of other stationary vehicles burdened with snow. He glanced around him. A shot shattered the car's windscreen. Glass and snow flew. The girl waved to him from a nearby shop doorway, her gloved hand raised beside a heavy grille. He waved back, gun raised, gesturing her to begin retreating down the block. She shook her head, gesturing towards the other side of the street. She'd seen where the shots originated.

He gestured to her, crouched only a matter of yards away, turning his wrist as if turning a key. She pointed at the car. He signalled understanding with a raised thumb, then he heard shouting.

The flames from the club belched through the shattered windows and the open door, to be lashed and sculpted by the storm. Panshin was standing in the light of the nearest street-lamp, waving frantically, his figure bulky, recognisable.

Lock opened the passenger door of the car and slid into the seat. He moved awkwardly over the brake and gear lever, roughly brushing the seat as he shuffled himself into a half-lying position behind the wheel. Panshin was still on the pavement, arms waving, dinner jacket whitened with snow. He raised himself in the driving seat, feeling for the ignition. You'll have to be better than most Russian cars, he thought. A lot better.

He turned the key, hearing two shots in the moment before the engine caught. He watched Panshin's body slowly, heavily, collapse into the snow and become half-buried, knowing that he had witnessed an execution. They'd *known* who it was, and he'd died because they were house-cleaning. He thrust the gear lever into reverse and let out the clutch. The car squealed and swung, lurching backwards like a drunk.

Two shots careened off the snow-covered bonnet. The storm half-blinded him through the shattered windscreen. He sensed the prick of glass in his buttocks and thighs from the partly littered driving seat. Shots against the door, impacting, distorting metal and padding. The car swerved, slid sideways, skidded. He was sweating feverishly, his hands slippery inside his gloves. The window behind him shattered.

The car would afford protection for only seconds now. It bucked as he accelerated in reverse, the rear wheels spinning wildly against a huge ridge of rutted ice. He waved frantically at Marfa, a white blob of a face – waving her to keep pace with the car but not to get in. Yelling:

'Keep behind the car, *behind* the car!'

He thrust the gear lever into second and accelerated forward, braked and then threw the car again into reverse. Once more, it bucked against the obstacle but wouldn't surmount it. A rear window shattered behind his head and he heard the ominous, dead pluck of bullets into the upholstery.

A rotund little bear jiggled on a short length of elastic in the rear window, its arms wide in hopeless surrender. He thrust the car forward again, the tyres squealing, then accelerated once more in reverse. Marfa's face, as she crouched behind the car's moving shield, was white and astonished, as if she feared he was trying to expose her to the unseen marksmen. The car bucked like a horse kicking out with its back legs and then mounted the ridge in the road and skidded away like an escaping animal because his foot was still jammed down on the accelerator. It careered across K Street towards the buildings that housed the snipers.

Marfa was left stranded and exposed. Bullets struck the car. Panshin's body, suddenly a hundred yards away, was slowly being covered with snow.

He stopped the car in a skid, then accelerated back across K Street towards Marfa. As the car mounted the pavement only feet from her, he saw her gesturing towards a dark, narrow alleyway beside a bar where neon struggled. *Cowboys' Bar*. Seeing her gestures, he realised they had a better chance on foot.

The car shunted against the grille across the windows and came to a halt. He switched off the engine, opened the passenger door and scrambled out onto all fours, rising like a sprinter to dash into the shelter of the alley. He slid into a tangled heap with Marfa as he collided with the girl.

He caught at his expelled breath. Marfa's chest was heaving. With an effort, he got to his knees, gripped the collar of her coat, and dragged her deeper into the alley. Her arms flailed in protest. Finally, he let her drop and staggered back against the alley wall, exhausted, his breathing coming in great, uncertain gouts, the icy air hurting his throat and lungs. The girl lay as if floating on water, incapable of movement.

Eventually, recovering his breath, he said: 'Come on, let's get moving. I want a limo – understand? I want an *expensive* car, so find one for me.' Marfa was glowering at him as her shock diminished. 'We'll exchange insurance companies and I'll pay for the damage to your car, OK?' He grinned wetly. 'Now, come on!'

Bakunin stood over the body of Valery Panshin, which the snow was inexorably and tidily masking, and considered the rightness of the whim that had ordered the club owner's demise. The snow melted on Bakunin's cheek and settled on the epaulettes of his uniform greatcoat and on the crown and brim of his cap.

It had been correct, sensible, inspirational even. Turgenev had kept him in ignorance regarding the American, Lock, and the extent of his knowledge and influence. His danger was unimportant, despite his temporary escape from the marksmen. Already, his troops were flooding that alleyway and the whole area around the burning club in pursuit of Vorontsyev and Lock and their feeble entourage. Bakunin could now feel the heat from the fire welcomely on his face. No, his position of massive ignorance, deliberately imposed by Turgenev, was intolerable. It could have exposed him. Panshin – the worthless, cretinous, greedy Panshin – might have already told, confessed. However, in the event that he had not, he had been put beyond any ability to do so. Opportunity, means, motive – Panshin was bereft of all three with two neat holes in his forehead.

Whatever Panshin knew was imprisoned in that broken vessel that had leaked a small amount of blood and brain tissue into the snow. He stirred the body with his foot. Then he looked up.

'Find them quickly,' he snapped, 'and finish them. Reinforce the roadblocks – and warn whoever's in command at the airport.

Do it without publicity, on a *secure* channel. You understand?' The lieutenant, his features frozen by cold and obedience, nodded. 'Good. He *may* have let something slip, but I imagine they're interested in nothing greater than their own skins. However, it doesn't do to be sloppy, Lieutenant.'

Turning away from the junior officer and the body, he strode through the snow towards his staff car.

'Alexei, for God's sake, get into the boot of the car!'

Dmitri Gorov's patience was as exhausted as his heavy frame. Vorontsyev stood in the driving snow, staring into the well of the old car's boot, unmoving and silent. Lubin was absent, hiding the BMW amid the detritus of a building site which wouldn't see the resumption of activity until the blizzard ended. He and Vorontsyev were in a narrow slit of a street, poorly lit, between blocks of workers' flats. Three streets from the flat in which the drug courier, Hussain, had been murdered by an explosive hidden in a paraffin heater.

'Not yet,' Vorontsyev replied. 'Dmitri –!' he burst out, turning to Gorov. 'There has to be something else we can do. The airport will be guarded.'

'And Turgenev himself will be there,' Dmitri offered seductively, immediately whirling round at the sound of someone approaching. Lubin appeared, hands raised in mock surrender, then passed out of the light of the lamp into shadow.

'That's a guess, Dmitri, nothing more. Is the car well hidden, youngster?'

Lubin grinned and nodded, his teeth chattering with cold, his boots crusted with dirty snow.

'It's a *good* guess, Alexei. It's his plane they'll be using, and only his muscle will get it airborne in this blizzard, weather window or no weather window. He'll need the runway cleared, the plane de-iced, the pilots briefed . . . I think he'll be there, if only to make sure *we* aren't!'

'OK, OK – it doesn't matter anyway, does it? We don't have any alternative. I'll get in – in a moment.' He smiled. His ribs ached slightly less now that his breathing was level, unexcited.

The escape had been quite straightforward, given the circum-

308

stances. The big BMW had got them out of the trap of the alley in a rush and they'd skirted the one car that had attempted to block the exit before it could get into position. The pursuit had been organised, but slow to react. Arrogance, over-confidence. They'd slipped into the canyons of the town's poorest quarter and into the storm before they could be effectively tailed.

Now, they had to bluff their way through the roadblocks and drive into what amounted to a trap already set. Dmitri's theory concerning Turgenev was probably rubbish, but it comforted, even inspired him, so let that be. For himself . . . ? One passenger intercepted while boarding would be enough, one nuclear physicist to wave like a flag. The security people would swamp this place, the UN would have apoplexy, Yeltsin would destroy Turgenev to maintain his own credibility and clean hands towards the West . . . they needed just one, or the *evidence* of one.

'Dmitri, if all else . . . doesn't work out, buy a camera and some film in the airport shop, will you?' He looked intently at Gorov, who understood and nodded.

'We'll get something out of this, Alexei – something.'

'Of course. Right, then – let's get moving. Lubin, you say you can hotwire this heap – you can drive it, too. And, Lubin, you did well, back there.'

'Sir!'

God, the enthusiasm of youth. All he had ever wished was to be saved from the fervour, as if he had menopausally passed the age where he could be impregnated with a cause, a sense of right. Now, it was just as Lensky the pathologist had predicted for him – he had become *a middle-aged idealist* . . . But he was mortal, vulnerable, and knew as much only too well. His arm, dulled by painkillers, confirmed that much! He was sensible about life, knew that it ended quickly enough without taking risks. Now, he was doing just that. He shrugged.

'What's wrong, Alexei?'

'Someone just walked over my grave,' he replied sombrely. 'Let's get on with it,' he added brusquely. 'You two help me in – I can't do it for myself.'

*　　　*　　　*

309

It was a black Cadillac, hardly even a half-stretch limo. So unexpectedly American that it amused him, despite his hunger and exhaustion. It was sitting on the snowy drive of a large dacha which appeared totally out of place. It was surrounded by high-rise blocks of flats encroaching on the poorly lit outskirts of the old town. A narrow street of six-storey blocks was the umbilical that connected this wooden house with its older, shabbier country cousins, which trailed out towards the tundra like uncertain spectators of vastness.

'Whose car is it?' he asked.

They crouched in the shelter of a builder's skip, one of as many as a dozen scattered like dice in the space between the blocks of flats which rose like dark draped curtains behind the storm. The few lights showing at five-thirty in the morning were like rents in their material rather than signs of habitation.

Marfa whispered hoarsely: 'He used to consider himself a gangster, a *biznizman* – in the early days. Two telephones in the house and a pink bathroom suite and he was the tsarevich.' She snorted. 'He was bought or frightened out of business, but they let him keep the car and gave him the money to build this place. He was a pimp, about Teplov's level, but in those days the girls were still on the streets. He used to have a couple of ramshackle caravans parked around here which served as the accommodation.' She sniffed. 'He wasn't a talented crook.'

'Not like Pete Turgenev, the prince of tides, uh?' She looked blankly at him. 'Not as smart as Turgenev,' he explained.

'No, not that smart.'

'OK, I can get that car to start – it looks just about good enough for a gas company executive. We'll take it. No deposit, nothing to pay for six months, right?' Again, she seemed nonplussed. 'Forget it. Let's get the car. Does he have a dog, this guy?'

'I don't think so. Just an old woman to look after him. His wife died of AIDS – she was his first girl. Nothing but the usual transmissible diseases for years, then –'

'Don't tell me, the Americans arrived and brought their diseases with them!' Lock snapped. 'Let's get the car.'

As they came out from behind the skip, the wind ripped at

them, growling with renewed threat. There seemed not the slightest chance that there would be a break in the weather. Which suited, anyway. He wanted the airport closed in all day. He leaned against the force of the wind, stepping high through the snow like a child exaggerating the difficult new art of walking. Marfa huddled beside him, using him as shelter without any suggestion of contact or companionship.

The drive sloped slightly. The Cadillac, mapped like a cow by its colour and the blowing snow, stood in front of closed garage doors. Lock sidled furtively beside the driver's door and removed a short length of lead pipe from his overcoat pocket. The things you can pick up off the sidewalk . . . He fitted it over the old-fashioned door handle and jerked it violently downwards. The lock broke and he tugged the door open.

The car alarm bellowed at him —

'Carefully now,' Dmitri warned. The GRU vehicle's headlights blared through the snow, picking them out moving along the airport road at a snail's pace. 'Just pull over and wait.'

The road had been cleared the previous evening and would be cleared again, he presumed, at first light. At six in the morning, it was clogged with the night's fall and drifts, a tumbled landscape in miniature. Beside him, he could hear Lubin breathing hoarsely, quickly.

'Calm down, lad, calm down.' Then, almost mischievously, and to release his own tension, he added: 'And get ready to run if they don't like the look of us.' He was chillingly aware of Vorontsyev in the boot.

The UAZ jeep drew alongside them, its canvas hood white under the weight of snow, its wipers flicking like drowning arms. A face inspected them with minimal curiosity from behind a streaked driver's window. It was, for a moment, apparent that the jeep would pass on down the road towards Novyy Urengoy.

Then it stopped and Dmitri heard its brake being dragged on. His heart thudded in his chest.

'We're maintenance men at the airport — really security, right?' he reminded Lubin.

'Yes, yes!' the young man replied with quick nerves.

Dmitri wound down the window of the old car. A decayed Mercedes now only fit for the scrapheap; which meant the Turks and Pakistanis in Novyy Urengoy. He hoped it hadn't yet been reported stolen. On the other hand, Police HQ wouldn't give a toss if the caller had an Asian accent.

'Yes?' he asked the frost-featured soldier who leaned down to the half-open window. There was no deference in his voice. 'What's the problem?'

'Security. We're checking for – criminals,' he concluded, as if remembering an item of rote learning that meant nothing.

'Criminals, eh? Our business, too, as a matter of fact. Out at the airport.' He flipped open his wallet, displaying a piece of plastic to which was attached his photograph. Something he'd had for years, a temporary posting out to the airport in the early days of heroin smuggling, when the most daring they had been was to disguise themselves as maintenance people. 'OK?' he asked. 'We'll be late clocking on if we hang about here.'

The soldier indicated that he wished to see the ID once more. A corporal's stripes on his greatcoat. His word would be enough for any officer in the jeep or nearby. Come on, *come on* –

Dmitri gestured as if to close the wallet again, and the corporal nodded. The snow was melting between his collar and his cap as he bent to the window and he resented his discomfort.

'OK,' he grumbled. 'I wonder you buggers didn't stay in bed on a day like this!'

'Double shift – lots of overtime,' Dmitri replied, sensing Lubin's tension mount after a momentary sense of relief. 'Thanks, mate. Good luck.'

Lubin drew slowly, very slowly, away from the UAZ. It diminished in the mirror, swallowed by the storm as the corporal was still engaged in climbing back into the rear of the vehicle. His breathing clouded the windscreen, despite the puffing of the heater, and Dmitri leaned across to wipe it clear. Snow rushed into the headlights as if the blizzard had gathered new strength.

'We're through, boy – we're through!' He raised his voice and turned in his seat. 'We're OK, Alexei – on our way!'

*   *   *

The last block of flats had disappeared into the snowstorm like a drifting liner, the few scattered dachas looked like boxes abandoned in the snow. And immediately there was the roadblock; two long-necked lights on parked dollies, the red and white pole, even the glow from some kind of trailer vehicle that served for accommodation. It was disconcerting, appearing as if it had been in place for some considerable time and had well-rehearsed routines. Marfa was catlike in her display of nerves in the driving seat.

He put his hand on her shoulder and her whole frame flinched at the contact. 'Take it easy,' he murmured, excluding all emotion from his voice.

They'd had the old Cadillac off the snowbound drive and down onto the street before a light had come on in the old *biznizman*'s dacha. No other lights, no flicking of curtains; people chose not to know. He'd gotten the bonnet open and found the alarm circuit. Ripped it out, silencing the noise. The door of the wooden bungalow was cautiously, fearfully opening as Marfa accelerated away. Yet somehow the noise, the hurry, had unsettled her more than the action on K Street, when she might have been killed so easily. Perhaps she'd just run out of resistance? Lock didn't know —

— didn't have time to care right now, he reminded himself.

A door in the side of the trailer vehicle, army drab showing where the snow had melted on its flanks, opened and light spilt out, gleaming through the snow. The girl shivered and Lock made as if to grip her shoulder once more, then resisted the impulse. His own nerves might be betrayed through his fingers.

Two guards, both armed with folded-butt assault rifles. Reluctant in the snow, but obedient. A corporal and a private by the flashes on their greatcoats.

Lock had damaged the door where he had broken in, denting it purposely to give the appearance of an impact by another car.

Marfa, masquerading as his Russian driver, wound down the window as the corporal leaned close to it.

'Papers? What are you doing out here, this time of the morning?' The private yawned, but his eyes never moved from the girl, the car, the shadowy passenger behind her. 'Well?'

Marfa said: 'I'm just the driver – taking someone out to the airport. Gas company business.' She managed the sentences as if they were in a foreign language, awkwardly but with a stiff, correct fluency. They might just believe her.

'Who's your passenger?'

He'd told her the name on the last of the passports. *Paul Evans*. She was hesitating, as if searching her memory for something long forgotten. Quickly, he wound down the window. He hadn't wanted to antagonise them, but –

'What's the hold-up, fella?' he asked, his accent broadly Texan, his tone impatient. 'Let's get going, uh?' he added to Marfa, making shooing gestures the two soldiers would clearly see. 'Jesus, these guys in uniform.' It was added quietly but the contempt would carry, even if they didn't speak English.

The corporal snapped in Russian at Marfa.

'How can you stand driving this prat around?'

'What's he saying, honey?' Lock enquired.

The corporal smirked, catching the tone that indicated a lack of Russian. Then he spat into the snow beside the car and said: 'OK, Yankee!' His accent was thick but the English was decipherable. 'You get out now – quick!'

'I'm not stepping out in a snowstorm for some jumped-up asshole in a uniform!' Lock replied in assumed outrage. 'You want to see my papers, fine! Anything else, forget it!'

The corporal's rifle nudged above the door sill. It was held casually at his hip. The barrel gleamed wet in the diffused glow of the overhead lights. He had successfully distracted them away from Marfa. The corporal's face was eagerly angry. He wanted to take *this Yankee* inside the hut, humiliate him.

There hadn't been anything else he could do. Which was no comfort.

'Out!' the corporal ordered, and the rifle waggled, a baton waved merely to attract attention. 'Mr American – out.' He stepped back, expecting instant obedience.

Lock snorted loudly and clambered out into the storm. There was an officer in the doorway of the trailer now, watching the small drama.

'What is it, fella – your haemorrhoids giving you problems?

You got a nasty temper on you –' Lock's breath was driven from his body as the rifle's muzzle was jabbed into his stomach. He raised his hands. 'What's gotten into you people?' he demanded. 'Listen, fella, I'm an executive with –'

'Inside!'

He was shunted towards the steps of the trailer. He glimpsed Marfa's worried features and his left hand gestured her to silence. Then his foot slipped on the steps and the corporal helped unbalance him by a prod in the back with the rifle. The officer had already retreated to his foldaway desk halfway down the cramped, harshly lit interior. Fuggy, heady with warmth.

He'd seen two other armed GRU soldiers outside and there was a sergeant at a smaller desk. He and the officer watched him with the anticipation lechers might have extended to a young woman. Lock clamped his nerves, held them still.

'You're the head honcho, right?' he drawled angrily. 'You got the say-so – so what is this? Some kind of stick-up? A frame? I got business to attend to out at –'

'Sit down!' The officer indicated a hard chair placed before the desk. With obvious but abashed reluctance, Lock sat. 'Good.'

'Look, Captain, what gives? There ain't usually roadblocks on the edge of town –'

'No.'

'Then, what's the problem?'

'We are looking for an American.' The captain's manner was theatrically pleasant, his English expressed in a slight American twang.

'I don't get you.'

'Perhaps I get you?' The officer smiled, offered a cigarette which Lock declined, then lit one for himself. Marlboro.

'Me? Look, Captain, here's my US passport. That ought to be good enough.' He handed the passport over. 'See. Paul Evans –'

'And who is he?'

'Me.'

'And who are you?'

'What?' He forced the anger as if from a small waterhole of confidence, one rapidly evaporating. 'Oh, yeah. I'm the guy in charge of shipments, *materiel* . . . ? Equipment coming in. For

315

SibQuest, the oil-gas company.' He managed to grin. 'We're small but we're sure growing!' SibQuest had Americans and Canadians as well as Europeans working for them, even though they were a Qatari company with Australian partners. As yet, they weren't important in the Siberian gasfields.

The captain was looking up the name on a typed list in a folder of stiff polythene sheets. His finger ran along his lower lip with the regularity of a typewriter carriage. What if he had the names of the executives –? How could he? The captain looked up.

'You expect shipments to arrive in this weather?'

Lock shrugged.

'No. But some came in before the weather changed. I've only just gotten around to them.' He grinned.

'It seems a very early time of the day to be troubling yourself and your driver,' the captain mused, his eyes straying to the window. In a clear patch in the porthole-like window, Lock saw Marfa's shadow within the car and two of the GRU soldiers leaning down to the driver's window. He hoped fervently their interest was sexual. And that Marfa's nerve would hold up.

'Sure.' He gestured expansively with his hands, appeared shamefaced. 'OK, so someone higher up, a V-P, kicked ass. I have to get out there on the double. My job might be on the line.'

The military contempt for the chicanery of civilian life was evident, like a bruise on the captain's features. This disorderly application of pressure, authority, made him contemptuous of the man Lock was assumed to be.

'Can I get going?' Lock asked tentatively.

The captain toyed with the passport, opening and closing it, his dark features narrowed in concentration. How much did he know? He didn't have descriptions, maybe, but he knew an American was involved. The cramped interior of the trailer seemed hotter, almost stifling, the storm very distant despite the occasional quivering of the vehicle in the wind's buffets. Lock felt the seconds elongate, as if time dripped like a faulty tap.

316

Then the captain threw the passport onto the desk.

'Very well, Mr Evans. You may continue with the work of saving your career. Sergeant, show the gentleman out.'

'Thanks.'

Lock stood up and made for the door. The sergeant intercepted him, tugging on a parka and pulling the hood over his head as he did so. Then he came down the steps behind Lock, following him to the car. The two soldiers rose to slouched attention beside it.

'She's your driver, yes?' the sergeant asked.

'Sure.'

They stood beside the car. Marfa's features were small with cold and tension.

'You're in a hurry?'

'Yes –'

The sergeant was inspecting the car. He bent by the rear wheel and took the tyre valve between his fingers. Then he looked up, his broad, thick-nosed face intent, greedy.

'OK, so how much?' Lock asked, then remembered to protest: 'The captain know you play this game every time there's a roadblock?'

'You will tell him?'

'This place is corrupt as hell!' Lock protested.

'And everyone in it,' the sergeant added philosophically.

Lock got out his wallet and took two ten-dollar bills from it. The sergeant shook his head. He took out another ten. The sergeant, snow epauletting his shoulders, rose to his feet and took the bills, slipping them at once into his pocket.

'A good remainder to your journey,' he said, smiling. Then he held the door of the car open like a hotel porter.

Lock collapsed into the rear seat and the door was shut behind him. The windows instantly clouded. His heart thudded in his chest as he said: 'Pull away slowly – *slowly*.' The sergeant's arm was raised and the barrier imitated his gesture, sliding upwards towards the two giraffe-necked lights. The rear wheels skidded. 'Slowly, dammit!' he growled, his own tension uppermost.

The car wobbled beneath the upraised barrier. Gradually, as Lock turned in his seat, the glare of the lights diminished back

317

down the road, the snow pouring more and more thickly behind the Cadillac.

'Sorry,' he mumbled. 'Sorry.'

The girl said nothing. Lock felt no relief, no anticipation, only an exhausted weariness – and a sense of foreboding.

FOURTEEN

Blue Remembered Hills

Even in Afghanistan, at the height of a winter snowstorm, the mountains had periodically and reassuringly loomed out of the blizzard and driving sleet; implacable and familiar. Here, he realised, there was nothing. There just wasn't a landscape, hardly even a shadowy clump of stunted firs. The tundra stretched flat and empty all the way to the Gulf of Ob and the Kara Sea; and began at the perimeter fence of Novyy Urengoy's airport.

Lock shuddered in the rear of the old Cadillac. The heater was little more than a futile protest against the weather that enveloped them. Marfa sat blowing on her woollen-gloved hands in the driving seat. Dmitri's mobile phone – or was it the Major's? – was pressed against Lock's cold cheek, so that the stubble rasped. Beyond the fence against which Marfa had parked the car, aircraft looked as small and lost as gulls sitting out a storm on unmoving pack ice.

'You think that's feasible?' Lock asked, breathless at the proposition. Perhaps his encounter with the GRU in their trailer had unnerved him more than he suspected or admitted. He could not be certain – maybe it was the narrowing perspective Vorontsyev's plan offered, the run up the blind alley. 'There's no way out, once we do that.'

'It's the only way,' Vorontsyev explained patiently. 'We then won't have to confront Bakunin's troops. We got here an hour ago. Lubin's been scouting. He counted three APCs, a half-dozen UAZs, even a piece of medium artillery, parked behind a commissary truck. That means as many as fifty GRU troops in the immediate area. I suggest we avoid the airport buildings, Lock.' There was a pained, cynical irony in his tone.

'OK, OK!' Lock blurted in irritation. 'I'm just saying there's no way out of your locale, none at all.'

'It hinges on Turgenev. If he's there, then we can use him to get us out. At least, keep us alive. If we can't take off . . . It is a damn aircraft, Lock, in case you'd forgotten!'

'So, Bakunin lets us fly out, no problem?'

'Bakunin takes his money, power and orders from Turgenev. Once we have Turgenev, we have checkmate. *If* you let Turgenev remain alive, Lock. Dmitri, Lubin, Marfa – ' The girl's head twitched at the sound of her name, as the car rocked in a buffet of the wind. ' – and myself, would be trusting you with our lives, once we got aboard the aircraft. Can we do that, Lock?'

It was absurdly simple, even if he didn't like it. He had to agree to let Turgenev live, or effectively kill them all. There was no other way of gaining Vorontsyev's vaunted *proof*. He clenched his free hand into a fist beside his thigh, grinding the knuckles into the denim-clad muscle. It was *that*, above all, that he did not want – Turgenev as a hostage, Turgenev continuing to breathe . . . and being taken to Moscow or somewhere else where he would have influence, connections, powers of bribery and escape. He would, he knew, be letting Turgenev make a home run. Beth's murder would never be avenged.

'Lock? Well, what's your answer, Lock?'

'He'll get off, scot free!' he protested in a wailing voice that startled the girl upright in her seat.

'Maybe. Maybe not. He'll be *stopped*, Lock. Isn't that what you want?'

'I want him dead,' he admitted.

'And us, in that case,' Vorontsyev replied gloomily, almost as if he accepted the implacability of Lock's hatred.

Vorontsyev was parked inside the airport perimeter, near the cargo hangars. Even with night-glasses, Lock would not have been able to see that far through the flying, pre-dawn murk. He could see only dim, retreating lights that seemed to be swallowed by the storm and the darkness, and a short length of the fence in either direction. And a solitary clump of twisted, snow-laden firs.

'OK,' he offered eventually in a choked, reluctant voice. Then more strongly, 'OK. I agree. It's the only way.'

'*Good.*' The relief was apparent, even in the pinched, maidenish voice given him by the mobile phone connection. Lock even heard the sigh of his next breath. 'That's good. You'd better come in.'

It was as if they had barred his membership to something, leaving him uninitiated and an outsider.

'You think the gate will swallow my story one more time?' he asked. 'Do I risk it?'

'They're relaxed, confident,' Vorontsyev reported. 'But, if you don't want to try, rip out a length of the perimeter fence and walk here –' He paused, listening to someone, either Dmitri or Lubin. Lock could vaguely hear another voice, then, more closely, Vorontsyev's agreement. 'Maybe you should walk. Just in case. Marfa knows the airport layout. We're next to a line of fuel bowsers.'

'Turgenev has to be with them, Vorontsyev.'

'Of course. We're behind the Russair cargo hangar. Don't keep us waiting.'

Lock switched off the humming phone and tapped the girl on the shoulder. 'You OK?' he asked solicitously, even though his mouth was sour with what he could only regard as defeat.

'Yes!' she snapped.

'Don't bite my head off, lady. I just wanted to know whether you could handle this or not.'

'I can handle it.' She turned in her seat. The windscreen beyond her was blank with snow. 'I'm all right. Really, I'm all right.'

'Sure,' he replied without irony. 'OK, let's go.'

'What about the car?'

'It's just a shape against the fence – leave it where it is.'

He opened the door and clambered out into the blizzard, staring around him in the darkness. No murky dawn was yet rivalling the dim glow of the perimeter lights. He turned up his collar and thrust his gloved hands into the pockets of his topcoat. Hunched into himself, he began to trudge along the fence, looking for a gap, a torn piece of mesh, the girl plodding behind him.

There'd be plenty of breaks in the wire, the small-scale smugglers would have made them over the months and years of cigarette and hashish illegalities.

The weight of a sense of betrayal strengthened, bowing his shoulders. Beth's murder was to go unrequited, Turgenev was going to get away with it. The taste of that was colder than the snow on his tongue. God damn it to hell, he cursed. God damn it all to hell . . .

His interior landscape, stretching into the future, was as empty and featureless as the tundra that reached away around him on every side.

Hamid was standing beside the grey Mercedes like a chauffeur, but that was not the image that came back to him as he was shrugged into his topcoat by one of the servants. Instead, he heard his mother's voice, her annoyance with him merely her fear of displeasing his father. *Pyotr, the car is* waiting *for you –* Pyotr! The last more as a plea than an injunction.

As a boy, he had stepped out of the main door of the block of flats in Moscow on many snowy pre-dawn mornings like this, and a man clapping his hands together for warmth would have been standing beside a battered *minibus*, his face pinched and angry at the delay. It had not been a *car*, whatever his mother's affectations beyond the pretensions of middle-ranking Party membership. His schoolfellows' faces would be peering through the fugged and iced row of windows, some of them smirking. *You'll be late for school – again* . . . So would run the litany of her peculiar orthodoxy of obedience – to his father, the Party, the Kremlin; to everybody she knew to be superior in status to herself and her husband. And his mother had known, with the nicety and obsession of a stamp collector, every minute gradation of office, income, accommodation among the various circles of the Inferno that had been the Secretariat of the Soviet Communist Party, its civil service.

He donned his fur hat. Glanced at the murky sky, still more lit by rig flames and the glow of the town than by the dawn. But the snow was easing, he was certain, and the wind, though it remained forceful in its gusts, was more fitful, coquettish almost after the directness of the blizzard. The weather window would open and Hamid and the scientists would be gone . . .

He became aware of the reason for the memory. It did not lie in his irritation with Hamid, or the Iranian's pose beside the limousine. It was that the scientists, all six of them, were seated in a minibus parked behind the Mercedes. It had arrived at the lodge only minutes earlier. The windows were tinted and he could not see their faces. But that vehicle had evoked his childhood in Moscow. He smiled, but with lingering bitterness. The memory of his stifling, orthodox, unquestioning home had never been rendered neutral by the solution of time. It remained acidic, stinging. He remembered Leonid Turgenev's *gratitude* for his Party card and his menial promotions and millimetric measurements of financial improvement, his ruthless driving of his only son to succeed in just the same manner as himself . . . his disappointments at the young Pyotr's love of sport, his laziness at school, his poor reports, his indiscipline. The beatings, the harangues, the lectures, the instilling of creeping, blackmailing guilt . . . then his irrational pride when his son became a trainee officer in the KGB 1st Directorate School.

He had hated his father. Towards his mother, the cipher, the imprint of her husband, he had felt the smallest tenderness and the greatest irritation. They were both dead now. He grinned as he approached the car, so that the Iranian was puzzled by the expression of humour. Wouldn't that be a simple, even simplistic explanation for his joy in capitalism? The antithesis, the complete refutation, of his father's crabbed, servile ideological loyalty, his puritanism, his utter lack of hedonism.

He slapped Hamid on the shoulder, surprising the man.

'In two hours, my friend, you'll be above the clouds and on your way to Tehran. Don't look so damn gloomy!' he laughed. There was no longer any sense of humiliation, or subservience to the Iranian; no reminder of meniality and the past.

Memories of his father always turned on their axis like this. They still possessed an initial sting, like a needle being inserted into a forearm vein . . . but the effect was like a narcotic drug. Pleasure, a dreamy confidence, a *joy* at his power, authority, wealth. How his father would have *hated* him now, and what a crying shame the old bastard hadn't lived to see – well, the Mercedes would have been enough, pulling up outside that grimy concrete block of flats!

'Come on, Hamid – let's get you on your way!' he called in the greatest good humour as he climbed into the limousine.

Lock chewed on the lumps of baguette, filled with a hard, rindy cheese and moistureless tomato, swallowing them gratefully, each mouthful awakening rather than abating his hunger. Vorontsyev was watching him with a sardonic amusement that did not occupy his flinty grey eyes. Behind the forced humour, the Russian's face was drawn and grey with the enervation of the pain in his arm and ribs. The dawn seeped slowly, an ineffectual thin dye, into the cloud-heavy sky. The snow no longer blinded, but blew like flimsy material through which the contours of the airport were visible. Snow-laden aircraft, the tower, the terminal building, the snowploughs, a tank, a piece of self-propelled artillery, petrol trucks.

There was no sense of increased or urgent activity. They were not expected. However, Lock accepted that Vorontsyev's estimate of around fifty troops was probably correct. They were alone in the car, which smelt of dirt and cracked plastic seating and stale food and bodies.

'Can't be done, it's too risky,' Lock said eventually, when he had eaten the last of the baguette. The front of his overcoat was covered with big crumbs. 'We'd be walking into a blind alley, with no way out. Can't you see that?'

'Lock, I'm tired. I don't need this . . .' Vorontsyev shifted his body in the rear seat, wincing with pain, breathing in snorted, nasal breaths. 'We're already in the blind alley, and our backs are against the wall. The plane is the gate we didn't expect to be there. We have to get away from here, right away. Can't *you* see that?'

Lubin was in the terminal building, dressed in a cleaner's overalls he had commandeered. Dmitri was somewhere on the terminal roof, watching the road by which the scientists would be brought to the airport, *if* they came. Marfa was scouting the hangar which housed Turgenev's Learjet, and the dispositions

of the GRU. Listening to their occasional reports over R/Ts they
had stolen from a secure locker in the police room in the terminal increased Lock's sense of the utter futility of their presence. Vorontsyev's crazy scheme of hijacking Turgenev's plane
and flying out of Novyy Urengoy seemed hardly more impracti-
cal than any alternative.

What alternative?

'Well?' Vorontsyev prompted. 'What's your answer?'

'That's crazy —!'

'What else is there?'

They glowered at one another like sparring animals, cats with
raised backbones, stiff fur. Then Lock relaxed, sipping at the
coffee in the plastic beaker. The warm, sweet liquid trickled
down a narrow unfrozen track in his gullet.

'I don't see it that way,' he said quietly. 'Turgenev may not
come — we don't know he's going to be here!'

'Lock — listen to me.' Vorontsyev's left hand gripped the sleeve
of Lock's coat like that of a remonstrative parent. 'Do you want
to walk out of here, or not? Does it matter to you, staying alive?'

'Why?'

'Because I'm not here by myself, that's why!' He snorted.
'Look, I probably care almost as little as you do about what
happens next, but I have a responsibility to the other three. I
had enough trouble persuading Lubin he wasn't abandoning his
wife and kid! None of my people deserves obliteration. Understand?' His eyes were hot and bleak, his lips quivering with rage.
'I won't let you do that. You owe Dmitri your *life*, damn you!'

Lock tugged at the damp scarf around his throat.

'This idea of mine,' Vorontsyev continued, 'may be lunacy,
but it's *safer* than any other way.'

'It depends on Turgenev being here! Otherwise, they'll just
shell the plane with that tank or the self-propelled gun! Christ,
haven't you thought of that?'

'I've thought that if Turgenev does come, you'll kill him out
of hand, and then they'll simply cut us down. I've thought of
that, Lock. Have you?'

'What if he doesn't come?'

'Then if we can get aboard the aircraft, quickly enough,

without giving ourselves away, we might just make it anyway.'
Vorontsyev looked down, as if shamefaced at a lie he had told.

'If Turgenev doesn't come himself, I won't come with you.'

'I know that.' He was silent for some moments, and then he said: 'I might not make it myself.' He was staring down at his broken arm, tightly buttoned inside his topcoat and at the slack, uncomfortable posture of his body in the seat.

'This is your only way back, Lock – take it,' Vorontsyev announced after another long, tense silence. 'You agree on that, at least?'

'Yes.'

'Right. What time is it?'

'A little after seven. Dawn.'

Vorontsyev clumsily picked up the R/T that lay between them on the cracked plastic seat. He pressed it against his cold, unshaven cheek.

'Dmitri – anything?'

The howl of the wind behind Dmitri's small voice. 'Nothing, Alexei.'

Vorontsyev craned to peer through the rear window, out towards the runway. The old car, with its weight and disguise of snow, had become unsuspicious, parked with other cars belonging to airport staff. The snowploughs remained stationary at the end of the runway. Their last run had been an hour earlier, headlights staring through the snow and darkness, the snow flung aside in great fountains.

Panshin was dead. Lock had told him that. Turgenev didn't know they had been told of the airport and the flight to Tehran.

'OK. Keep watching, old friend. Lubin?'

The young man's voice was a hoarse, secretive whisper. 'Nothing, Major. No increase in activity, no increase in tempo. Idle bunch of bastards,' he added, as if to dispel his own nerves rather than to reassure.

'OK – Marfa?'

Again the howl of wind, audible to both himself and to Lock, who instinctively rubbed his gloved hands together against the thought of the cold.

'They're still carrying out the routine patrols. The aircraft's

326

been inspected, but it hasn't been fuelled —' Vorontsyev felt a sick hollow in his stomach. 'I haven't seen any sign of the pilots.' She, too, was whispering.

'Where are you?'

'In the hangar. Behind some crates of spares.'

'Has food been taken aboard?'

'I think so.'

'Stewards, cabin staff — any sign?'

'Just one. No, there were two, a man and a woman. They're on board now, I can't see them — *wait*!' Her excitement jolted both of them. Then she was whispering less audibly. Lock leaned towards Vorontsyev to try to hear. 'A car's just pulled into the hangar, two people getting out — uniforms, caps.' A tense pause, then: 'They're going aboard. Small suitcases, charts — the pilot and co-pilot?'

'Must be. Don't move, but keep calling in. Dmitri, stay where you are until you can see something you can confirm. Lubin, get back here now!' Vorontsyev glared triumphantly at Lock. 'They *must* be coming, man! They have to be.' He chuckled, but the sound turned to a painful cough. He waggled his hand, and continued breathlessly: 'Turgenev's providing us with the rope we can hang him with!'

Lock looked round wildly at the noise of big engines starting. One of the snowploughs was on the move. 'Can we take the scientists inside the hangar?'

'Where will they fuel up?'

'In the hangar or —' He watched the second snowplough begin to rumble towards the runway. The first snow was gouting from the leading machine in a great wave. 'Maybe the runway. It's safer, out in the open. Where, *how*, Vorontsyev?'

'Alexei — two vehicles. A Mercedes and a small bus, by the look of it. Blacked-out windows. Turgenev's car?'

'Keep watching, Dmitri!' Vorontsyev sounded breathless.

'Major, an APC has just pulled up at the hangar, soldiers getting out of it!' they heard Marfa report. 'Eight, *ten*! Spreading out —'

'Shit!' Lock raged. 'Where now, Vorontsyev? Uh — *how*?'

*   *   *

'Yes, Bakunin. We're heading directly for the hangar. Where are you?'

Over the car telephone, Bakunin sounded as if he were donning a familiar, stiff, subordinate uniform.

'Half a mile from the airport.'

'Our *friends* – where are they?'

'Lost them, temporarily. I have given orders, made dispositions. They're hiding out somewhere. It won't be long before – '

'Panshin?'

'Dead.'

'What did they learn from him?'

'Nothing that will be of any use. He wouldn't have talked. He was aware we were outside, had the place surrounded. He would have been too frightened.'

'Very well.' Turgenev rubbed his nose. The thought of Lock's continuing freedom irked but did not unsettle. 'Check the whole security operation and then let me know when you've done so. We won't start engines until I have your all clear.' He smiled at Hamid beside him. 'Don't waste time.' He put down the telephone.

'The hangar's been put out of bounds, Vorontsyev! Don't you understand? Your bright idea isn't going to pan out!'

They were standing beside the car, in the bitter wind. Occasional flakes of snow plucked against their cold cheeks, but the blizzard had all but quietened. Low cloud still pressed threateningly. The snowploughs were hundreds of yards down the cleared runway. Lubin hovered on the other side of the car like a child ignored while his parents quarrelled. Lock saw Dmitri scuttling towards them with a crab's wary haste.

'Let me think, Lock,' Vorontsyev ground out between clenched teeth. 'Let me *think*.'

'Well, Alexei –!' Dmitri blurted as he reached them, red-faced.

Vorontsyev turned on him. 'Shut up, Dmitri,' he warned. He had erred, he realised. Perhaps fatally. He rubbed his unshaven cheeks with his still-damp glove. Stamped his feet against the cold, as he wandered away from the car.

'Marfa?' he whispered into the R/T.

'Yes? The GRU troops are all outside the hangar, but you won't be able to get in now.' He scowled at the information. 'There's a fuel truck, and one of those tugs they use to tow aircraft. Oh, and a fire truck.'

'The pilots?'

'I can see them in the cockpit – the flight deck,' she corrected herself.

'Anything else?'

'No.'

'Keep me informed – tell me when Turgenev and his passengers arrive.'

He turned back to look at his three companions, huddled in argument, Lock waving his arms in derisive dismissal. The anger wearied him, and was futile. Like everything else. Turgenev was here, bold as brass in his Mercedes, tsar of all he surveyed, just about to hand his tame nuclear physicists onto the boarding steps, ushering them away to Iran or Pakistan or even Iraq, wherever he had contracted to send them. His plane would probably bring in another consignment of heroin when it returned! And *he* – he was standing amid a line of snow-laden cars stamping his feet like a discarded mistress!

Marfa's voice interrupted his flagellatory recriminations.

'The Mercedes is here – with a small bus behind it. Is it them?'

'Yes!' he exploded. Then: 'Where exactly are they?'

'Outside. Waiting. The aircraft's being towed out of the hangar now. There are men around the fuel truck. The fire-fighters are standing to attention –!' It was all so damned easy for Turgenev. He was, truly, truly untouchable. Only hundreds of yards away but immune. 'The plane's cleared the hangar – coming to a stop. The fuel truck's alongside it now.' How long did it take to fuel a Learjet? God, there was an aircraft out there with a range of maybe three thousand miles and more, two pilots on board, a gift from the gods –! He ranted inwardly. 'The fuelling's started, by the look of it,' he heard.

'Be careful,' he warned.

'Turgenev . . . it's *him*!' she whispered. 'He's watching the fuelling. There's a smaller, dark-featured man with him, and some people are getting out of the bus.'

'How many?'

'Four, five – six. That's all . . . Just a minute, I'll try to change my position, get a better look.'

He waited in furious but impotent impatience. As if events raged beyond a thick wall or tinted, unbreakable glass. He was divorced from them; they continued without him.

'That's better.' She was breathing harshly. 'I'm near the hangar doors, there's no one left inside. There's – I can see six of the GRU from where I am. The others must be out of my line of sight. The six passengers from the bus are going on board . . . When are we going to move, Alexei?' She asked her question in a peremptory, agitated manner. 'Turgenev – he's . . .' She paused, then: 'He and the dark-skinned chap are going aboard, too!'

Turgenev could not, simply could *not*, be taking them to Tehran personally. The other man would be doing that. But he was on board, they were all *together*, just as he had hoped and planned.

And there were ten armed guards, and fifty more within shouting distance . . .

Lock was at his side. He twitched with impatience. 'What's happening?' Then he heard:

'Yes, they're all on board now –'

'What?' His eyes burned. 'They're leaving while we stand around here?' He drew the Makarov pistol from inside his topcoat and thrust a round into the chamber. 'You can kiss my ass, Vorontsyev! If you won't do something, I will!'

'Are you coming?' they heard Marfa ask.

'I am, lady – I am!' Then he added: 'Your boss doesn't have the *chutzpah* for it, apparently, honey!' He scowled in contempt.

'Wait!' Vorontsyev cried.

'What for, man? Hell to freeze over?'

'The aircraft's engines have been switched on, they're running them up,' Marfa reported. 'The GRU are scattering like mice!' Then she sensed the situation; or the quarrel between Vorontsyev and Lock impinged at last. 'What are we going to do, Alexei?'

'We're coming!' he snapped. 'All of us. Two minutes –!' He grabbed Lock's arm. They reached Dmitri and Lubin. 'The hangar. Come on, let's get moving!' He retained his hold on Lock's sleeve, as if to prevent the man from bolting, or firing the pistol he held in his hand. 'We must try to stop the plane.'

'How?'

'The tower?'

Lock shook his head. They hurried across snow that was barely disturbed by footprints, through a scattering of warehouses blazoned with Cyrillic script and English. A tank creaked across their path, a hundred yards away, imperious and oblivious. 'There's no way to stop the plane except by ramming it,' he admitted breathlessly.

They passed the first of the long row of hangars. The clouds seemed a lighter grey, though no less thick. There was little more than the scent of snow in the air.

'The plane's beginning to taxi!' Marfa's voice was high with excitement, then suddenly filled with disappointment. 'Alexei, Dmitri – come *on*!'

Lock ducked back at the corner of a hangar, waving the others to a halt. Someone grabbed his arm to prevent themselves overbalancing. Then he peered round the edge of the building. The soldiers had passed out of sight. The APC stood as if abandoned fifty yards from them. He saw Turgenev's Mercedes and the empty bus next to it . . . And the Learjet sliding gracefully as a swan across the perspective between the two hangars.

Where was Turgenev? The plane was beyond reach, but –

'Where's Turgenev?' he snapped into Vorontsyev's R/T.

'Still aboard –'

'Oh – Christ!' he wailed, staring at the lowering sky.

The Learjet began taxiing away from the hangar, slowly increasing its speed. Yellow-painted self-propelled passenger steps followed servantlike in its wake, out towards the taxiway. The fuel bowser moved off, puffing grey fumes. The APC, the bus, the Mercedes . . . The driver was standing beside it, smoking –

– scattered pieces. He couldn't make the jigsaw come together. Mercedes, relaxed driver, plane, Turgenev, plane, Mercedes, driver still smoking, in no hurry to leave, waiting, waiting for –

'The car! *His car* – for God's sake, we can use his car! Look,

331

it's waiting to pick him up. He's not going anywhere! He's getting out before it takes off, has to be —!'

Then he was running along the side of the hangar, its corrugated wall a hypnotic blur, disorientating him. The driver had his back to him, he heard the sound of laughter, presumably from a soldier he could not see. He heard his breathing, his heart thudded in his chest and the blood pounded in his ears. He had no idea whether or not they were behind him. He could see the aircraft, dazzling against the grey sky like a great dove, its flank emblazoned with the logo of – *Grainger-Turgenev*. His throat was dry, he could not swallow, could hardly breathe. It was as if it was put there to mock him. *Grainger-Turgenev*.

Rage, desperation, compulsion – all expressed in the swing of his arm at the surprised, half-turned face of the driver, all weighted in the strength of the blow he delivered to the man's face with the barrel of the Makarov.

He was still looking at the body when hands grabbed him and thrust him into the car's leather-scented interior. Someone, grunting with pain, got heavily in beside him, there was a third, wearing the chauffeur's uniform cap, in the driving seat. Dmitri, the first he recognised, was in the front passenger seat. Marfa flung open the door and clambered in, squashing Vorontsyev, who yelled with pain. His face was ashen with effort. The car was heavy with tension, exhilaration.

'*Slowly!*' Vorontsyev cried, still in pain, clutching his ribs.

Lubin steered the Mercedes forward. Lock glanced through the rear window. The driver's unconscious form was clearly visible, lying in the snow between the two hangars. They passed the GRU soldiers, clustered around a truck painted olive-drab. They were drinking coffee or vodka, oblivious to the passage of the car. Lubin turned onto the taxiway behind the self-propelled passenger steps that had followed the Learjet. Turgenev was going to get off the airplane before it took off, and his Mercedes would be waiting for him.

The aircraft reached the end of the taxiway and turned onto the runway. The main passenger door, behind the flight deck, opened as a dark gap. Lock could only snatch at his next breath.

'*Slowly*,' Vorontsyev insisted, his breathing less ragged.

The passenger steps were twenty yards ahead of the Mercedes. The Learjet was poised at the end of the runway. Lock heard his own sharp intake of breath as a tall, fur-hatted figure in a well-cut, dark overcoat appeared in the gap of the open passenger door. Turgenev. The name filled his mouth with saliva, like the anticipation of food. The terminal building was a wall of dull glass against which the tank and the self-propelled gun were posed. The passenger steps drew up beside the plane and their hydraulics jiggled the top step into alignment with the open door. Everything seemed slowed down and made distant; the effect of the car's tinted windows or perhaps his own anticipation. Vorontsyev was watching him anxiously. The Mercedes drew to a halt near the bottom of the steps.

'Just me,' Lock said. 'When he's halfway down the steps. Not till then, not –'

'Don't *kill* him, Lock.'

Lock made no reply, his hand poised on the door handle. They watched him like an audience, each one of them still, tense. Turgenev waved a hand back into the passenger cabin of the plane, then stepped onto the short flight of steps.

'Look!' Marfa breathed, pointing back towards the hangars. 'They've found the driver!'

The GRU uniforms were clustered in a tight knot between the two hangars, small as a gathering of ants around a dead fly. A UAZ jeep was pulling up beside them. Lock turned back to the steps and saw, to his horror, that Turgenev had paused near the top, one gloved hand on the metal handrail. He was unalarmed, merely curious, squinting towards the hangars. The familiar car, parked beside the steps, reassured.

The Iranian would be armed, Turgenev probably not . . .

. . . *now*.

He thrust open the door, climbed out, skidded on wet slush, then pushed himself towards the bottom of the steps. As he looked up, he knew at once that Turgenev had recognised him. The Russian turned quickly to regain the aircraft. Lock's boots pounded on the metal steps as the man retreated. His breath was laboured, his feet slippery beneath him. Turgenev was quicker than he, having passed through shock into action in an instant.

333

Other boots on the passenger steps. Turgenev, turning in the doorway, his hand reaching into the breast of his coat. The distance too great, the time too short, his sensation of being slow, old, hardly moving –

– released as he blundered into Turgenev, catching the scent of his cashmere overcoat, and his aftershave. Then he collided with a locker's metal, dizzying himself, his head shrieking with pain. His hands fumbled for Turgenev, who slipped them with a matador's grace and was gone, through a drawn curtain into the forward passenger cabin. Lock held his head, something wet on his gloved fingers. Lubin and then Dmitri loomed in the doorway, Marfa's head bobbing behind them.

Lock pointed forward, then staggered through the curtain. Turgenev was at the other end of the small cabin, at the door to the flight deck. And turned to watch him. Hunted, alarmed – and strangely aloof. The Iranian was on his feet, on the starboard side, rising from his seat, staring wildly at them. Armed. Gun in his hands, held out stiff-armed, no shock-delay, pure professionalism.

Lock fired twice and the Iranian's blood splashed the cabin ceiling and the wall behind his head. Lock's left arm almost torn from its socket by the impact of the single shot the Iranian had had time to fire. He staggered, sat heavily on the arm of a chair. A terrified, middle-aged face stared up at him from behind thick-glassed spectacles.

'Stop him!' Lock groaned.

The flight deck door had closed behind Turgenev. Foreboding. There was no way the man would allow himself to be taken hostage, allow the airplane to –

'Christ, *stop* him –!' he bellowed.

Dmitri had reached the door, his hand was on the handle, his face careless of his own safety, when Lock heard the first shot. Dmitri threw back the door. The second shot echoed in the cabin. Someone whimpered in terror. Through the open door, Lock could see Turgenev standing between the two pilots' seats, each of which held a slumped, still form. He'd shot the pilot and co-pilot. They couldn't, now, fly anywhere.

Then Turgenev turned away to shut down the engines. Dmitri

seemed startled into rage at the movement and struck at Turgenev's arm with his gun. Turgenev's pistol clattered to the floor
of the flight deck, his features expressing a snarling anger for
an instant. Then he shrugged, rubbed his arm, and raised his
hands in a mockery of surrender. Dmitri wore ashen shock on
his round features. Turgenev entered the passenger cabin and
Dmitri closed the door on the bodies.

Someone screamed, as high-pitched and alien as a siren.
Vorontsyev turned, to see Marfa slap the stewardess across the
face, then hold her tightly against her. The woman's shoulders
heaved, her face buried in dark hair and the stuff of Marfa's
coat.

Lock looked down at his wounded arm. There was blood on
the sleeve of his coat. There was hardly any pain, surprisingly.
His arm was still in traumatic shock. He let his hand rest on
his lap, oblivious of the stunned imprinted fear on the face
of the bespectacled man in the seat beside him. He coughed
at the tickle of burned powder from the gunshots. A gout of
blood splashed down onto his hand. Blood ran from his lips,
down his chin. He gingerly opened his topcoat. The breast
of his check shirt was darkened with blood. He felt a numb
terror – the salty blood on his tongue, filling his mouth again.
The Iranian's one shot had passed through his arm – and his
lungs.

Vorontsyev was looking at him in horror, even as Turgenev
announced:

'It seems, gentlemen, our flight has been delayed indefinitely.'

Vorontsyev raised his pistol in his left hand, but did not strike
Turgenev. Instead, his imagination sensed the isolated aircraft,
the runway, the fleeing passenger steps, the tower, the terminal,
all spreading out around them. The game was lost. The aircraft
had been sabotaged.

'It hasn't worked – Major.' Turgenev was smiling. 'You're
stuck. Dead stop.' His eyes, as he spoke, were studying Lock
with an intense, hot anger; and growing satisfaction. He seemed
unconcerned by their numbers, his own situation.

'Your friend Bakunin can get us another pilot,' Vorontsyev
replied. 'In exchange for you.' He sensed his words like soft

335

hands pushing at a great door he could not hope to open. Turgenev shook his head.

'I don't think so. Besides, this time the hijackers have to negotiate with the hostage, isn't that so?' Casually, he removed his gloves and, wrapping his coat around him as neatly as a woman might have done, he sat in the one empty seat in the forward cabin.

'Lubin, Dmitri — check the other cabin — close the passenger door,' Vorontsyev said mechanically, gesturing with the useless pistol.

Dmitri glanced almost angrily at him, then abandoned the silent, pale-featured Lock and passed through the curtain behind Lubin. They heard the noise of the door being closed and locked. Marfa pocketed her gun and moved towards Lock, who hunched away from her on the arm of the seat. It was obvious to Vorontsyev that she was making a great effort to keep her features inexpressive as she saw Lock's wound. The American growled once like a dog suspicious of further harm, then allowed her to unbutton his shirt, inspect the wound. Vorontsyev, in the strained, heightened silence of the cabin, distinctly heard the small, ugly noises of the bloodsoaked shirt against Lock's skin.

He turned to Turgenev, who seemed distracted by memory or reflection. Marfa moved quickly to the lockers, opening and slamming them shut, until she found the first-aid box. She glowered at one of the scientists until he abandoned his seat as nervously as a sheep, then helped Lock into it. The man's face was grey with pain. Vorontsyev turned away, unwilling to witness the extent of the wound, to acknowledge that Lock was, effectively, Turgenev's prisoner — the man needed an emergency operation, transfusions . . . might even be dying. He ground his teeth in impotent rage.

Then, surprisingly, Turgenev moved to stand beside Marfa, as if to supervise her attentions to Lock.

As Dmitri re-entered the forward cabin, Vorontsyev said: 'Get these two back with the others — they can sit on each other's laps if they have to. Lubin can keep an eye on them.'

'I'll start finding out who and what they are.' It was as if

336

Dmitri, like himself, had stumbled upon a piece of defensive play-acting, the role of a clerk or customs official which would keep reality at bay, at least for some moments.

Vorontsyev picked up a briefcase which had slipped to the floor from the Iranian's seat. The dead man sat hunched like an abandoned doll against the bulkhead. Vorontsyev tossed the briefcase to Dmitri. 'It'll be in here. Terms and conditions of employment, previous experience, the lot –' He tried to smile, knowing it was at best a sickly, defeated expression. Dmitri merely nodded, tapped the two passengers on the shoulder and herded them through the curtain to the four-seat rear passenger cabin.

Marfa had completed her bandaging of Lock's arm and chest. Turgenev, hypocritically, shook his head. 'Hospital, very soon – or not at all. Maybe not at all, anyway.' Marfa's quivering lower lip confirmed the callous, detached diagnosis. Perhaps Lock was dying anyway, but delay would kill him for certain . . .

. . . as surrender would kill *them*, his people who had followed him into this prison. He could not bargain *anything* for Lock's life, for the only counter he had was Turgenev himself. The scientists, whoever they were and however eminent and valuable, were mere *goods*. Turgenev and Bakunin would be indifferent to their survival. There was only Turgenev, the hostage and the negotiator.

He turned at a voice from beyond the flight deck door, startled. Saw Lock's ashen face, and snapped at the still distraught stewardess, who seemed obsessively afraid at the imminent opening of the door:

'Give him some brandy – hurry up, girl!'

The young woman scuttled to obey her orders. He opened the door of the flight deck to the smell of blood, even in the cold air, and Bakunin's voice, tinnily irrelevant, from the radio. Turgenev had followed him, and the man flinched at a defensive jab of the pistol in his direction. Turgenev again mockingly held up his hands, then fiddled with the radio, handing a headset to Vorontsyev, who motioned him into stillness against the door. Half-turned in the small, awkward space, leaning over the pilot's head with its drying leak of blood, he growled:

337

'Yes, Bakunin, what do you want?' It was as if he had been interrupted from important work.

'Vorontsyev, what the hell do you think you can achieve by this?' Bakunin barked. 'You're not going *anywhere*!'

Vorontsyev saw the flash of Turgenev's confident grin, and the black, flylike dot of a helicopter through the windows. It was closing slowly, traversing a surveillance rather than attack course.

'Listen to me, Bakunin. Prince Turgenev –' Turgenev snorted with suppressed amusement. '– the local tsar, is here with us. He thinks he can bargain his way out of here, but he can't do it unless *we* go, too. OK?'

After a pause, Bakunin said: 'Then why haven't you taken off? You don't really need my permission, do you?'

The helicopter minced back and forth across the windows. The clouds seemed lower, a darker grey. The airfield stretched away around the isolated Learjet, a slow, hesitant fog seeming to cling just above the blank snow. The runway gleamed blackly ahead of the aircraft like a taunt.

Turgenev leaned beside Vorontsyev.

'Bakunin,' he said, 'it's me. I'm all right. But there is an evident shortage of pilots aboard the plane at the moment.' Bakunin chuckled. 'You understand? Our friend here doesn't seem to know what to do –' Vorontsyev listened, without making any effort to interrupt Turgenev. '– but that makes him doubly dangerous. We'll be in touch.' He switched off the radio.

Immediately, Vorontsyev flicked the radio back on. 'Bakunin, unless you want to see the money tree cut off at the roots, arrange a pilot for us!'

Turgenev shrugged, then announced imperiously: 'Now you've told him what he should have been allowed to realise in that slow, saurian brain for himself. We are *all* helpless out here –'

Vorontsyev pushed Turgenev through the door into the passenger cabin, the pistol prodding the back of the man's cashmere overcoat. 'Why should that be?'

'What choice does he have? If this aircraft takes off, if any of you managed to get away, *he* is ruined. Do you think he has houses round the world and their accompanying bank accounts?' Turgenev laughed. 'He probably keeps it under the mattress, everything I've ever paid him!' He paused, then added: 'Something of a problem, mm?'

Turgenev seated himself once more, his smile fixed. Vorontsyev inspected Lock's sick, hanging face, then Marfa's distress.

A snowflake, large as a jellyfish it seemed, appeared on one of the porthole windows of the cabin. Then a second and a third. Vorontsyev closed his eyes in anguish. When he opened them, the stewardess had retreated from the forward cabin. Dmitri was standing between the two cabins, revealed like an actor by the drawn-back curtain. Marfa was attempting to read a file. He glanced at the digital clock on the bulkhead. It had been less than ten minutes since they had boarded the plane. Ridiculous . . .

He bent over Lock's seat and the American's eyes fluttered open. Vorontsyev was appalled at the violence of his decline. He touched the American's hand.

'Christ, this hurts, and it's strange . . .' Lock muttered, blood at once dribbling from his lips so that he snatched his hand away from Vorontsyev and wiped the side of his mouth with a bloodsoaked handkerchief. There was almost nothing left of Lock, apart from the hot, burning eyes, reddened and blinking in and out of focus. Lock wanted nothing, nothing but to kill Turgenev. There was no gun near his hand, Vorontsyev realised with relief, then immediately wondered whether Lock still had the gun somewhere. He hoped not. He patted the hand that had returned to his and stood up. His arm and ribs seemed a long way from him, their jolts and naggings of pain undemanding.

'They're top people,' Marfa whispered, leaning towards him and offering the file. 'Two from Semipalatinsk, one from that newish place south of Moscow – two top-grade technicians.' She swallowed. 'They're bomb builders, Alexei.' She was strangely animated. 'They could have made a real difference.' She was flicking the files like cards in an illusion. He saw two heads crowned by military caps. He turned to Turgenev.

'Nothing but the best,' Turgenev said. He withdrew a cigar case and lighter from his pocket. 'The sign's not on, is it?' he

339

mocked, and puffed at the Cuban cigar contentedly, a paradigm of the capitalist.

The windows behind his blond head were streaked with melted snow running like tadpoles. The telephone embedded in the arm of Turgenev's seat blurted in alarm. Turgenev gestured at it, and Vorontsyev nodded.

'Yes? Ah, Bakunin —' He smiled at Vorontsyev, as if in apology for the unwelcome interruption of their conversation. 'No, I don't think that's necessary. I think the situation's realities are sinking in —' He broke off, attracted by the violent, blood-foamed coughing from the seat across the narrow aisle. He turned to face Lock, who was holding the Makarov pistol quiveringly towards Turgenev. 'Just a moment —'

Ugly swallowing noises, the soughing of Lock's breaths, and their uncertainty.

'Pete —' He paused, but managed to still the threatened coughing fit. 'Tell the guy I'm dying, uh? Tell him I'm the wild card, unre — *liable* . . .' He paused again, for a longer time. His eyes glared briefly in Vorontsyev's direction. 'Tell him there isn't a lot of time. If I — think I'm going to — black out . . . you're coming with me. OK?'

He fell back against the seat, exhausted. Turgenev moved to a more upright position, as if to spring, his eyes enlarged with adrenalin like those of a cat. He glared at Vorontsyev —

— who grinned. Turgenev appeared momentarily unnerved. It was out of the question that Lock should be allowed to kill Turgenev, their only letter of credit, their passport . . . Yet, Lock's last desperation frightened the man.

Vorontsyev had to use it.

'I'll get back to you, Bakunin . . . What? No, nothing's wrong!'

Lock was wearing a beard of blood, but his mouth was smiling with a luxurious, impervious satisfaction. The Makarov was rested heavily, almost numbly, along the arm of his seat, pointed unwaveringly at Turgenev.

'Well?'

'Well what?' Turgenev snapped.

'Do we get a pilot?'

'I only have to wait — what? Fifteen minutes, maybe half an

340

hour, and the only man in the room who poses the slightest threat will be dead!' He was leaning towards Vorontsyev, whispering savagely. 'What is there to concern me?'

'Me, Pete,' Lock announced faintly, with a detached, fey amusement. 'Me. Get the guys a pilot. They won't stop me killing you — but you know that, uh?'

Vorontsyev maintained his stony expression for a moment, then shrugged. 'Up to you.'

Snow flew past the windows behind Turgenev. The fuselage quivered infinitesimally in the increased wind. The slight tremor seemed to transfer itself to Turgenev's frame.

'His lungs are filling up with blood, like a swimming pool,' Turgenev hissed. 'I don't have to wait long.'

'But he worries you — he's nothing to lose.'

'You won't let him kill me, Vorontsyev. You don't want to die.' Turgenev's voice was a hoarse whisper. He was leaning forward intently, but seemed distracted by Lock, who wiped the latest blood from his chin, then waved Marfa's solicitations aside. And Lock was studying the conversation as closely as if lip-reading. Vorontsyev was increasingly aware of his detached, Olympian manner. 'We both know that,' Turgenev continued, his priorities buzzing insectlike in the tense, cramped space of the cabin. Vorontsyev was worried by Lock's control of the situation. 'So, we wait. Bakunin won't give you a pilot . . . you can only deal through me.' Turgenev leaned back, but his confident assurance was something being rehearsed in a large mirror.

Turgenev wondered if he could buy them off . . . then the thought made him smile. He need only string them along until Lock coughed his way into oblivion. Even Bakunin, out there behind the swiftly returned blizzard, was too greedy ever to contemplate a solution that involved harming Turgenev.

There was only Lock . . .

. . . and the evident fact that Vorontsyev and his people seemed subservient to Lock's priority. They were becoming no more than observers of the scene.

Yes . . . It was that that was unsettling, the creeping foreboding that they might act too late. They may hesitate just long

341

enough for Lock to kill him before their sense of their own survival awoke . . .

Bakunin glanced around him at the detritus of the control tower, its litter of operators and managers, his second in command, the GRU troops. The tinted windows of the tower were blind with driving snow. The idiot who stood beside him, taller, slimmer, younger, had suggested storming the aircraft. *Special troops*, he had replied, then added an assertion that *We can handle the situation*. The captain had accepted his decision, probably without a moment's reflection on his own small accumulation of bribes, kickbacks, payments for looking the other way, even the occasional squalid, unimportant murder.

But Bakunin had reflected. Special troops would be under outside command. Other people would have to have the situation explained – the American, the town police, Turgenev, all of it would have to be justified. It was too dangerous to himself to involve a specialist anti-hijacking unit.

And his own troops couldn't cope with it, couldn't pull it off . . .

. . . even though – and the thought returned like a wasp he could not rid himself of on a hot afternoon – no one could be allowed to come off that plane alive, with the sole exception of Turgenev.

Finality. Vorontsyev, the stupid, lazy, time-serving policeman who'd got something akin to religion over Turgenev . . . and especially the American, whoever and whatever he was or had been. Acting or hoping to act as a nemesis. The incident had to be wiped from the tarmac and from reality, just as Panshin had been despatched, falling into the snow, a bullet through his forehead. For safety's sake.

'What do you estimate visibility to be?' he asked his second in command.

'Around twenty to twenty-five metres, sir.' Georgian accent. He distrusted Georgians, but the man was efficient after the manner of his own dim certitudes.

'Very well. Have the aircraft surrounded by armed troops in a forty-metre perimeter. Anyone trying to come or go – have

342

them stopped.' He glared at the younger man. 'You understand me, Josef? These people must be neutralised. A closed incident is what we must achieve – together with the safety of Turgenev, of course.'

'Will you try to negotiate them out?'

The storm made the windows fiercely blank, writhing outside the octagonal enclosure of the tower like fanned smoke from a conflagration. He shook his head.

'Turgenev is making his own arrangements, Josef. I do not intend to jeopardise –' He shrugged. '– the man makes the rules here. If he feels in any real danger, he will begin negotiations.'

'The pilots?' the captain asked, looking much like a bemused boy as he spoke. 'He – just, well, he killed them? Himself?'

'That's it, Josef. Admirably decisive, mm?' He laughed. 'They haven't any idea of the kind of man they're playing with. None whatsoever!'

'Should we – you, call him again?'

Bakunin thought for a moment, then said: 'In ten minutes. If he wants something, or is in the unlikely position of having to ask for help, he'll call us. The others don't want to talk to us – he's in charge. He never let them gain control of the situation.' He disliked the admiration in his voice. 'The weather has this place in a vice for the next twelve hours, minimum. Now, get that plane encircled, just in case they try to run for it.'

The captain saluted and turned away. Bakunin moved towards the blind windows and their rushing snow. The whole tower quivered in the wind's force.

Brilliantly ruthless, killing the pilots.

What would he do? Buy them off? Just sit and wait? Expect to be rescued?

Offer them an alternative victim, a smaller scandal?

His suspicion was spreading and inflating like a wasp sting –

It began with the blinking, the effort to keep the small cabin in focus. His eye movements were becoming more exaggerated, more frequent. Before that, there had been a kind of exhilaration in the pain, a fierce clarity of sensation and thought. Or perhaps that had come from his understanding that he was dying, and deteriorating very quickly. Now, the cabin swam in and out of clarity, as if it were sometimes there around him and at other times outside the streaming, blind windows.

The girl, Marfa, was an unwelcome nurse. Rather than seeming solicitous, she loomed now as a reminder. *Memento mori.* Vorontsyev's pain was another signal of his decline which he resented, having been so detached only minutes earlier. He had been above and outside it all, controlling them.

He coughed, a gout of blood fell onto his lap and he disregarded it, fighting for breath. Gradually hearing the appalling, liquid noises in his chest. The girl had propped him up with pillows from one of the lockers. He was bleeding into one of them, his head resting on another. She had wrapped a blanket around him because he was feeling colder. It would be difficult to talk, but he must – to Vorontsyev first, and then and only then to Turgenev.

Lock pointed with the pistol, unnerving Turgenev, alarming the Russian policeman. He essayed a smile, shook his head. He gestured Turgenev out of the cabin with fierce little shakes of the gun. Vorontsyev nodded and Dmitri took Turgenev into the rear cabin. The scientists in there were irrelevant, he had seen that very clearly; the files would be sufficient for their purposes. But not important, not like the obligation to ensure the survival of these people who had placed him in a position to kill Turgenev . . . and who, if he didn't get rid of them now, would prevent him from achieving that last goal.

Vorontsyev sat in the nearest seat, leaning forward. Marfa gave Lock a drink of tepid water, which he managed to swallow, fighting off the dangerous tickling it caused in his throat.

He had to be made to understand . . . but Lock was afraid of squandering his remaining strength and consciousness. He blinked. It required shorthand, they had to attend very closely, understand him at once –

'Go,' he announced, then pointed at the files on one of the seats. 'All – you need, there.' There was a bout of coughing after that huge effort, yet he hated more the girl's sympathetic, anguished breathing beside his face and wished he had the redundant energy to push her away.

344

Vorontsyev shook his head. Lock nodded vehemently.

'All – you. Use – use the *car* . . .' His breathing unnerved him, the long wet inhalations and exhalations like a tide, drowning him as he sat helpless.

Again, Vorontsyev shook his head. Then he said:

'If we leave, it's with you. Hospital –'

Lock shook his head.

'No – good.'

'Then we'd need to take Turgenev, bargain our way out.'

'No.' Once more, the room was starkly clear to him. Dmitri stood behind his seat, the girl crouched beside him, Voronts-yev looked as lugubrious as any deathbed mourner. The pain seemed like light rather than heat. He saw their situation with the identical, fierce clarity that had been his wound's first gift. 'Mexican – standoff,' he announced. 'Only chance – go now.'

Vorontsyev's scheme had trapped them all. Turgenev was fated to survive. They'd get no pilot, there'd be no storming of the plane. Eventually, they would try, as Vorontsyev evidently planned, to exchange Turgenev for their freedom. Turgenev would have them eliminated as soon as he had been released. They all knew that. He had the power, the influence, the weight of numbers. They'd never be allowed to survive.

'You – want to break him. The files,' he said. 'Storm will hide you – don't wait.'

Vorontsyev's eyes admitted the bleak truth. The storm was the only thing on their side. Once it blew itself out, they'd be as exposed as tumours on an X-ray plate, to be surgically extinguished. They couldn't take him – and he wouldn't surrender Turgenev to them.

Vorontsyev knew that Lock was offering them their lives – or some slight chance of their lives – in exchange for the murder of Turgenev. He maintained an expressionless look. Lock would ensure they had their best chance of escape by forcing himself to remain conscious. He would wait until the very last flicker of consciousness, the final moment of his own life, before he shot Turgenev. Then, on the edge of the dark, he would execute his enemy.

He glanced towards the files. If they got out, managed to make it to Moscow or some other city, maybe someone would listen; maybe the authorities would act. Regard Turgenev's empire like rot in an old building – treat it; kill it . . . It seemed a romantic notion.

Lock smiled at him. It was obvious the American knew he had made his decision.

'See?' he said. 'You have to – uh?'

Then he began an appalling fit of coughing, his whole frame heaving, blood staining his lips and chin and the front of his shirt. Eventually, he subsided further into the seat as Marfa, no longer resented, cleaned his face and inspected his wound with nimble, afraid fingers. Vorontsyev realised that Lock would be dead in minutes. He got up and went to the window.

Beside the plane, the Mercedes was a white lump, something covered with a heavy sheet. He strained to see beyond the violence of the storm, but the scene was featureless, empty. They might already have the plane surrounded – they certainly would do before the blizzard subsided. He could feel the tension, the claustrophobia of the cabin.

Then he turned to Lock.

'Yes,' he said, picking up the files. 'Everything we need is in here.' He looked at Marfa and Dmitri.

'What about the others? The cabin crew, the six – ?' Dmitri began.

'They'll be more interested in escape than anything else. Just like us,' he added with a bitter smile. 'Tell Lubin to bring Turgenev back in here, then talk to the steward. Tell him they're all being released. As soon as we've left, they can leave.' Dmitri nodded and retreated to the aft cabin.

Turgenev was alertly suspicious as he re-entered, aware that some decision had been reached; concerned, but still confident, pleased at the evident decline of Lock.

'Hi, Pete,' Lock greeted him, his supineness suggesting relaxation rather than exhaustion.

His tone startled Turgenev.

'Well?' he sneered. 'What idiotic solution have you agreed on?'

'The – deal,' Lock announced, 'you for them . . . They – go, we . . . stay –' He swallowed noisily.

Turgenev turned on Vorontsyev. 'You'll never get off the airfield!' he snapped. 'Not even under cover of this weather.'

'We'll see. Lubin – you drive. Dmitri, open the door –' He shuffled his own forgotten broken arm to greater comfort. They'd have to drop onto the snow-covered tarmac but that wouldn't kill any of them. He glanced at Lock. 'Do you want him tied in his seat?' he asked. Lock slowly shook his head. 'Very well. Marfa?' She nodded.

The noise of the passenger door being opened and the bellowing entry of the storm drowned all sound, all thought. The curtain flared in the wind. Vorontsyev pushed Turgenev into his seat, paused for an instant beside Lock, who merely smiled, a boyish, unworried expression. He heard Lubin jump, then saw Marfa disappear through the door. Dmitri glanced back at Lock and Turgenev, then disappeared. Vorontsyev paused at the raging gap in the fuselage, blinded and disorientated, then jumped, collapsing at once into the new snow, his ankles shot though with pain.

He was helped to his knees and looked back. The stewardess and her companion were standing in the doorway. He waved his pistol and their figures vanished. He heard the engine of the Mercedes fire. Dmitri was sweeping the snow from the windscreen with swinging movements of his arm. Marfa was beside him and he shook off her proffered hand. They reached the car as Lubin began revving the engine. Snow was flung out by the rear wheels and the car skidded slightly sideways.

'Get in!' he bellowed to Dmitri who was still clearing snow from the windows. 'Lubin – straight down the runway, don't stop until you reach the fence, then go through it! Understand –?'

Then he heard distant, toylike detonations. The car seemed plucked at, assailed by small pebbles. Dmitri's features flattened into caricature against the passenger window, then slid out of sight.

'*Dmitri –!*' he yelled, opening the door, looking down to

347

inspect the dead features that stared up at him. Two shots passed above his head, shattering the window on the other side of the car.

'Go, go!' Marfa was screaming at Lubin.

'*No!*' Vorontsyev cried out, but the car lurched forward, leaving Dmitri as a shapeless lump in the snow, diminishing. More shots –

Lock heard the shooting, at first with great clarity, then more distantly as the steward slammed the passenger door shut. He heard the Mercedes accelerate, then that noise, too, was lost in the babble of panic from the aft cabin. He switched his attention – slowly, with a great effort of concentration – to Turgenev.

And shook his head.

'Don't call – them, uh? Stupid –'

Turgenev sat back in his seat. Lock had no more than minutes now; his blinking the cabin into focus was a nervous tic, regular and compulsive. His face was ashen, there was blood on his chin which he had not bothered to wipe away. His breathing was irregular, less of a struggle but like a fading signal from a distant transmitter. Turgenev knew he had only to wait for five, ten minutes –

– gestured with his eyes to warn the steward, who had appeared behind Lock. The man nodded his understanding and retreated behind the curtain.

'Don't count on it,' Lock said quietly.

Lock listened to the subsiding babble from the other cabin. Soon, they'd open the door and bellow their identities into the storm, hoping not to get killed. Or they'd tell Bakunin or whoever was out there they had only one dying man to content themselves with . . . Soon.

'You'll never know if they made it,' Turgenev offered.

'Neither will you – Pete.' He suppressed a threatened fit of coughing. He heard his lighter, slower breathing. It wouldn't be long now, not long at all. 'Beth. *Why?*'

'What? Oh – that was handled badly, John. It shouldn't have happened.'

'It did, though . . .'

348

'Yes, it did. Look, John, I can still save your life!' It was talk, just talk. 'I can get you to hospital, I can keep you *alive*, John!'

'You – emptied my . . . life, Pete. It isn't anything – any more.' He heard the steward move behind his seat and managed a louder voice: 'Crazy to try!' He smiled as he heard the man retreat to the aft cabin. There was the silence of a tense audience in the rest of the Learjet.

'John, this is crazy. *You're* crazy. This revenge thing. It isn't how things *work* . . .' His voice insinuated. There was a not-unkindly authority in its tone. 'Lock, you – people like you – you're just romantics . . . This doesn't solve anything, even begin to. The world is shit, Lock. Everywhere, in every way. You used to think Afghanistan was a *good* war, that you had God on your side, that you were helping . . .'

Lock watched Turgenev lean closer to him, as if confiding some important truth.

'It was bad through and through, John, that war. It was the world in microcosm . . . Let me *help* you –'

Lock blinked with a furious, futile rapidity. He felt himself retreat from the cabin. The ringing of the telephone set in the arm of Turgenev's seat was very distant and quiet.

Turgenev's hand moved to the phone. Lock struggled to attend to the movement, lurching more upright – to be doubled up in a blind, uncontrollable fit of coughing. Blood on his hands, on the gleaming barrel of the pistol . . . Then hands on him, a hand grabbing for his pistol –

– which fired. Lock saw nothing, heard the noise of the gun, twice, felt a weight fall crushingly onto his back . . . lost consciousness.

The steward snatched up the receiver, gabbled into it. Turgenev's body had toppled sideways into the narrow aisle. Lock's had slid down in his seat so that his blind eyes stared up at the steward. His young, expressionless face saw blood dribbled down the dead man's chin.

'Yes, yes –! Both dead! *Both* – we are all safe, yes, Colonel, we are all safe!'

Relief coursed through the steward. He put down the receiver,

349

then stepped over Turgenev's sprawled body towards the door. He opened it, shivering in the icy cold.

A moment after the impact of the projectile, the aircraft was engulfed in flame.

POSTLUDE

'The superiority of the rich, being . . .
unmercifully exercised, must inevitably
expose them to reprisals.'

William Godwin:
Enquiry concerning Political Justice

Wrapped in his overcoat, he sat on the barrel of one of the cannons ranged before the façade of the Arsenal; the cannons had been captured from Napoleon's army during its terrible winter retreat from Moscow. He stared up at the windows of the Palace of Congresses. Light snow flurried between him and the towers and pinnacles and massive buildings of the Kremlin.

Lubin's baby was grumpily cold, wrapped like a bundle of washing in his mother's arms, held up beside her cold, pretty dark face. Marfa, hands thrust into the pockets of her grey coat, long scarf wrapped again and again around her neck and shoulders, studied him in a silence as weary as his own.

'What did the deputy minister have to say?' she asked eventually. Hooded crows cawed from the high gutters in a mockery either of her question or his anticipated reply.

'He said the Interior Ministry, the whole Federation, owed us a great debt.' He shrugged and grinned acidly. 'He told me I'd been promoted to Colonel, you and Lubin to Detective First Class. He hinted we could all look forward to Moscow postings, just as soon as the papers came through.'

He looked up at them. The news had not disturbed the lines of cold and disappointment on their faces. Katya Lubin alone appeared innocently pleased.

He had been released from hospital a week ago. He had spent those seven days in an endless round of pointless debriefings and meetings; now, he felt the sour, disillusioned ennui of an unsuccessful salesman, someone peddling religious tracts. No one *really* wanted to listen. After all, they insinuated, Turgenev was dead, the American's body or what was left of it had been

353

flown home, and Bakunin was to be disciplined for his *excess of zeal* and poor judgement in storming the plane. But even that was *understandable*, for there appeared to have been a *bomb on board* . . . He had struggled not to laugh aloud at that politest of fictions.

Turgenev's criminal activities had been a profound shock and a temporary embarrassment. The smuggling of nuclear scientists had to be stopped at all costs. The other criminalities of which he had been guilty were of much less account.

He shrugged.

'Waste of time,' he murmured, more to the late autumn temperature and the light snow than to his companions. 'We made the trip for nothing.'

Their escape had been easier than he had expected. From Novyy Urengoy to Nadym at first, then skirting the Gulf of Ob to Salekhard. The blizzard had blown itself out during their journey. They'd waited less than two hours for a flight to Vorkuta, and from there had flown direct to Moscow. If there had been any organised pursuit, they had never been aware of it.

I'm sorry, John Lock, he thought. *I'm sorry.*

Dmitri was dead, and he carried that weight on his back like a great rock. Lock — only Lock had achieved something; his revenge.

'The American was the only one who got what he wanted,' he announced.

Marfa snorted angrily.

'You're feeling very sorry for yourself, *Colonel*!' she snapped. 'That bastard Turgenev's dead, the smuggling of the scientists has been broken up — *we* broke it up! — and the heroin supplies have been disrupted for months, maybe even for a year. That's *something* — isn't it?'

'That's right — sir,' Lubin chorused, rubbing his gloved hands as if before a warming fire. His wife appeared anxious to return to the hotel. 'We did achieve something —'

'Quite a lot, in fact,' Marfa persisted.

Vorontsyev shifted on the cannon. His bruises still ached. His ribs protested as his good hand slapped the gun's old metal. He stood up, adjusting the sling on his broken arm.

Grinned.

'You're sure, are you, children?' Marfa's anger was evident. Lubin merely smirked. Vorontsyev raised his hands. 'OK – we did it. We got one of the bastards. One of the very biggest . . .' He gestured towards the Kremlin. 'They're out there – hundreds, thousands of them. The politicos, the old *apparatchiks*, the mafiosi and the *biznizmen*. This country's endemically corrupt –'

'We're not – you're not!' Marfa snapped at him. 'We *won*!'

After a silence, he put his good arm around her shoulder, then began walking across the cobbles towards the nearest gate in the high Kremlin wall, beyond which lay Moscow. Katya Lubin, holding her husband's hand, trotted beside them, clutching the baby against her.

'Very well,' Vorontsyev announced. 'But before the next crusade, I think a dinner to celebrate your promotion. I'll pay!'

He did not feel lighthearted. Dmitri and Lock rubbed against him in memory, preventing the dissipation of his mood. But Marfa was right. Turgenev was dead. And there were other crooks out there easier to catch and convict. A *lot* easier. Yes, they had done something – won a battle if not the war.

He patted their shoulders, grateful for their innocence.

355